The Man with the Golden Torc

"Packed with enough humor, action, and plot twists to satisfy fans who prefer their adventure shaken, not stirred. . . . Readers who recognize the pun on Ian Fleming's James Bond title will find the secret agent in question has more up his sleeve than a fancy car and some high-tech gadgets." —*Publishers Weekly*

"The author of the Deathstalker and Nightside series introduces a hard-boiled, fast-talking druidic James Bond, who wields ancient magic instead of a gun . . .a witty fantasy adventure." —*Library Journal*

"An action-packed paranormal mystery. Engaging . . . [with] snappy dialogue adding a touch of black humor." —Monsters and Critics

"Take some James Bond, and throw in some of Green's own Nightside, and mix liberally with the epic over-the-top action of his Deathstalker novels, and you're somewhere in the right neighborhood for describing *The Man with the Golden Torc*. It has everything one has come to expect from Green's work: distinctive characters, stylized ultraviolence, more mad ideas per page than most writers get in a lifetime, and a wild roller-coaster plot that doesn't let up." —The Green Man Review

"There's no one who's consistently more entertaining writing that subset of contemporary fantasy that involves the wizards and creatures that secretly live among us . . . [a] blend of humor and high adventure." —Critical Mass

"Green launches another strong contemporary fantasy series. . . . Fans of high-speed urban fantasy with a smart-aleck hero, fighting impossible odds are sure to enjoy it." —SFRevu

"Readers who enjoy the Nightside series will also love *The Man with the Golden Torc*. There is a [enough] dry wit, romantic humor, and colorful villains to keep readers turning the pages. Green has another hit series." —The Best Reviews

For
Heaven's
Eyes Only

Simon R. Green

A ROC BOOK

ROC
Published by New American Library, a division of
Penguin Group (USA) Inc., 375 Hudson Street,
New York, New York 10014, USA
Penguin Group (Canada), 90 Eglinton Avenue East, Suite 700, Toronto,
Ontario M4P 2Y3, Canada (a division of Pearson Penguin Canada Inc.)
Penguin Books Ltd., 80 Strand, London WC2R 0RL, England
Penguin Ireland, 25 St. Stephen's Green, Dublin 2,
Ireland (a division of Penguin Books Ltd.)
Penguin Group (Australia), 250 Camberwell Road, Camberwell, Victoria 3124,
Australia (a division of Pearson Australia Group Pty. Ltd.)
Penguin Books India Pvt. Ltd., 11 Community Centre, Panchsheel Park,
New Delhi - 110 017, India
Penguin Group (NZ), 67 Apollo Drive, Rosedale, Auckland 0632,
New Zealand (a division of Pearson New Zealand Ltd.)
Penguin Books (South Africa) (Pty.) Ltd., 24 Sturdee Avenue,
Rosebank, Johannesburg 2196, South Africa

Penguin Books Ltd., Registered Offices:
80 Strand, London WC2R 0RL, England

Published by Roc, an imprint of New American Library, a division of Penguin
Group (USA) Inc. Previously published in a Roc hardcover edition.

First Roc Mass Market Printing, June 2012
10 9 8 7 6 5 4 3 2 1

Copyright © Simon R. Green, 2011
All rights reserved

ROC REGISTERED TRADEMARK—MARCA REGISTRADA

Printed in the United States of America

CHAPTER ONE

The Prisoner

t was half past November, but I couldn't sleep.

I wasn't sure how long I'd been sleeping, but it felt like a long time. As though I'd been hibernating through the winter, wrapped up safe and warm, sleeping soundly and deeply through the dark and the cold. But something wouldn't let me rest and so here I was, up and about, walking down a long, empty corridor in a silent, empty house.

There was no transition: One moment I was fast asleep; the next I was wandering aimlessly down a cosy-looking corridor with rich carpeting, wood-panelled walls, and great wide windows. I sort of recognised where I was, but I couldn't put a name to it. Couldn't even put a name to myself. I had no idea who I was, but strangely it didn't seem to bother me. I had no memories and no plans. No needs, no worries. Just me walking in an empty place. The setting was familiar, and a slow curiosity led me to study the painted portraits hanging on the walls I passed. The faces were familiar, too, but I couldn't put a name to any of them. They seemed friendly, supportive, like . . . family. I couldn't decide whether I felt vaguely comfortable in the silent and empty setting, or obscurely threatened. Or both.

Who was I? What was my name? I stopped and concentrated, scowling till my forehead ached, and eventually something came to me. Drood . . . What was that? Was it even a name? What the hell was a Drood when it was at home? I started forward again, and soon came to the end of the corridor. I turned right, and another long corridor stretched before me. I kept walking. It was something to do while I tried to get my thoughts in order. Was this whole place empty except for me? A standing suit of medieval armour loomed up before me, and, moved by some obscure impulse, I stopped before it. The solid steel was well polished, but it bore all the dents and scrapes and hard knocks of a long working life. Someone had worn this armour in the past, used the gleaming sword and shield that stood propped up beside it, in some long-forgotten conflict. I frowned again. The suit of armour . . . meant something to me. Something special. I leaned in to study it more closely, and only then realised that the whole suit was covered in thick whorls of hoarfrost. I reached out to touch the heavy steel breastplate with a single fingertip, but I couldn't feel the metal or the ice.

I stepped back and looked around me. The floor, the walls and the ceiling were all covered with layers of frost and crusted ice. Even the huge windows were coated with heavy, fern-patterned hoarfrost. So why didn't I feel cold? I looked down at myself. I was wearing a plain white T-shirt and generic blue jeans. My arms were bare, but I didn't even have gooseflesh from the cold. I moved over to the nearest window and rubbed away the frost with my bare forearm. I didn't feel a thing. I looked out the window, and winter was everywhere. For as far as I could see, great sweeping waves of snow covered the grounds, smooth and untouched by any mark of man or beast. A great billowing ocean of white, stretching off for as far as I could see. No snow fell, though a light grey mist curled and heaved around the base of the house.

Here and there in the rising and falling of the snow were distinct shapes that might have been snow sculptures. Winged horses, gryphons, and a really massive dragon. Very detailed, but utterly still. Scattered across the snowscape like watchful guardians. There was a massive hedge maze, too, all its complicated runs and turns one big pattern when seen from above. White lines and dark shadows. And then I saw something moving inside the maze, something that raged up and down the narrow ways, striking out at the snowy hedgerows with savage strength. It swept this way and that, moving too quickly for me to identify, except to know for a fact that it wasn't in any way human. There was something bad, something wrong, something horribly monstrous about it, but even as it struck out at the endless white hedgerows around it, it wasn't able to damage or disturb them. For all its obvious strength and power, it was clearly trapped inside the maze. I watched it prowl up and down and back and forth, never stopping, never able to find an exit. I wondered what it was, and why I was so scared of what would happen if it should ever find a way out.

I looked up at the open sky. A huge moon, full and blue, hung alone in a dark, dark sky with no stars. No stars at all. I backed away from the window, and the blue moonlight fell through the glass, illuminating some of the corridor. For the first time I realised the blue moon was the only light there was. Blue moonlight, shimmering ice and dark shadows filled the corridor, and not a sign of life anywhere. I moved quickly down the corridor, checking each window, but I always saw the same thing. The exact same view, from the exact same angle, never changing no matter how far I walked . . . Which should have been impossible.

I turned and looked back the way I'd come. Although the rich carpeting was crusted with a thick layer of hoarfrost, I hadn't left a single footprint behind me. No mark, nothing, to show I'd passed this way. I stamped my foot hard, but it didn't disturb the frost beneath me, and the sound was oddly flat, strangely muffled.

Was I a ghost, haunting this place? Or was this place haunting me? It seemed . . . dead. And why did the only cold I was feeling seem to come from within me, rather than from without?

I called out, "Hello! Anybody there? Anybody?" No answer. The silence seemed heavier and more oppressive than ever. I shivered abruptly, and not from the cold. It occurred to me that my voice had sounded strangely flat, and I realised it was because my voice hadn't echoed at all. It should have. One more impossible thing in an impossible place. I breathed heavily, but my breath didn't steam on the air before me.

I hurried down the corridor, trying every door I came to. None of them would budge; the door handles wouldn't even turn in my hand, no matter how much strength I used. I beat on each door with my fist, but no one answered. I ran on, rounding another corner, and then I stopped abruptly before a huge grandfather clock. Tall and solid in its ornate oakwood case, it had a wide face and hanging brass weights. It was utterly silent, not a tick or a tock, and after a moment I realised the face didn't even have any hands. I checked my wristwatch. The digital display was completely blank. Had I come to a place where time had stopped, where there was no time left?

Farther down the corridor I came across a full-length mirror set in a filigreed silver frame, shining bright in the blue moonlight. I stood before the mirror, and it reflected everything in the corridor except me. My heart pounded in my chest, and my breath rasped harshly in my throat. I pressed one hand hard against the cold glass, but the mirror refused to acknowledge any part of me.

I fell back from the mirror and turned to run again, pounding down the corridor, though my feet made no sound at all and I didn't slip or slide on the icy carpeting as I should have. I threw myself round the next corner, and then came to a sudden halt as I found myself down on the ground floor, in the entrance hall, facing the great double doors that led outside. I stood very still, not even breathing hard, staring at the doors. This was wrong. An upstairs corridor couldn't connect directly to a downstairs hall without benefit of stairs. But right then I didn't care. The way out was in front of me, and I'd had enough of this empty house. I ran to the doors and tried the handles, and of course they wouldn't move. I rattled the handles so hard that it shook the double doors, but they wouldn't open. I slammed my shoulder against them, again and again, but I couldn't even feel the impacts on my shoulder. I finally stopped and leaned against the doors, hot tears of frustration burning my eyes. And then a voice behind me said:

"You can't leave, Eddie. There's no way out for you. You're confined here, a prisoner in Drood Hall."

I spun round, and there, standing in the hall, calm and civilised and immaculate as always, was Walker. The man who ran London's Nightside in every way that mattered. Dressed like someone Big in the City, smartly and expensively tailored, right down to the bowler hat and the rolled umbrella he was leaning on. A man past his best days, perhaps, but still the ultimate authority figure, with a polite smile and cold, cold eyes. I knew him immediately, and suddenly a whole bunch of my memories came flooding back. I was Eddie Drood, also known as Shaman Bond, the very secret agent. Field agent for that most ancient and powerful family, the Droods; trained from childhood to protect Humanity from all the dark forces that threatened it.

This was my home, Drood Hall. Though I'd never known it so deserted, so abandoned. I remembered a lot of things now, but not how I came to be here, or what the hell was going on. So I struck my most comfortable and assured pose and gave Walker a cold glare of my own.

"A prisoner?" I said. "In my own home? I don't think so, Walker. And how the hell did you get in? We're really very particular about who we allow into the Hall."

"Ah," said Walker. "Let's say . . . I am here representing certain powerful and vested interests who have questions they want me to put to you. There are things they want to know about you and your family. The things you've done and intend to do. All the secrets you and your family have kept from the world. They want to know . . . everything. Just tell me, Eddie, and all of this will be over. You must realise there's no point in fighting me, or those I represent. You're a reasonable man. . . ."

"No, I'm bloody not," I said. "I'm a Drood field agent, licensed to take names and kick supernatural arse, and being reasonable never gets you anywhere against the forces of evil. I've got questions of my own, Walker. Starting with, what's happened to Drood Hall? And where the hell is everybody? Did I miss a fire drill?"

I felt the need to back up my questions with a little authority of my own, and so I subvocalised the activating Words that would call up my armour, the special golden armour that was my family's greatest secret and most powerful weapon. But to my surprise and shock nothing happened. My hand went to my throat, and the golden torc wasn't there. I think I cried out then, as though part of my soul had been ripped away. Droods receive their torcs shortly after birth, and are never without them. I clawed at my throat with both hands, but it stayed bare. For a moment I couldn't breathe, and then I clamped down on my racing thoughts with an iron will. I was a trained field agent, and I was damned if I'd panic in the face of the enemy. Even if I had never felt so helpless in my life, so vulnerable, so . . . unmanned.

For the first time I knew how the rest of my family had felt when I took their torcs away.

I glared at Walker. "How dare you? How dare you steal my torc? And what's happened to my family? What have you done with them?"

Walker smiled calmly back at me. "I'm here to ask questions, Eddie, not answer them. My current lords and masters require your obedience. Tell me your secrets, Eddie. Every last one of them. And then this nightmare can end."

I stood my ground and considered him thoughtfully. Losing my temper with Walker would get me nowhere. You can't run a spiritual cesspool like the Nightside with a reasonable manner and good intent. Walker believed in the iron fist in the iron glove, and had always been a very dangerous man. Certainly I couldn't hope to intimidate him without my armour. But the day I couldn't think rings round a soulless functionary like Walker, I'd retire from the field and raise bees. According to the media there's a shortage these days. . . . I gave Walker my best cocky, crafty grin, the one that says, *I know something you don't know. . . .*

"Haven't seen you since that nasty business with the independent agent," I said. "So, still keeping the lid on the Nightside, are you? Running back and forth trying to make all those gods and monsters play nicely together?" And then I stopped, and frowned, and looked closely at Walker. "Didn't someone tell me . . . you'd been killed?"

Walker shrugged. "Comes to us all, in the end. No one gets out of life alive. All that matters here and now is that I serve new masters; and they want information from you. Past cases, victories old and new, everything there is to know about the notorious Drood family."

"Yeah," I said. "That'll be the day. So, new lords and masters, is it? And who might they be, exactly?"

"You don't need to know," said Walker. "It doesn't matter; we all have to serve someone, in the end. It's all right for you to talk to me, Eddie. The secrets we hold in life aren't important anymore, once we're dead."

I stared at him. "Someone really did kill you? I didn't believe anyone could take down the legendary Walker."

"I got old," said Walker, "and perhaps a little careless with someone I trusted. Still, he'll make a good replacement."

"And . . . I'm dead?"

"Of course. Don't you remember the disguised Immortal stabbing you? No? Well, I'm sure it'll come back to you. You're probably still in shock."

"I am not dead! I'm breathing; I can feel my heart pounding. . . . I can't be dead!"

"You must be," said Walker. "Or you wouldn't have come here among dead people."

A sudden shudder went through me, and I looked quickly about the entrance hall, splashed with deep shadows and blue moonlight.

"There are dead people here?"

"Oh, yes," said Walker. "Old enemies and older friends: some you may remember, some not. The past is full of strangers with familiar faces. People whose lives you touched in passing, for good or bad. The lives you saved and the lives you ended. And all of them want what I want. Answers. Secrets. Information. You must tell me what I need to know, Eddie. Tell me."

"I'm damned if I'll tell you anything!"

"You'll be damned if you don't," Walker said calmly.

I looked past him suddenly, as I glimpsed a familiar face. Standing quietly in the blue moonlight as though he wasn't sure he ought to be there, a tall, thin figure stared sadly back at me. Wrapped in a long grey coat, with a thick scarf wrapped round his neck to keep out the cold, Coffin Jobe nodded sorrowfully in my direction. Jobe was a necroleptic; he kept falling down dead and then getting over it. We knew each other, but I wouldn't call us friends. And he certainly had no business in Drood Hall.

He approached me in a reluctant sideways sort of way, and came to a halt beside Walker, who moved away to one side, as though afraid he might catch something. Lot of people felt that way about Coffin Jobe. I always thought it was the coat; it looked like it could start a new plague all on its own.

"Hello, Jobe," I said. "Is this where you go to when you're being dead?"

"I don't know," said Jobe. "I never remember where I've been once I'm alive again. There are rules, apparently. But I don't think I've ever been here before. In fact, I'm getting the distinct feeling I shouldn't be here. Of course, I get that feeling in a lot of places when I'm being alive. . . ." He looked at me accusingly. "I liked you better when you were being Shaman Bond. I always knew where I was with Shaman. Just another face on the scene, another chancer, like me. Not important at all. But it turned out you were a Drood all along. Laughing at us from behind your Shaman Bond mask."

"No," I said. "That's not how it was, Jobe. . . ."

But he was already gone, disappeared in a moment, back in the land of the living again.

A door opened to one side, and out of his private office stepped the Drood family's Sarjeant-at-Arms. The previous Sarjeant, who'd died so very bravely on the Damnation Way, buying the rest of us time to escape. Big and muscular and brutal, exactly as I remembered him, with half his face still a mass of scars from where my girlfriend, Molly Metcalf, wished a plague of rats on him. He'd deserved worse. He stood beside Walker and looked at me coldly, his gaze as inflexible and judgemental as always.

"You were a thug and a bully when you were alive, Sarjeant," I said. "And it would appear death hasn't mellowed you."

"You never did understand duty, Edwin," said the Sarjeant. "You should never have been allowed to run the family. You took away our torcs. You made us weak."

"The family had become corrupt," I said. "Drifted too far from who and what we were supposed to be. I did what I had to do to save the family from itself."

"By destroying its Heart."

"The Heart was rotten. It lied to us. I was the only one left who cared about what the family was supposed to stand for. What did you ever care about, except disciplining those weaker than yourself?"

"You never understood duty," said the Sarjeant-at-Arms. "The family has to be strong to do the things it has to do. I tried to make you strong by beating the weakness and rebellion out of you."

"Weakness?" I said. "You mean things like compassion, and honour, and doing the right thing?"

"Yes," said the Sarjeant. "Everything the family

does is right, because we're Droods. Nothing else matters."

"We're supposed to protect Humanity, not rule them!"

"Sheep need shepherds," said the Sarjeant. "And a little culling now and then, to improve the stock."

I strode right up to him and punched him in the face. But my hand passed straight through him, as though he were only a vision or a ghost. I snatched my hand back, and the Sarjeant looked at me almost sadly.

"Good punch, Edwin. Just like I taught you. But that won't help you here. You can't fight us. You can't stop us. Tell us what we want to know. Tell us all your secrets. It's the only way you'll ever be free of this place."

"You're not the Sarjeant-at-Arms," I said. "He'd die before he betrayed a single Drood secret to an outsider."

"You can't escape us," said Walker.

"Yeah?" I said. "Kiss my arse."

I sprinted past him, up the stairway and onto the next floor. Only the next floor wasn't there; instead I stumbled to a halt inside the War Room, the nerve centre of the family, where all the really important decisions are made: looking after the hundreds of field agents out in the world, stamping out supernatural brush fires and slapping down the bad guys. Brown-trousering the ungodly, as my uncle James liked to put it. The War Room was usually packed with people at their work, full of sound and fury; but now it was deserted, silent. All the workstations were empty, the computer monitors and the scrying balls left unattended. All the lights were out on the great world map, and all of the clock faces, showing the time in every country in the world, were blank, without hands. Time had stopped here, too.

The work surfaces were layered with frost, and the communication systems were thickly coated with ice. (Part of me wondered where the blue moonlight was coming from to illuminate the War Room, but I'd made a conscious decision to worry only about those things that mattered immediately.) I wrote my name with my fingertip on the frost covering one monitor screen, but I couldn't feel the cold of the ice. I looked up sharply, as one by one the monitor screens on the walls that should have shown trouble spots across the world turned themselves on, and vaguely familiar faces appeared on the screens, looking down at me, watching me with cold, angry, judgemental eyes. When I looked at any face directly it vanished, reappearing when I looked somewhere else. I was surrounded by a sea of faces, grim and condemning, but none of them could face me directly. I looked quickly back and forth, but all I could do was catch glimpses of my accusers out of the corners of my eyes. Glimpses of cold, scowling faces watching me with bad intent.

I almost jumped out of my skin when I suddenly realised there was someone in the War Room with me. I spun round, putting my back against the nearest workstation, and there facing me was the Blue Fairy. Half elf, thief, traitor . . . sometimes a friend, and sometimes not. That's often how it is, out in the field. He looked very smart, almost fashionable, in his own ratty way; but his face was ravaged by time and far too much good living. He looked at me and shook his head sadly.

"Eddie, dear boy, what are you doing here, pursued by the dead, at the mercy of old friends and enemies? So much bitterness and unpleasantness, and all for a few secrets that probably never mattered that much, even when we were alive." He looked about him. "Terrible place, no sense of style. Tell them what they want to know, Eddie, and then we can both get the hell out of here. I don't like this place. Don't like being dead, for that matter. When I first discovered what being dead was like, I cried and I cried and I cried. . . ."

"There has to be a way out of here," I said. "Help me. I helped you. . . ."

"Did you, Eddie? Did you really? Yes, you rescued me from the depths of depression and disgrace, gave me new life and purpose . . . but did you think I'd be grateful? You should have left me as I was: a broken man, dying by inches and not giving a damn. You woke me

up, gave me hope . . . just so I could die anyway a few
years later in one of your stupid spy games. You should
have left me as I was. It would have been kinder."

"You always did make bad decisions, Edwin," said
another familiar voice.

And out of the deep, dark shadows of the War Room
came my grandmother, Martha Drood, Matriarch of
the family. She stood tall and stiff and proud before me
in her neat grey twinset and pearls. Looking at me with
her cold eyes and colder face. No sign of the awful
wound that killed her in her own bed, soaking the whole
front of her in blood. She looked me up and down and
sniffed briefly. Another familiar sound. It tore at my
heart. I hadn't realised I'd missed it so much.

"You ran away from the Hall to be a field agent, and
what good did that do you? All because you didn't have
the discipline to buckle down and do what you were told,
like everyone else. I was grooming you to take a high
position in the family, but you turned your back on us.
You were always such a disappointment to me, Edwin."

"I avenged your murder," I said steadily. "I caught
your killer, the Immortal disguised as your husband,
Alistair. I killed him for you, Grandmother."

"I'm still dead," she said. "All because you weren't
paying attention. Too caught up with your new girlfriend. I never approved of her."

"You never approved of me, Edwin," said Alistair
Drood, stepping forward to stand beside Martha. "You
were responsible for my death too. I was only trying to
do the right thing and protect my wife. You watched me
burn in hellfire, and did nothing to save me. Tell them
what they want to know, Edwin. Let your grandmother
and me know peace, and rest at last."

"Tell them," said Martha Drood. "Tell them everything, Edwin."

"Tell them," said the Blue Fairy. "Or we'll never
leave you alone."

"None of your deaths were my fault!" I yelled at
them, and then I turned and ran out of the War Room.

And straight into the Armoury, even though it was located in a whole other wing of Drood Hall. I looked quickly behind me, but no one had followed. I moved slowly forward, checking every dark shadow for a new accusing face. The huge stone chamber seemed strange and unsettling, far too quiet without the usual hustle and bustle of the Armourer and his lab assistants. Always busy working on new weapons and devices of appalling destruction. Or raising hell and getting themselves into trouble for the fun of it. It isn't a successful day in the Armoury unless someone's been transformed into something distressing, or exploded, or committed some brave new crime against nature. But the workstations were empty, and the weapons-testing ground was unnaturally quiet. I moved quickly through the Armoury, looking for something I could use as a weapon. There were always nasty destructive things lying about in the Armoury. But the few dark shapes I could make out were welded to surfaces by the extreme cold, buried under thick layers of ice. I tried to pry a few of them loose, but no amount of effort would budge them. I beat at the crusted ice with my fist, but couldn't even crack or splinter it.

A sound behind me spun me round, hands up to defend myself, half expecting Uncle Jack, the Armourer. But instead it was my uncle James. The greatest field agent the family ever produced: the legendary Grey Fox. Dead, because of me. He stood there smiling, tall and dark and handsome in his splendid tuxedo. Every inch the master spy I never was. Looking just as he had before I got him killed.

"No," I said. "Please. No. Not you, Uncle James. I can't stand it. . . ."

"Relax," said Uncle James. "It's all right, Eddie. I forgave you long ago."

For a long moment, I couldn't say anything. Uncle James nodded understandingly.

"It's good to see you again, Eddie. I understood why you did what you did, even when I was alive. Ah, the things we do for the family . . . I don't hold grudges.

You see things a lot more clearly once you're dead. You did for the family what I should have done long before."

"Why are you here?" I said. "Are you a prisoner in this place, like me?"

"No. I was called here, like the others. But unlike most of them, I'm on your side."

"Do you think I should tell Walker what he wants to know?" I said. "Tell him all my secrets, and those of the family?"

"Of course not," said Uncle James. "Walker always was too ready to bow down to authority, or to anyone with a public-school accent. Tell him to go to hell, Eddie."

I had to grin. Death had not mellowed Uncle James. "Do you know whom Walker's working for? Who it is who wants my secrets?"

Uncle James frowned. "It's hard to be sure of anything here. Hardly anyone or anything is necessarily what they appear to be."

"Even you?" I said.

He shrugged easily. "Hard to tell. I think I'm me, but then I would, wouldn't I?"

I put out my hand to him, but when he went to shake it, our fingers drifted through one another.

"Am I a ghost?" I said. "Give it to me straight; I can take it."

"Not even close," snapped another familiar voice. "You shouldn't be here, boy."

And suddenly standing next to my uncle James was Jacob Drood, the family ghost. He wore a battered Hawaiian shirt over grubby shorts, looking older than death itself. His face was a mass of wrinkles, his big, bony skull graced with a few flyaway hairs. But his eyes were as sharp and fierce as ever. He nodded brusquely to Uncle James, and then fixed me with his glare. "I'm the only ghost here, Eddie; but I can't help you. There are rules even the dead have to obey. Perhaps especially the dead."

I studied him carefully. He looked more solid and

more real than anyone else I'd met in this empty Hall. "Are you really here, Jacob?"

"Yes. But not everyone else is." He looked at Uncle James, who smiled easily back. Jacob sniffed loudly and glared about him before piercing me with his sharp gaze again. "Someone's running a game on you, Eddie. Even I can't tell who the players are, for sure. You need to get out of here, boy. You don't belong here. Bad things are on their way, attracted by the light."

"The blue moonlight?"

"Your light, boy! Get out of here! Run, while you still can!"

I looked at Uncle James, and he nodded quickly. That was enough for me. I turned and ran back through the Armoury, and almost immediately found myself in the Sanctity, the great open chamber that served as a meeting place for the ruling council of the family. Once it was home to the Heart, the huge other-dimensional diamond that gave the family its power, and its original armour. As long as we fed it the souls of our children. I put a stop to that and destroyed the Heart, and now the Sanctity was only a room. But there was no trace of the rose red glow that usually suffused the chamber, the physical manifestation of the other-dimensional traveller called Ethel, who came to the Hall to replace the Heart and supply our new armour. The good angel I'd found to replace the bad. Except that angels always have their own agenda, and don't always give a damn for merely human concerns. . . .

The Sanctity felt cold and desolate without Ethel's comforting glow. I called out to her, but no one answered. I nodded quietly to myself. One final proof that this place wasn't, couldn't be, the real Drood Hall. No one could have kept Ethel from answering me in the real Hall.

"Always running, Eddie," said yet another familiar voice. "Never staying in one place long enough to take responsibility for your actions."

I took my time turning around, and there was Penny

Drood, tall and slender in her usual white sweater and slacks. She looked at me with cold, desperate eyes.

"You let him kill me. That old monster from old London town. My blood is on your hands. You must make amends, Eddie. Tell Walker what he needs to know."

"I did warn you about Mr. Stab," I said. "I told you what he was, but you were so sure you knew better."

"You've always got an answer, haven't you, Eddie?" said Alexander King, the independent agent, stepping forward to stand beside Penny. "Typical Drood. Always ready to blame the bad things in the world on someone else."

"In your case, I was right," I said. "Nasty old man, squatting on your stolen secrets, guarding your hoard like a dragon in its cave. Yes, I killed you. Do it again in a minute. After everything you were responsible for, you deserved your death."

"Tell them what they want to know," said King. "You can't keep anything from Walker or those he serves. They have all the power here. They know where all the bodies are buried."

Suddenly the entire great chamber of the Sanctity was full of people crowding in around me. Matthew and Alexandra Drood, who did their best to have me killed in the name of Zero Tolerance, and died trying to stop me from saving the family. And more faces, and more: all the men and women who'd died at my hands, or because of me, because I was an agent of the Droods. All the bad guys, and those who thought they were good guys but chose a bad cause to follow, and all those in between. All the Accelerated Men, who died trying to storm Drood Hall and kill the family. All the teenage Immortals, who died trying to rule Humanity, or because they planned to unleash the forces of Hell by opening the Apocalypse Door. All those I'd fought to save the world from. I hadn't realised there were so many of them. Hundreds of dead men and women surrounding me with cold, pitiless eyes, many of them with their death wounds still fresh and bloody. I stood my ground, glaring around me, refusing to accept the guilt they were trying to impose on me.

"There isn't one of you here who didn't deserve your death," I said. "I did my duty. To the family, and to Humanity. You all needed killing."

And one by one they faded away, unable to face the certainty in my gaze.

"Harsh words, Eddie," said one final familiar voice. "Hard and harsh, even cold-blooded. I always knew you were an agent, but I never knew you were such a successful assassin."

Philip MacAlpine of MI-13 stood before me, middle-aged and rumpled, but still every inch the professional spy.

I glared right back at him. "What the hell are you doing here? Did someone in your own department finally shoot you in the back?"

He grinned. "Wouldn't you like to know? You must allow me my little secrets, even if you can't be allowed to hang onto yours. It's your own fault, Eddie; you shouldn't have led such an interesting life. Or acquired so many fascinating secrets. You must have known you couldn't hang onto them forever. You mustn't be greedy, Eddie. You must be a good boy and learn to share. Tell Walker what you know. Or you can tell me, if that's easier."

I laughed in his face. "Yeah, right. That'll be the day. At least Walker has some integrity in him. You sold your soul long ago, to any number of masters. I wouldn't give you the time of day."

"How very hurtful," murmured Philip. "We're not really so different, Eddie. Both of us secret agents, operating in the shadows because we don't belong in the light. You served an ancient family with its own hidden agenda, while I was a blunt instrument for government policy. Doing all the hard and dirty things that needed to be done to hold the world together. And perhaps manage a few good deeds along the way, when we could."

"The difference between us is that I took the bigger view," I said. "I never let politics get in the way of what needed to be done. I protected Humanity from those who would prey on it. Which, as often as not, turned out to be politicians."

"We don't all have that luxury," said Philip. "Must be nice to look down on us like gods and decide what's best for us, while the rest of us scrabble around in the gutter, getting our hands dirty from all the rotten little jobs you can't be bothered with. You can make as big a mess as you like, with your marvellous golden armour, stepping in to save the day and then disappearing, leaving the rest of us to clean up after you. Well, now all your sins have come home to roost, Eddie. You've upset a lot of very important persons, and now that you're . . . vulnerable, they're determined to wring you dry. They want everything you know, and they will get it, sooner or later. You're a prisoner here, with no armour and no family to protect you. You're on your own, Eddie, facing a legion of tormentors."

"And if I don't feel like talking?" I said.

"It's the only way you'll ever get out of here," said Philip. "Wouldn't you like to be free of all this? Free to lie down and rest, and be at peace at last?"

"Peace is overrated," I said. "And why should I want to leave? This is my home, isn't it? My family home, Drood Hall. Needs a bit of cleaning up, got to fix the boiler, and there're a whole bunch of gate-crashers I have to give the bum's rush to. . . ."

Philip scowled at me. "You are in the hands of your enemies, Eddie. You can't stop them. They are endless, they are multitudes, they are legion. They will be at your back and at your throat and they will never stop coming for you, forever and ever and ever. By hook or by crook, they'll tear every secret you know out of you, even the ones you didn't know you knew, and they will laugh at your screams as they do it."

"Over my dead body," I said.

I punched him in the face. I meant it as a gesture of defiance, expecting my clenched fist to pass straight through him, but it collided with solid flesh and bone. I heard his nose break, and saw blood fly from his pulped mouth, and it felt good, so good. Philip fell backwards, crying out in shock and pain. I laughed out loud as I strode past him and out of the Sanctity. For the first time, I felt like I was getting a handle on the situation.

The moment I left the Sanctity I was back in the entrance hall again, approaching the firmly closed doors. Walker was still there, smiling easily at me, leaning on his rolled umbrella. He stood between me and the doors, blocking my way. He didn't say anything. He didn't have to.

"I'll never talk," I said. "You of all people should understand. My secrets don't belong only to me; they belong to the family. Our secrets keep people safe, keep people alive, help protect them from people like you and your secret lords and masters. I wouldn't let my family down while I was alive, and I'm damned if I'll do it now. Droods stand between Humanity and their enemies, alive or dead."

"I have my Voice," said Walker. "The Voice that commands and cannot be disobeyed. I could make you tell me."

"No, you couldn't," I said. "Because if you could, you would have done it by now. You can't con a con man, Walker."

"Perhaps," said Walker. "But I was always so much more than just a man with a commanding Voice. I have always known a great many unpleasant ways to make people tell me what I need to know."

I believed that. I backed slowly away as Walker advanced on me. I was thinking hard, looking all around me, trying hard to call up any information I had about the Hall that Walker couldn't possibly know. Something I could use against him. The painted portraits on the walls caught my attention. The images were moving, changing, faces with crazy eyes and distorted expressions. Becoming nightmare images, glimpses into Hell, as though all my ancestors were trapped and damned and suffering. I turned my head away, refusing to believe that.

Matthew and Alexandra appeared again, walking down the long hall towards me.

"Go on," said Alexandra. "Kill us again. You know you want to. But you can't. Tell Walker what he wants to know."

"I didn't kill either of you," I said, and then stopped and stared at them both as that thought struck home. I hadn't killed them; Jacob had. But these two hadn't known that, so they couldn't be who they appeared to be. Jacob and Uncle James had both said not everyone in this Hall was who or what they appeared to be. . . .

"You're not real," I said firmly. "I don't believe in you."

I glared at Matthew and Alexandra, and they faded away in the face of my certainty. I turned and looked at Walker.

"Just you and me now, Walker. Or perhaps it always was. If you are Walker."

He considered me thoughtfully, as we stood facing each other. Two men in an empty hall, the prisoner and his inquisitor. Walker sighed briefly, and adjusted one spotless cuff.

"There's nowhere you can go, Eddie. And I have all the time in the world to break your will and learn what I need to know. Everyone talks, eventually."

"Use your Voice," I said. "Go on. But you can't, can you? Because you're not really Walker. And this isn't Drood Hall. Is anything here real? Is anyone? Or is this all just a clash of wills between me and whoever you really are? You can't get anything out of me unless I offer it freely, and I'll never do that."

"Never is a long time," said Walker. "I can walk out of here, go about my business, and come back whenever I please. Might be a few days, or a few years, maybe even a few centuries. Or perhaps I'll stay away until you're so desperate for another human voice, for human contact, that you'll beg me to come back. Beg to tell me everything you know, to relieve the awful solitude. Hell isn't other people, Eddie. Hell is an empty house, forever and ever and ever."

"And I will always defy you," I said. "Forever and a day. Remember the Drood oath: 'Anything for the family.' We mean it, Walker. That's what makes us strong, not our armour."

"Anything for the family?" said Walker. "I think I believe you, Eddie. Ah, well." He tipped his bowler hat to me and started to turn away.

"Hold it," I said. "Are you really Walker? Are you really dead? Am I?"

He smiled vaguely. "Who can say, in a place like this?"

"If I am dead," I said, "and this is a place of the dead . . . why haven't I seen my parents?"

"Charles and Emily?" said Walker. "Whatever makes you think they're dead?"

He opened the doors, stepped through them, and was gone. I started after him, and then stopped short as a great blaze of pure white light swelled up before me. And out of that light stepped Molly: my sweet, wild witch, Molly Metcalf. She smiled widely at me, rushed forward, and threw her arms around me, holding me tight, so tight I thought she'd never let me go. I held her just as tightly, even as a terrible sadness stabbed my heart like a knife.

"Oh, Molly," I said finally. "How did you die? Who killed you, to send you here?"

She let go of me immediately, and pushed me back so she could stare into my eyes. "I'm not dead, sweetie. Neither are you. Though you came bloody close."

"So this isn't Drood Hall? Or some cold place in Hell?"

"Not even close," said Molly. "This is Limbo. And I am here to take you home."

She embraced me again, and the light blazed up, and finally I felt warm again.

CHAPTER TWO

No Place Like Home

And I woke up safe in my Molly's arms, bursting back into consciousness like a swimmer rising up from the depths and breaking the surface of the sea. I was back in the real Hall, back in the real Sanctity, basking in Ethel's rose red glow, sitting up on the floor beside Molly, surrounded by my family. The Armourer was there, my uncle Jack, a middle-aged man in a stained lab coat, looking shocked and concerned but trying to hide it. The Sarjeant-at-Arms, big and brutal and permanently angry. My cousin Harry, slick and supercilious in his neat grey suit and wire-rimmed glasses. And my other cousin, Roger Morningstar, the half-breed hellspawn, dark and sardonic in his Armani suit. And Molly. My sweet, wild witch and free spirit, a delicate china doll with big bosoms, bobbed black hair, and a mouth red as sin. My own true love, for my sins.

She looked intently into my eyes, trying to keep the anxiety out of her smile, one arm round my shoulders, the other hand patting my chest comfortingly. I managed a shaky smile for her, and we leaned forward so our foreheads touched, resting against each other. I felt safe and happy, and so damned alive I might burst apart into clouds of sheer joie de vivre at any moment. Brief shivers and shudders came and went, and I was breathing hard, but the cold was slowly seeping out of me, replaced by Molly's warmth and the uncomplicated comfort of Ethel's rose red light.

I was home again.

I remembered everything now. Remembered the Immortal bursting into the Sanctity, disguised as Molly's sister Isabella. A transformation so perfect it even fooled the Hall's many layers of defences. I remembered the Immortal stabbing me. How the knife felt as it sank into my flesh and pierced my heart. Remembered the pain and the blood, and falling, and dying . . . I clutched at my chest, and fresh blood ran down my wrist as I crushed the torn shirtfront with my hand. The whole of my shirt was soaked in blood. But when I pushed the material aside, the skin underneath was undamaged. I ran my fingers over my chest, searching for the deep wound I remembered, but it was completely healed. I felt fine. I looked at Molly.

"It's all right, Eddie," she said, reassuring me with her eyes and her smile as well as her words. "You're fine. Everything's fine now."

"Look at this shirt," I said numbly. "Ruined. And it was my favourite shirt, too."

"I never liked it," said Molly.

"You never said. . . . All right. I'm back. Now, what the hell just happened?"

The Armourer moved in and offered me his hand. I grabbed onto it, and he hauled me to my feet. My legs threatened to shake for a moment, and then steadied. Molly stood close beside me, in case I needed her. The Armourer looked me over closely, and then pulled me into his arms and hugged me fiercely.

"I thought we'd lost you, Eddie; I really did. And I couldn't bear the thought of your being dead. I've lost too many already."

I hugged him back, awkwardly. We've never been a touchy-feely family. He let go of me abruptly and stood back, in control again.

"Do you remember what happened, Eddie? While you were . . . gone?"

"I was in Drood Hall," I said slowly, "but it wasn't the real Hall. It was a cold, empty place . . . full of dead people. Walker was there, and Grandmother, and Uncle James."

"A near-death experience?" said Harry. "How very fashionable."

He shut up as the Armourer glared at him. "Fascinating," Uncle Jack said briskly. "I've always wanted to record one of those. What did James have to say to you? Did he forgive you?"

"We forgave each other," I said.

"You weren't really dead, as such," Molly said quickly. "Your spirit was in Limbo. And not everyone you encountered there was necessarily who or what they appeared to be. And Walker almost definitely wasn't Walker."

"Might have been," said the Armourer. "He's dead, all right. I got a letter."

"What happened to him?" I said.

"Someone killed him. An old enemy, or an old friend. Possibly both. It's like that in the Nightside. So I'm told."

"He still shouldn't have been there with you, Eddie," said Molly. "Not if you were in a semblance of Drood Hall. He's never been here."

Roger Morningstar sniffed loudly. "You don't understand Limbo any more than I do, Molly. It's neither Heaven nor Hell, not a place for the living or the dead: more of a spiritual waiting room . . . a place between places. Who knows who has access to it? If the living can enter, why not the dead? It could be that everyone you saw there, Eddie, was exactly who they seemed to be."

"You do so love to stir it, don't you?" said Molly. "Trust you to play Devil's advocate."

"And trust you, Eddie, to have a near-death experience that's completely unlike everyone else's," said Harry.

"Back to life for only a few minutes, and already you're annoying the crap out of me, Harry," I said.

"Now button your lip while the grown-ups talk, or I'll supply you with a near-death experience of your own. Ethel? Are you there?"

"Eddie, Eddie, Eddie!" said the disembodied voice of our very own other-dimensional entity. "Where did you go? I couldn't see you anywhere, and I can see into dimensions you people don't even know exist!"

"The Hall was very different without you," I said. "So cold . . . I called, but you couldn't hear me."

"How terrible for you," said Ethel, completely sincerely.

"Yes," I said. "It was."

I started to shake again. Molly quickly slipped an arm through mine and squeezed it against her. The Sarjeant-at-Arms stepped forward and glared at both of us.

"I demand an explanation as to what exactly happened! Why aren't you dead, Eddie?"

"Try not to sound so disappointed, Cedric," I murmured. "Though I think I could use an explanation myself. Molly?"

"You were stabbed through the heart," said Molly. "But you were never completely dead. Try not to be too mad at me, Eddie. I did it for your own good."

"Did what?" I said. "Tell me."

"Like every other witch," Molly said carefully, "at the start of my career I worked a very special magic to store my heart somewhere else, technically separate from my body, but still connected. And then I hid my heart somewhere very safe and secure and secret, so my enemies could never find it. And as long as my heart remains separate, I am very hard to kill. I can recover from every wound, every attack, no matter how apparently deadly. That's how I survived that assault by the Drood mob stirred up by the Immortals." She glared at the Sarjeant there, and he had the grace to look a little guilty. He's supposed to prevent things like that from happening. Molly took a deep breath. "I performed the same magic on you, Eddie, some time ago."

"What? Without even telling me?" I said, rather loudly.

"Yes!" said Molly, meeting my fierce gaze with her own. "I didn't tell you because I knew you'd react like this! I knew you wouldn't agree if I suggested the idea to you, even though it was obviously the sensible thing to do . . . and I wasn't prepared to risk losing you. So I did it while you were asleep. Because I needed you to be safe."

"When, exactly, did you do this?" I said. "How long ago?"

"I'm not going to tell you," said Molly, folding her arms firmly below her breasts. "Not until you've calmed down a little. Or perhaps even a lot."

"I can't approve of this," the Sarjeant said flatly. "A Drood's heart in the hands of an outsider? Completely unacceptable! As long as the witch knows where your heart is hidden and you don't, she'll always have power over you."

"He does have a point," said the Armourer. "What if the two of you had a big row? Or even split up?"

I looked at Molly. "The things we do for love . . . My heart belongs to the family. That's the way it has to be. You have to put it back."

"Oh, all right," said Molly, pouting. "Men. Never appreciate anything you do for them. There. It's back."

I looked down at my chest. "Just like that?"

"Of course! It's no big deal. One of the first magics I learned. Your heart was never actually missing, after all. It was . . . separate. And safe."

"Did you check it for cholesterol?" said the Armourer.

Molly glared at him. "I'm a witch, not a cardiologist!"

"All right, all right! Only asking! We do have a problem with cholesterol levels in the family, and I was just wondering if . . . Shutting up right now. Sorry."

I didn't feel any different. A thought occurred to me, and I looked consideringly at Molly. "Where exactly did you put my heart? Tell me you didn't hide it in that private forest of yours, with all those overintelligent and highly curious animals. What if one of the squirrels had dug it up while looking for nuts? You know the squirrels have never approved of me!"

Molly gave me her best haughty glare. "We are definitely not discussing this until you are in a much calmer state. And don't even think of raising your voice to me like that if you ever expect to see me naked again."

Women never fight fair.

"I will agree to change the subject," I said. "But only because I'm still waiting to hear what happened to me after I was stabbed!"

"Your spirit went to Limbo," said Molly. "You weren't, properly speaking, alive, but I'd seen to it that death couldn't claim you. So Limbo took you until my magics could supercharge the healing process and repair your body enough for your spirit to return. You were in . . . spiritual shock. Neither in one condition nor the other. Limbo isn't a place, as such. When you go there, your mind creates its own setting. It's perfectly possible"—and here she broke off to scowl at Roger for a moment—"that all the people you saw there were really only parts of your own mind, talking to one another. Working out old issues and unresolved conflicts. Psychotherapy for the soul."

"I don't think so," I said. "Some of them, maybe. But there was definitely another presence there. Walker . . . was very much Walker. He wanted to know things. Secrets . . . mine, and those of the family. He said he represented someone else. He had new lords and masters now, and they were determined to rip every secret I had out of me. Whatever it took."

"Walker is quite definitely dead," said the Armourer. "I'll show you the letter, if you like."

"I want to see that letter," the Sarjeant-at-Arms said immediately. "I never knew you had such close contacts with the Nightside."

"Later, Cedric," said the Armourer. "And don't pout like that. It's unbecoming in a man of your age." He nodded to Molly. "Carry on, my dear. We're all listening."

"While you were in Limbo, Eddie," said Molly, "and

spiritually vulnerable, it is possible that some enemy of yours could have launched an attack on your spirit, trying to overpower your defences."

"Did you tell them anything?" said the Sarjeant.

"No," I said steadily. "I know my duty to the family."

"Of course you do, Eddie," said the Sarjeant. "My apologies. But we have to know; we need to find out: Who were these enemies? And how did they know you were in Limbo, and therefore vulnerable to this kind of attack?"

He turned his stern gaze on Molly, who actually stirred uncomfortably.

"Look," she said, "I'm no expert on Limbo, all right? Don't know anyone who is. But to reach Eddie, and enter the construct his mind had made there, and push him around . . . they'd have to be really powerful."

"As powerful as the Droods?" I said.

"I thought we'd killed off everyone as powerful as us," said Roger.

"There's always someone," said the Sarjeant darkly.

"Anyway," said Molly, "as soon as I'd repaired your heart, Eddie, and got your body back in good working order, I was a bit surprised your spirit didn't return immediately. That's what's supposed to happen. So I went after you. I've been to Heaven and to Hell; Limbo doesn't scare me. I spent some time there myself, recovering from what the Drood mob did to me. I don't remember what it was like, though. You won't either, after a while. It's not something the living are supposed to know about."

I didn't say anything, but I hadn't forgotten a thing. The whole experience was as fresh and clear to me as when I was there. Every detail, every moment, every word. Because it was important that I remember. Someone had tried to steal my secrets, and those of my family, and I was determined to find out who. And . . . there was something else.

Charles and Emily? Walker had said. *Whatever makes you think they're dead?*

Harry was talking. "You always have to be the centre

of attention, Eddie. You can't even die in an ordinary way. Though I did think we really might have lost you, for a while."

"Disappointed?" I said.

"Oh, perish the thought," said Harry.

"What was it like in Limbo?" said Roger. "I've never been there. I'm banned."

Molly looked at him incredulously. "Banned? How the hell do you get banned from Limbo?"

"Boisterousness," Roger said vaguely. "Bad behaviour. You know how it is."

"The memories are slipping away," I said carefully. "I have to say, I'm happy to see most of them go."

"What do you remember?" said Molly.

"Cold," I said. "So very cold . . ." I shuddered briefly, and Molly moved quickly back to hold my arm again. I smiled at her. "How long was I gone? It seemed like ages. . . ."

"Maybe twenty minutes," said Molly. "Longest twenty minutes of my life."

I had to fight not to shudder again.

There was a polite and very deferential knock on the Sanctity doors, which then opened to reveal two of the Sarjeant's security men. I looked quickly at him, and he gestured for his people to close the doors and stay put. They did so, quietly and efficiently. The Sarjeant taught his people well. I glared at them anyway, on general principle, in case the Sarjeant had summoned them to take me away for interrogation. He can be very single-minded when it comes to the security of the family. That's his job.

"My people are here to take away the dead Immortal," said the Sarjeant, accurately interpreting my thoughts. "It's important we examine the body thoroughly."

"You mean dissect him?" I said.

The Armourer smiled happily, rubbing his bony hands together. "Know thy enemy . . . and make bloody sure he's dead. We don't know nearly enough about how the Immortals change their shapes to take on other people's identities. I always assumed it was some form of projective telepathy, making us see what they wanted us to see, but this flesh-dancing thing they do seems more like shape-shifting: actual physical change, right down to the DNA. Now, I could provide you with any number of useful devices that could do that, but the Immortals did it through sheer willpower and inherited ability. . . . All right, I'll stop talking now."

"Some Immortals still remain at large, out in the world," the Sarjeant said heavily. "Watching us with bad intent and no doubt plotting their revenge against us. We didn't kill them all at Castle Frankenstein. Unfortunately."

"I need to know everything there is to know about the Immortals," the Armourer said briskly, "if I'm to build a reliable detector to prevent this kind of thing from happening again. And to make sure that everyone in this family is exactly who and what they're supposed to be. I don't want any more nasty surprises."

"Hear, hear," I said solemnly.

I moved over to look down at the dead Immortal. Molly stayed close beside me. The man who'd tried to murder me looked very young now. Almost harmless. Just another teenage boy, like all the Immortals who never aged. Black froth had dried and crusted round his mouth, from where he'd taken poison rather than be captured. His eyes were still bulging; his face was contorted, his body racked by muscle spasms. He'd fouled himself in death, and the smell was pretty bad.

"I usually know the people who try to kill me," I said finally. "But I never saw that face before. Presumably he wasn't at the castle when we went in; and that's how he survived when the others didn't."

"He looked like my sister," said Molly. "Moved and sounded like Isabella. I was completely fooled. He couldn't have managed such a close match . . . unless he'd had access to the original. He must have known my sister."

"Perhaps the remaining Immortals are holding her prisoner," I said.

Molly grabbed hold of my arm so hard it hurt. "We have to go find her, Eddie!"

"Of course we do," I said. "You came and found me. But where do we start? Any surviving Immortals will have scattered across the world by now. If they've got any sense. The only base we ever knew about was Castle Frankenstein, and that's in the hands of the Bride now, and the Spawn of Frankenstein." I stopped as a thought hit me. "Molly, could you use your magics on this body, and get some information out of him?"

"Not really," said Molly, which I had to note wasn't an unequivocal *no*. "My powers are life-based. Mostly. I was never that interested in necromancy."

"I am," said Roger. "Death and damnation are my business."

I looked at him. "You can raise the dead?"

"I can make a corpse sit up and talk," Roger said carefully. "There's a difference. And only with the very recently departed, where the soul is still close by."

"Walker could do it," said the Armourer.

"He only did it that one time!" said Roger. "And he had the Voice. I'm only a poor half-breed hellspawn, so I'll have to do it the old-fashioned way."

He looked around at all of us, making sure he had everyone's agreement. Not that he gave a damn for our approval; he wanted to make sure we were all implicated in the unnatural and condemned thing he was about to do. None of us said no. My family has always been able to do the hard, harsh, necessary things. Roger crouched over the dead Immortal, smiling down at the corpse and muttering something under his breath in a language I didn't even recognise. The air seemed to slowly darken around him, as he revealed the side of himself he usually kept hidden. His other, perhaps even truer self: his demonic aspect. Stubby horns thrust up out of his forehead. His eyes caught fire, sulphurous yellow flames leaping up from glowing eyeballs. His fingers grew sharp, vicious claws, and his feet were suddenly rough cloven hooves. Where he stood, the wooden floor began to smoke and smoulder. Dark shadows seemed to wrap themselves around Roger Morningstar, despite Ethel's rose red glow. Where Roger was, the light seemed bloodred.

Roger's father may have been my uncle James, the legendary Grey Fox, but his mother had been a lust demon out of Hell. I never did get the full story on that. But looking at Roger now, with all his evil aspect up front and in your face, it was hard to see how we'd ever been able to take him in as one of us. I'd accepted his presence in the family because he was Harry's love and partner, and because Roger had fought on our side in the past . . . but now, seeing all the darkness in him let loose, I had to wonder if perhaps we'd made a terrible mistake.

He looked like what he was: a hellspawn set free from the Pit to walk up and down in the world, spreading horror and evil among us like some spiritual cancer.

Harry looked at Roger with something very like shock, and I realised Harry had never seen this side of his lover before. He watched, fascinated and appalled in equal measure, as Roger Morningstar pulled back one elegant shirt cuff and cut open a vein in his wrist with one clawed fingertip. Steaming-hot, dark blood streamed down into the corpse's open mouth, quickly filling it and spilling out over the sides. Roger sealed the wound in his wrist with a touch, and then he leaned forward over the body. He was smiling a happy, satisfied smile, as though he was enjoying doing something he didn't often get to do these days.

"Blood of my life for you, Immortal, for a time. My life to move within you and raise you up to do my bidding and my will. Sit up and speak, little dead man, and tell me what I want to know."

The corpse's mouth snapped suddenly shut, and its throat worked convulsively as it swallowed. The eyes turned to stare unblinkingly at Roger, and then the corpse sat up, the body making loud complaining sounds as it fought the stiffening of rigor mortis. The corpse looked into Roger's burning eyes. And then the dead man screamed horribly, a lost, terrified, trapped sound.

"Stop that," said Roger, almost casually, and the scream cut off immediately. The corpse worked its mouth, stained with the poison it had taken and Roger's dark blood, and when the dead Immortal finally spoke, its voice sounded as though it travelled some unimaginable distance. It sounded like something trying to remember what a human voice sounded like.

"Who calls me back?" it said, and suddenly I didn't want to hear whatever else it might have to say.

"I do," Roger said briskly. "Talk to me, Immortal."

The corpse's mouth moved slowly, adopting an awful smile. "Do you want to know the secrets of life and death? Shall I tell you the awful knowledge of the Shimmering Plains and the Courts of the Holy, or perhaps the Houses of Pain, in the Pit?"

"Don't waste my time," said Roger. "I probably know more of that than you do, at this point. Stop showing off and tell me: Who sent you here to murder Eddie Drood? Are there other Immortals out there in the world plotting attacks on Drood Hall?"

"There are only a few of us left now," said the corpse, still looking only at Roger. "Scattered. Hiding. I don't know where they are. This was all my idea. If I couldn't be a real Immortal anymore, a man of privilege and power, I decided I'd rather die, taking my hated enemy with me." He turned his head slowly to look at me, and it was all I could do not to flinch back from the sheer hatred in that look. "We were masters of the world, and you took it all away. The barbarian at the gates of Rome. The savage who didn't even understand the glory he destroyed. I wanted you dead, Drood, and I came so very close. . . ." He tried to spit at me, but nothing came out of his black-crusted mouth.

The Sarjeant-at-Arms moved forward to stand between me and the dead man. He was capable of small kindnesses, when he chose.

"How did you get in here," he growled, "past all the Hall's defences?"

"Rafe was one of us," said the corpse. "He told us everything. Do you really think he was the only one?"

"I have got to get that detector working properly," said the Armourer. "Sort out who's who once and for all."

Molly pushed forward to glare coldly into the dead man's face. "You made yourself look like my sister Isabella. Where is she? Are you holding her somewhere? Where is she? Where's Isabella?"

"Damned if I know," said the corpse. "I never had her. Didn't need her. I could duplicate anyone I ever met, and I knew Isabella of old. She worked with us several times on matters of mutual interest."

"Your sister worked with the Immortals?" I said to Molly.

"Oh, hell, Eddie," said Molly, "Iz has walked along with everybody, one time or another."

"Even worked with us, on a few occasions," the Armourer said cheerfully. "On matters of mutual benefit. I made some very useful devices for her, none of which she ever returned. You went out with her for a while, didn't you, Cedric?"

We all looked at the Sarjeant-at-Arms, but he had nothing to say.

"If we could stick to the matter at hand, people," said Roger. "You don't think what I'm doing is easy, do you? The body is already starting to fall apart. Anything else you want to ask, ask quickly. He won't last much longer."

We all looked at the dead Immortal. His skin was blotched and cracking, thick fluids seeping out of him as Roger's dark blood burned him up from the inside out. His eyes had sunk right back into their sockets, nothing but a mess of black jelly now. The corpse moved his head blindly back and forth.

"Don't leave me like this. Please. Don't leave me here, trapped in a decaying body."

"Why not?" said Roger. "You deserve it."

"No," said Molly. "Let him go."

Roger looked her and raised a sardonic eyebrow. "Mercy, from the wild witch of the woods?"

"No," said Molly. "Not mercy. Why keep him from

Heaven's judgement, and Hell's punishments, one moment longer?"

"Hard-core," said Roger, smiling.

"You tried to murder my Eddie," Molly said to the dead man. "Burn in Hell."

I looked at her, disturbed by the savage and uncomplicated hatred in her face and in her voice. I liked to forget that my Molly had her own dark side, like Roger; but sometimes she wouldn't let me. I couldn't say anything. It wasn't my sister the Immortals had used.

Roger straightened up and stepped back, snapped his fingers lightly, and just like that the dead man was simply a corpse again. We all watched it carefully for a while, but it lay there, cracking slowly open, leaking all kinds of unpleasant fluids and stinking the place out. The Armourer sniffed loudly.

"You haven't left me much to dissect, Roger."

I looked at Molly. "The Immortal lost most of his family. I think it was grief that moved him, as much as revenge. God has mercy."

"I don't," said Roger. He was still maintaining his demonic aspect, defying any of us to say anything. Perhaps because it felt so good not to have to pretend anymore. He smiled widely at Harry, showing rows of pointed teeth. "This . . . is who and what I really am, Harry, my dear. It's as real and as relevant as the human face I usually wear to show the world."

"We all have our dark sides," Harry said steadily.

"Not like mine," said Roger.

He took on his human aspect again, resuming the dark, sardonic and lightly mocking face he'd always shown before. And then he turned his back on all of us, including Harry, and walked away to be on his own. Where he'd been standing, his cloven hooves had scorched deep hoofprints into the wooden floor. Smoke curled slowly up from them, and on the air there was the smell of blood and sulphur and sour milk. The stench of Hell.

"Damn," said the Armourer. "I'll have to get the industrial sander out again."

It's hard to impress my uncle Jack.

"All right," I said. "What now?"

"An attack on you is an attack on the family," said the Sarjeant-at-Arms. "I'll have the family psychics run some tests on you, see if they can pick up some traces of who or what might have been threatening you in Limbo."

"Later," I said. "I'm tired."

The Sarjeant sighed heavily. "You've never had any faith in the family psychics, have you, Edwin?"

"Well, they didn't predict my bloody death, did they? I wouldn't trust that bunch of poseurs and wannabes to guess my weight!"

"Later, then," said the Sarjeant, entirely unfazed. "In the meantime, I will organise the family's resources to search for the missing Isabella Metcalf. We have people everywhere, Molly. We will find your sister for you."

"Eventually," I said.

The Sarjeant didn't actually shrug, but he looked like he wanted to. "It's a big world."

I looked at Molly. "Do you have any better ideas?"

She frowned. "My younger sister, Louisa, could find Iz easily, but last I heard, she was off exploring the Martian Tombs."

I had to blink. "Really?"

Molly did shrug. "With Louisa, who knows?"

"I've got it!" said the Armourer. "The Merlin Glass, Eddie! It can find anyplace you needed to get to, so technically there's no reason why the Glass shouldn't be able to locate any individual person you want to find and show you where they are! Try it!"

I reached into the dimensional pocket I store the Merlin Glass in, at least partly because the damned thing creeps the hell out of me, and held the hand mirror out before me. The image in the Glass quickly cleared to show Isabella Metcalf, her own bad self: a tall muscular woman in crimson biker leathers, with short-cropped black hair and an intense, sharp-featured face. She was lurking in a fairly ordinary-looking business office, leafing through papers on a desk in a way that suggested she didn't have anyone's permission to do so. She looked up, startled, to see Molly and me watching her through the Merlin Glass.

"Iz!" said Molly. "You're all right!"

"Of course I'm all right! And keep your voice down," Isabella said urgently. "No one's supposed to know I'm here!"

"We're coming through to join you," said Molly.

"Don't you dare!" said Isabella. "You'll blow my cover!"

But I'd already shaken the Glass up to its full size, and Molly and I were stepping into the office with her.

"Eddie!" roared the Sarjeant-at-Arms behind me. "You can't just rush off! You have responsibilities here!"

But Molly and I were already gone.

CHAPTER THREE

Hell Hath Fury

As offices went, this one hadn't even made an effort. Just an ordinary, everyday business office with characterless furniture and all the personality of a brick wall. Not even a potted plant in the corner to cheer the place up. When Molly and I arrived, Isabella was busily thumbing through a thick sheaf of papers. She didn't have the grace to look even a little bit guilty, and glared at Molly and me as though we were the ones who had no right to be there.

"What the hell are you two doing here?" she said, keeping her voice down.

"Oh, we happened to be passing," I said easily. "Thought we'd drop in, say hello. . . ."

I busied myself shutting down the Merlin Glass and stowing it safely away while Molly advanced on her sister to give her a big hug. Isabella dropped the papers on the desk and stopped Molly in her tracks with an icy glare.

"What's the matter with you? It's not my birthday."

Molly then launched into an impassioned account of what had been happening. She hit only the high points, but it still took a while. I used the time to take a good look round the office. It was all very neat, very tidy, and everything had that sheen of newness, as though everything had been moved only that day. The office felt . . . strange, incomplete, unfinished. As though someone had put everything in this room that they thought an office should have, but no one had actually moved in yet. The computer was the very latest model, the monitor was wide-screen and HD, and the keyboard didn't have a speck of dust on it. I considered the computer thoughtfully, wondering whether it was safe to try cracking its systems open with my armour. Luther Drood, the Los Angeles field agent, had shown me a neat little trick using Drood armour that could make any computer roll over on its back, begging to have its belly rubbed. I reluctantly decided not to try anything just yet, on the grounds that Isabella would have already cracked the computer if it were that easy. The bad guys do love their booby traps. And if I set off an alarm while Molly was busy persuading her sister what a great guy I was, I'd never hear the end of it.

So I leafed quickly through the papers on the desk, looking for whatever had caught Isabella's attention. Damned if I could see what she'd found so interesting. Pretty standard business correspondence: job openings and opportunities, accounts and invoices and memos covering the upcoming week's meetings. But all very bland, very vague, almost too generic to be true. What was more interesting was what wasn't on the desk: namely, not a single personal touch. No photographs, no coffee mug with an amusing saying on the side, not a mark out of place. Nothing on the walls, either: not a portrait or a print . . . or a window. Only a featureless box for someone to sit in and do . . . businesslike things. No, this wasn't an office. It was something set up to look like an office, enough to fool an outsider.

Molly was rapidly approaching the end of her story, so I took the opportunity to quietly study her sister Isabella. The crimson biker leathers looked well lived in and hard used, like she'd done a lot of travelling in them, and she looked muscular enough to bench-press a Harley-Davidson without breaking a sweat. Even standing still she burned with vitality, as though she couldn't wait to be out and about doing things. And, given that she was one of the infamous Metcalf sisters, probably wild and destructive things. She was handsome rather than pretty, had a hard-boned face stamped with character and determination, and wore surprisingly understated makeup. She had a certain dark glamour about her. A dangerous glamour, certainly, but there was something about Isabella that suggested she could be a whole lot of fun, if you could keep up with her.

She was the only woman I knew who had a worse reputation than my Molly. A supernatural terrorist, a twilight avenger, the Indiana Jones of the invisible world, been everywhere and done everyone. Isabella had given her life to the uncovering of mysteries and the pursuit of truth, and she didn't give a damn whom she had to walk through or over to get where she was going. Always out in the darker places of the world, digging up secrets and things most people had enough sense to leave undisturbed. Just to ask questions of the things she dug up, and kick them in the head if they didn't answer fast enough. She was looking for something, but I don't think anyone knew what. Maybe not even her. I think she liked to know things. And if Molly was the wild free spirit of the Metcalf sisters, Isabella was by all accounts the tightly wrapped control freak who always had to be in charge.

I knew we weren't going to get on. But she was Molly's sister, so . . .

Having finally understood why Molly was so pleased to see her alive and well, Isabella grudgingly allowed Molly to hug her, but only briefly.

"So," she said coldly, fixing me with an implacable gaze, "someone impersonated me? Someone actually dared? My reputation must be slipping. I did hear there was a rumour going around that I might have mellowed, and I can't have people saying things like that about me. I can see I'm going to have to go out and do something appalling. Even more appalling than usual, I mean. Can't have people thinking I've got soft; they'll take liberties."

"Trust me, Iz," said Molly, "no one thinks you've got soft. There are still religions in some parts of the world where they curse your name as part of their regular rituals."

"Well," said Isabella, "that's something. You have to keep the competition on their toes in this game. There's never any cooperation when it comes to digging up graves, despoiling tombs and desecrating churches. It's every girl for herself, and dog-eat-dog. Or perhaps that should be god-eat-god. . . . It's all based on fear and loathing and a complete willingness to take risks no sane person would even contemplate. You still haven't explained what you're doing here, interrupting my work."

"I thought you'd want to know that the Droods now know you know how to get past their defences," said Molly. "I hate sentences like that; they're always trying to get away from you. I had to tell them, Iz; they wanted to know how your duplicate was able to penetrate Drood security so easily. I had to tell them that to avoid telling them other things."

"Other things?" I said suspiciously. "What kind of other things?"

"Later, sweetie," said Molly.

Isabella looked at me, and then shrugged briskly. "Don't take it personally, Drood. I don't give a damn about you or your family; I wanted access to your Old Library. I did ask nicely, but when that snotty, stuck-up, dog-in-the-manger family of yours turned me down, I had no choice but to find my own way in. Partly because no one tells me to get lost and gets away with it, but mostly because I wanted to read some of the wonderful old books you're supposed to have. You Droods sit on all kinds of information that would make my job a lot easier—because you can."

"You've been strolling around the Old Library?" I said.

There must have been something in my voice or my face, because Isabella actually looked away for a moment.

"Well, I haven't personally been in there, as such. Not yet. But I'm working on it!"

"You're welcome to try," I said. "But once you're in there, watch your back. There's something living in the Old Library: something very powerful and very scary. It almost killed an Immortal who was masquerading as our assistant Librarian."

"You see!" said Isabella. "That's the kind of secret I want to know about!"

"Let us change the subject," I said, "on the grounds that I have been here for what seems like ages, and I still don't know why. What are you doing here, Isabella? And where is here, anyway?"

"Can we please all try to keep our voices down?" said Isabella. "This really isn't the kind of place where you want to attract attention to yourself. This is Lightbringer House, deep in the financial area of Bristol. As far as the rest of the world is concerned, Lightbringer House is only another ugly, anonymous office building, where businesspeople do business things. Except they don't. This whole building is a front, a place for people to come and do things in private that would get them hanged from the nearest lamppost if they even mentioned them in public. This office, and all the others, are for show, something for people in authority to see if they have to be given the grand tour. Everyone here works on the same thing: a purpose so secret even I haven't been able to scare up a whisper of what it might be."

"Yes," I said patiently. "But what are you doing here? Who are these people? What makes them so important?"

Isabella looked at Molly. "Just once, I wish you'd go out with someone who doesn't need everything spoon-fed to him." She looked back at me. "I've spent over a year now investigating a secret underground Satanist conspiracy. And don't look at me like that, Drood! There are still such things. I'm talking about a worldwide, highly organised cabal involving very highly placed people from all walks of life. All of them worshipping the Devil, and dedicated to the destruction of civilisation as we know it."

"I thought that kind of stuff was an urban legend," I said. "Something for the tabloids to get excited about on slow news days."

Isabella smiled smugly. "That's what they want you to think. And who do you suppose owns most of the tabloids these days? If people could see the birthmark on the back of Rupert Murdoch's head, they'd shit themselves. All right, I can see you're not convinced. Quick history lesson. Pay attention and don't make me repeat myself, or I will slap you a good one, and it will hurt."

"She will, too," said Molly. "I'd stay out of reach, if I were you."

I sat down on the edge of the desk, conspicuously within reach of Isabella, and smiled politely. "Go ahead. I love being lectured by strict women wearing leathers."

"Oh, Eddie," said Molly. "You never said. . . ."

"Later, sweetie," I said.

"Young love," said Isabella. "The horror, the horror. Anyway, the last really big Satanic conspiracy took place during the nineteen twenties and thirties, back when all those bright young things were looking for something new to believe in. Most of them had the good taste to become Communists or sexual deviants; the rest sold their souls to the Devil because they were bored. . . . The whole thing crashed to a halt when they backed Hitler and the Nazis, and everybody else backed the Allies. After the war, people had too much else to think about. There were some brief surges in the sixties, but it's hard to get people excited about sin when nothing's a sin anymore."

"What about the eighties?" I said.

"No," said Molly. "The Satanists weren't behind that. It only seemed that way."

"Right," said Isabella. "Back then, people were throwing their souls away every day, of their own free will. The Devil didn't have to do a thing."

"I'm not always sure I believe in the Devil, as such," I said.

"You'd better," said Isabella. "He believes in you. Where was I? Oh, yes, the Satanists are back now, and organising with a vengeance. They see the Droods as dithering, without real leadership, and preoccupied with other things. Like the Loathly Ones and the Immortals. So the Satanists have quietly launched a major comeback, while you're too busy to notice."

"Pardon me if I'm not too impressed," I said. "I can't help seeing Satanists as so . . . old-fashioned. And what are they doing here? Planning bad business practices? Plotting better ways to avoid paying taxes?"

"It's a really good cover," said Isabella. "But it's still just a cover."

"What brought you here?" said Molly, attacking the question from another front.

"You know me," said Isabella. "I need to know things. Secret things. Especially when someone else doesn't want me to know them. I was looking for something and found something else, which is always the way. I was investigating a local legend of a town where everyone was a werewolf, in Avignon, France, which led me to the abandoned Danse Academie in Germany's Black Forest that had been a feeding ground for one of the Old Mothers; and that in turn brought me to an outbreak of ancient forces around a circle of standing stones in darkest Wales. But in each case, by the time I got there, someone else had already been there and put a lot of effort and a lot of money into cleaning it all up so that not one trace remained of what had happened there. Everyone I talked to smiled and shook their heads and lied right to my face. Someone had spread some serious money around in a major cover-up that would probably have fooled anyone else.

"I didn't know who these people were, or what they'd wanted in these places, and I hate not knowing things, so I started digging. I went underground, into the city subcultures, showing my face in the kinds of places the powers that be like to pretend don't exist, because people aren't supposed to want such things. . . . And there I asked a whole bunch of awkward questions, stirring up the mud to see what was underneath. A word here and a name there put me on the trail of something unusually big and organised, and after that it was a case of 'follow the money. . . .' I followed the bribes through the corrupt officials and the compromised authorities, rising higher and higher, until it led me here, to an office building that had nothing to do with business. Lightbringer House may be only the tip of the iceberg, but this is where the Satanists come to get their orders. This is where things are decided and things are sworn in Satan's name.

"One interesting side note: According to the official records, all the businesses in this building are subsidiaries of Lightbringer Incorporated. Which, if you look back far enough, was once known as Fallen Star Associates. The main front for the nineteen thirties Satanist conspiracy. These people are back, and this time they mean business. They have a plan, and I want to know what it is."

"Okay," I said. "All very interesting, and possibly convincing, but I don't see anything in this office to back it up. The papers on the desk are boring to the point of bland, and it's not like there's a knitted sampler on the wall reading, 'I Love Lucifer.' Are you sure this isn't paranoia and scaremongering? We see a lot of that in the Droods. In fact, it's pretty much business as usual."

"If Iz says there's evil here, there is evil here," Molly said firmly. "No one knows evil better than Iz. She's never wrong about things like this. Except when she's wrong."

"Molly, do me a favour," said Isabella. "Stop trying to help. Look, the evidence is here somewhere! I just haven't found it yet. They'd hardly leave it lying around, would they? The trail I followed led me to this floor, and this office. Orders come from here, and payments, and even a few not very discreet threats."

"If this really is as big a conspiracy as you believe," I

said, "I don't think we should do anything to let them know we know. I think we should all return to Drood Hall and discuss a more . . . organised response."

"Put myself in the hands of the Droods?" said Isabella. "Yeah, right, like that's going to happen! Never trust a Drood!"

"Why not?" I said, genuinely taken aback by the anger in her face and the venom in her voice.

"Your family killed our parents, remember?" said Molly. "Isabella isn't as forgiving as I am."

"I still don't know what you're doing with this one," said Isabella. "I mean really, Molly, a Drood?"

"He's different," Molly said stubbornly. "He's . . . special."

"You always say that," said Isabella. "And you always end up sleeping on my couch, crying your eyes out. You have the worst taste in men. . . ."

"Molly and I have something in common," I said. "It's possible that my family was responsible for the death of my parents, too."

Isabella looked at me sharply and then shook her head. "None of this is important. The truth is here, and I will find it, even if I have to tear this whole office apart."

"Oh, not again . . ." said Molly.

Isabella glared at both of us. "Get out of here. Both of you. Go back to your precious Drood Hall. I don't need your help, and I don't want you here."

"Too late," I said cheerfully. "I'm intrigued now. The return of the Satanists! It's all so very Dennis Wheatley. . . . Molly, my dear, do you think you could keep a lid on any booby traps I might set off by persuading this computer to talk nicely to me?"

"Don't see why not," said Molly. "Silicon sorcery's always been a specialty of mine."

"You haven't gone back to cloning credit cards, have you?" said Isabella.

"Of course not!" said Molly. "I'm into a much higher class of lawlessness now."

"If you could concentrate on the computer, Molly . . ." I said.

"Oh, sure! No problem!"

I half expected her to work some dramatic chaos ritual over the computer, or sprinkle fairy dust on it, but she sat down before the machine, fired it up and worked some subtle magic through the keyboard, until the computer dropped its pants and showed her everything it had. Molly pushed back the chair, grinned at me and got up so I could take her place.

"There you go. Ask it anything you want. I've got the security systems eating out of my hand. You could pry this computer open with a crowbar and piss in the back, and it wouldn't shed a single tear."

"You always did have a delicate touch," I said.

"Later, lover," said Molly.

I subvocalised my activating Words, and sent a tentacle of golden armour racing down my arm from my torc, until it formed a gleaming golden glove on my right hand. Isabella watched, fascinated. Not many outside the family get to see Drood armour at work. And live to tell of it. I set one golden fingertip against the computer, pressing lightly, and delicate golden filaments shot through the computer's silicon guts, bending them to my will. I had no idea how my armour's strange matter did this; I supply the willpower, and the armour does everything else. Which has been known to bother me now and again. When I got the chance, I was going to have to ask Ethel some very pointed questions, though I was pretty sure I wasn't going to like the answers.

I asked the computer some blunt questions, and the answers appeared on the monitor screen in swift succession. Of course, there was so much information in the computer that the trick lay in asking exactly the right questions, and I was operating pretty much in the dark. But with Molly and Isabella leaning over my shoulders and yelling suggestions in my ears, it didn't take me long to scare up a whole bunch of records and secret files I wasn't supposed to be able to get at. Passwords and encryptions are no match for Drood armour.

And it turned out, everything Isabella had said was true. Lightbringer House was the central meeting place for Satanist groups from all over the world. This anonymous office building was where policy was decided and all important decisions were made. This was where they came to talk to one another, to boast and brag of all the awful things they'd done and the worse things they planned to do. This was where they came to kneel in dark churches and worship the Devil, and celebrate evil in appalling ways. Lightbringer House organised everything and was the motivating force behind a horribly large number of plots and conspiracies buried deep within all the governments of the world.

I jumped from file to file, my stomach muscles tensing painfully as I took in the sheer size and scale of the operation. These people wanted to rule the world, and they were going about its slow and certain corruption with cold, focused precision. It soon became clear that there had been a lot of comings and goings from Lightbringer House recently. Really important people, familiar names and faces from politics and big business and a dozen other spheres of influence, were in the building right now, discussing . . . something. There was no specific information in the computer about this, only a sealed file name: "the Great Sacrifice." And a whole bunch of serious new security measures that had been placed throughout the building to keep this meeting secure and very private. Molly leaned forward suddenly, pointing at the screen.

"There! What was that? Go back, go back. . . . Yes! The big meeting is being held in the main boardroom, directly down the hall from here! And given the sheer number of high-level Devil-worshipping scumbags attending, I think it behooves us to go and take a look and listen in."

"And possibly slaughter the whole lot of them, on general principle," said Isabella.

"Given the sheer amount of magical and technological weaponry that's been installed, specifically to keep people like us out, I don't think we can afford to start anything," I said firmly. "We need to discover exactly what's going on, and then concentrate on getting that information out of this building and into the hands of those who can best decide what to do about it."

Isabella looked at Molly. "Is he always this stuffy?"

"A lot of the time, yes," said Molly. "It's one of his more endearing qualities."

"Let us go look in on this meeting," I said resignedly. "But nobody is to start anything until we've found out what this Great Sacrifice is all about."

I retracted the golden strange matter into my torc and shut the computer down. Molly quickly removed her interventions, and when we went to leave the office there was no sign the computer had ever been tampered with. I'm a great believer in not leaving any traces behind; you never know when they might turn up again to bite your arse. Isabella eased the office door open a crack, looked out and then nodded quickly. We moved out into the corridor, shut the door carefully behind us and strode down the corridor towards the boardroom as though we had every right to be there.

I'd half imagined the Satanists' building would be all dark shadows and gothic gloom, but the corridor was as anonymously banal as the office. The lights were almost painfully bright, the carpet was a dull grey and the walls were bare. There were a few people about, presumably too low-level to be allowed into the big meeting: regular-looking businesspeople in neat suits, going about their business and paying us no attention at all. First thing a field agent learns: Act like you belong somewhere, and most people will assume you do. Simple confidence will take you farther than even the best fake documents. But even so, it was a bit odd that no one paid any attention to Isabella's crimson biker leathers and my torn and bloodstained shirt. Presumably Satanists were used to seeing strange things on a regular basis.

And . . . there was something about these ordinary, everyday businesspeople, as though they weren't necessarily people at all. But maybe something else, pretending to be people.

In fact, the whole corridor was making me feel distinctly uneasy. It was all too bright and cheerful, with not one thing out of place. More like a film set than somewhere people actually lived and worked. Even as I strode along, nodding and smiling to the men and women who nodded and smiled at me, something was making all the hairs on the back of my neck stand up. My flesh crawled. There was a growing sense of threat and menace, unfocused but very real, and very near, as though something might jump out at me at any moment. Walking down that corridor towards the boardroom felt like walking along a tightrope knowing someone was right behind you, waiting for a chance to push you off. Or like walking across a series of trapdoors, any one of which might drop open at any moment, letting you plummet into some awful trap, or perhaps letting you fall and fall forever. . . . My problem is I've got far too good an imagination. Well, one of my problems . . .

Still, even my torc was tingling uncomfortably, as though trying to warn me of some imminent danger. The closer I got to the boardroom and the people waiting in it, the more worried I became that not only was I in danger from the building's many weapons and protections, but I was heading into an area of actual spiritual danger.

I murmured as much to Molly, who nodded vigorously. "Yeah, something about this place is creeping me out big-time, too. Which is weird; it's usually the other way round. This is a bad place, Eddie. I don't think these Satanists are using the name for shock value. I think they're playing this for real. I'd raise my Sight and take a proper look at what's going on here, but I'm pretty sure it would set off every alarm in the building."

"Took you long enough to work that out," said Isabella. "I felt that the moment I got here, which is why I was reduced to checking out papers that happened to be lying around. This is a bad place full of bad people with bad intentions. Can we take that for granted and move on?"

If Isabella was feeling the same sense of threat and danger I was, it didn't seem to be bothering her much. She led the way right to the closed door of the main boardroom. There were no guards, or at least no obvious ones. I tried the handle on the off chance, but the door was locked.

"Don't try to force it," Molly said quickly.

"I know," I said. "Alarms. I have done this secret-agent thing before, you know. It bothers me there aren't any guards."

"They must think their defences are so good they don't need human guards," said Isabella. "Either that, or the real guards are invisible and waiting to pounce on us."

"Really wish you hadn't said that," said Molly, looking quickly about her. "I feel naked without my Sight."

There was a single sign, saying MEETING. ONE P.M. START. NO ADMITTANCE AFTER THE MEETING HAS BEGUN.

"One p.m.," said Molly. "The thirteenth hour. Satanists are always big on tradition. Probably because their greatest victories are all in the past."

"We have to get in there," said Isabella. "Find out what this is all about. I hate not knowing things! Eddie, can you use that golden-finger trick on the lock?"

"Almost certainly," I said. "But again, I'm guessing the presence of strange matter this close to the movers and shakers would set off every alarm there is. I think we're better off doing this low-tech."

I produced a single golden brown skeleton key from my pocket, made from real human bone by the Armourer. (I didn't ask whose bone. One learns not to ask questions like that around the Armourer.) Molly and Isabella moved quickly to cover me while I worked on the lock, blocking the view of anyone who might happen by. Though this end of the corridor was disturbingly quiet and empty. The skeleton key had the lock open in a moment, and I tucked it away again before carefully turning the handle. Isabella glared at me.

"I want one of those! It's not fair. You Droods have all the best toys."

I gestured for her to be quiet, and then eased the door open a few inches. I waited, braced for any alarm or attack, but nothing happened. I peered through the narrow gap. The main boardroom was big enough to pass for a meeting hall, and was packed from wall to wall with rows of chairs, every single one of them occupied by rich and powerful and famous people. Names and faces you'd know, along with a whole bunch only people like me are supposed to know about. They were all staring with rapt attention at the man standing on the raised dais before them, commanding the room with fierce authority. Everyone there seemed absolutely fascinated by what they were hearing, hanging on his every word. But there was also something about them that suggested they were scared—either of the man on the dais or of what he was saying. What could he be suggesting? What could be so extreme that it could frighten even hardened Satanists? I pushed the door open a little more, and when no one reacted I squeezed through the gap and stood at the back of the hall, behind the rows of chairs. Molly and Isabella moved quickly in after me, leaving the door ajar, just in case. We stood very still, hardly breathing, but no one looked back. All their attention was fixed on the man on the dais.

Tall, dark and compelling, he strode confidently back and forth on the dais. In his expensively tailored suit, he looked and sounded a lot like one of those well-rehearsed motivational speakers, working his way through a series of points and positions on his way to the bit where we all get rich. He smiled a lot, showing perfect teeth, and his regular handsome features had that slightly stretched look of subtle plastic surgeries. His hair was suspiciously jet-black for a man well into his forties. But his voice was rich and sure and utterly compelling, holding his audience in the palm of his hand. I leaned in close to Molly and Isabella and murmured in their ears.

"Either of you know this guy?"

"The face is familiar," said Molly, frowning.

"So it should be," said Isabella. "That is the one and

only Alexandre Dusk. Big man in computers. A millionaire before he was twenty, and a billionaire before he was twenty-one. No one knows how rich he is now, but when he talks, governments listen. If they know what's good for them. But . . . he hasn't been seen in public for years. People have to put up millions just to ask him questions over the phone. Most have to settle for an e-mail. So what the hell is he doing here, in person?"

"If you'd belt up and let us listen, we might find out," said Molly.

So we shut up and listened. Dusk could talk, though he sounded more like a politician than some self-made computer geek. He spoke well and fluently, pinning his audience to their seats. He was selling them a vision. He'd clearly already been talking for some time, getting his audience worked up. They really wanted what he was selling. Dusk prowled back and forth before them, his voice rising and rising as he gestured with increasing assurance. And when I realised what he was talking about, I was fascinated, too, even as a slow, cold horror crept over me.

"The Droods have removed themselves from the game," said Alexandre Dusk. "They're effectively leaderless now, and fighting among themselves. They may have marvellous new armour, but they don't know what to do with it. They are yesterday's men; we are the future. The Immortals are a dead end. Most of them are gone, the few survivors scattered and on the run. The Droods did us a favour there by removing the one organised and influential force that might have been able to stand against us. Right now, every government and leader in the world is looking for a chance to struggle out from under the Droods' oppressive heel, looking to seize the chance to think and act for themselves. They want to be powers in their own right, and they'll listen to anyone who can show them a new way. And that's going to be us."

"You see?" Molly murmured in my ear. "You set the governments of the world free, for the first time in history, and the first thing they do is plot to stab you in the back."

"Of course," said Isabella. "They're politicians."

"No good deed goes unpunished," I said.

"This is our time, come round again!" said Dusk. "It is our duty to take advantage of this situation, all this marvellous chaos and confusion, and take the reins of power for ourselves, as it was always meant we should. But not by replacing these governments and leaders. We've tried that, and it's never worked. The sheep always rebel when they realise they're headed for the slaughterhouse. No, my friends, we've always made better kingmakers than kings. The power behind the throne. Harder to detect, harder to fight, harder to find out what our true agendas are until it's far too late. You can get much more done when you're not in the public eye, and there's no one to be horrified by the methods we use. And it's always good to have a leader around to use as a fall guy if it all goes wrong and we have to make a swift exit by the back door.

"So we have become the latest generation of advisers, political consultants, focus groups, lobbyists, personal assistants. . . . We are the people who really decide what gets done. And now that the politicians have come to rely on us, now that they're ready to listen to anything we have to say as long as it keeps them in power . . . it's time for the Great Sacrifice. The final willing degradation of Humanity, a spiritual crime so great it will damn all their souls and give our lord Satan his final victory over mankind. Then we will dispose of the leaders and take their place as kings of the new Earth!"

The crowd went mad. They rose to their feet, shouting and screaming, pounding their hands together, almost out of their minds with excitement and anticipation. The whole room was full of a wild, vicious, malignant hysteria.

I looked at Molly and Isabella. "Is he serious? Are they serious?"

"Sounds like it," said Isabella.

"What the hell is this Great Sacrifice?" said Molly. "Whom are they planning on sacrificing?"

Isabella glared at the howling crowd, her upper lip curled. "Look at them. Typical Satanists. The little men, the cheats and bullies who'd never rise to the top through their own abilities. They want to be king of Shit Heap, and take their revenge on the world and all those people who stand between them and the things they want, the things they think they deserve. The secret plotters and the backstabbers . . . They want power because at heart they're cowards, afraid of everyone who has power over them."

"The worst evil always comes out of small people," said Molly. "Small-minded, small-souled, vicious little turds."

"Satanists," I said. "I do get it, Molly, really."

And then the whole boardroom went quiet, and we looked up to find everyone in the crowd had turned around and was staring at us. Dusk pointed a dramatic finger in our direction.

"Intruders! Strike them down in Satan's name!"

"Damn," I said. "Ladies, I think it is time we took our leave."

"Try to keep up," said Isabella, already halfway out the door.

Molly and I were right on her heels. I slammed the door shut behind us and crushed the lock with an armoured hand. It wouldn't hold off the crowd for long, but it should buy us some time. I spun round, and then swore dispassionately as a demon dog came pounding down the corridor towards us. I have encountered such things before, but this had to be the biggest I'd ever seen: a great mountain of night-black flesh almost filling the corridor from wall to wall, its hunched back brushed against the ceiling. The whole corridor shuddered under the thunder of its approach, great clawed paws slamming against the floor. Isabella glared at me.

"I told you not to come here! It must have smelled your torc!"

"Oh, sure," I said. "Put all the blame on me."

"I'd run, if there were anywhere to run," said Molly.

"Oh, ye of little faith," I said, stepping forward to face the demon dog.

It was almost upon us now, great slabs of muscle moving smoothly under its dark hide. It had a flat, brutal face, with flaring hellfire eyes and a wide slash of mouth packed with more vicious serrated teeth than seemed physically possible. It snorted and grunted hungrily as it ran, and already it was close enough that I could smell the blood and brimstone on its breath.

It came straight at me like a runaway train, lifting its ugly head to howl its fury: a terrible, primitive sound, all hate and rage and spite for everything that lived. A disturbingly human sound, rather than anything animal, because a demon dog only looks like a dog. I armoured up, the golden strange matter covering me from head to toe in a moment. And like that I felt stronger, faster, sharper, like coming fully awake after dozing all day. I never feel more alive than when I'm wearing the family armour, boosted far beyond human limitations, to defend Humanity from all the things that threaten us. But even as I moved forward to face the demon dog, I wasn't actually sure any of that would be enough to stop several tons of advancing demon dog.

They're not real, not natural. They're physical constructs: made, not born, in special labs, created to be strong enough to hold and contain a demon out of Hell. A muscular machine possessed by a demon, trained to go for the soul. Fortunately, the shape itself limits what a demon can do. Because they're possessing a dog's shape, they're limited by the natural laws of this world to take on the nature of a dog. Which means they're vicious as hell, but not terribly bright. They fight and attack like an animal, with no thought of strategy.

Still bloody strong and hideously powerful, though.

So I ran straight at the demon dog and punched it right in its ugly face. My golden fist sank deep into its night-dark forehead, piercing the flesh and cracking the heavy bone beneath. The demon dog howled with pain and shock, skidding to a halt as it pushed me ahead of it. Molly and Isabella scattered to get out of its way, pressing their backs against the corridor walls we as passed them. I held my balance till we both came to a halt, and then ripped my armoured hand out of its head. Dark, steaming blood ran down the demon dog's face, briefly catching fire as it passed over the flaring eyes. It growled deep in its chest and swung its head back and forth, throwing the blood off. Where the dark blood hit the walls, the surface blistered and bubbled. The wound was already healing, the dark flesh knitting back together.

And while the dog was busy thinking about that, I extended my right hand into a razor-edged golden blade and jammed it into the dog's flaring left eye. The flames snapped out as the eyeball exploded, drenching the front of my armour in stinking gore, which ran quickly down to pool on the corridor floor and eat holes in the carpet. The demon dog jerked its head back, howling miserably, shaking its great head back and forth as though it could shake off the pain that filled its simple mind. I stood poised, waiting for my chance, and then lunged forward and sank my golden blade deep in its remaining eye. The demon dog reared up, slamming its head and shoulders against the ceiling and lifting me right off my feet. I clung to the dog's head with my other hand and pulled my blade out. Long strings of dripping musculature clung to my sword, and I flicked them away as I jumped back from the demon dog.

The dog surged forward again, and I backed quickly away from it. Even blind, it could still smell where I was. The flat, brutal face slammed into me like a runaway car, the force of the impact lifting me up off my feet and carrying me before it. I forced myself down until my golden feet made contact with the floor again, and then I dug them in, gradually forcing the dog to a halt. My feet left deep grooves in the wooden floor, but it still took all my armour's strength to hold off the demon dog as it forced its way forward. I punched the demon dog's head again and again, the sound of rending flesh and splintering bone horribly loud in the corridor. Stinking dark blood drenched my armour, only to fall helplessly away, unable to affect the golden strange matter. But the wounds I made kept healing, and an eye suddenly rose up to fill the empty left socket, and caught fire. The demon dog could see again.

It still couldn't force me backwards, large as it was; it had no room to manoeuvre in the corridor. It flexed its great neck muscles and threw me backwards. I travelled several feet before I landed, and braced myself, but the dog stayed where it was, regarding me ominously with its one flaring eye. It was growling constantly now, like a never-ending roll of thunder. It charged forward, moving impossibly quickly, and its huge jaws closed with vicious strength on my chest and left shoulder. They closed like a steel press, bringing incredible pressure to bear; but it couldn't breach my armour. Huge teeth broke and shattered as the jaws tried to break through. The demon dog whipped its head back and forth, flailing me around like a rat, and all I could do was hang on desperately with both hands, golden fingers sunk deep into its dark flesh. The massive jaws clamped down, but my armour held. There aren't many things that can pierce Drood armour, and a demon dog's teeth don't even come close, I was relieved to discover.

The jaws opened to try another bite, and I jumped backwards, using the armoured strength in my legs to put a reasonable distance between me and the dog. It surged forward again, mouth gaping wide. I waited till the last moment, and then thrust my hand into the open mouth, grabbed its tongue, and tore the writhing thing out by the roots. Blood shot out like a fire hose as the dog dug all four paws in and skidded to a halt. It howled in outrage, the sound half-choked and interrupted by gushing blood, but still deafeningly loud in the confined space. The ripped-out tongue thrashed and squirmed in my hand, and then wrapped itself tightly around my arm. Serrated teeth on the underside of the tongue broke and fell away without even scratching my armour. I crushed the tongue in my hand into a bloody pulp, tore the rest away from my arm and stamped the remainder into a nasty mess under my feet. Some things can gross out even a hardened field agent.

But while I was preoccupied with that, the demon dog swung its wounded head against me, lifting me up off my feet and pinning me against the corridor wall. I hung there, feet dangling helplessly in midair, my arms trapped at my sides by the great weight of its bulk. The corridor wall cracked beneath me, ruptured by so many tons of pressure. My armour still protected me, but I couldn't break free. All the demon dog had to do was hold me there until the Satanists got out of the locked room, and then . . .

Molly and Isabella popped up out of nowhere, glowing blades in their hands, and hit the demon dog from both sides at once. Their witch knives sank deep into the dog's throat. Blood spurted thickly, steaming on the air, and Molly and Isabella moved quickly back to avoid it, without removing their knives. They forced the blades deeper in, and then jerked them across the dog's throat until they met in the middle. The dog tried to howl, but they'd cut its voice out. Dark blood gushed across the floor, and the pressure on me began to weaken. Suddenly all the strength went out of it, and the demon dog collapsed. Molly and Isabella stepped back, regarding the dog warily. I pushed the body away from me. It didn't react. It was panting harshly now, and the flames had gone out in its eye. It took one last snap at me, for spite's sake, and then it stopped breathing.

Right on the edge of my hearing I heard a despairing scream as the possessing demon was forced out of the dead dog and sent plummeting back into Hell to face its punishment for having dared fail.

The dog lay still, nothing but a great slab of muscle now, dead and empty. Molly glared at it.

"Bad dog."

I armoured down and stretched tiredly. Fighting the dog had taken a lot out of me. The armour has the strength, but I still have to operate it. Isabella scowled at me.

"Typical Drood. Had to armour up, didn't you? That much strange matter has set off every alarm in the place!"

"Big dog," I said a bit plaintively. "What was I supposed to do, let it use me as a chew toy? Hit it on the nose with a rolled-up newspaper? And I don't hear any alarms."

Molly snapped her fingers, and I could hear all of Lightbringer House's secret alarms going off at once. Bells, sirens, flashing lights, the works. And in the background, an endless inhuman howl that had nothing to do with any alarm system.

"I think we woke something up," said Molly. "And I don't think we should stick around to find out what."

"Yeah," Isabella said reluctantly. "I can always come back again."

"Curiosity killed the cat," I said.

"And satisfaction brought her back!" snapped Isabella. "Now how are we going to get out of here before that boardroom door finally gives way and lets loose a whole crowd of angry Satanists?"

"No problem," said Molly. "Eddie has the Merlin Glass. We can step through it, out of this building and into Drood Hall, and then shut the Glass down before anyone can follow us. They won't even know where we've gone."

I already had the Merlin Glass out, and was shaking it up to full size. Isabella glowered at it jealously.

"The Merlin Glass? How the hell did you get your hands on that, Drood? I've been looking for the Glass for years. . . . Trust the Droods to keep all the best toys for themselves. You have to let me examine it!"

"Maybe later," I said. "If you're good."

"You want a slap?" said Isabella.

"Hands off the boyfriend, Iz," said Molly.

But I was concerned over a new problem. No matter

what I tried, the Merlin Glass stubbornly refused to show me anything other than my own reflection. I tried shaking it back to its original size, and then shaking it hard, on general principle, but it remained just a looking glass. I finally said something harsh but justified, and put the Glass away again.

"Houston, we have a problem," I said heavily. "It would appear this building has put up some really heavy-duty shields, now that the alarms have gone off, and the Glass can't access the world outside. We're not going to be able to leave that way, after all."

"It's been that kind of a day," Molly said wistfully.

"Terrific," said Isabella. "You're a bloody jinx, you know that, Drood?"

And then we all looked round sharply. From somewhere not nearly far enough off came the sound of a great many raised and furious voices, heading our way at speed. The Satanists had finally got out of the boardroom. I looked quickly round the corridor. No turnings, no windows anywhere, and the corridor ended some twenty feet on in a blank wall. The other way was blocked by several tons of dead demon dog, frustrating us even in death. The sound of the oncoming mob was a lot closer. I looked at Molly and Isabella.

"I am open to suggestions."

"I can't teleport us out," said Molly. "Not past these shields. Iz?"

"Took everything I had getting in here," said Isabella. "I was expecting to stroll out unrecognised."

"How high up are we?" I said. "How far is it to the lobby and the main exit?"

"We're on the twenty-second floor," said Isabella. "One elevator at our end of the hall, and a stairway."

"Really don't like the idea of being trapped in an elevator," I said. "And the stairway is bound to be guarded." I looked thoughtfully at the end wall. It didn't look that tough. "I could punch through that wall, grab the pair of you and jump. . . . I'd survive the fall, and if you stuck close enough to the armour, it should protect you as well."

"Have you actually tried this before?" said Isabella.

"Not as such, no."

"Then I am not trusting my life to a *should*," Isabella said firmly.

"We'll take the elevator," I said.

"Witches and sisters first," said Molly.

We headed quickly for the end of the corridor. The shouts and howls were dangerously close behind us, but I didn't look back. It wouldn't help, and I didn't want to be distracted. And then bullet holes exploded in the walls to either side of us, and I immediately armoured up again and fell back a little, so I could stand between the witches and the bullets. I did try to do it subtly, for their pride's sake. I was pretty sure Molly wouldn't allow herself to be taken out by some mere bullet, but I wasn't taking any chances. I don't, where Molly's concerned, no matter how mad she gets afterwards. Some things are nonnegotiable. It's a guy thing.

We got to the elevator, and Isabella hit the call button with her knuckle. (Old burglar's trick: using the knuckle instead of a finger, so you don't leave fingerprints.) I turned and looked back. Beyond the body of the demon dog the corridor was full of angry people with flushed red faces and snarling mouths. A dozen or so had guns, though luckily the bulk of the dead dog was protecting us from a straightforward attack. They had to shoot round the massive bulk, and they weren't very good at it. But some had already reached the body and were trying to force their way past it, snapping off shots as they did. I stood facing them, trying to be as wide as possible. Half a dozen men and one woman opened fire on me from almost point-blank range, blasting away indiscriminately. I stood firm and my armour absorbed every bullet that hit me, soaking up the impact and sucking them in. The Satanists kept firing, but I could tell they were impressed. There's something very off-putting and downright intimidating about an enemy who stands there and lets you shoot him. Especially when he's staring back at you with a featureless metal mask that doesn't even have any eyeholes.

But the Satanists kept firing, and I couldn't move or even back away to get to the elevator without leaving Molly and Isabella vulnerable to a lucky shot. Bloody bullets can go anywhere in a firefight. Especially in a confined space like this. And then, as so often happens during extended firefights, they all ran out of bullets. The guns fell silent, and the Satanists stopped and looked dumbly at their empty weapons. One actually shook his gun, as though that might help. Such things never happen on television. People behind them yelled for them to get back out of the way and let someone else have a go. Presumably they had more guns, with bullets. I risked a look back over my shoulder.

"Is that elevator here yet?"

"Something's wrong with it!" snapped Isabella. "I've hit the call button till it's started whimpering, but the floor lights aren't working and the door won't open."

"Buy me some time, Molly," I said.

Molly stepped forward to stand beside me, snapped her fingers sharply and the Satanists closest to us suddenly disappeared, replaced by a dozen very surprised-looking toads. Really ugly, warty toads. The next-nearest Satanists fell back, ducking into doorways to give themselves cover.

Isabella sniffed loudly. "Toads. I thought you'd outgrown that, Molly."

"Never mess with a classic," said Molly. "And never argue with success. People will risk bullets, but show them a bunch of their friends suddenly catching flies with their tongues, and suddenly everyone's very happy for someone else to go first. Eddie, I think we've waited long enough for that elevator. You get the doors open, while Isabella and I show these Devil-worshipping shit-stains what happens when you get the Metcalf sisters mad at you. Iz, you in the mood to do something awful and downright distressing?"

"Always," said Isabella.

I expected them to smite the Satanists hip and thigh with destructive spells and really messy magics, but instead Molly and Isabella strode down the corridor side by side, walked straight through the dead dog as though they were ghosts and then threw themselves at the nearest Satanists. Basically, the witches beat the shit out of the poor sods, their small fists flying with appalling speed and precision. Blood flew, bones broke and the air was full of horrid sounds as the Metcalf sisters knocked the Satanists down with much malice aforethought and trampled them underfoot. The Satanists had braced themselves for a magical attack, but two fist-fighting young witches were a bit too close and personal. Molly and Isabella pressed forward, laughing harshly in the face of the demoralised enemy.

Behind my golden mask I had to grin. Never get a Metcalf sister mad at you.

Some of the Satanists remembered they had guns, and opened fire again. Molly and Isabella stood their ground, whipping their hands back and forth in mystical patterns, and bullets turned into flowers and fluttered to the floor. Some Satanists ditched their handguns for automatic weapons, but it didn't make any difference. Just meant more flowers. Still, while it was good to know Molly and Isabella could defend themselves, I also knew they couldn't keep it up for long.

I'd started to give my full attention to the closed elevator doors when the building's main security systems finally kicked in. Great sliding panels opened in the corridor walls, and I had to blink a few times. I would have sworn they weren't there a moment before. Really large gun barrels emerged from gun emplacements inside the walls, and turned quickly to orient themselves on Molly and Isabella. I ran forward and put myself between the gun barrels and the witches just as the guns opened fire.

The bullets pounded away at me, targeting my head and chest and gut, and while my armour easily absorbed the bullets, the sheer intensity of the fire meant I daren't move, for fear of exposing Molly and Isabella. This was serious weaponry, pumping out bullets in a steady stream. They chewed up the walls behind me on both sides, blasting jagged holes in the doors and blowing them off their hinges. Some hit the dog's body and blew the dark flesh apart in a series of explosions. Meat confetti blew everywhere, and dark liquids splashed up and down the corridor. The smell was appalling, as the bullets blew away muscles to reach the organs within.

Wave after wave of bullets slammed into me and were absorbed, doing no damage. I was starting to feel a bit cocky, a bit *Is that all you've got?* when the gun barrels suddenly fell silent and retreated into the walls. To be immediately replaced by even bigger new guns, firing explosive flechettes at thousands of rounds a second. The dead dog blew up, blown to fragments in a moment. I stood my ground, bracing myself and leaning slightly forward into the solid stream of bullets, my armour sucking up the bullets with continued enthusiasm. When I was sure my armour could handle that much concentrated punishment, I advanced slowly forward into the pounding fire, grabbed each gun barrel in turn and ripped them right out of their emplacements. I tied the last few in knots, to make a point, before throwing them on the floor. Suddenly it was very quiet in the corridor. Followed by a wild round of applause from behind me, and a wolf whistle from Molly.

Another panel slid open in the wall beside me. A gun barrel started to roll out. I grabbed it and forced it back inside. The gun emplacement exploded, flames and black smoke belching out into the corridor. None of which troubled me inside my armour. Back down at the other end of the corridor, the Satanists were all bunched together, maintaining a safe distance from Molly and Isabella and me. They'd given up on guns. Something in their faces seemed to suggest that they felt that what I was doing was somehow unfair. I shouldn't have been able to shrug off their no doubt very expensive weaponry.

I was so busy looking for more sliding panels in the walls, I was completely caught by surprise when trapdoors started dropping suddenly open the whole length of the corridor. Great squares of flooring fell away, silently and without warning, and apparently at random. I braced myself, legs akimbo, and looked quickly to Molly and Isabella. I shouldn't have worried. Several trapdoors opened beneath the two witches as they strolled unconcernedly back to join me; but Molly and Isabella walked right over the open spaces as though they weren't even there, tripping lightly across the deep drops without even looking down. Isabella sniffed loudly as she rejoined me by the elevator doors.

"Trapdoors? What is this, amateur night?"

"Right," said Molly. "I mean, please. That's one of the first tricks I learned."

"Can you walk on water, too?" I said, honestly curious.

Molly laughed. "Hell, sweetie, I can tap-dance on swimming pools! For a while, that was my favourite party piece."

"A great improvement over the old one," said Isabella. "And a lot less trouble cleaning up after. You always were a show-off. She was the same as a girl, Drood. She and her precious unicorn."

I had to look at Molly. "You rode a unicorn?"

She grinned briefly. "Not for long."

I looked back up the corridor. It seemed safest. The satanic business types had regrouped, many of them now carrying really big guns, and what looked like grenade launchers and flamethrowers. The only reason they hadn't already come after us was that they were too busy arguing among themselves as to who should have the honour of approaching us first. Everyone seemed very keen to give that honour to someone else. It's nice to feel appreciated. Some bright spark produced a grenade, pulled the pin and lobbed it along the floor towards us. The trapdoors immediately snapped shut, one after another, to help the grenade along its way. I waited till it had almost reached us, to be sporting, and then bent over, picked the grenade up and held it to my chest with both hands. The grenade went off, and my armour absorbed all of the blast and most of the smoke. I looked back up the corridor and waved cheerfully to the one who'd lobbed the grenade; and he actually stamped his foot in frustration, turned away and had to be comforted by the other Satanists. I don't think they'd encountered Drood armour before. Certainly, it wasn't doing their self-confidence any good. Several looked like they wanted to burst into tears.

"Stop showing off and open the elevator doors!" said Isabella.

"No sense of fun," said Molly. "She was the same as a girl. She and her enchanted motorbike."

I turned back to the elevator doors and considered them thoughtfully. And while I was doing that, a horrifically bright light flared up in the corridor: a fierce, incandescent and definitely unnatural glare brighter than the sun. Almost bright enough to overpower my armoured mask, which had to cloak my vision in darkness for a few moments to protect my eyes. Molly and Isabella cried out in shock and clung to each other, momentarily blinded. And while we were all disoriented, new panels slid open in the corridor walls, revealing dark, concealed places full of things very like trapdoor spiders.

Large, hairy things the size of cats, with far too many legs and eyes, and snapping fanged mouths. They came swarming out of the walls, poison dripping from their mouths, eager to get at us while we were still helpless. But my mask was already back to normal. I moved quickly forward to block their way, and they swarmed all over me, clinging to my armour with their sticky legs, trying to force their fangs through the strange matter. I shuddered and squirmed inside my armour. I've never liked spiders. I made myself stand still till they were all over me, surging and pushing and pressing their deadly mouths against the outside of my mask; and then I seized them in my golden hands, crushing their pulpy bodies and tearing them away from my face. I slapped at them, and they fell away dead. Some dropped off and tried to run, and I stamped them all underfoot. When I finished, I was breathing hard, and my heart was going like a trip-hammer. *Never* liked spiders. I looked at the openings in the walls, and they all slid swiftly shut. Molly and Isabella blinked gingerly around themselves as their vision cleared.

"What the hell just happened?" sad Isabella. "What's all this mess on the floor? And what is that dripping from your hands, Drood?"

"Trust me," I said. "You really don't want to know."

"I've had enough of this place and its nasty little surprises," said Molly, knuckling one watering eye. "Time we were leaving. Open those elevator doors, Eddie, and don't be polite about it."

"Love to," I said.

I jammed one set of golden fingers between the two doors, making a gap big enough to get both hands in, and then I forced the doors apart. Metal shrieked and crumpled under my armoured strength. I looked down what should have been the elevator shaft, and swore mildly. I hadn't expected the elevator to actually be there; I'd been thinking more along the lines of grabbing one of the elevator cables and then sliding down it with Molly and Isabella hanging on. I could do that. Unfortunately, there were no cables and no shaft. The whole mechanical business was gone, and the shaft itself had been replaced by a long, pulsing pink throat, complete with thick purple veins, a handful of staring eyes and several rows of swiftly rotating teeth. A curling acidic haze filled the throat, suggesting some kind of stomach at the bottom. Dropping into the throat would be like passing through a meat grinder. And a hungry one, at that. I was pretty sure my armour would survive, but I couldn't say the same for Molly and Isabella. A series of low sucking sounds drifted up the throat. Something was feeling peckish.

"If I had the time, I'd piss down you," I told the throat, and then turned back to Molly. "We're taking the stairs."

"That's still a bad idea," said Molly. "But apparently the lesser of two evils."

"I hate this place," said Isabella.

We headed for the door to the stairwell. I insisted on going first. I stood before the door for a few moments, looking it over carefully and checking for any new surprises, and then slammed it open with one heave from my armoured shoulder. The door slammed back against the inside wall, making a hell of a din that echoed down the long stairwell. There was nothing obviously dangerous waiting, so I started down the rough cement steps, with Molly and Isabella close behind. I didn't hear any sounds of pursuit, which rather worried me. If they weren't coming after us, it could only be because they didn't need to. Because something was waiting for us.

We made it down the first few floors without incident, the only sound that of our feet pounding on the bare steps. And then I stopped and held my hand up for silence. We stood and listened, and from below came the sound of feet ascending the stairs. There was something not quite right about the sound. Flat, unhurried, almost shuffling. And not a word, not a human voice, to accompany them. The Satanists we'd encountered before hadn't been at all diffident about expressing themselves. I leaned out over the drop and peered down the stairwell. And up the stairs came twenty or thirty naked men and women.

I looked at Molly. "Why are they wearing no clothes? I don't think I like the idea of being attacked by naked people. I mean, satanic nudists? What's that all about?"

"You don't get it, Eddie," said Molly, not even smiling. "They're not wearing clothes because they don't need any. They're dead. They're all dead."

I leaned out and looked again. They were closer now, close enough for me to see the terrible wounds that had killed them. Great holes in their chests from where their hearts had been ripped out. Ragged nubs of bone protruded from the gaping wounds, and long streaks of dried blood crusted their pale grey torsos. Their faces were blank and staring, their eyes unblinking. They were dead, and they were coming for us.

"These are what's left over from human sacrifices," said Isabella. "Not even zombies, really, because there's nothing left in them. Just bodies raised up and moved around by an external will. I don't know why the Satanists kept them. Waste not, want not, I suppose. The raised dead do make excellent shock troops against the living. Very psychologically effective. Shock-and-awe troops, if you like."

They were only a floor or so below us now, close enough that I could see other things that had been done to the dead bodies. Some had missing hands; some had no feet and stomped along on what was left of their ankles. Some had no eyes, or teeth, or lips. And all of this had clearly happened before they died.

"Why do that?" I said.

"Satanists just want to have fun," said Isabella.

I looked at her. "You think this is funny? Torture and mutilation and human sacrifice?"

Molly put a gentle hand on my arm. I couldn't feel it, but I could see it. "You know how it is, Eddie. We have to laugh in situations like this, or we'd go mad."

"Yes," I said. "I know. It . . . got to me, for a moment there."

"That's the idea," said Isabella. "One thing about Satanists; they really know how to push your buttons."

"You don't have to worry about hurting them, Eddie," said Molly. "There's no one left inside them to hurt. It's only . . . bodies."

"You take care of them," I said. "I can't seem to work up the enthusiasm."

"Sure, Eddie," said Molly. "No problem. You stand back and let the Metcalf sisters get to work."

The two witches leaned over the stairwell, chanted something in unison and extended their hands. Great waves of fire burst from their fingertips, gushing blasts of hot yellow flames that shot down the shaft and incinerated the dead bodies coming up. Fire filled the shaft, so hot the air rippled around it and the stairwell walls blackened. There was a brief stench of burnt meat, and then even that was gone. The flames snapped off. The air still shimmered with heat haze, and I had to wait a few moments before I could take a look. All the dead men and women were gone. Nothing left behind to mark their presence but some scorch marks on the steps below, and a few ashes floating on the air.

"Fire purifies," said Molly. "If you do it right."

"I'm wondering where they stored the bodies," said Isabella. "Maybe they have really big freezers in the basement."

"I think they kept them around to gloat over," said Molly. "That's Satanists for you. You all right now, Eddie?"

"Yes," I said. "It's just that . . . some things are *wrong*."

"Hold everything," said Isabella. "Something else is coming up the stairs."

"Of course there is," I said. "It's been that kind of day. Are they at least wearing clothes this time?"

"Yes and no," said Molly, leaning too far out over the stairwell for safety. I pulled her back, and she glared at me. "What's coming up next isn't really real, as such. Though they are quite definitely present."

I leaned out for a look. A whole group of human shapes were marching up the stairs in perfect lockstep. They were like . . . plastic impressions of people: the right shape but no detail, with grey and colourless, blank faces. There was something really odd about them, though it took me a moment to realise what. You could see them only from the front. From the side, they were barely an inch or so thick. And from behind, they were only a concave gap. I leaned back to look at Molly.

"Okay, ten out of ten for weird. What the hell are they?"

"Husques," Molly said succinctly. "Experienced sorcerers can shed them, like a snake sheds its skin. Really experienced sorcerers can throw off ten or twenty husques at a time, and send them out to do their bidding. A physical extension of the sorcerer's will. Better than zombies, because the sorcerer can experience what his husque experiences, but more dangerous, because what happens to the husque can affect the sorcerer who throws it. They're inhumanly strong, and there do seem to be rather a lot of them."

"So, if we damage enough of these husques, we can hurt, maybe even kill the sorcerers?" I said.

"Got it in one," said Molly. "You want me and Iz to fry them for you?"

"No," I said. "I have some serious anger issues to work off, and I feel the need to vent."

So I strode down the steps and waded right into the husques. They swarmed forward like rabid dogs, eager for the kill, and I was ready for them. I punched the first one to reach me right in the face. My golden fist smashed through and out the other side. The husque was only an inch or so thick. The husque flapped about on the end of my arm, its hands flailing uselessly against my armour. I tore it apart with hardly an effort, and it shredded like paper. I made my way steadily down the stairs, beating the husques down and tearing them apart. They were all over me, clawing at me with inhuman strength and perseverance, even as I destroyed them, but they couldn't touch me through my armour. I ripped them to pieces, smashing them down and trampling them underfoot, and it felt good, so good. I thought of Satanist sorcerers screaming and dying; and I smiled inside my golden mask. It wasn't a good smile. It took me three flights of stairs before I finally came to a halt, because I'd run out of husques. Molly and Isabella came tripping down the stairs to join me. The air was full of something very like confetti.

"Feeling better now?" said Molly.

"Much," I said. "It's easier fighting monsters. They're just what they are. But people shouldn't make themselves into monsters."

"Boy Scout," said Isabella, not unkindly.

"Something else is coming up the stairs," said Molly. "And it sounds . . . really nasty."

"I have had enough of this," I said. "They're sending things against us to wear us down, so that when we finally have to face the big shots, down in the lobby, we won't have anything left to hit them with. My armour is endlessly strong, but I'm not. And you're using up your magics. You can bet they've got something really special waiting for us on the ground floor, and we need to be in shape to face it. So we can't keep fighting these things."

"I'm not ready to give up yet," said Isabella, bristling.

"Neither is he," said Molly. "Eddie's pointing out that even our powers aren't infinite. And if we use them all up fighting proxies, he isn't sure he can defend us from what the Satanists will have waiting down in the lobby."

"I'd die trying," I said.

"Of course you would," said Molly.

"All right, all right, I'm convinced," said Isabella. "This one's a keeper, Molly. Now tell me you have a better idea, Drood."

"Well," I said, "I don't know about better, but it's definitely an idea." I looked down the stairwell. "It's only seventeen floors or so. I think we should jump."

"What?" said Molly. "That's your great alternative? I take it all back. You're crazy, Eddie, and dangerous with it."

"I thought that was what you liked about me," I said.

"I am not jumping seventeen floors! I can't fly! And I do not want to hear any sentence from you that includes the word *broomstick*."

"To make it completely clear," said Isabella, "I don't fly either."

"You don't have to," I said, in that patient, manly tone that drives women absolutely insane. "It's really very simple. I take you in my arms and jump. You cling tight to the armour, and the sheer proximity should protect you, too."

"There's that word *should* again," Molly said dangerously.

"Things aren't that desperate," said Isabella.

"Something really nasty is coming up the stairs," I said. "And there's undoubtedly worse to follow."

"All right, things are that desperate," said Isabella. "I'm still not going to do it."

"I think we have to, Iz," said Molly.

"No!" said Isabella.

"Why not?" I said.

"I hate heights!"

"Oh, come on," I said. "The fall will probably kill you."

I grabbed them both, took a firm hold and jumped. We plummeted down the stairwell, the two witches clinging desperately to me with both hands. They chanted something more or less in unison, and I could feel subtle magics wrapping around us, bonding them to my armour. Good idea. Might even work. The stairways whipped past us faster and faster, Molly's and Isabella's voices Dopplering away above us. Various unpleasant things stared blankly at us as we dropped past them, and I was quite happy to give them a miss. I'd had enough of fighting the Satanists' attack things. I wanted to slap the big guys down and then get the hell out, so I could pass on the information to my family. That was what mattered.

The last few floors swept past in a blur, and then the ground floor slammed up against my feet like a hammer blow. My armoured legs flexed, absorbing the impact, and the armour protected me from the shock. I hardly felt a thing. Molly and Isabella slumped bonelessly in my arms, but their magics seemed to have done the trick. I straightened up, holding the two witches to me until they could get their breath back and their legs under them. They finally straightened up and pushed me away, almost angrily. They made a point of standing unsupported on their own, and then giggled suddenly, and high-fived each other. A thought struck me.

"All this time I've been running back and forth, putting myself between you and all danger, but you're both witches. You keep your hearts somewhere separate and safe. Have you really been in any danger, so far?"

"Don't be silly, Eddie," said Molly. "We can still be hurt, still die, if we're hurt badly enough. You saw what happened to me when the Drood mob attacked me. I was ages getting over that."

"Right," said Isabella. "Keeping your heart separate is another ace up the sleeve. I'm a witch, not a goddess."

"Speak for yourself," said Molly. "What a ride! Let's go back up and do it again!"

"Maybe later," I said. "I think there are some people here who want to talk to us."

We'd finally reached the lobby of Lightbringer House. It was packed with people. On most occasions, the lobby was probably a wide-open space, light and airy, big enough to impress without being actually intimidating. Just the place to put new arrivals in the right frame of mind. But now it was packed from wall to wall with businessmen and -women in smart power suits, loaded down with all kinds of really heavy-duty weapons, some so big it took two of them to aim the things.

There were security forces, in generic black uniforms, with guns. They all looked very professional. Scattered through the crowd were men and women with magical weapons, everything from pointing bones to glowing blades to Hands of Glory. Hundreds of people, all with weapons trained on Molly and Isabella and me. They had us outnumbered and outgunned, and they knew it. They were smiling: really nasty, unpleasant smiles. They didn't want to kill us unless they had to. Not right away. They were looking forward to taking us somewhere private and doing awful things to us until we died of them. Maybe even sacrifice us to their lord and master. And then make use of our bodies afterwards. I looked around the lobby, and then laughed right in their faces.

"You know," I said loudly, "the good thing about killing Satanists is that you never have to feel bad about it afterwards. There's no such thing as too many dead Satanists."

I struck a pose and held up an armoured fist. Sharp spikes extruded from the golden knuckles, gleaming brightly. There were a few shocked gasps from the watching crowd. Encouraged, I continued, concentrating on refining my armour, shaping it into a more aggressive form through sheer willpower. I couldn't hold the changes for long; but they didn't know that. Rows of thick, solid spikes rose up from my arms and shoulders, and heavy golden spikes jutted from my elbows. I turned slowly, so everyone could get a good look at how nasty Drood armour could be.

Not to be outdone, Molly struck an equally impressing pose beside me. Lightning flashed on the air, slamming down around her again and again, filling the lobby with its sharp actinic glare. Lightning danced around Molly Metcalf and never touched her once. And then it stopped as suddenly as it started, leaving harsh blue-white energies roiling around Molly's hands, spitting and crackling on the still air.

Isabella stamped one foot down hard on the lobby floor. The heavy marble cracked and shattered under the impact, and a series of ripples spread out from her, distorting the marble floor, rising up in sharp ridges under the Satanists' feet.

The three of us moved leisurely to stand back-to-back, so between us we could cover the whole lobby. To my right, the lobby ended in massive glass windows, but they were opaque now, to make sure no one outside could see in. I was pretty sure they'd be soundproofed, too. Whatever happened in the lobby stayed in the lobby.

"So," I said. "Who's first?"

"I think that would have to be me," said a familiar voice.

A narrow aisle opened up amid the packed Satanists, and Alexandre Dusk came strolling forward to face me. He looked calm and assured, and perhaps even a little bored: a great man called away from important business to deal with some trivial, minor matter. He stopped a safe distance away from me and gave me his best professional smile.

"You must realise this is over, Drood. You can't kill us all."

"Want to bet?" I said cheerfully. "I'm certainly ready to give it a bloody good try."

A certain ripple of unease ran through the crowd. They may not have encountered Drood armour before, but they'd certainly heard things about it. There was a lot of looking at one another, and a general willingness to let somebody else be the first to start something. Some of them were even trying to hide behind one another. To his credit, Dusk didn't seem at all impressed. He stood his ground and gave me his best smile.

"We might or might not be able to kill you, Drood. But we can quite definitely kill your companions, the infamous Metcalf sisters."

"Watch your language, Dusk," said Molly. "We are not infamous; we are legendary."

"Right," said Isabella. "Especially legendary when it comes to taking out the trash. Hands in the air, people; who wants to die first in an interesting and possibly explosive way?"

"I'm bored with turning people into toads," said Molly. "What's ickier than toads?"

"How about worms?" said Isabella. "They make such a satisfyingly squishy sound when you tread on them."

"Locusts are good," said Molly. "They go crunch!"

"You talk a good fight," said Dusk. "But we have the numbers. And the weapons, and the magics, and all the powers of darkness. Armour off, Drood, and let us take you prisoner. Or you can watch us pull your little friends down, and kill them by inches right in front of you."

"You'd kill them anyway," I said. "You're Satanists, and so by definition your word is worthless. But you won't kill them, Dusk."

"Really? Why not?"

"You really want Louisa Metcalf mad at you?" I said.

Another ripple ran through the crowd. They'd all heard of Louisa Metcalf. A general feeling of unease was making itself apparent in the crowd. They'd thought this was going to be easy. I don't think any of them had ever been in a real fight before. Some were backing away; some were lowering their weapons and looking around for the exits. The confidence was oozing out of them. I had to fight an impulse to shout, *Boo!* just to see how many would faint or wet themselves.

Dusk must have realised what was happening. His voice cracked like a whip. "A witch is just a witch, and a Drood is only as strong as his armour! We . . . are so much more. We are the blessed children of the dark."

"A few of you, maybe," I said. "Most of your people look like they're up way past their bedtime."

Dusk shrugged. "You simply can't get good followers these days. But there's enough of us here to get the job done. Surrender now, and we'll hold you somewhere secure till we can contact your family and make a deal. I'm sure they've got something we'd like that we can swap you and the witches for. I don't want to have to kill you, not when you're worth so much more to us as bargaining chips."

I considered him thoughtfully. "Droods don't surrender. You must know that. You're stalling; buying time to hit us with some big secret weapon. You really think you can take us?"

"Anything will break, if you hit it hard enough and often enough," said Dusk.

"It's going to get messy," I said. "Loud and messy. You ready to draw that much attention from outside?"

"The building is very thoroughly shielded," said Dusk, confirming my suspicions. "I could sacrifice a busload of blind orphans in here, and no one outside would see or hear a thing. Don't think we can't hurt you inside that armour, Drood. We know all there is to know about hurting people."

I had to laugh. "Droods have been honing their fighting skills for centuries. You're amateur night."

Dusk looked me over thoughtfully. "So which Drood are you, exactly?"

"Any Drood is every Drood," I said.

"You think we fear the Droods?"

"You do if you've got any sense."

A wild-eyed young man ran suddenly forward out of the crowd, screaming at the top of his lungs and wielding a long glowing sword. He brought the blade swinging round in a vicious arc, moving almost too fast to see.

It hit me on the side of the neck and shattered into a dozen pieces. The young Satanist stood there with only the hilt in his hand. I leaned forward a little, so he could see his own reflection in my featureless golden mask.

"Run," I said.

He sprinted back into the crowd and disappeared. I looked at Dusk, who shrugged.

"There's always one."

"There'll be one fewer if he tries that again," I said.

"I'm curious," said Dusk. "Why didn't you kill him?"

"Because I kill only when I have to," I said. "That's the difference between us."

"Oh, I think we're a lot closer than you care to admit," said Dusk. "We're both quite capable of doing whatever we consider . . . necessary. And you can't stop us."

"I wear the Drood armour," I said. "You can't stop me."

"Oh, please," said Dusk. "There's nothing about you that couldn't be cured with the right kind of can opener."

"And there's nothing about all the people in this lobby that a good kicking couldn't help to put right," I said. "Shall we get started?" I looked about me, and people actually fell back. "I mean, come on! Worshipping the Devil? When has that *ever* been a good idea? I put it all down to poor toilet training, myself."

Dusk looked at Molly and Isabella. "Since your companion seems impervious to good sense, have you anything useful to say?"

"Fuck off and die," said Molly.

"Apparently not," said Dusk.

"Why are we still talking?" I said. "Are we waiting for your marvellous secret weapon to make its appearance? Or has one of its wheels come off?"

"No," said Dusk. "I'm curious. I've never met a Drood before. Don't know anyone who has. You're the urban legends of the invisible world. How did you come to be here? How did you know I was going to be here today? Which of my people betrayed us?"

I had to smile behind my mask. I could have told him it was all down to chance, but he wouldn't have believed it.

"Wouldn't you like to know?" I said, to sow a little mischief.

"At least my power is my own," said Dusk. "How does it feel, knowing that your only power comes from your armour? That you can have power over the world only by sealing yourself off from it? We glory in our power, and know sensations you can only dream of."

"It's not the armour," I said. "It's never the armour. It's the Drood inside it. And to attack one of us is to attack the whole family. Are you really ready to declare open war on the Droods?"

There was a long pause. He was actually thinking about it. I really wasn't sure what he would do next. He had the numbers and the weapons . . . but he wasn't sure. I was still a Drood in my armour, and Molly and Isabella both had reputations for blood and mayhem. It would be a brave bookie who'd set the odds on this one. I was ready to fight if I had to, but I was really hoping I wouldn't have to.

"Let them go," Dusk said finally. "It's not as if they know anything important. Run back to your family, Drood. Tell them their time is almost over."

He gestured with his left hand, and his people obeyed him immediately, falling back to open up a narrow aisle between us and the lobby entrance. Molly and Isabella and I moved slowly but steadily over to the doors, not dropping our guard for a moment. Molly pushed the doors open, and she and Isabella slipped quickly out onto the street beyond. I paused to look back at the watching crowd.

"You did a lot of damage while you were here, Drood," said Dusk. "There will be a reckoning."

"Send the bill to Drood Hall," I said. "And we'll all take turns officially ignoring it."

I left the lobby, and the doors slammed shut behind me. There was the sound of a great many locks slamming shut. I quickly armoured down, before any passersby could notice, and then Molly and Isabella and I strode perfectly normally down the street, away from Lightbringer House. It felt good to be back in the real world again, in the natural sunshine and the easy calm of everyday life. I could feel my muscles slowly unbunching as I was finally able to relax. That had all been a lot closer than I cared to think about.

"I could have taken him," Isabella said suddenly.

"We could have taken him," said Molly.

"You want to go back in and try?" I said. "I'll hold your coats."

"Not right now," said Isabella.

"Maybe later," said Molly. "There were an awful lot of them, weren't there?"

"I counted three Hands of Glory, several death charms and something that looked very like a monkey's paw," I said. "Drood armour's good, but it does have its limits."

"If we hadn't been there," Molly said slowly, "and if you hadn't had to worry about us, would you have fought them anyway, and to hell with the consequences?"

"No," I said. "The important thing was to get out of there alive with the information we gathered. My family doesn't know anything about this, and they need to know. I'm more concerned about you now. They've seen your faces; they know who you are. They'll never stop coming after you. I think you both need to come back to Drood Hall with me. You'll be safe there. My family doesn't take any shit from jumped-up Devil worshippers."

"Put myself in the hands of the Droods?" said Isabella. "I don't think so!"

"Then what will you do?" said Molly.

"I have my own leads to follow," said Isabella. "This was my case, and my business, long before you stuck your noses in."

"And if they do come after you?" I said.

Isabella smiled briefly. "I could always go spend some time with Louisa."

She strode off down the street, head held high, not looking back. People moved quickly to get out of her way.

"Well," said Molly. "That was . . . interesting. Whose great idea was this, anyway?"

"Yours," I said.

"Why do you listen to me?" said Molly. "I wouldn't."

CHAPTER FOUR

Too Many Secrets for One Family

B
ack at Drood Hall, I walked into the Sanctity to find the ruling council already assembled and waiting for me. Somehow, I'm always the last to arrive. I'd like to take the credit and say I do it deliberately, so I can make a big entrance and be sure everybody's attention is fixed on me . . . but the truth is that no matter how hard I try, they're always there first. I sometimes think they must all get together secretly beforehand and agree to actually start the meeting ten minutes earlier, so they can all look at me disapprovingly for being late again. But, truth be told, I'm always late. For everything. It's a gift.

And these days nobody glares at me too much when I walk in late with Molly Metcalf on my arm, because Molly glares right back at them. And it's never a good idea to upset someone who can turn you into something small and squishy with warts on your warts by looking at you in a Certain Way. I, of course, do not have to worry about this happening to me, because I have learned the magic words, *Yes, dear.*

They were all there, sitting round the great table in the middle of the Sanctity. The ruling council of the

Droods, self-appointed on the run after the Matriarch's murder, because someone had to keep the
wheels turning while the family got on with its job.
Family politics come and go, but duty and responsibility go on forever. My uncle Jack, the Armourer, was
sitting at the head of the table in his usual lab coat,
fresh that day but already marked with scorch marks
and chemical burns, over a grubby T-shirt bearing the
legend, *Give Me a Lever and a Place to Stand, and I'll
Beat the World into Submission.* The Sarjeant-at-
Arms sat stiffly in his chair, back straight and head
erect, big and muscular in his black suit and spotless
white shirt, like a bouncer who'd taken over the night-
club. A thug and a bully and proud of it, the Sarjeant
was a very busy man who could still find the time to be
disappointed in me.

William the Librarian sat slumped in his chair, wearing a battered dressing gown that must have had a pattern on it once upon a time, and a pair of sloppy bunny
slippers. It was immediately clear that he wasn't wearing anything under the dressing gown, and even before
I reached the table, the Armourer had to tell the Librarian to keep the damn thing closed. There was something about the bunny slippers that disturbed me. They
were white, and most bunny slippers are pink. In fact, I
was pretty sure that the last time I'd seen them, they
had been pink. But now they were white. Which felt like
it should *mean* something . . . that I should remember
something . . . but the memory remained elusive, so I let
it go.

And finally there was cousin Harry, looking more
like a defrocked accountant than ever in his neat grey
suit and wire-rimmed spectacles. Quiet, clever, dangerous cousin Harry. And his partner, Roger Morningstar.
Who, by long tradition, was not allowed to actually sit at
the main table with the council. Because although he
had much to contribute, he was only half Drood. And
so, like my Molly, he could attend council meetings, but
not sit at the table. The two of them had to sit on separate chairs a respectable distance away. Petty, I know,

but that's tradition for you. When a family's been around as long as the Droods, you acquire a lot of traditions along the way, rather like barnacles on a ship. It's the long-held traditions like this one that make me wonder whether we're getting a bit too inbred.

Molly always got her own back by bringing a really massive bag of popcorn to every council meeting and crunching the stuff loudly during the boring bits. Roger sat loosely in his chair, calm and entirely at his ease, and we all did our best not to notice that his half-demonic presence was still potent enough to set fire to the chair he was sitting on. Little grey streams of smoke drifted up into the air, and I hoped someone had reminded Ethel to turn off the sprinklers.

Ethel, as our very own other-dimensional friend insisted we call it, manifested in the Sanctity as a pleasant rose red glow. Bathing in that ruddy glare was enough to calm the spirit and ease the heart. Didn't stop us all from arguing, though.

I sat down in my assigned place at the far end of the table and immediately launched into my tale of what had gone down at Lightbringer House. Only to be as immediately stopped by the Sarjeant-at-Arms. Meetings have to have agendas, in his world, and that meant my late-arriving news would have to wait until we'd dealt with existing business first. All the others went along, because the Sarjeant was quite capable of out-stubborning us all when it came to matters of precedence. So I sank down in my chair and sulked, with my arms folded tightly across my chest, while he worked his way through the business of the day. It wasn't easy feeling sullen and thoroughly pissed off under Ethel's soothing red glow, but then, I've had a lot of practice. When it comes to trying your patience, my family could make Mother Teresa drink vodka straight from the bottle while drop-kicking a leper.

"We have to decide what to do next, now that our Matriarch is dead," the Armourer said heavily. "Grandmother's been gone some time now, and we can't keep putting this off. I've been carrying most of the load, with Harry's help, staying on top of the day-to-day problems, because I'm most senior. . . . But I have my own work to be getting on with, in the Armoury! I never wanted to be in charge. I'm not good with people. When I'm faced with a problem, my first response has always been to hit it with something heavy. Which works fine with machines, but not so much with people."

"Exactly," said the Sarjeant-at-Arms. "I'd hate to think you were encroaching on my territory."

"Someone's got to be in charge," Harry said firmly. "We've lost direction. The family is undermanned and overextended. There's no overall strategy, and no long-term policy. Someone's got to be in a position to make the important decisions."

"Someone like you, Harry?" I said. "That didn't work out too well, the last time you tried."

"I've been studying," Harry said coldly. "Reading up on the family history, and all kinds of useful background knowledge."

"He has," said Roger. "I never knew there were so many books on the principles of leadership. I particularly enjoyed the Machiavelli."

"Not really helping there, Roger," said Harry.

"The council can continue to oversee the usual day-to-day stuff," said the Sarjeant. "But only until a new leader is elected."

"Harry has proved himself very competent in handling such matters," said the Armourer.

"I always knew you'd make a good housekeeper, Harry," I said.

"At least he gets involved!" snapped the Sarjeant. "It's all very well to sneer at paperwork and bureaucracy, but you can't run a family this size without it! If people like Harry didn't keep on top of all the little things, our departments would grind to a halt, and you'd be left with no backup at all!"

"Oh, indeed," I said. "It's a wonder I get anything done. . . ."

The Armourer cleared his throat meaningfully, and

I shut up. Only my uncle Jack could still make me feel like an errant schoolboy.

"If we are to hold another election," said Harry, "then I must respectfully insist that all candidates be allowed sufficient time to campaign properly."

"You want to bring politics into the Hall?" said the Armourer, scowling heavily. "Didn't we have enough problems with the Zero Tolerance faction?"

"How will everyone know how good I'd be for the family unless I'm allowed to explain it to them?" said Harry, in his most reasonable voice.

"I love a good campaign," said Molly, past a mouthful of popcorn. "I've already got a great slogan in mind. How about, 'Vote for Eddie or I'll Turn You into a Dung Beetle'?"

"I wish I thought she was joking," said the Armourer.

"Any attempt by you to interfere with the family's electoral process will result in your being banned from the Hall," said the Sarjeant-at-Arms, glaring at Molly.

"Love to see you try, Cedric," said Molly, glaring right back at him.

"Really not helping, Molly," I said.

"Whatever the result of the election," said the Armourer, "should we also decide on a new Matriarch? As a constitutional position, perhaps? The family has always had a Matriarch. . . ."

"Tricky," said Harry. "Do we appoint the next in line, or should the new Matriarch be elected, too?"

"Who is next in the line of succession?" I said. "I've never really kept up with that side of things."

"Technically," said the Armourer, "the Matriarchy is supposed to pass from mother to daughter, or granddaughter. Your mother would have been next in line, Eddie, but with her gone, and you her only child . . . the direct line of succession is broken. If James or I had produced a daughter, she would have been next in line. But I had only one son, and while James had many . . . offspring, only one has ever been acknowledged by the family, and that's Harry. And before you say anything, Harry, yes,

I know you have an absolute multitude of half sisters, by various mothers, but none of them can be accepted as legitimate successors."

"Tradition," said the Sarjeant, nodding solemnly.

"Daddy Dearest did put it about rather a lot," murmured Harry. "I haven't even met all my half brothers and half sisters."

"He was very romantic," the Armourer said firmly.

"We can't simply appoint a Matriarch," said the Sarjeant. "If we must have one, and I think we must, then tradition demands she be part of the line of descent, no matter how . . . fractured. Traditions are all we have to hold the family together."

"My aunt Helen was Mother's sister," said the Armourer. "And she had a daughter, Margaret. I suppose . . ."

"Don't recognise the name," I said. "The family's getting far too big. . . ."

"I could always organise a cull," said the Sarjeant.

We all looked at him. He didn't appear to be joking.

"Moving on," I said. "Uncle Jack, what does Margaret do in the family?"

"Wait a minute!" said the Sarjeant. "You mean Capability Maggie! She's in charge of landscaping the Hall grounds, maintaining the lawns and the lake and the woods, and all the creatures that live in them."

"That's her," said the Armourer. "Devoted to her job. Raised a hell of a fuss when I dug up half an acre to bury that massive dragon's head you sent back from Germany, Eddie. I mean, I covered it over again. . . . I think a new barrow adds personality to the garden. And it is the only part of the garden that can actually have a conversation with you when you walk past it."

"Does she have Matriarch potential?" said Harry.

"She runs the gardeners with a rod of iron," said the Sarjeant. "Sometimes literally. And she chased me twice around the Hall with a pitchfork that time I walked across her new seedlings."

"Now, that I would have loved to see," I said. "Hell, I'd have sold tickets."

"I still say she should have put up a sign," said the Sarjeant. "I'll have a word with her. From a safe distance. Sound her out, see how she feels."

"Are we still talking about a constitutional Matriarch?" I said. "Because I'm damned if I'm having some new Matriarch ruling over me with a pitchfork. What exactly would her powers and responsibilities be?"

"To be decided by the family, I suppose," said the Armourer. "Or whoever the family elects as its new leader."

"What's she like, this Margaret?" I said, trying to hold the Armourer's gaze, even as he seemed not to want to.

"Downright vicious, if you tread on her seedlings," said the Sarjeant.

"Very . . . forceful," said the Armourer. "Doesn't suffer fools gladly. Or at all, really."

"Exactly the right sort," said Harry.

I looked at him thoughtfully. "Will you be standing for leader in this new election, Harry?"

"Of course. I live to serve the family. How about you, Eddie?"

"The only reason I'd stand would be to prevent your taking command again, Harry."

"How very unkind," said Harry.

"The next item on the agenda," said the Sarjeant quickly, "is the continuing problem of the Librarian."

Everyone looked at William, still sitting quietly at his end of the table, lost in his own little world, as always. Even allowing for the dressing gown and bunny slippers, he looked fairly presentable. His hair and beard were neatly trimmed these days, because his new assistant Librarian, Ioreth, did it for him. But he still looked like he wasn't eating nearly enough. William had a first-class mind some of the time, but he couldn't always remember where he put it. He worked best when left alone with his beloved books in the Old Library, but here and now . . . He raised his great grey head suddenly and looked at me . . . and he had the cold thousand-yard stare of a soldier from some terrible forgotten war.

He hadn't contributed a single word to the council meeting so far.

"How are you feeling, William?" I said, a bit loudly.

"Who can say?" William said sadly. "I'm here, because the Sarjeant said I was supposed to be here. Settle for that."

I looked up into the rose red glow that marked Ethel's presence. "I had hoped springing him from that asylum and bringing him home to the family might help him."

"Sorry, Eddie," said Ethel, her calm and kind voice seeming to come from everywhere at once. "I'm doing all I can to soothe his troubled brow, but someone has done a real number on this man's mind. I can barely see into his head, and I can see into dimensions you don't even have names for yet. Trying to sort through his thoughts is like drowning in a bucket of boiling cats. There's a lot going on inside his mind, but it's all going on at the same time. It's a wonder to me he can even see the real world. He is fighting it, Eddie; but I think he's losing. And . . ."

"Yes?" I said, after the pause had gone on a little too long for my liking.

"There're . . . other things in his head, too," Ethel said reluctantly. "Shadows . . . things I can't even identify. I've no idea what they are."

"Terrific," said Harry.

"I do wish people wouldn't talk about me as though I weren't here!" said William, sitting suddenly upright. "All right, some of the time I'm not. I know that. But it's the principle of the thing! I shouldn't be here. . . . Put me back in the Old Library. I can focus there. I can cope. I can contribute to the family. Nothing else matters."

"I really thought you'd feel better once I got you home," I said.

"Oh, it is better here," said William. "Don't think I'm not grateful, Eddie. I am, I am. . . . But the Heart broke me, you see, and even though I ran away from the Heart and the Hall and the family . . . I couldn't run away from what it did to me. I'm still broken. . . . And all the Droods' horses and all the Droods' men couldn't put me back together again."

I looked around the table, glowering at everyone. "This has gone on long enough! William is family, and he needs our help. And now that the Matriarch's no longer here to block it, I say it's time to hire a professional telepath and see what he can do to put William's mind right."

"I do understand, Eddie," the Armourer said gently. "I remember how William was before he left. He was my friend, and I miss him. But I have to say . . . what if the Matriarch had a good reason for saying no?"

"Like what?" I said.

"I don't know!" said the Armourer. "Don't look at me in that tone of voice, Eddie! I did discuss the matter with Mother on several occasions, but she always refused to explain her reasons. She didn't have to, after all. She was the Matriarch."

"I also raised the matter with her," said the Sarjeant. "I was . . . concerned about my uncle. She also refused to explain her thinking to me. She said, very forcefully, that allowing a telepath access to William's mind was completely unacceptable. She was . . . very curt about it. I assumed it was a security issue; that William must have something in his head, family secrets, that no outsider could be allowed to know."

"Doesn't seem likely, does it?" I said. "What could William know that the rest of us don't?"

"That's rather the point, isn't it?" said the Sarjeant. "But for once, you and I are in agreement, Edwin. This has gone on far too long. William is family and must be helped. Nothing else matters."

"Who do we have in mind for the job?" said Harry. "The family's psychics—"

"Aren't up to the job," I said firmly. "What's inside William's head would eat them alive. We need someone with real power, someone who can punch their weight."

"The London Knights are always boasting about their first-class telepath, Vivienne de Tourney," said the Sarjeant. "Apparently they use her to maintain communications among the Knights when they ride out to war in other worlds and dimensions, where our science doesn't always work. She can maintain telepathic contact among hundreds of Knights simultaneously, so they can talk to her, and one another, and never once get muddled. A first-class brain. I could talk to her. . . ."

"You've been drinking with their seneschal again, haven't you?" the Armourer said accusingly.

"I do like to get out now and again, yes," the Sarjeant said, matching the Armourer glare for glare. "A little private club for those who serve. I do have a life outside the family."

"I thought that was forbidden, on security grounds?" I said, amused despite myself.

"It is forbidden," said the Sarjeant. "For everyone except me. I don't have to worry about breaking security. I am security. And I can drink their seneschal under the table any day of the week."

"Bloody London Knights," growled the Armourer. "Do we really want to go cap in hand to those snotty, stuck-up little prigs? Always so high and mighty—last defenders of Camelot, my arse! They give themselves such airs and graces. . . . We're the real defenders of Humanity! Because they're always off fighting somewhere else!"

"What about the Carnacki Institute?" said Harry. "They have any number of telepaths working for them."

"The Ghost Finders?" said the Sarjeant. "I don't think so. They'd want payment in more than money. They'd want information, secrets, sources. . . . And I've never really trusted them. I don't think anything we gave them would necessarily stay with them. They've always been too close to the Establishment for my liking, for all their protestations."

"If we have to hire someone," I said carefully, "I say we hire the best. And that means Ammonia Vom Acht."

Everyone reacted, and none of them favourably. The Armourer pulled a sour face, and the Sarjeant shook his head firmly. Harry and Roger looked at each other, and neither of them looked pleased by the prospect. William was back to staring off into space again. I looked at Molly, and she made a point of being very interested in the remaining contents of her bag of popcorn.

"All right," I said. "Agreed, she's a poisonous, vicious and really quite appalling woman, and those are her good points. But you know you're going to get your money's worth with her."

"I should hope so," said the Sarjeant. "Given how much she charges."

"How do you know how much she charges?" I said.

"I have made my own overtures," said the Sarjeant. "Once it became clear that we were going to have to do something about William."

"I'm still here!" said William.

"Only just," said the Sarjeant. "But can we really risk allowing *that woman* into Drood Hall? She could rip the secrets out of everyone's head in ten seconds flat."

"I wasn't thinking of letting her into the Hall, as such," I said. "I thought perhaps something more like neutral territory—namely, the Old Library. Teleport her straight there, through the Merlin Glass. She'd be cut off from the rest of the Hall and the rest of the family. I'm sure Uncle Jack could whip up something I could wear to keep Ammonia out of my head."

"What?" said the Armourer. "Oh. Yes. Of course, no problem. I'll take it under advisement. I think I may go and hide somewhere the day she arrives."

"Lot of people feel that way about Ammonia Vom Acht," I said.

"I still want to know who or what is living in the Old Library, along with the Librarian," the Sarjeant said determinedly. "I am referring to whatever it was that scared the crap out of the Immortal posing as Rafe. You were there, Eddie, when whatever it was stopped Rafe from killing the Librarian. What did you see?"

"I keep telling you," I said, "I didn't see anything. All I could feel was this . . . presence. Big and powerful and dangerous, but not like anything I've ever encountered before. William . . . William! Do you have anything you want to contribute?"

"Something's there," said William, nodding wisely. "Something very old, I think. Watching me, or watching over me. It's so hard to be sure. . . . It steals my socks, you know."

"We can't have someone or something unknown running loose in the Old Library!" said the Sarjeant.

"We've already run the exorcism engine three times!" said the Armourer. "None of my equipment was able to detect anything!"

"Why not let the Vom Acht woman have a crack at it?" I said. "If she really is the top-ranking telepath she's always claimed, she should be able to pin it down. Or at least tell us what it is we're dealing with."

"She might not survive such a close encounter," said the Armourer. "You saw the state of the Immortal after we dragged him out of the Old Library."

"Get her to work on William first," the Sarjeant said wisely. "Then have her scan the Old Library. And she might die, you say? Excellent. A plan with no drawbacks."

"You've got cold, Cedric," said the Armourer.

"I was born cold," said the Sarjeant-at-Arms.

"Some days you can't breathe in here for testosterone," said Molly.

"Have we finally finished all the family business?" I said. "I really would like to talk about my encounter with the first well-organised, worldwide Satanist conspiracy in sixty years!"

"It's always about you, isn't it, Eddie?" said Harry.

"Far more often than it's about you, Harry," I said.

I ran through everything that happened at Lightbringer House, with Molly chipping in now and then to add details. There were certain parts I chose to leave out, mostly concerning Isabella, but I couldn't leave her out entirely. I was pretty sure she'd be inviting herself back in again at some point. William actually brightened up a bit at the mention of her name.

"Very healthy young girl!" he said loudly. "Got a good pair of legs on her. They go all the way up to her arse. I don't know why you insist on keeping her out of the Old Library, Sarjeant. She can come and visit me anytime. . . ."

"She can't have access, because she isn't family," said the Sarjeant.

"Oh, let the girl in," said William. "I could show her a few things. Oh, yes. I may be insane, but I'm not crazy."

"Dirty old man," said Molly, in a not entirely disapproving way.

"Moving on," I said deliberately. "I'm mostly concerned about Alexandre Dusk, and the Great Sacrifice he was talking about."

"It is a worry, yes," said the Sarjeant. "But I don't see anything serious enough in this that we should make it a top priority."

"*What?*" I said. "Are you out of your mind, Cedric? A Satanist conspiracy involving every government in the world, talking about a satanic coup so big it could debase all Humanity, and let loose the Great Beast himself . . . and you don't see that as a top priority?"

"It's just Satanists," said the Sarjeant. "They always talk big. We'll keep an eye on them, certainly. Gather information, see who's actually involved and what they might have going for them. . . . I'll delegate one of our field agents to infiltrate Lightbringer House."

"I could do that!" I said immediately. "I could go in as Shaman Bond!"

"The council has a far more important mission in mind for you," said Harry. "Important and urgent. You'll need to be ready for insertion first thing tomorrow morning."

"*What?*" I said. "I've only just got back from being dead!"

"No rest for the wicked," the Armourer said solemnly. "I can always whip up one of my special pep-you-up tonics, if you like."

"No, I do not like," I said. "Grandmother used to

dose me with your tonics all the time I was growing up, and they always tasted *vile*."

"That's how you know it's doing you good," said the Armourer. "You always got a nice chocolate afterwards, didn't you?"

"There isn't a chocolate in the world that could take away the taste of your tonics!"

"It's nice to be appreciated," said the Armourer. He shook his head slowly. "An actual Satanist conspiracy, after all these years. I always have trouble taking them seriously. It's all a bit too much Dennis Wheatley, as far as I'm concerned."

"Who?" said Harry.

"You know," said Roger. "*The Devil Rides Out*, that was him. The old Hammer horror film we watched on DVD last week. Most of the people in my circles think it's a classic. We all love Charles Gray as the coven leader, Mocata. Very sinister. He made being a Devil worshipper look so damned *cool*. Mocata was supposedly based on Aleister Crowley, but I am here to tell you, Crowley was never that impressive. Or even that dignified. Hell of a mountain climber, though."

"Have you heard anything about this new conspiracy?" I said. "These are your people, aren't they?"

"Oh, please! Hardly," said Roger. "They're nothing but wannabes, whereas I am the real thing. There have always been satanic conspiracies, but none of them were ever as powerful or as important as they liked to think."

"Yes, well," said Molly, "you would say that, wouldn't you? Do you know anything about Alexandre Dusk and his proposed Great Sacrifice?"

"Haven't heard anything," said Roger.

We all waited, but he had nothing more to say. Even Harry was looking at Roger thoughtfully, but he didn't seem to care.

"I have to ask," I said, looking round the council. "Given that there is an unquestionably real satanic conspiracy, is there, in fact, a good-guy equivalent? Apart from us, obviously."

"There are other organisations on the side of the Light," said the Sarjeant-at-Arms. "And any number of powerful individuals, like the Lord of Thorns, in the Nightside; and the Walking Man, the wrath of God in the world of men. . . ."

"I was thinking of something more specific," I said. "Are there agents of good in the world, to match the agents of evil?"

"Unfortunately, yes," said the Armourer. "There is . . . the Emmanuel."

Everyone seemed to sit up a little straighter. Even William was giving the conversation his full attention, such as it was.

"Emmanuel," said William. "Literally, 'God with us.'"

"Is that a person or an organisation?" I said.

"Good question," said the Armourer. "Nobody knows. Or at least, no one knows for sure. This family has had dealings with the Emmanuel, down the centuries. When we knew for sure that we were in way out of our depth. According to family records, and these are very secret and very private records, the Emmanuel is extremely powerful, and not to be summoned lightly."

"All right," I said. "What's the big secret here? What does the Emmanuel do?"

"He answers questions," said William. "Truthfully. He knows everything there is to know about people, places and the true nature of reality. Which can be . . . very upsetting. Not to mention downright disturbing. We do have a book of his recorded sayings in the Old Library. It's locked shut, in half a dozen different and very thorough ways, and on the front cover someone has stamped the words 'Do Not Open Till Doomsday.' I for one can take a hint."

"He can do . . . pretty much whatever he feels like doing," said the Armourer. "I never met him, but Mother did. She said he was a man with no restraint and no limits. A man who would do absolutely anything in the name of the good. Which is why this family has only ever made contact with the Emmanuel when we were really deep in the shit, and going under for the third time. Apparently being around him can be . . . damaging."

"Why?" I said.

"Because he scares the crap out of us," said William.

"Of course," said Roger. "Agents of the light, the ones who draw their power directly from the Most High, can be as cold-blooded, single-minded and dangerous to be around as any agent of the dark. Neither side really cares about people; it's always the long view for them. Whatever's best for Humanity as a whole, and God help the poor individual. Always ready to sacrifice today, in the name of tomorrow."

"Anyway," said the Sarjeant, "according to family records, we've only ever met the one man. And whether that is the Emmanuel or the representative of a larger organisation . . . we have no way of knowing. Certainly the family has always been very glad to see the back of him. Apparently, he has only to look at you and you want to blurt out every bad thing you've ever done, or thought of doing, and then throw yourself at his feet and beg for mercy. We had to be very careful about whom we let talk to him. Even the best of us came away from such meetings . . . disturbed."

"I have heard of the Emmanuel," said Roger, and something in his voice made us all turn to look at him. "I've never met him. Don't know anyone who has. But then, of course, we don't move in the same circles. . . . He's even more of an urban legend in the invisible world than the Droods. Often talked about, rarely encountered, best left strictly alone. Everyone knows someone who claims to know someone who's met the Emmanuel; but when you try to pin them down . . . Where he comes from, nobody knows, but we're all really glad when he goes back there. Extreme good can be just as scary, and just as dangerous, as extreme evil. All of my kind . . . the half-castes, the hellspawn and the Nephilim, and every possible combination of the natural and unnatural worlds, have good reason to stay well clear of such ... archetypal forces. Neither good nor evil has any use for shades of grey. ..."

"On a somewhat connected matter," I said, after we'd all taken some time out to consider Roger's words, "I was told that this family has long-standing pacts with Heaven and Hell. Is that right?"

"Oh, yes," said the Armourer, entirely casually. "Very old pacts with the Courts of the Holy and the Houses of Pain. What about them?"

"Why?" I said. "And a whole side order of, *How?"*

"You never did pay attention in history class, did you?" said the Sarjeant.

"This is very old family history," said the Armourer. "Going back to the really early days, when our armour was still new and we were still making a name for ourselves ... And we needed all the help we could get. The details of how contact was made, and even exactly what we get out of it, are kept locked away in Very Secret, Need to Know, Move Along, Nothing to See Here files."

"I'm getting really tired of hearing that phrase, *need-to-know,*" I said. "I used to run this bloody family, and the sheer number of things it turns out I didn't need to know is getting on my tits big-time. Who does know?"

The Armourer and the Sarjeant-at-Arms looked at each other, their faces unreadable. Finally, the Sarjeant said reluctantly, "The Matriarch knew. And ... one other."

"William," said the Armourer. "As Librarian, he knew."

We all looked at William, and he looked back with surprisingly clear and thoughtful eyes. "The original contracts, or compacts, are still on file in the Old Library. They make very interesting reading. Which is why I've filed them away in such a manner that no one will ever be able to find them again without my help. Trust me on this, Eddie: You don't need to know what's in them. No one in the family does. It's enough to know ... that we have contacts, and perhaps even friends, in high and low places. And Jacob, of course."

"What?" I said.

"The ghost, Jacob," William said patiently. "He knew. He wasn't supposed to, but then, it's hard to keep secrets from the dead."

"Could we use these . . . contacts?" I said. "To try to find out what's happening with this new Satanist conspiracy, and what they're up to?"

"No," said William.

We all waited, but he had nothing more to say.

"The family must be protected," the Sarjeant said heavily. "Some things must stay secret."

"Like the source of our original armour?" I said. "Or the pact our ancestors made with the Heart? We did make some really bad decisions, back in the bad old days. That's always been the trouble with this family. Too many secrets."

"I think you're pushing this too far, Eddie," said the Armourer.

"Am I?" I said. "I don't think I'm pushing this nearly far enough! What about those secret departments within departments that most of the family isn't even supposed to know exist? You told me about them, William; have you remembered anything else?"

"I don't know!" said William. "Don't push me! I know what I need to know, when I need to know it, and on good days that includes where to find the chemical toilet. I know some things . . . but I'm not entirely sure I trust them. There are . . . agents, yes, more secret than the field agents, sent out to do the kinds of things the family would rather not admit to, even to itself. Perhaps especially not to itself. But I don't remember who they were, or are. Maybe I never knew. . . . Only the Matriarch knew everything."

"And she's gone," I said. "Which raises a very interesting question: Who's running these special agents these days, and what exactly are they doing in the family's name?"

"Eddie has a point," the Armourer said reluctantly. "We've let things run loose far too long. Admittedly, we have been a bit busy lately, but still . . . Someone has to take charge. Someone has to set overall policy of what is and is not acceptable, and make sure the family's left hand knows what its right hand is doing."

"Once the family has elected a leader, they can take control," said Harry.

"Can we wait that long?" I said. "Are we supposed to let these secret departments run themselves, without anyone knowing what they're doing?"

"I know," said William. "I've always known. Of course, I don't always remember what I know. Or even if what I remember actually happened."

"I don't care what he may or may not know; we are not putting him in charge of anything," the Sarjeant said firmly. "No offence, Uncle William."

"Oh, hello, young Cedric," said William. "Do you want an ice cream?"

"Uncle Jack," I said, looking firmly at the Armourer, "you're the senior man here, with actual field agent experience. You'll have to take charge. Dig up these secret departments and rein them in. Only till someone can take overall charge again."

"You do like to put me on the spot, don't you, Eddie?" The Armourer scowled and drummed his fingertips on the table for a moment, but in the end he nodded shortly. "All right. There are people I can talk to. And they'll talk to me, if they know what's good for them."

"I should be involved in this," said the Sarjeant. "It involves family security."

"Yes, it does, and no, you shouldn't," said the Armourer. "You tend your own briar patch, Cedric."

"Hold it," said Harry. "Don't we get to discuss this? The Armourer gets to be in charge because he's the oldest here?"

"Because he has seniority, because he has actual field experience and because he knows who these special agents are. Don't you, Uncle Jack?" I met his gaze steadily. "You have to know who they are, because you're the one who supplies them with all the necessary weapons and gadgets before they go out on their missions. Right, Uncle Jack?"

He smiled suddenly. "You always were smarter than you let anyone realise, Eddie. Yes, I know who they are. Now all I have to do is persuade them to tell me whom they work for; who gives them their orders and sends them out on their missions. As if I don't have enough work on my plate . . . Engines big enough to drive the moon out of its orbit don't build themselves, you know."

There was a pause.

"I thought we'd agreed that you were going to table that one, for the time being," I said tactfully.

The Armourer sniffed loudly. "Man's allowed to have a hobby, isn't he?"

I looked at Roger. "We are about to change the subject. What do you know about the family's pact with Hell?"

"Not a thing," said Roger. "Way above my pay scale."

"Is there anyone you could talk to who might know what Dusk is up to?"

"I don't think they'd tell me, even if they knew," Roger said carefully.

"Even though you're half Drood?"

"Especially because I'm half Drood. Besides, consider the source. Hell always lies."

"Except when a truth can hurt you more," said Harry.

"What did happen on your recent trip to Hell?" I asked Roger. "Did anything come of that?"

"Not really," said Roger. "I had to call it off and come back in a hurry when everything started kicking off here with the Accelerated Men attack."

"I think we've spent quite long enough talking about Hell," said the Sarjeant. "It's time to move on to more immediate business. Our immediate top priority is the Supernatural Arms Faire, currently being held in the mountains above Pakistan."

"What?" I said. "What's that got to do with us?"

"It's still mostly called the Supernatural Arms Faire, even though most of the weapons on display these days tend towards superscience," said the Armourer. "I go every year; never miss it. Last year they were giving away Shock and Awe in the goodie bags! It's a very old affair, Eddie; goes all the way back to Roman times. Or at least, that's when it first appears in an official report. Enthusiasts such as myself did take to calling it Harmageddon back in the eighties, but it never really caught on. Everybody who's anybody who's involved in weapons of mass destruction goes there to see what's new and nasty. The Internet's made a lot of things more readily accessible, but there's still nothing quite like the joy of browsing."

"What has this got to do with me?" I said. "And why do I know I'm really not going to like the answer?"

"Must be turning psychic," the Armourer said cheerfully. "Now pipe down and pay attention, or there'll be a short, sharp visit from the slap fairy. You need to know this. All the world's most talented weapons makers turn up at the fair every year to show off their latest creations. And take orders for the coming year. We can often figure out what the bad guys are planning by studying their shopping lists. The location of the Supernatural Arms Faire changes every year, attendance strictly by invitation only. But it does keep coming back to the mountains over Pakistan, if only because they're far enough from anywhere civilised that if something should go *bang!* unexpectedly, it won't do too much damage. Do I really need to tell you that they've never even heard of Health and Safety? And the organisers do like to keep the fair as far as possible from the world's prying eyes."

"What organisers?" I said. "Who's behind the fair?"

"The Gun Shops of Usher," said the Sarjeant. "Very old firm. Older than us." He fixed me with a cold stare. "We're sending you in this year to observe and take notes, because you're the most experienced field agent we've got left. Who isn't busy with something else."

"Why does it always have to be me?" I said plaintively. "Why can't I ever get a case that involves loafing about at the seaside?"

"I could go," said Harry.

"No, you couldn't," I said quickly. "I need you here, taking care of the day-to-day business. So I don't have to."

"Every man to what he does best, Harry," said the Sarjeant.

"If you only knew what he does best . . ." murmured Roger.

"Not now, dear," said Harry.

"How am I to get in, even as Shaman Bond, if I don't have an invitation?" I said craftily, to show I had been paying attention.

"I visit the fair every year," the Armourer said cheerfully. "I have a long-standing invitation to attend, because I have established a cover as a weapons enthusiast and retired nerd. You can get in on my ticket. Take Molly; I'm allowed a plus-one. Ah, I always have a great time wandering round the stalls, quietly sneering at new inventions I created or overcame years ago. And I always bring back a few good ideas. . . . Steal from the best, and call it research!"

"Do they know you're a Drood?" said Molly.

"Of course not! They'd shut everything down and leg it for the horizon. Or try to kill me. Probably both. No, they think I'm another of those very keen trainspotter types who always turn up at affairs like these. Making endless notes, jotting down serial numbers . . . and exclaiming over unexpected obsolete makes, and proudly comparing their to-see lists. The fair security people could keep us out if they really wanted to, but the weapons makers like to have us around so they can show off in front of us and feel like stars. They'd miss us if we weren't there. But this time it has to be you, Eddie. I'm too busy. You can go in as Shaman Bond, and no one need know you're a Drood. I'll give you the coordinates, and you can drop in through the Merlin Glass. In and out, no problem."

"But what am I supposed to do there?" I said. "What is so important that an experienced field agent has to attend the Supernatural Arms Faire?"

"Because there are rumours, very serious rumours,

that someone has come up with a high-tech equivalent to Drood armour," said the Sarjeant. "And that they will be showing off the prototype at this year's fair."

"And we can't have that," said the Armourer. "Of course, people have been promising Drood-type armour for years, but no one's ever been able to deliver."

"Several normally trustworthy sources were very sure that this year, someone might have something," the Sarjeant said firmly. "And, Eddie, if they have, you are to grab the prototype and bring it back with you, so the Armourer can hack it open and see what makes it tick. Before one of us has to go head-to-head with it in the field."

"Who's supposed to be behind this new armour?" I said.

"If you find out, bring them back, too," said the Armourer.

"All right," I said reluctantly. "But after I come back, I want to talk a lot more about Dusk and his proposed Great Sacrifice."

"Of course," said the Armourer. "We should have more definite information on the conspiracy by then."

I sighed heavily. "First the Loathly Ones, then the Invisibles and the Accelerated Men, and now a brand-new Satanist conspiracy. How many conspiracies are there?"

"How long is a superstring?" said William.

We all looked at him, but he had nothing else to say.

"Any more business?" the Sarjeant-at-Arms said finally. "No . . . very well. Meeting adjourned. I'll look into who's properly next in line to be Matriarch; Armourer, I want a full report on whatever you discover about the secret departments; and Harry, I want a fully thought-out position paper from you on how we're going to run the next election. We need some new ideas; the last election was really a shoo-in for the Matriarch. I'd like to see more of a fight this time. William . . . why don't you go and have a nice lie-down, and see what else you can remember? And then write it all down. Before you forget it again."

"Good idea," said William. "I'll get Rafe to help me."

"Rafe is gone," I said carefully. "You have a new assistant Librarian—Ioreth. Remember?"

"Oh. Yes," said William. "I'd better write that down."

The council broke up, everyone going their separate way with a certain amount of relief. The Sarjeant called in his security people to escort William back to the Old Library, and to put out the chair Roger Morningstar had been sitting on. I used the Merlin Glass to transport Molly and me straight to my room on the upper floor. Molly put her hands on my shoulders and started to say something, but I placed a fingertip on her lips and shook my head urgently. I leaned in close, so I could whisper in her ear.

"Molly, I need you to put up all your best privacy spells right now. I need protections so strong that no one will be able to overhear what I have to tell you. Do it now."

"Who are you worried will listen in?" said Molly, as she stepped back and struck a series of mystical poses, her hands moving so quickly they left shimmering trails on the air.

"Everyone."

"Including your own family?"

"Especially them."

Molly made a final gesture and the whole room shuddered. The floor seemed to drop away an inch or so beneath my feet, and then steadied. There was a faint but very real tension on the air. Molly nodded briskly.

"Done and done. You can talk freely, Eddie. Gaea herself couldn't overhear us now. What's so important?"

I took both her hands in mine and had her sit down on the edge of the bed, facing me. "Remember when I was trapped in Limbo, and Walker was interrogating me, trying to make me give up all my secrets?"

"Of course," said Molly. "We still need to figure out who was really behind that. Could it have been Dusk, do you suppose?"

"I did consider raising the subject with him," I said. "But it never seemed the right time. I'd hate to think he was actually that powerful. . . . The point is, Walker said something to me right at the end. I said, 'If this is where the dead people go, why aren't my parents here?' And he said, 'What ever makes you think they're dead?'"

Molly's eyes widened, and then she squeezed my hands reassuringly. "Eddie . . . it would be wonderful if there were hope. But it probably wasn't Walker. You can't trust anything you see or hear in Limbo."

"It started me thinking," I said. "I never did see the bodies of my parents. . . ."

"I never saw the bodies of mine," said Molly. "They were killed by your family, fighting alongside the White Horse Faction, and the Droods never gave us anything to bury. There often aren't bodies in our business, Eddie. You know that. I'd like to believe my parents could be alive, too. . . . But you have to let go. You have to move on."

"But what if my parents are still alive?" I said. "In hiding, perhaps? Or even being held captive somewhere? I don't like to think they would have left me here, all these years, if they were still alive. I like to think they would have rescued me from the family. But if they are still out there . . . and my family has been lying to me all this time . . ."

"We'll look into it," said Molly. "Find you the truth about what really happened to your mother and father. But do you really believe your family could have hidden this from you all these years?"

"Of course," I said. "There are far too many secrets in my family."

CHAPTER FIVE

Weapons of Mass Distraction

The knock on my door came far too early in the morning. I was awake and up and about, but only just.

I'd been up barely half an hour, forced out of an extremely comfortable bed by a raucous alarm clock and Molly's relentlessly good-natured presence. It was still dark when I looked out the window. The Hall grounds swept away before me like some strange night country. It reminded me of the view I'd seen from the windows in the Winter Hall, in Limbo, and I shuddered despite myself. No full moon here to light the grounds, though; the family never leaves such things to chance. Two long lines of electric lights lined the long driveway up to the Hall, and floating, shimmering spheres drifted silently across the great lawns in regular patterns. Balls of plasma energy, generated by some machine deep in the basements of the Hall, designed by the previous Armourer. Before that it was all paper lanterns and will-o'-the-wisps generated by a magical stone, by long tradition. The previous Matriarch put a stop to all that, in the name of efficiency. Some of the older Droods were heard to grumble that they preferred the old lights, that they were warmer and more comforting. But no one paid any attention. We've always been a very practical family.

There were guards out there in the dark, even if I couldn't see them. There are always guards on the grounds. We all take a turn from the time we're sixteen. It's one of the things you look forward to, growing up in the Hall. The first time you're designated a sector and sent out into the night is a great feeling. It means you're an adult at last, with an adult's responsibilities. Protecting the family while they sleep. I can still remember how that felt: making my rounds in the quiet of the early morning, the grass damp with dew under my feet, head snapping round at every unexpected sound.

And I could remember lying in my bed, tucked up tight and toasty warm, half-awake in the dog hours of the morning, part of me feeling sorry for the poor bastards out in the cold, and part of me happy to be able to relax, to feel safe and protected. Of course, the vast majority of the Hall's defences are mechanical and magical in nature, everything from force shields to robot guns in their bunkers under the lawns, to the gryphons in the woods and the undine in the lake; but there always has to be the human element to be the last line of defence. Because protective systems can be sabotaged—from without and within.

We're a very practical family.

When the knock on my door came, I'd barely finished shaving. All Droods do that the old-fashioned way, with lots of shaving cream and a straight razor. It teaches us to have steady hands and nerves. I wasn't even dressed yet, bumbling around the room in my jockeys and one sock, looking for the other sock, and waiting for Molly to get out of the adjoining bathroom. I hadn't yet progressed from grunting noises to actual words. I am not a morning person. Molly, on the other hand, had already been up for an hour, and had worked her way through a full British fry-up breakfast of sausages, beans, bacon, eggs and fried bread, sent up from the kitchens through the dumbwaiter. She did offer me some, but my stomach never wants to know about food till at least eleven o'clock. I had a big mug of hot black coffee, to jump-start my heart, and forced down some All-Bran with milk. (The mug bore the legend *Worship Me Like the Goddess I Am*. Molly gave it to me.) The heavy breakfast smell still lingered in the room, and I allowed myself to sniff it now and again.

Molly was on the toilet, dress hiked up and knickers round her ankles, reading the latest *Heat* magazine. God knows where she found it, certainly not in my room. I knew she was doing this because she insisted on having the bathroom door wide-open. Because, she said, she liked being able to always see me. Now, I enjoy her company, and I'm not the most inhibited of people, but there are still some things I feel should remain private. When I finally got to use the toilet, I was quietly determined that the door was going to stay shut, even if I had to barricade it from the inside.

The knock on the door came again, and I went to answer it, glancing at the ornate Italian clock on the wall. Coming up to seven thirty a.m. Someone was going to pay and pay dearly for disturbing me at such an ungodly hour. Did I mention that I am not a morning person? I hauled the door open and glared out into the corridor, and there was my uncle Jack, beaming at me cheerfully.

"Hello, Eddie! Isn't it a marvellous morning? Ready for the off?"

I growled at him, and tried an even fiercer glare, but it didn't faze him in the least. He strode forward, and I had to step aside to let him in or he'd have run right over me.

"What are you doing here, Uncle Jack?" I finally managed. "Is there some emergency? I didn't hear any alarms."

"Oh, no, nothing like that. This is the day of the fair, my boy, and you don't want to be late. I've decided I'm going with you."

I realised I was still holding the door open, dressed in only my underwear, and there was a hell of a draught.

I looked up and down the corridor, but there was no one else about, nothing to suggest any kind of trouble. I shut the door and looked blearily at the Armourer as he looked around my room and tried not to look too distressed at the state of it. I didn't care. My room. If I want to live like a pig, it's up to me. The Armourer stopped dead as he looked through the open bathroom door, and quickly turned his back to the sight of Molly on the loo. I managed a small smile.

"You take us as you find us this early in the morning," I said. "I'm only up because Molly's an early riser. Probably comes from living in a forest most of the time. Now, what's this about the fair?"

"I'm going with you," the Armourer said firmly. "I haven't been out in the field for thirty-five years, and the odds are I never will again, now that I've been given the secret departments to run, as well as the Armoury. So I am seizing the opportunity for one last adventure, and to hell with Cedric. Who does he think he is, ordering me around, the bloody Sarjeant-at-Arms?"

"I didn't know you missed working in the field," I said. "I thought you were happy terrorising people in your Armoury."

"Well, yes, but then there's happy, and then there's . . . happy," said the Armourer, still carefully keeping his back to Molly. "All this talk about the fair has got the old adrenaline going again. I always thought of my yearly visits to the Supernatural Arms Faire as my own territory: the one time I could justify leaving the Hall and getting out into the world again. I need to do this, Eddie. I need to get out into the field and get my hands dirty one more time. Before I get old."

People tend to forget that my uncle Jack was a field agent for many years, second only to the legendary Grey Fox himself, my uncle James. And that Jack was an agent during the coldest days of the Cold War, when every mission was life-and-death, and every decision you made mattered. And now, after all these years as the family Armourer, he'd heard the call again, like an old dog by the fire pricking up his ears as the pack runs past in full cry; and he had to show us all, had to show himself, that he could still do it. Who was I to say him no?

"All right," I said. "You know the ground; glad to have you. But what about the invitation? If you're going to use it . . ."

"I'm entitled to plus-one," he said cheerfully. "And no one's going to be that upset if I make it plus-two. I'm a familiar face. They know me."

Molly came out of the bathroom, properly attired, with her magazine tucked under her arm. "I heard all that. When are we going?"

"Right now," said the Armourer. "Halfway across the world, the Supernatural Arms Faire has already opened for business." He looked at me. "I should wrap up warm, though, Eddie. It's bitter cold where we're going."

The Merlin Glass dropped us off halfway up a mountain in Pakistan. It was midday, but the sky was grey and cloudless and the sun wasn't even trying. It was a grey world, all rock and stone and dust, and not a sign of life anywhere. The air was fiercely cold, burning my lungs as I breathed it. I shivered, even inside my heavy sheepskin jacket, and stamped my boots against the cold, hard ground. It was a good thing I'd listened to the Armourer's warning; leaving the Hall for here had been like stepping off a balmy beach and into a freezer.

We'd arrived some way along a rough dirt track heading down into a deep valley, where the Supernatural Arms Faire was already set up. Row upon row of stalls and booths and tents, swiftly erected and easy to tear down when leaving. It was like a small town, thrown up overnight. Crowds of people were already milling about, filling every inch of space between the various sellers. Someone with a sense of humour was flying from their stall a black flag with the skull and crossbones.

Molly leaned heavily against me, shuddering violently despite being wrapped from chin to toe in a long coat of ermine fur, topped with a fluffy white hat she'd pulled down to just over her eyes. Her face had gone white from the cold, with bright pink spots on her nose and cheeks. She looked adorable.

"You look adorable," I said.

"I never know what to wear to these formal occasions," she said. "Bloody hell, it's cold. My nipples have gone hard."

"Not in front of the Armourer, dear," I said.

Uncle Jack was almost unrecognisable, buried in the depths of a heavy black duffel coat. He was peering happily down into the valley, rubbing his bare hands in anticipation. He smiled back at us.

"Cold? This isn't cold! Seven years ago, when the snows came early and a wandering polar bear was heard to remark that it was a bit nippy, that was cold! This is merely bracing! Get a good lungful of that crisp mountain air. There's no pollution out here."

"Of course not," I said. "It couldn't survive the cold. I can't feel my ears."

Molly looked down at the arms fair and sniffed loudly. "Is that it? A bunch of tents, and not even an open café to sit around in? Not exactly big on creature comforts, are they?"

"It's an arms fair, girl, not a fashion show!" said the Armourer. "You don't come here to sip your Starbucks and enjoy the ambience; you're here to look at guns and wonder how best to buy up all the good stuff before your enemies find it."

"Gun nuts," she said sadly. "Weapons geeks. The horror, the horror . . ."

The Armourer made a big show of rising above her. "Follow me, and watch your footing on the path. Even the local mountain goats have been heard to mention that the going can get a bit tricky underfoot; and it's a long way down. And be careful if you have to exert yourself; at this altitude, the oxygen can get a bit thin. So don't be too proud to mention if you start feeling light-headed or confused. There are oxygen stations set out at regular intervals; use them. Coin operated, but they take all the major currencies. Except the yen.

Don't ask. Now, let's go see what surprises await us this year. Oh, and Eddie, I know you're passing as Shaman Bond here, but . . . don't show me up. I want to be able to come back here again next year."

I glared at him. "I'm an experienced field agent. I know how to behave."

"No, you don't. You've never known how to behave. That's why we made you a field agent, so you could work off your anger doing nasty things to bad people. And, Molly, please don't kill anyone. Not unless you feel you absolutely have to."

"Of course," said Molly, smiling cheerfully.

The Armourer set off down the narrow trail with the ease of long familiarity, leaving Molly and me to stumble along after him. We clung to each other for comfort and support, and to share body warmth. I'd got too used to my armour insulating me from the harsher environments of the world. The surrounding mountains were massive grey walls of rough stone, with ragged cracks and crevices and not a sign of life anywhere. A suitably grim setting for a fair dedicated to death and destruction. The mountaintops had dustings of snow, picked up and tossed around by gusting winds too high up for us to feel.

And up above the mountaintops, I could make out the shimmering heat haze of heavy-duty force fields hiding the fair from the outside world. Force shields were necessary to hide the various energy systems and magical emanations from the exhibits on display. So many new energy spikes in one place would have raised eyebrows and set off alarms in every tracking station in the world. The Armourer said there were also a whole bunch of magical protections in place to hide the presence of the force fields. Because the sudden appearance of such powerful energies would arouse suspicion in themselves. As in, *What have you got to hide?* The Supernatural Arms Faire had been around for a long time, and it survived by being very thorough and very paranoid.

"If your family has known about the fair for such a

long time, why haven't they done something about it?" said Molly, holding on to my arm with a death grip as a stream of pebbles shot out from under her foot.

"Better to let it be, so we can keep an eye on what's happening," I said. "If we spook them, they'll shut it down, wait a few years, and then start it up again somewhere new, even more secret and underground. And then we'd have to waste precious time and resources hunting them down again. This way we get to see who's producing what, and who's buying it, whilst at the same making sure all of our weapons are as up-to-date as we like to think."

I glanced back the way we'd come, just in time to see a long straggling line of local people passing by on a much higher trail. Men, women, children and donkeys, all heavily laden. Some of them glanced down into the valley, but it was clear they didn't see a thing. As far as they were concerned, they were alone on the mountain, following the trail their ancestors had laid down centuries before. The fair's protections were working. The locals kept going, carrying on with their everyday lives as they had for generations, with no idea of how close they'd come to one of the world's most dangerous secrets.

By the time Molly and I finally reached the bottom of the valley and the outskirts of the fair, the Armourer had already flashed his invitation around, reassured the fair's security people, forewarned them about me and Molly, and was off chatting happily with old friends. He walked around quite openly, nodding and smiling to people who nodded back quite cheerfully—people who would have done their utmost to kill him on the spot if they'd even suspected he was a Drood. But then, he had the best kind of cover; he really was what he was pretending to be . . . just another weapons enthusiast.

He strolled up and down the long rows of stalls and booths, peering at everything, picking up the occasional item to study it more closely and ask detailed questions, clearly enjoying himself tremendously. Every now and again he'd meet up with some old acquaintance from previous fairs, and then they'd stop right in everybody's way for long conversations about what was worth looking at. No one made any fuss. Like the Armourer said, the fair liked having the enthusiasts around. They added character. All the people Uncle Jack knew were clearly in the same line of work as him; the outfits and the accents might differ, but they all had the same boyish smiles and wide-eyed enthusiasm when it came to various means of murder and mayhem.

They thought the Armourer was one of them: a retired old weapons maker with too much time on his hands, filling his retirement with happy interests. I made a point of standing close enough that I could eavesdrop on what was being said. There's nothing quite like standing before some stall, apparently browsing, to let you hang around with your ears wide-open. One of the Armourer's old friends used to work at Area 52 in the Antarctic, while another was a Russian exile who used to work at a secret Soviet science city in what was now the wilds of Georgia. Others worked for corporations, or secret agencies, or certain well-known names with delusions of grandeur and more money than sense. But no matter who they were, or used to be, the refrain was always the same: The fair was not what it used to be; the stall and booths used to be bigger and more varied, there was far too much hype and not enough substance, and the youngsters showed no respect at all.

After a while I let the Armourer go; he knew what he was doing, and I wanted to look at the weapons. The first booth I stopped at specialised in steampunk technology, featuring outmoded weapons of mass destruction from a calmer, more civilised age, when arms could also be works of art. What was once cutting-edge had become cute and interesting, passed by and superseded by relentless science, now brought back as antiques and curios—and collectibles, of course. Nothing like a patina of history to add layers of value.

Standing beside the booth, and actually lowering over it, was a great steam-powered automaton, the Iron

Mann of the Plains. still in working order, claimed a sign set out before it. Blue-black steel, gleaming and polished to within an inch of its life, with flaring red eyes in its immobile face, and huge arms and legs. In its day, the sign proclaimed, the Iron Mann of the Plains could outrun a steam train and lift the heaviest of weights, and had a Gatling gun built into its chest. Unfortunately, the booth owner confided, you had to keep stoking the thing with coal to keep the steam pressure up or it clanked to a halt. And then it was a real bugger to get it going again. Brilliant, but never very practical, its time in the sun over almost as soon as it had begun.

The booth owner was very keen to show me a series of series of carefully polished lenses from thirteenth-century Arabia, which when properly arranged could focus sunlight into a laser beam. But he didn't seem particularly keen to demonstrate the effect. Perhaps it wasn't sunny enough. Beside me, Molly had got interested in an eighteenth-century phlogiston flamethrower. Molly raised an eyebrow.

"Science proved that phlogiston didn't actually exist."

"It worked perfectly well until then," said the booth holder.

We moved on. A surprising number of people recognised one or the other of us. Sometimes both. No one was in the least surprised to see Shaman Bond at the Supernatural Arms Faire; I'd gone to great pains to establish his reputation for turning up anywhere. I've always liked being Shaman Bond; my cover identity doesn't have my restrictions or responsibilities. And people are nearly always happy to see Shaman Bond, whereas if Eddie Drood turns up it always means trouble for someone. Several of those we met were surprised to see Molly and me together: the notorious chancer and the infamous wild witch of the woods. In fact, one passing acquaintance actually leaned in close so he could murmur, "Too much car for you, Eddie," in my ear. I didn't hit him. It would only have attracted attention. It didn't help that Molly found the whole situation hilarious. And then I came to a sudden halt as our way was blocked by a very wide, wide loud person I knew only too well.

"Shaman Bond, as I live and breathe!" said a familiar fruity aristocratic voice. "Delighted to see you again, dear boy! What the hell are you doing here? Wouldn't have thought you had the wherewithal to use the bloody pay toilets here! Eh? Eh?"

Augusta Moon stood before me, grinning broadly. A larger-than-life professional troubleshooter and monster hunter, Augusta looked like one of P. G. Wodehouse's more frightening aunts. Tall and wide and heavy with it, Augusta dressed like some old-fashioned maiden aunt who'd read too many Lord Peter Wimsey mysteries: a battered tweed suit, stout walking shoes and a monocle jammed firmly into her left eye. If Augusta had ever heard of fashion, makeup and femininity, it was only as things other people did. If the cold was bothering her, she hid it remarkably well. She carried a stout oaken walking stick with a heavy silver head that still had dried blood crusted on it from her last encounter with the forces of evil. She also wasn't above poking people with her stick when she wanted to make a point. People who knew her were usually careful to stand out of arm's reach. She grabbed my hand and gave it a good mauling, laughing heartily all the while. Some monster hunters are more frightening than others.

Augusta Moon travelled the world doing good, and to hell with whether other people appreciated it.

She finally released my aching hand and scrutinised Molly through her monocle. "Didn't know the two of you were an item! Hmm. Didn't see that one coming. Blessed be the world that still has such surprises in it! Look after this one, girl. A hard man is good to find. Eh? Eh?"

"What's a lady like you doing in a place like this?" I said.

"Oh, doing a little shopping, looking for something new and nasty to put the wind up the ungodly. Not everything responds to being hit over the head with a stout stick, though the Lord knows I've tried the method on practically everything under the sun, or hiding from it. I once used this very stick to make a shish kebab out of a vampire. It was his own fault for bending over."

"You are an appalling person, Augusta," I said solemnly.

"Only in a good cause, dear boy. What are you doing here, Shaman? Looking for a little something for an engagement present, perhaps? Eh?" She dropped Molly a roguish wink. "Hold out for a ring, dear, and then use it to pierce something exotic! These modern gels, eh, Shaman?" She looked at me thoughtfully. Augusta had a magnificient brain behind her chosen facade. "Wouldn't have thought you were the gun-running sort, old cheese."

"I'm here representing someone else," I said smoothly. "Someone who doesn't want their face seen, because it would only push the price up. You know how it is." I gave her my best knowing look. "You aren't here by chance, Augusta. What are you really looking for?"

She gave her harsh bark of laughter again, and prodded me right above the navel with her walking stick. "No fooling you, eh, Shaman? No, no . . . I was in Delhi last week, searching for the Golden Frogs of Samarkand. Bloody things have gone walkabout again, and the usual rush is on to find them first and claim the bounty. And keep them out of the wrong sort of hands. Ugly-looking brutes, but no accounting for taste, as the vicar said when he kissed the verger. Anyway, the trail ran stone-dead cold in Delhi, but a backstreet encounter in Calcutta pointed me in this direction. So if you should happen to spot the bloody things here, hands off! They're mine!"

"You're welcome to them," I said. "I don't want golden warts on my unmentionables."

"Then I'll see you around. Be good, my dears, and if you can't be good don't do it in front of witnesses!"

She crushed my hand again, slapped me on the shoulder hard enough to rattle my teeth, and barged between Molly and me. Still laughing, she disappeared into the crowd, which immediately fell back to give her plenty of room. Molly and I headed determinedly in the opposite direction.

"Nice friends you have," said Molly.

"I thought she was a friend of yours," I said.

"Are we looking for anything specific?" said Molly, linking her arm companionably through mine, though I could barely feel it through the thicknesses of two very heavy coat sleeves. "I mean, apart from the duplicated Drood armour, which we are not going to find, because it never actually appears, no matter what the rumours say."

"To be honest," I said, "I think this is the family's way of getting me out of the Hall for a while. I did wonder at first whether Harry was up to something and wanted me out of the way.... But it's more likely the council thinks I need some time off for rest and relaxation. A little holiday after my near-death experience. And God knows I could use some serious downtime, after all the shit that's been raining down on me recently. As missions go, this is almost certainly a waste of time. So let us enjoy ourselves and take it easy for once."

"All right," said Molly. "I can do that. Hell of a place for a holiday, though."

"That's my family for you," I said.

We strolled on for a while, taking it easy, taking in the sights. The air was still bitterly cold, except for when we walked through brief gusts of heat generated by the stalls' heaters. Some booths actually had steam rising up from them. The walkways between the displays were covered with simple wooden boards, and there were no signs or directions. As centuries-old fairs went, this one didn't impress me as being at all well organised. There was certainly no lack of interested customers gathering excitedly before the various stalls, money clearly burning a hole in their pockets. They chattered happily with each other, argued over provenances and delivery routes, and nearly always seemed to end up with the age-old refrain, *Anything off for cash?* Some people stared in awe at the more impressive offerings, too intimidated to even inquire after the price. I recognised a surprising number of faces from all sides of the tracks: good guys and bad and every shade of grey in between. Everyone needs weapons, no matter what side you're fighting on.

"Buy me something," said Molly, after a while.

"Other girls want chocolate or flowers," I said. "Or shoes."

"Oh, I want those, too," said Molly. "But you can't come to an arms fair and not buy anything. I'm pretty sure there's a law against that."

So we looked around to see what there was.

One stall was offering assorted alien technology: from things that fell off the back of an alien starship, or stranded Greys and Reptiloids, or things that fell through dimensional doorways when the wind was blowing in the wrong direction. It was all dumped on the benches set out before us, in random heaps and piles. Large, blocky shapes of unfamiliar metal; warped crystal things with strange lights flickering deep inside; semiorganic bits and blobs trailing metallic filaments like tentacles. It could have been the secrets of the universe laid out before us, or the biggest bunch of junk and tat ever assembled in one place. The stall owner cheerfully admitted he had no idea what any of it did.

"It's old stock, picked up from a fire sale in the Nightside. Got to be worth something, hasn't it? It's alien! Pick something, and we'll fight over a price. You should be able to reverse-engineer something useful out of anything here. Hey, you! No touching!"

The big, hulking man standing next to me sneered haughtily at the stall owner and prodded a weird, wobbling thing with a disdainful fingertip. There was a sharp clap, like a very localised thunderstorm, and then he disappeared, leaving behind a space where he used to be. Air rushed in to fill the vacuum, while for a moment everyone's hair stood on end. The stallholder blinked a few times, and then recovered wonderfully.

"See! See!" he said, addressing the surrounding

crowd. "How useful is *that*? Wouldn't you like to make someone you know disappear?"

We left him haggling with a very interested crowd, while I wondered how he was going to sell the thing without handing it over, or how the buyer was going to carry it away. . . .

Another store boasted an exhaustive display of crystals, magic stones and balls in every shape and colour you could think of. Molly oohed and ahhed over them, but I couldn't see anything to get excited about. Not one decent aura among the lot of them. According to the middle-aged woman behind the stall, dressed in what she no doubt fondly imaged was the very latest Gypsy chic, everything on the table had a fascinating history or legend attached to it. Well, she would say that, wouldn't she? Mind you, she spotted me as an unbeliever straightaway, and concentrated her sales pitch on Molly.

"See this one, dearie? The shimmering sphere with the bloodred flaw? That is the original Scrying Stone that Dr. Dee used to learn the artificial language Enochian, created expressly so that men could talk directly with angels. If you could only reestablish contact with the same spirit that spoke with Dr. Dee, who knows what secrets you might learn?"

"I think the key word in that sentence was *if*," said Molly. "Do I look like a rube? You'd have a better chance of contacting the spirit world if you banged your head against the wall."

"Well!" said the Gypsy lady, drawing herself up. "I never did. . . ."

"Oh, you must have," said Molly sweetly.

I took her firmly by the arm and we moved on. Next up was a twee affair almost buried under displays of fresh flowers, offering a wide range of elven artefacts and weapons at really quite reasonable prices. I pointed a few things out to Molly, but she shook her head immediately.

"Never trust an elf, or anything they leave behind.

You can bet most of it's boody-trapped, ready to do something transformative and allegedly humorous to whatever poor fool picks it up without industrial-strength gloves on."

"They've got a wand," I said. "It looks very nice."

"Traps are supposed to look inviting. Elf wands are just the sugar coating on the trap, because they're one of the few elven weapons a human could actually use."

"I know a private investigator in the Nightside who uses one," I said. "Larry Oblivion."

"Yes, but he's dead!" said Molly. "There's not a lot more the wand can do to him! Hey, how is it you know someone from the Nightside? I thought Droods weren't allowed in the Nightside."

"We have agreed not to enter," I said. "There's a difference. We could go in if we wanted to; we choose not to. Wouldn't be seen dead in the place, myself. I know Larry because he and his brothers did some work for the family recently."

"Rather you than me," said Molly. "That Hadleigh Oblivion gives me the creeps."

Microsoft had a really big presence at the fair; but then, Microsoft has a really big presence everywhere.

I paused before a simple open booth representing the Gun Shops of Usher franchise. It seemed odd that the family who'd bankrolled the Supernatural Arms Faire for so many centuries should have such a modest presence. The man standing behind the counter was Mr. Usher himself. I looked him over thoughtfully, and he nodded politely.

"I thought you ran the gun shop in the Nightside," said Molly.

"Oh, I'm there, too, my dear," said Usher, a small grey man with a small grey voice. The man behind the Gun Shops of Usher, the greatest supplier of murder and mayhem to the world, was a reputable man in a regulation suit, with a broad, square face, a professional smile and a cold, passionless stare from behind wire-rimmed glasses. He looked like what he was: a businessman interested only in business. "I'm there, and I'm here; I'm everywhere there's a gun shop, Miss Molly. Because there's always someone who needs a gun."

"You run them all simultaneously?" I said. "What are you, an avatar of slaughter?"

"Nothing so grand, Mr. Bond," said Usher. "I'm . . . necessary."

I looked over the weapons spread out on the table before me. Guns: special, individual, significant guns from throughout history and legend. The Walther PPK that Hitler used to shoot Eva Braun before he turned it on himself. Billy the Kid's old nickel pistol. The first rifle used to kill an American Indian, and the first rifle sold to an American Indian. Half a dozen guns that had turned on their famous author owners, each one neatly labelled and autographed by the writer. And a rifle from a book depository. Magic bullets extra.

"I see you carry a Colt repeater, Mr. Drood," said Usher. "Your uncle does very good work."

"Don't use that name again," I said coldly. "I'm here incognito. You blow my cover in front of this crowd and I will blow you away."

"Of course, Mr. Bond. Your secret is safe with me. You'd be surprised how many secrets I keep."

Molly and I moved on to the next stall. I wasn't sure putting a bullet through Mr. Usher's head would actually kill him, but the formalities have to be observed. Molly gave me a sideways look.

"You don't like guns, do you? Sort of strange, that, in a secret agent."

"I can use a gun if I have to," I said. "But I'm an agent, not an assassin. I kill only when I have to, and I try really hard to take no pleasure or satisfaction from it. Walk too far down that path and you end up in groups like Dusk's. Because that's where you belong."

"Guns don't kill people; people kill people?" suggested Molly.

"People with guns kill people," I said. "Guns make it easy for people to kill people. It should never be easy to take someone's life."

"Pacifist!" sneered a passerby.

"Hardly," I said, but he was already gone.

At the next booth, a scientist in the traditional white coat was demonstrating description theory with a blackboard and a piece of chalk, to an only mildly interested crowd. He didn't seem to have anything to sell, but he was so earnest and determined that people were willing to listen. They watched, frowning, as he stalked back and forth before his blackboard; like so many dogs being shown a card trick, they could sense something clever was happening, but couldn't follow it.

Basically, the scientist explained, description theory says that if you can describe something exactly, using mathematics, then the maths is the object, and vice versa. So if you change the maths, you change the object. His theory had many applications when it comes to weapons: Description theory bombs, where the maths can persuade a city it isn't there anymore. Or even transportation, where the maths can persuade the universe that people are where the maths says they are.

By this time, the scientist had the crowd hanging on his every word, and he scurried back and forth before the blackboard, adding a symbol here and taking away one there as he carefully rewrote his maths, getting closer and closer to his objective. He finally added one last symbol with a flourish, and the blackboard disappeared. The crowd gave him a massive round of applause.

"No! No!" yelled the scientist, throwing his chalk on the ground and stamping on it. "That isn't what's supposed to happen!"

Molly and I moved on and left him to it. I don't like to see a grown man cry.

Not too far away, another scientist was trying to persuade a sceptical crowd of the value of quantum uncertainty devices. Only every time he adjusted the controls on the device in front of him, he changed into somebody else. The scientist became another man, who became a woman, who became something tall and blue, before disappearing completely. Leaving only a disembodied voice saying, "Hello? Hello? Is there anybody there? Oh, bloody hell, not again . . ."

There were a great many other interesting things to be seen. A bottle of cheap djinn, a rifle that could shoot round corners and a pack of crazy ghosts who'd been conditioned to work as attack dogs. These last were a miserable-looking bunch, held in place by shimmering chains of reinforced ectoplasm. Their faces were blank and their eyes were empty, and their semitransparent bodies drifted in and out of one another as they stirred restlessly in the limited space of their tent. Their handler was an Armani-suited Sicilian with an easy, charming manner and a chilling ruthlessness in his sales pitch.

"Imagine, my friends," he said. "The enemy you have whom no one can reach . . . is now reachable. Ghosts can go anywhere: through walls, through barbed wire, through all kinds of security systems, walking in straight lines straight to their targets. They do whatever you tell them to do, with no back talk. They have no identities left; I've beaten that nonsense out of them. They're spiritual attack dogs now, suitable for defence or offence. Ectoplasmic collars and chains can be provided at little extra cost."

"Have you no respect for the dead?" said someone in the crowd. "What if they were members of your family?"

"They are my family," said the Sicilian. "Why should they rest while they can still make money for the family?"

"What if one of them should happen to wake up?" said Molly, almost lazily. "What if they should happen to remember who they are and what you've done to them?"

The Sicilian grinned his easy, supercilious grin. "Not going to happen, pretty lady. You want a big brute, perhaps, just for yourself? They can be trained to do almost anything. . . ."

"When people can be as appalling as this," said Molly, "is it any wonder I prefer animals, on the whole?"

The Sicilian stopped smiling. He tugged on the chain

of one of the ghosts, and it surged forward to crouch beside him. The Sicilian pointed at Molly and muttered something under his breath. The ghost suddenly snapped into focus. Its face was sharp and distinct, the eyes full of a mad rage. It snarled, and its mouth had vicious teeth. It raised a hand, and the fingers ended in claws. It looked entirely solid and substantial. The Sicilian slipped loose the chain, but before the ghost could move forward Molly fixed it with her gaze, holding its eyes with hers. For a moment neither of them moved, and then all the rage went out of the ghost's face, and it cringed back to hide behind the Sicilian, whimpering. The Sicilian cuffed it round the head and glared at Molly.

"Hey! You break it, you pay for it!"

Molly ignored him, looking thoughtfully at the pack of ghosts. They moved restlessly back and forth, frowning under her gaze. Molly looked back at the Sicilian.

"What if they should all wake up and remember what you've done to them . . . ?"

She snapped her fingers once, and then turned unhurriedly away. The Sicilian screamed horribly as the pack swarmed over him, but he didn't scream for long. I gave the crowd a warning look, in case anyone felt like getting involved, but they all had urgent business elsewhere. I caught up with Molly and walked along beside her.

"Can't take you anywhere," I said after a while.

"Some shit I won't put up with," said Molly, staring straight ahead.

"You sweet, sentimental old thing, you," I said.

She smiled suddenly, like the sun coming out. "Yes," she said. "I am. And I'll kick the crap out of anyone who says otherwise."

The next booth was a technological wonder, all brightly polished steel with flashing lights and electronic sound effects. The booth operator was trying to persuade passersby to step inside the booth and be made over into a perfect new version of themselves. Results guaranteed. Strangely, no one seemed interested. The operator was working himself into an absolute

lather of excitement, but no one even stopped to en-
quire about the price. I looked at Molly.

"It's a con," she said briskly. "You step into the booth
and disappear forever. What steps out is a Thing from
Outside transformed into a perfected version of you. It
then goes out into the world to gather information before an invasion by the rest of its kind. No one's fallen
for it in years, but they keep trying."

"If the fair knows about this, why do they allow it to
go on?" I said.

Molly gave me a pitying look. "Because they've
paid."

"Ah," I said. "Of course. Silly me." I looked at the
transformation booth. "I knew I'm supposed to be on
holiday, but I really don't think I can allow an alien invasion to happen right in front of me. Distract the operator for me; there's a dear."

"Can't take you anywhere." Molly sighed. She
walked up to the operator and glared right into his face.
"Hey! You! My sister walked in there ten minutes ago
and she hasn't come out yet! What's your game?"

And while the operator was sputtering and protesting his innocence, and offering to open the booth so
that Molly could see her sister wasn't in any way in
there, I strolled round the back of the booth, glanced
casually around to make sure no one was watching and
then concentrated on my torc, muttering the activating
Words under my breath. As I concentrated, a slender
filament of golden strange matter eased out of the torc
and slid across my shoulder and down my arm, till it
could jump off my fingertip and into the open workings
at the back of the booth. I whipped the filament back
and forth, ripping and tearing at the delicate parts
within, and there was a sudden flash of discharging energies, followed by a burst of thick purple smoke. I
quickly pulled the strange matter back into my torc and
stepped away as purple smoke enveloped the booth.
The operator forgot all about placating Molly, and
howled something inhuman as he saw what was hap-

pening to his transformation device. It suddenly im-
ploded, sucked inside itself by whatever was happening
within, and alien forces pulled the whole thing back
into its home dimension. Molly gave the operator a
good shove from behind, and he tottered forward, to be
sucked in by the imploding energies. In a few moments
booth and operator were both gone, and Molly and I
were some distance away, not even looking in that direction.

"I know," said Molly. "Some shit you won't put up
with."

"Damned right," I said.

And that was when the Satanist conspiracy made
their appearance at the Supernatural Arms Faire. A
group of about twenty large and menacing men in dark
suits appeared out of nowhere, striding purposefully
through the fair, looking quite ready to trample over
anyone who didn't get out of their way fast enough.
They weren't even trying to hide what they were; each
wore a large inverted cross on a chain. As they drew
nearer, I realised they were wearing formal tuxedos,
and very smartly fitted, too. Nothing like a tuxedo to
add that touch of class and dignity to a bunch of Satanist scumbags. Molly and I stood well back to let them
pass. They all seemed very serious, very focused, very
determined. I got the giggles.

"Look, everybody!" I said loudly. "They all look like
waiters! No, penguins!"

And I moved in behind them and waddled along in
the rear, flapping my arms at my sides and making
plaintive *feed me!* noises in penguin. The crowd loved
it. They went apeshit, laughing and cheering and joining in with penguin noises of their own. The Satanists
kept going. They couldn't stop and look back to see
what was going on; that might make them look weak. So
they increased their pace, trying to leave me behind. So
I made plaintive *wait for me!* noises in penguin and hurried after them. Until Molly grabbed me by an arm and
hauled me away, forcefully pushing me into a side turn-

ing, out of sight of the Satanists and the wildly applauding crowd.

"We're not here to attract attention!" said Molly. "Especially from a whole bunch of probably highly trained satanic foot soldiers! You're supposed to be a secret agent, so act secret! Stick close to me, and observe what the bastards are up to from a safe distance. They wouldn't have shown up here in such an ostentatious way unless they were up to something important!"

"You mean, like, make friends and influence people?" I said. "Or are they here to buy weapons like everyone else? I know! Let's grab the smallest one, haul him off somewhere private and hit him in the head until his eyes change colour, or he starts telling us things we want to know."

"What's the matter, Eddie?" said Molly, looking searchingly into my face. "This isn't like you."

"Lightbringer House," I said. "They made us run away with our tails between our legs. I'm not taking that from a bunch of Devil-worshipping scumbags."

Molly shook her head slowly. "Testosterone must be such a curse. No one is supposed to know there's a Drood here, remember? You're Shaman Bond. Who fortunately has a reputation for eccentric behaviour."

I smiled briefly. "I put a lot of time and effort into building that reputation. Lets me get away with all kinds of things that would otherwise require explanations."

"You're not going to do the penguin thing again, are you?" said Molly.

"Almost certainly not," I said. "Satanists bring out the worst in me. They're so straight-faced. We can still sneak along behind them and spy on them, can't we?"

"Oh, sure," said Molly. "I can sneak with the best of them."

So we caught up with the Satanists and strolled casually along behind them, observing their every move from a respectable distance. We weren't alone. A lot of people were interested in why Satanists had come to the arms fair. The tuxedo group walked up and down the stalls and booths, row after row, looking over the exhibits on display, but never buying anything. They seemed much more interested in the people behind the stalls, especially the weapons designers and manufacturers. Quite often the Satanists would make these people a more than generous offer to come and design weapons for them. Most of the weapons makers turned them down. Even they had a line they wouldn't cross. The Satanists never made a fuss, never tried threats or intimidation, only smiled politely, gave everyone their card and moved on to the next stall.

They did buy a few things, after it became clear people wouldn't talk to them if they didn't, and by eavesdropping shamelessly at the next stall, I was able to ascertain that the Satanists had established a major line of credit with the fair before they arrived. Which made me wonder who was backing them. You can't set up a major conspiracy without extensive funding. A question to raise with the family once I got back. Certainly the stallholders seemed only too happy to take the Satanists' money, even if none of them seemed to be taking the tuxedo guys particularly seriously.

One of the Satanists broke away from the group, attracted by a stall offering cloned monkeys' paws. He spoke briefly with the stallholder, who spoke briefly in return. Then somebody must have said something, because it all kicked off, with the two men shouting into each other's faces and the insults flying thick and fast. The rest of the tuxedos got involved in a hurry, backing up their own with cold, glaring eyes and a heavy, threatening presence. The stallholder must have hit a silent alarm, because almost immediately the fair's security people were making the scene. The crowd backed quickly away to give both sides room to manoeuvre, but not so far that they might miss any of the excitement.

The Satanists stood shoulder-to-shoulder, several ranks deep, their tuxedos almost crackling with indignation that anyone should dare to stand against them. They faced off against the fair's security people, who turned out to be a small army of bald-headed monks in scarlet robes. They outnumbered the Satanists, but only just. They had no obvious weapons, but were very clearly That Kind of Monk. The kind who didn't need weapons because they've trained themselves to be weapons.

"The Bloodred Guard," Molly murmured in my ear. "They've been enforcing polite behaviour at the fair for centuries."

The Satanists and the monks stood their ground, facing one another down with cold, impassive faces, and then one of the tuxedos revealed himself to be the leader, or at least spokesperson, by stepping forward to address the monks in an actually quite polite and reasonable tone of voice.

"You know who we are. You know whom we represent. And you know what we can do. Are you really ready to throw down against us over a single obnoxious stallholder who threatened one of us to his face?"

"Of course," said one of the monks, stepping forward to meet him. "That's our job. We protect the fair. Are you ready to be banned from the fair, forever, over one of your own who can't control his temper? You know who we are. And what we can do."

"We're protected," said the Satanist.

"We are protection," said the monk.

The Satanist leader considered for a moment, and then shrugged easily. "We shall show our peaceful intent by making a sacrifice, for the good of all."

He turned around to face his group and beckoned forward the one who'd started all the trouble. He came forward and stood before the spokesman, scowling sullenly.

"I'm not apologising."

"No one's asking you to," said the leader.

His hand came up suddenly, holding a long, slender blade. He stabbed his own man in the eye, driving it in deep and twisting it. Blood spurted out, soaking his cuff and sleeve. He jerked the blade out, and his victim crumpled bonelessly to the ground and lay still. The leader flicked a few drops of blood from the blade, then made it disappear again. He then cleaned his hand and wrist fastidiously with a monogrammed handkerchief. He smiled at the monk.

"Is that acceptable to you?"

The monk nodded slowly. I think even he was a bit shocked at the calm and callous way the Satanist had put an end to the problem. The crowd seemed equally disturbed. There are some things you don't expect to see, even at an arms fair. The monk nodded to his people, and the Bloodred Guard separated into two groups, taking up positions to line the walkway, to hold the crowds back as the Satanists moved off. Not one of them looked back at the one of their own they left lying in the dirt. The Bloodred Guard waited until the Satanists were a fair distance away, and then silently disappeared back where they'd come from. The watching crowd fell on the dead body and stole everything he had, including his clothes, his underwear and, when nothing else was left, even the body. I looked at Molly.

"Hard-core," she said finally. "These new Satanists don't mess around, do they?"

"What could be so important here that the Satanists couldn't risk being thrown out?" I said. "So important they'd even kill one of their own over it?"

Molly shrugged. "Satanists do what Satanists do. You know what? I'm hungry. There's a food stall over there. Buy me something."

"Didn't you bring any money?"

"Why would I need money? I've got you. Buy me something hot and spicy, and earn yourself some major boyfriend points."

I escorted her over to the food stall, which offered steaming-hot curries with rice, and bowls of a dark brown soup with things floating in it. I looked at the grinning little Gurkha behind the stall, with his *Eat the Corporations* T-shirt.

"What kind of soup is that?"

"Hot!" he said cheerfully. "Fresh! Eat!"

So we had two big bowls of the soup, followed by a beef madras for me and a chicken vindaloo for Molly, with lashings of brightly coloured pilau rice. No utensils—it came on a paper plate, and you used your fingers. My fingers were so cold I could barely feel the heat anyway. I drank the soup straight from a paper cup, and it went down very well. Could have been mulligatawny, though I still wasn't prepared to be quoted on what the floating bits might have been. There are some things man is not meant to know if he wants to sleep easily.

When we finally moved off again into the bustling crowds, it quickly became clear that something was in the air. Everyone seemed sure something special was in the cards, even if no one was too sure what. I asked about the possibility of the Drood-type armour making an appearance this year, subtly at first, and then increasingly openly, as it became clear this was the hot topic on everyone's lips. Even though the new armour had been promised for years, and had never once shown up, the general feeling was that this might be the year. And no one wanted to miss it.

Molly and I followed one particular rumour right to the edge of the fair, but it turned out to be a young enthusiast showing off his new exoskeletal armour. Impressive to look at: a series of reinforced steel braces connected by microprocessors, powered by a hulking great power box on his back. But the first time the young inventor powered it up, it coughed and spluttered and then broke his left arm in three places. His moans of pain were drowned out by the laughter of the crowd. Tough audience. His assistants were still trying to prise him out of the exoskeleton when Molly and I moved away.

Since we were on the outskirts of the fair, we took the opportunity to look over the larger items on display, too big to be contained within the fair itself. A vertical-takeoff plane took up a lot of the valley floor, huge and gleaming, with really impressive-looking engines. Half a dozen flying motorbikes with antigrav generators instead of wheels. Even a giant robot some fifty feet tall. They had it sitting down, to keep it inside the fair's force shields. It was Japanese, of course. They do love their giant robots. But since this one was made by Toyota, no one was taking it too seriously. There was even a massive U.S. Army tank that could be remote-controlled by the operator's thoughts. It was a prototype, of course, and the current owner was very keen to sell it and disappear, before the U.S. Army turned up looking for it.

Molly and I found the Armourer holding court with a group of his fellow enthusiasts, making disparaging comments about everything on display, and enjoying the general laughter. He was quite happy to see Molly and me again, though he made a point of not knowing who we were in front of his friends. He couldn't resist showing off in front of us, though, explaining exactly what was wrong with all the oversize items.

"The VTO is a great idea," he said grandly. "Rises up like an angel, flies like an eagle, steers like a cow. The flying motorbikes are an even better idea, but the antigrav outriders run off batteries that need recharging every twenty minutes, and God help you if the power runs out while you're still in midair. Don't even get me started on the giant robot."

Molly and I took an arm each and steered him firmly away so we could talk to him on his own, and brief him about the appearance of the Satanists.

"Could their appearance have anything to do with these big items?" I said.

"Oh, no, stuff like this turns up every year," said the Armourer. "It's not supposed to be practical; it's engineers showing off. They're always saying they've finally fixed the design flaws, but they never have. Never met a giant robot yet that didn't trip over its own feet. Satanists, though, that is new. What do they want here?"

"Weapons?" I said. "Like everyone else?"

"People like them usually work through second or even third parties," said the Armourer. "Never let the left hand know what the left hand's doing, and all that. And they've always been behind-the-scenes types, never showing off in public. Something's up. . . ."

We were heading back into the fair proper when the

massed tuxedos rounded a corner right in front of us. And I recognised one of them. I grabbed Molly and the Armourer and hauled them into a concealing side walkway. The Satanists marched right past us without pausing.

"I recognised the big guy next to the leader," I explained. "From Lightbringer House."

"Are you sure?" said the Armourer.

"He got really close to me with a flamethrower," I said. "You never forget the face of someone who's tried to kill you. I had my armour on at the time, so he won't know me; but they all saw your face, Molly. . . ."

She looked after the Satanists and smiled unpleasantly.

"Want me to lure him away from the others and turn him into something soft and squishy?"

"No," I said. "But if we could lure him away from the pack and scare some information out of him . . . about the Great Sacrifice, for example . . ."

"Sounds like a plan to me," said the Armourer.

"Hold it, hold it," said Molly. "You can't be involved in this. He can't see your faces. I'm no problem; he's already seen mine. So you two hold back, and watch a professional at work."

The Armourer looked at me. "Is she always like this?"

"Pretty much," I said.

He grinned broadly. "Lucky boy . . ."

We set off purposefully after the Satanists, Molly out in front. But even before she could make a move, something alerted them and they all slammed to a halt as one. Their heads came up like hounds scenting the air, and then they all turned round as one and pointed at Molly. Who was so surprised she stood there and let them do it. The Armourer grabbed me by the arm and hustled me off to one side. I didn't like leaving Molly on her own, but I couldn't afford for Shaman Bond to get involved. If people got a good look at what he could actually do, they might start making comparisons with the Droods . . . and I'd never be able to be him again. I liked being Shaman Bond. Molly would understand.

Hell, she'd probably be really mad if I butted in and stole her thunder.

She didn't seem particularly troubled that all the Satanists had her in their sights. In fact, she was smiling her really dangerous smile.

"All right," she said. "Let's do it. Let's see what you've got, boys."

And to the watching crowd's surprise, the Satanists turned and ran. They sprinted up the walkway, the leader stabbing his finger at every stall he passed; suddenly every stallholder, every weapons maker and designer blinked out of existence. Molly and the Armourer and I pounded after them, and the crowds scattered to get out of our way. The massed tuxedos broke up, little groups of them charging up and down the narrow walkways, stabbing their fingers at the stalls and disappearing every scientist or engineer who worked on the fair's weapons.

That was what they'd come here for. Their plan was becoming clearer to me by the moment, now that they'd been forced to commit themselves. Why steal the fair's weapons when you could steal all the weapons makers and put them to work for you? That was why their leader hadn't been too concerned when he kept being turned down. He gave them each his card! Probably contained some tracking device, some signal for their teleporter to lock onto. I kept running after the Satanists, and man after man disappeared.

The Satanists had worked this all out in advance. They'd been doing really well until Molly got too close.

The Bloodred Guard came running again, but far too late. The Satanists had made their way right through the fair, from one side to the other, and taken everyone they'd tagged. I looked at the Armourer, and he nodded sharply. We ducked into the concealing shadows of an abandoned booth, subvocalised our activating Words, and armoured up. The freezing cold disappeared in a moment as the golden strange matter swept over me, and I felt like I was fully awake for the first time. I looked at Uncle Jack and saw myself reflected in his gleaming armour: a golden agent of law and order. Or at least, Drood law and Drood order.

We burst out of the booth, and a lot of people started screaming. The crowd took one look at us and scattered, running full-pelt for the exits. The Bloodred Guard stopped dead in their tracks. Uncle Jack and I tore off after the Satanists. One turned, took up a magical stance and thrust a splay-fingered hand at us. A brilliant flare erupted in the air between us, an incandescent glare so bright and vivid my mask had to shut itself down completely, sealing me in darkness to protect my eyes. I could hear people crying out and panicking all about me. I stood still, waiting, and the mask quickly adjusted to the fading glare and cleared again. People were staggering around, clutching at their ruined eyes. The Bloodred Guard were dazed, but recovering. Hard stock, these monks. The Satanist was gone, running full-pelt to catch up with the others at the edge of the fair. The Armourer was already heading after them, and I hurried after him. All across the fair, those who hadn't been blinded were already charging towards preprepared teleport gates and dimensional doors. None of them wanted anything to do with Droods. Even the stall and booth operators were rabbitting. They thought we'd come to shut them down.

"We let ourselves be played," the Armourer said harshly as I ran alongside him. "All the time we were laughing at the tuxedos, they were preparing to snatch the weapons makers right out from under our noses! This is bad, boy, really bad."

"Not least because everyone else thinks we're responsible for all this!" I said. "Sooner or later, someone is going to get really aggressive with us."

"We have to stop the Satanists!"

"If we can catch them," I said.

There was chaos everywhere now, as the whole fair went crazy. Everyone who didn't have access to the teleports or the dimensional doors was running for the hills, or, more properly, mountains. The telltale shimmer overhead was gone, which meant the force shields were down. No point in hiding, now that the Droods were in the fold. And an increasing number of really pissed-off people weren't even trying to run. They grabbed the nearest weapons and opened fire on the Armourer and me. And Molly, who'd caught up with us. I moved quickly to put my armour between her and the gunfire. The Armourer dropped back to cover the rear. All kinds of guns opened up on us from every direction at once. The din was deafening. Bullets hammered into me. My armour absorbed them all easily, and the Armourer sucked up punishment behind me. Molly ducked down between us and peered interestedly out to either side.

"I think we've upset them," she said. "I've never had so many guns aimed at me at one time before. It's really quite exhilarating. Are you going to call in reinforcements from your family?"

"I hardly think so," said the Armourer, turning calmly this way and that so his armour could absorb bullets more efficiently. "Two Droods are more than enough. I think we need to shut this event down, Eddie. Preserving the fair is no longer a credible option. Take as many of them alive as you can; we can use their information. And some of them are old friends, after all. . . ."

"You have to admire his ambition," Molly said to me.

Half a dozen men pressed forward to the front of the crowd and opened up on us with heavy-duty automatic weapons. The bullets hammered into my armoured chest and head, and flew past me to chew up the nearby stalls. One of the flimsier structures all but disintegrated, collapsing in a cloud of dust and pulverised wood and metal. I walked steadily forward into the hail of bullets, my armour soaking up the impact so I didn't feel a thing. The Armourer waded into the people in front of him, golden fists rising and falling, and unconscious and broken bodies crashed to the ground. Uncle Jack seemed to be quite happy to be back in the field again.

The armed men in front of me stopped firing and fell back to let someone else through. He was carrying a massive armament known in the trade as Puff the Magic Dragon. He was a big man, and he still had to strain to carry the thing and point it in my general direction. He opened fire, and the long barrel pumped out five thousand explosive rounds a second. The sheer pressure of so many bullets slamming into me at once actually pushed me backwards. My strange matter was absorbing every single bullet and suppressing every explosion, but the sheer impact pressed me back like a fire hose. Until I dug my golden heels in. The wooden boards shattered underneath me, and my golden feet dug deep into the hard, stony ground. My backward momentum slowed and then stopped, my golden feet leaving long, deep grooves in the ground. I held my position, leaning slightly forward into the thundering fire, like a swimmer breasting the tide. And then, step by step, I forced my way forward against the pressure of the bullets. They hammered into me, raking across my chest and gut and then up to my head, but none of them could touch me. Until finally I stood right before the man and his gun, close enough that he could see his white, wide-eyed face reflected in my featureless golden mask. And then I ripped Puff the Magic Dragon out of his nerveless hands, broke it over my knee and crumpled the two pieces into junk with my armoured hands.

"Run," I said. And he did.

I looked around, and Molly stepped out from behind a particularly sturdy booth. Even a Metcalf sister has enough sense to hide from that dragon. A man with an automatic rifle stepped out from a booth opposite and opened fire on her. I didn't even have time to react. Molly stuck out one hand, and the bullets turned into butterflies in midair long before they reached her. Pretty pink butterflies, like animated scraps of sugar floss. But Molly had been through a lot recently, and her magic resources had to be running low. And the man didn't seem to be running out of bullets. They inched steadily closer towards her before turning into butterflies and flying away. I left it as long as I could, for Molly's pride's sake, but in the end I couldn't stand it anymore. So I picked up the nearest booth and hit the man with it. He disappeared from sight without a sound. Molly lowered her hand, breathed heavily for a moment and then glared at me.

"I could have taken him!"

"Of course you could," I said. "I got impatient."

A man stepped out from behind another booth and pointed one of the cloned monkey's paws at us. He said the activating Words, and all its fingers fell off. The man threw what was left on the ground and stamped on it, then realised Molly and I were still watching him, at which point he quickly removed himself from the vicinity. That's what you get for buying cheap knockoffs.

I looked around, but the walkways were deserted. The fair was almost empty. The crowds had seen what Drood armour and one really annoyed witch could do, and had lost all faith in the weapons the Supernatural Arms Faire had to offer. A great roar of engines overhead made me look up, and there was the vertical-take-off plane hovering directly overhead. Huge and sleek and shiny, it must have manoeuvred into position while I was distracted, its noisy approach covered by the sound of gunfire. It rotated slowly overhead, held up by the massive downdraught of its engines. The pounding air slammed against my armour, blowing up great clouds of dust and dirt to blind me. Molly had already retreated to shelter, and sent a brisk wind my way to disperse the clouds.

The plane's targeting system finally locked onto me, and it opened up with every weapon it had. Heavy machine-gun fire sprayed across me, followed by two supersonic missiles. My mask shut down again as the world disappeared in fire and noise. When I could see again, I was standing in a large open space, with all the surrounding stalls and booths blown apart or blown away. Quite a few more were on fire. Molly was standing some distance away, protected inside one of her special protective fields. But I didn't know how long she could keep that going, so I ran forward and jumped up into the air, propelled by the powerful strength of my armoured legs. I think the VTO pilot guessed what I was up to at the last moment, because the plane started to rise, but I was already there.

I grabbed onto the undercarriage with one extended golden hand, the fingers closing hard, sinking deep into the metal. I hung there for a moment beneath the plane, and then pulled myself up so I could get a good grip with my other hand. I hauled myself up onto the wing and stood up. The massive VTO engines roared deafeningly, trying to maintain balance as I strode along the wing, heading for the cockpit. I could see the pilot staring out at me unbelievingly. I grabbed the cockpit roof and tore it away, the steel shrieking as it ripped and buckled under my grasp. The pilot panicked and hit the ejection button. He shot up past me, his chair leaving a trail of flames behind it that washed briefly and ineffectually over my armour.

The plane lurched back and forth, its balance gone without the pilot to adjust the engines. The nose turned down, and the plane plummeted back to earth, heading straight for the fair. There were still a lot of people down there, stumbling lost and confused up and down the walkways. I couldn't let the VTO plane crash into the fair and kill them all. So I rode the plane down, leaning back and shifting my weight this way and that to guide its descent. The armour gave me the feel of the plane almost immediately, and a shift of my armoured weight at exactly the right times was all it took to steer it in the right direction. I rode the plane all the way down, over the fair and on into the valley, and then I jumped away at the last moment. I landed easily, my armoured legs soaking up the impact, and the VTO plane hit the valley floor hard and skidded along for some time in a billow of smoke before finally skidding to a halt in a shower of sparks. No fire, no explosion, nothing. I shook my head and ran back to the fair.

Still, what a ride . . .

I saw the Armourer facing off against the remote-controlled tank, and headed over to back him up. A great, hulking steel monster, the tank roared towards my uncle, who stood his ground and let it come. The tank fired shell after shell at him, each one dead on target, exploding against his armour without driving him back an inch. When the smoke from the explosions cleared, he was still standing where he had been, though some of where he had been standing wasn't there anymore. I could tell from the way he was posing, arms folded easily across his chest, that the Armourer was enjoying himself. It might have been thirty years since he'd seen action in the field, but he was still every inch a Drood agent. Besides, all those years working in the Armoury had probably made him rather blasé about being blown up. The Armourer waited until the tank was almost on top of him, and then he leaned forward, ducked underneath and lifted the whole front of the tank up off the ground. Its tracks turned helplessly, unable to get a grip. The Armourer walked slowly forward, step by step, raising the tank up and up until it tipped over onto its back. It hit hard, and a series of things went *bang* inside it. Streams of black smoke billowed out of cracks in its sides, along with bursts of flame from electrical fires.

I went to stand beside the Armourer, and Molly came tripping up to join us. She threw her arms around me and hugged me as best she could through my armour. I held her carefully, mindful of my armour's strength.

"How could you tell which was me?" I said.

"Your armour is quite different from everyone else's," she said, leaning against my chest. "You don't realise how much you change it subconsciously these days."

I looked at my uncle, in his basic old-fashioned skin-tight golden armour, and he nodded his featureless head. "She's right, Eddie. Your armour has an almost medieval affect. Like some Arthurian knight. I guess the Drood is in the details, these days."

A great shadow fell over us. The giant Japanese robot was up and on its feet and looming over us. Fifty feet tall, broad chest, massive arms and legs, hundreds of tons of steel and all the latest technology. The chest opened up to reveal row upon row of energy weapons, the squat barrels sparking and crackling with discharging energies. The face had been painted to resemble some old-time Japanese demon, and the eyes flashed fiercely. The giant robot raised its arms slowly and menacingly. It stepped forward, tripped over its own feet and fell flat on its face. The impact shook the ground like an earthquake. Molly and the Armourer and I watched it closely, but it didn't move again.

"Told you," said the Armourer.

We headed back to what was left of the Supernatural Arms Faire.

Those people who hadn't been able to leave or escape, or didn't want to abandon their stalls or merchandise, stood around in small groups for comfort and mutual support. They regarded us with suspicious eyes as we walked past, but said nothing, not wanting to draw attention to themselves. More than half the stalls and booths and tents had been destroyed or ruined, and the whole place was a mess. Fires burned here and there, and smoke drifted this way and that on the gusting wind. The Bloodred Guard appeared out of the ruins and spread out to stand before us. We stopped and bowed politely. The head monk sighed and turned to his fellow guards.

"Knock it off, guys. We are way out of our league. Everyone stand down and see what you can do to help the injured. There are still people here who need our help. If that's okay with you, Drood?"

"Carry on," said my uncle Jack. "But don't let anyone go. There will be questions."

"These people need doctors, not interrogators," said the monk.

"They'll get help," I said. "We're the good guys."

"Yeah, right," said the monk.

He and his fellow guards turned away to do what needed doing. There was a general air of *we're not being paid enough to fight Droods,* which was only reasonable.

The Supernatural Arms Faire was now officially over. Half of it was in ruins, the other half was still on fire, and there was no one left to sell anything to. A good day's work, I thought. Except there was no trace of the Satanists anywhere, or the people they'd kidnapped. We were going to have to do something about that.

"I'll call in the family," said the Armourer. "Medics first, and then support teams to Hoover up everything that's left. Can't have so many good weapons going to waste, after all."

"Boys and their toys," said Molly.

I handed the Armourer the Merlin Glass, and he opened it up to make contact with Drood Hall. I armoured down and walked off with Molly, shivering hard as the mountain cold hit me again.

"So much for a day off, and a nice little holiday," said Molly.

"Oh, I don't know," I said. "I had a good time. Didn't you have a good time?"

"Well, yes," said Molly. "But that's not the point! The satanic creeps got away with it again! Worked their plans right in front of us, and then disappeared, laughing, leaving us to clean up the mess. I am getting really tired of being caught on the back foot all the time, Eddie. I want to know what they're planning. I want to know what the Great Sacrifice is. And I want to take the fight to them, instead of always being one bloody step behind!"

"Exactly," I said. "We have got to get into the game fast, or the game could be over before we even get a kick of the ball."

CHAPTER SIX

Who's Been Sleeping in My Bed?

Like all proper missions, the next one started with a stop off at the Armoury, that heavily shielded cavern underneath the Hall, where the Armourer and his devil's assortment of highly motivated and only technically mentally disturbed lab assistants labour night and day to provide the Drood family with all the guns, gadgets and assorted weird shit that field agents need to carry out their missions successfully. Not the safest of places to visit, but where's the fun in safe, anyway? Certainly there's always something interesting going on in the Armoury.

The old place looked as it always did, when Molly and I wandered in the next day. All very different from the cold, silent, deserted place I'd seen in the Winter Hall. In what might or might not have been Limbo. Despite Molly's well-meant reassurances, I hadn't forgotten a single thing about my time in that place: what I'd seen and heard, and what people had said to me. I'd checked with the family's researchers; Walker was quite definitely dead. Had been for some time. So who was it who came to me in the Winter Hall, wearing Walker's face, to tell me my parents might not be dead after all?

A question . . . for another time. I had a mission to prepare for.

I found the familiar loud and violent circumstances of the Armoury strangely comforting as Molly and I followed the Armourer past the packed workstations and smoke-wreathed testing grounds. The lab assistants were all hard at work, creating appalling and distressing weapons for my family to throw at our enemies and damn all their underhanded schemes. Guns roared, swords glowed and things went suddenly *bang!* with all their usual nasty efficiency; and an oversize eyeball with big, flapping bat wings went fluttering down the main aisle, pursued by an assistant with a really big butterfly net.

The Armourer stalked through his territory like Daddy come home to see what the kids have been getting up to in his absence. He peered over shoulders, made useful suggestions and cutting remarks, and yelled right into people's faces when they weren't following the proper safety protocols. Which was a bit much, coming from him. I still remember the time he showed us his new handgun that fired black holes, and it took four of us to wrestle him to the ground and take it away from him before he could demonstrate it.

Uncle Jack was always convinced the lab assistants started slacking, or practicing their own self-destructive forms of one-upmanship, the moment he wasn't around to watch over them; but they all seemed as absorbed and homicidally inclined as always. One of them was wearing a T-shirt with the message *Blow It All Up and Ask Questions Later.*

One particular lab assistant, naked but for a lab coat unfortunately not buttoned up at the front, was sitting inside a chalk-drawn mandala on the bare floor, playing an electric bass with all kinds of weird tech plugged into it. I knew him of old. Eric was convinced he could make his bass guitar generate a chord so powerful it would make everyone who heard it crap themselves simultaneously. Psychologically effective and physically distressing at the same time. He hadn't had much success so far.

The best he'd been able to produce was a chord that acted as a mild but effective laxative. So every morning Eric went to the family hospital wards to play a short recital. Which, I understand, was always very well received by the patients.

A rather fierce young lady in a blood-spattered lab coat was walking up and down before a row of large, warty toads wired securely in place along a wooden plank. She was holding what looked like a souped-up soup ladle with many wires hanging off it, and every time she pointed the thing at a toad, the toad exploded. Messily. None of the other toads reacted. In fact, they all seemed quite resigned about it. Drugs will do that to you. Just say no. Especially to lab assistants with a funny look in their eyes.

"Ah!" the Armourer said happily. "I was wondering when Charlotte was finally going to get the kinks out of her protein exploder. Very efficient . . . The toads are all clones, of course, to avoid running out of test subjects."

"Why toads?" I said.

The Armourer shrugged. "Nobody likes toads. If it were kittens . . ."

"Don't go there," said Molly. "Just don't."

"Of course, it's all pretty basic for the moment," said the Armourer. "Simply point and die. But once Charlotte gets the fine-tuning right, she'll be able to blast the warts right off their backsides!"

"And when exactly would that come in handy?" I said.

"Early days yet, Eddie, early days . . ."

A rather upset-looking young man was being led away by the hand by a rather resigned-looking young woman. He'd somehow ended up with both eyeballs in one socket, and he was not being a brave bunny about it. I got the impression from the look on the young woman's face that this wasn't the first time she'd had to do something like this.

Molly picked up a small brass box covered in pretty flashing lights, from the top of a computer console. The Armourer almost jumped out of his skin.

"Don't touch that!"

"Why, what is it?" said Molly, hanging onto the box even more firmly.

The Armourer snatched the box away from her, looked at it and then shook it fiercely. Nothing happened, so he put it back on the console.

"Odd," he said. "It should have reversed your polarity. I'll have to work on it."

"You hit him," Molly said to me. "You're closer."

"I wouldn't dare," I said.

"I've got something for you, Molly," the Armourer said quickly. "Come and take a look at this little beauty."

He scrabbled among the assorted tech and junk cluttering up his worktable, tossed aside a pistol with five barrels and a fluffy gonk with an evil stare, and finally held up a golden crown: a simple circle of gold, with an intricate golden lattice containing dozens of brightly shimmering crystals. He offered the crown to Molly, and she looked it over while being very careful not to touch it. The Armourer preened proudly.

"Very nice," Molly said finally. "Expensive, but vulgar, vaguely Celtic in design, but aesthetically pleasing from every angle. What am I supposed to do with it?"

"You put it on your head!" said the Armourer. "It'll protect you from every known form of psychic attack, and make damn sure Ammonia Vom Acht can't prise any useful secrets out of your pretty little head."

Molly looked at him coldly. "I am supposed to put something you made on my head, and trust that my brains won't start leaking out of my ears?"

"That was a long time ago!" said the Armourer. "I wish people would stop going on about it. . . . Look, put the bloody thing on so I can fine-tune the settings to your personal aura. It has been very thoroughly tested, you know. What do you want, a guarantee in writing?"

Molly stuck her lower lip out and looked at me. "Why doesn't he have to wear one?"

"Because I have a torc," I said patiently. "And psychic protection comes standard. Please put the crown on, Molly, or I'll have to go without you. You go up against Ammonia Vom Acht with an unprotected mind and she'll rip your thoughts open and gut them like a fish, with one look."

Molly sniffed loudly, snatched the crown out of the Armourer's hands and lowered it gingerly onto her head. The Armourer ran his fingertips lightly over the various crystals, humming something he fondly imagined had a tune, until he had them all blinking and flickering at the same rate. He then grunted in a satisfied sort of way and stepped back. Molly immediately demanded a mirror to see how she looked. I held the Merlin Glass up before her so she could study her new look in the reflection.

"This really isn't me, Eddie. I do not do the fairy-princess look. People will snigger at me."

"No one would dare," I assured her.

"Ammonia won't think I'm . . . scared of her, will she, wearing protective headgear in her presence?"

"It won't even occur to her that you wouldn't be scared," said the Armourer. "Anyone with half a working brain in her head would have enough sense to be scared shitless of Ammonia Vom Acht. The most powerful telepathic mind in the world today . . . Well, human mind, anyway. If you were to enter her presence unprotected, even for a moment, she could read every thought you ever had, or make you think you were someone else and always had been, or plant secret hidden commands for future behaviour so deep in your subconscious even other telepaths wouldn't know they were there. Until it was far too late. Or, even worse . . . she might think of something funny to do to you. Ammonia's sense of humour isn't what you'd call normal."

Molly scowled unhappily, but left the crown where it was. I thought it did make her look a bit like a fairy princess. I liked it. I looked expectantly at the Armourer.

"Well, Uncle Jack? Don't I get any new toys before I set out on this extremely dangerous mission?"

"None of my guns or gadgets would do you any good against Ammonia Vom Acht," said the Armourer. "In fact, they'd only give you a false sense of security. Trust to your torc to protect you, and try not to antagonise her. You will anyway, but she might appreciate the effort."

"That's all the advice you've got for me?"

"Please don't kill her. She might be annoying, but she's very useful. We might need her help again someday."

I frowned. "Why would I want to kill her?"

"You haven't met her yet."

I waited, but he had nothing else to say. So I nodded good-bye, and he nodded vaguely and hurried off to show his lab assistants what they were doing wrong. I hefted the Merlin Glass in my hand, thinking hard. Molly looked at me.

"Ready to go, Eddie?"

"I don't know if *ready* is quite the right word," I said. "But I can't seem to come up with a good enough reason to put it off, so . . ."

"Aren't you going to armour up first?" said Molly. "You don't want Ammonia seeing your face; or would she be able to read your identity anyway?"

"No, the torc will protect me at all levels," I said, trying hard to sound calm and confident. "But it doesn't matter if she sees my face, or yours. She won't know me as Shaman Bond, because he doesn't move in her kind of circles. Ammonia . . . doesn't get out much. People come to her."

"She might not know you," said Molly. "But you know her; don't you?"

"I know of her; everyone in the secret-agent business does. And she'll probably know you by reputation."

Molly smiled smugly. "Lot of people know my reputation."

"And you say that like it's a good thing. . . ."

"You want a slap?"

I activated the Merlin Glass, and we watched our reflections disappear from the hand mirror as the Glass sought out Ammonia Vom Acht's location. The image flickered uncertainly for some time, struggling past her various protections, until finally an image appeared in the Glass: a rather distant image of an isolated cottage somewhere down in Cornwall. I tried to get the Glass to zoom in for a closer look, but this was as close as it could get. I sort of got the feeling that the Glass was afraid to get any closer. Which was . . . interesting. The cottage didn't look particularly threatening.

"The Glass is detecting really heavy-duty protections," I said. "We'll have to go through as is, and walk the rest of the way. And hope we don't set off any psychic land mines. Doesn't look too far. Weather looks nice. My torc and your crown should protect us."

"And if they don't?" said Molly.

"Then we improvise. Suddenly and violently and all over the place. That's what field agents do!"

"Don't you raise your voice to me, Edwin Drood!" said Molly. "Just because we're off to visit the witch in her gingerbread cottage. I have a really bad feeling about this. . . ."

"Situation entirely normal," I said.

It turned out that the greatest and most dangerous telepath of our time had chosen to live in a pretty little cottage down on the Cornish coast, on top of a hill looking out over the sea. Miles from anywhere, with acres of desolate-looking landscape between her and the nearest town or village. Molly and I stepped through the Merlin Glass and emerged onto the very edge of the cliff top. Two more steps and we'd have both been grabbing handfuls of fresh air as we plummeted towards the crashing sea. I couldn't really see that as a coincidence.

I have tried forming glider wings out of my armour, and I don't want to talk about the results.

Molly and I carefully moved back a few paces, and I put the Glass away. It had already shrunk down to its original size without being ordered to, as though it were afraid of being noticed. I put it away in its pocket dimension, so called because I keep the separate dimension in my pocket, and looked down. Hundreds of feet below, the heavy swelling sea smashed against dark and ragged rocks, foam flying on the air.

A cold wind was blowing out of the north, and gulls hung in the air above us, keening mournfully. There is an old legend that says the gulls are crying for the sins of the world, and that when we finally get our act together, the gulls will stop crying. It was easy to believe such a story in a desolate place like this.

The cottage looked to be a good half a mile away, as the crow flew: across a bare stone and scrub plain. Molly and I looked at each other and started walking. There wasn't a single living creature to be seen anywhere, and even the steady sounds of our footsteps on the stony ground seemed strangely muted. As we drew closer, I could see the cottage was fronted by a carefully laid-out garden. A low stone wall marked the boundaries, hand-built in the old style, and there were hedges and flowers and topiary trees. A splash of vivid colours in such a grey setting. We stopped before the wrought-iron gate that was the only entrance to the garden. Beyond the gate, a narrow gravel path led straight to the cottage's front door. A simple sign beside the gate said, trespassers will be violated. Molly and I stood before the gate, carefully not touching anything, peering between the bars. The garden looked lovely.

"I can feel industrial-strength protections and defences hanging in the air, waiting to be triggered," said Molly. "They feel . . . strange. No magic, no tech, only the power of one person's mind. I get the feeling we'll be safe as long as we stick to the path. She knows we're here, Eddie."

"I'd be disappointed if she didn't," I said. "Stay put for the moment. Let her get a good look at us and our protections."

"She's been watching us from the moment we arrived," said Molly, shuffling uncomfortably from foot to foot. Molly's never been one for standing around. Not when there's dashing in where angels fear to tread to be done. "I can feel her attention, like a great weight pressing down, or like staring into a blinding searchlight.

The sheer power I'm sensing is downright scary. And I don't usually do scary. Ah!"

"What?" I said, looking quickly around.

"It's gone. She's not watching us anymore."

The wrought-iron gate swung slowly open before us, the hinges making soft protesting noises. I knew Ammonia could have oiled those hinges, but chose not to, as a simple extra warning system. It was what I would have done. I strode forward, doing my best to exude confidence, and Molly stuck close beside me, head erect, eyes glaring in all directions. The gate swung noisily shut behind us, but I wouldn't give it the satisfaction of looking back. Our feet crunched on the gravel path as we headed for the cottage. The garden really was delightful: open and attractive, with all kinds of flowers, neat hedgerows, and trees trimmed into perfect geometric shapes. Someone had put a lot of work into this garden.

"A peaceful setting," I said. "For such a famously unpleasant woman."

"So all the stories I've heard are true?" said Molly, still scowling arond her.

"If they're distressing, awful and appalling stories, almost certainly yes," I said. "This is a woman who once called the current Anti-Pope a big-nosed idiot. To his face."

"An accurate description," said Molly.

"Well, yes, but you don't say something like that to a cult leader with a private army of fanatical followers. Not to his face."

"I do," said Molly.

"Well, yes again, but you're weird."

"You say the nicest things, Eddie."

"I do my best," I said.

The cottage loomed up before us like a dentist's waiting room; it might look pleasant enough, but you know there's trouble ahead. Actually, the cottage, in its delightful setting, looked as though it should be a photo on the lid of a jigsaw box. Say about a thousand pieces, nothing too difficult, you know the sort. A charming, old-fashioned cottage with a brick chimney poking up through the neatly thatched roof, roses curling round the front door, long vines sprawled across the creamy white stone of the facing wall. Two large bay windows on either side of the front door, which, as I drew closer, I could see had no bell or knocker. Ammonia Vom Acht always knew when visitors were coming.

Bees buzzed loudly over the flower beds, and brightly coloured butterflies fluttered by, but no birds sang. Which struck me as a bit odd. And possibly even disturbing. I stopped short of the front door and listened carefully.

"It's quiet," said Molly. "Perhaps even too quiet."

"Why aren't there any birds?" I said. "Even the gulls are steering well clear of this place. You're always saying you're one with the wild woods; what's wrong with this picture?"

"You're right," said Molly. "I'm not picking up a single living creature bigger than an earthworm anywhere near here. Not even a mole or a dormouse. And that's not natural."

"This means something," I said.

Molly looked at me sideways. "Why are you so nervous, Eddie? You've faced far worse than this in your time. I know; I was there. This isn't like you."

"I've always preferred dangers I can hit," I said steadily. "Telepaths . . . are sneaky. They come at you in unexpected ways, and they don't fight fair. And this is, after all, Ammonia Vom Acht we're talking about. You must have heard the stories. . . ."

"Pretend I haven't," said Molly. "Get it out of your system. What stories?"

"Some of her more famous cases, then," I said. "Just the high points. She was once asked to help resolve a case of split personality in a very important and well-connected person, where the two personalities were in conflict with each other. The dominant good guy versus the usually subordinate trickster type. Ammonia decided she liked the trickster personality better, so she made that the dominant personality and put the other one to sleep. Lot of trouble there, until he was finally removed from office with a lead ballot. Another time, she was hired to investigate an amnesiac, only to discover he'd already paid a substantial amount to a previous telepath to wipe all his memories, because he couldn't stand being the kind of man he'd become. Ammonia agreed, destroyed his memories again, only even more thoroughly, kept all the money the man's family had paid her, and defied them to do anything about it!"

"So far, I have no problem with any of this," said Molly.

"You wouldn't," I said. "But it gets worse. Having decided that she now knew better than anyone else what was good for people, Ammonia then went through a phase of overhauling the personalities of everyone she met. Rewriting their minds for the better . . . according to her lights. More like telepathic muggings. Some of these rewritings were successful; others weren't. A lot of people ended up killing themselves, because they knew they weren't who they were supposed to be. Some of them killed other people, because some subtle restraint had been removed. But by then Ammonia had moved on, never around to clean up the messes she'd made. She stopped only because practically every other telepath in the world got together and ganged up on her and made her stop. Such a gathering was made possible only through my family's intervention, and I'm not sure we could make it happen a second time. Getting telepaths to work together is like herding cats. It is possible, but only with the continued threat of immediate extreme violence. Which can be very wearing . . . I'm pretty sure Ammonia still blames us for stopping her fun. Anyway, after all this she went into a bit of a sulk and retreated from the world. Only comes out to work on cases no one else can manage; and then only for the challenge, and a truly massive fee.

"She lives all the way out here because she knows too many secrets. No one can keep anything from her, you see. And since she's met pretty much everyone who matters, at one time or another, there are always agents and assassins on her trail, either to kidnap her to force those secrets out of her, or to kill her to make sure her secrets die with her. She could hide herself so completely that no one could find her, but her pride won't allow that. And she does so love to prove she's still as powerful as everyone's afraid she is. So she stays here, and lets her enemies get close enough that she can have some fun playing with them. Sometimes she lets them get right to her gate before she makes their heads explode. Sometimes she mind-wipes them, and leaves them to wander the world as horrific living examples. And sometimes she rewrites them and sends them back to murder the people who sent them to kill her."

"Okay," said Molly. "You've said your piece. I feel very thoroughly lectured and warned. Do you feel better?"

"Not really, no."

We headed for the front door again. I didn't hurry, taking my time. Molly frowned.

"You're actually scared of her, aren't you?"

"Not scared, not as such . . ." I said, and then stopped. I could feel my heart hammering in my chest, and the cold sweat beading on my forehead. "If my torc isn't enough to protect me, the first I'll know about it is when Ammonia slips inside my head and makes me do things. Think what she could do with my armour. . . . All the terrible things she could make me do to you, or my family, while I was held helpless inside my own head . . ."

I stopped, because Molly was smiling at me fondly. "I have never known anyone who could find so many ways to feel guilty about things you haven't even done! None of that will happen, because I won't let it happen. You may not be able to trust your torc, but you trust me, don't you?"

"Yes," I said. "I can always trust you, Molly."

We were right outside the front door. I raised a hand to knock, and the door swung suddenly open before me. And there, standing in the doorway and very obviously blocking our path, was Ammonia Vom Acht herself. She didn't look pleased to see us.

The greatest telepath mankind has ever produced was under medium height, stocky, with a broad and almost mannish face under a frizzy shock of unrestrained auburn hair. She had piercing green eyes, a hook of a nose and a thin, flat mouth not really helped by a brief slash of dark red lipstick. There was a lot of character in her face, but no one was ever going to call her pretty. Or even handsome, unless the light was really bad. Someone once said she had a face like a bulldog licking piss off a thistle, and I could see why. She wore dull, characterless clothes with more than a touch of the masculine about them: a battered tweed jacket with leather patches on the elbows, over baggy trousers with earth stains still on the knees from working in the garden. Her shoes were stout brogues, with trailing laces.

I didn't run. I knew my duty.

When she finally spoke, her voice was harsh and clipped and almost emotionless.

"So. Edwin Drood and Molly Metcalf. I've been expecting you. I was busy gardening when I sensed you were coming, so this had better be worth it."

"Hold everything," I said, caught off guard despite myself. "We arrived instantaneously through the Merlin Glass."

"I sensed the Glass was about to open here," said Ammonia. "You have no idea what an impact that thing makes on the world when you use it. But then, you don't even know what it is, really, do you?"

"Do you?" Molly said bluntly.

Ammonia ignored her, which isn't easy. She looked us both over, eyes narrowed, and then nodded abruptly. "You're both shielded. Good. Nothing worse than a noisy mind. That's why I have to live out here, so far away from everyone else. Being the most powerful telepathic mind in the world isn't always all it's cracked up to be. I have trouble keeping everyone else out of my head. The world will keep pressing in. People will intrude . . . and all the shouting makes me tired."

She stepped back. "Come in. Brush your feet on the mat. Properly! And don't mutter."

She beckoned us into a wide, brightly lit hallway with bare wooden floors and faded prints of rare flowers on the walls. Molly and I slipped in, and the door closed itself behind us. Ammonia turned her back on us and headed for the door at the far end, gesturing brusquely for Molly and me to follow her. We did so. She didn't look back, but she did keep talking to us over her shoulder.

"You were wondering why there are only insects in my garden, and no beasts or birds. I scare them off. Have to. Can't stand to have anything with a mind around me. All that red-in-tooth-and-claw stuff; they can't turn it off, you know. The endless fear and appetite make me bad tempered."

I felt a chill run up the back of my neck. "Were you reading our minds just then?"

"No," said Ammonia. "I heard you talking about it in the garden. It's quiet in the garden. That's why I like it. Come through into the parlour. Meet my husband, Peter."

That last bit almost stopped me dead. There was nothing in any of my family's files about the infamous Ammonia Vom Acht being married. Molly shot me a quick look and mouthed the word *husband?* and all I could do was shrug helplessly.

The parlour was small and cosy, filled with modern, brutally styleless furniture that clashed loudly with the rest of the cottage. Bright sunlight streamed in through the great bay window. There were vases of fresh flowers on every flat surface, pleasantly scenting the air. A large and very modern electric clock dominated one wall, working silently away, while the other walls presented paintings by several masters. Ammonia, it seemed, was very fond of the Pre-Raphaelites. Payment for past services, presumably. Two large and very comfortable-looking armchairs stood facing each other across the real fireplace. Sunk deeply in one of the chairs was Ammonia Vom Acht's husband, Peter.

He rose languidly from the depths of his chair to greet us. He smiled vaguely in our direction, but didn't offer a hand to shake. He was a tall, diffident sort in an expensive three-piece suit with recent dinner stains on the waistcoat, a pale, bland face under thinning blond hair, and a calm, uncommitted smile. He had a large drink in his hand, though it was barely midday.

"This is Peter," said Ammonia. She might have been speaking about her accountant. "I married him because he's a psychic null. Born shielded from every form of telepathic contact. His thoughts stay inside his head. I can't hear him. I can relax around him."

"And I married her because she needed me," Peter said blithely. "And I do so love to be needed. Don't I, old thing?"

His voice was well educated, even aristocratic: that affected, bored drawl that gets on everyone's nerves.

"I can't hear his thoughts or sense his feelings," said Ammonia. "Everything he says and does is a surprise to me. You have no idea what a relief that is."

"So many compliments," said Peter. "You'll make me blush, dear."

Ammonia nodded slowly. "I'm not easy to live with. I know that."

"Some marriages are made in heaven," said Peter. "The rest of us do the best we can." He spoke vaguely, his voice trailing away. When he looked up from his glass to take Molly and me in, his eyes were frankly disinterested. "You mustn't mind Ammonia. She's only being herself. Her problem is, she's always had difficulty deciding where she stops and other people begin. The edges are never properly nailed down, for a telepath. Things sneak in: thoughts, emotions, intentions. . . . She has no people skills. None at all. I'm not even sure she is people, really."

"Peter . . ." said Ammonia.

"Yes, dear, I know. We have guests. Party manners! Can I get you people a little something? I'm having a little something. I always have a little something about now."

Molly and I declined. Peter nodded understandingly, knocked back what was left in his glass, and drifted over to the very modern sideboard to refill his glass from a functional but quite ugly crystal decanter that was already half-empty.

"Ammonia doesn't drink," he announced, turning lazily back to face his visitors. "She daren't. Whereas I . . . am rarely sober. I daren't . . . I drink like a fish, you know, like a spiny denizen of the deep. So would you, if you were married to the most powerful telepath in the world. It's not the person, you understand; it's the lifestyle. Oh, do sit down, both of you. You make the room look untidy. No use waiting for Ammonia to ask you. Such things simply don't occur to her. No people skills, remember? Not her fault, of course."

Peter slumped bonelessly back into his armchair, and Ammonia sank down into the chair opposite him. Not a single recognisable emotion had crossed her face so far. Molly and I pulled up two stiff-backed wooden chairs and sat down facing them.

"Given everything the poor girl's been through, it's a wonder she's as sane as she is," Peter said affably. It was off-putting, the way he talked about his wife as if sometimes she was there, and sometimes she wasn't. He smiled vaguely at Molly and me. "Do you know the story? It's not one of the better-known ones, but it is jolly interesting. Ammonia spent the first ten years of her life in a coma, you see. Self-inflicted, to protect her developing mind from the thoughts of all the world crashing in on her at once. She had to learn how to make a shield that would keep everyone else out, before she could decide on who she was. Think of the poor child knowing all there was to know about human nature at such a young and defenceless age. The good and the bad, the sane and the insane, the saints and the devils . . . Only an iron will kept her together. . . . That's what makes her such a marvellous curative telepath. She knows all there is to know about the demons of the mind, because she's been there. You're very good at what you do, aren't you, dear? Yes, you are."

"Peter . . ." said Ammonia.

"I'm telling them what they need to know, old thing."

Peter smiled conspiratorially at Molly and me. "I see you've noticed all the fittings and furnishings are terribly up-to-date. Have to be. Ammonia can pick up traces, echoes, from all the people who used to own old things. People imprint on everything, you see. She had to run a full-scale telepathic exorcism on the cottage before we could move in, wiping the stone tape recording clean, as it were. And all the furniture has to be replaced regularly, every twelve months, because they soak up memories. We hold a nice little bonfire for the old stuff, out back. Because you can never tell what another telepath might pick up from it. For a telepath like Ammonia, peace of mind is everything. Everything. Isn't that right, old girl?"

"Yes," said Ammonia.

"And she has to be a vegetarian," said Peter. "Because she can hear the dying screams and last terrified emotions of even the smallest piece of meat. Someone once told me that a plant screams when it's plucked from the ground, but apparently that's not true. Certainly not root vegetables, because we eat enough of the things. I haven't had a sausage in years. Can't even pig out when she's away. You always know, don't you, dear?"

"Does she always let you do all the talking?" said Molly.

"Mostly," said Peter, entirely unperturbed. "It's what I'm for. She has no small talk, poor old thing. And she doesn't trust anyone. All the time we've been sitting here, chatting so cosily, she's been trying to break through your shields, to see if she can. It's not that she wants to know things; she can't help herself. Have I distracted them enough now, old dear? Jolly good . . . I'll be quiet. Got some serious liver damage to be getting on with. . . ."

"I've heard of both of you," Ammonia Vom Acht said flatly, and my eyes snapped back to her. "Edwin Drood and Molly Metcalf. The Drood who thinks he's better than other Droods. Who thinks he's the first Drood to develop a conscience. But you're far from the first to try to redeem your family, Eddie. Power corrupts; always has, and always will. Those torcs of yours make you more powerful than people were ever meant to be.

"And you, Molly. The loudest and least of the infamous Metcalf sisters. Is there anything more obvious and pathetic than another young rebel without a cause? Who rejects everything so she doesn't have to commit to anything? And yes, Molly, I know my reputation, too. Is there ever anyone more rejected than the one who tells the truths that no one wants to hear?"

"Well," I said brightly. "That's told us! But I don't think I'll take any of it too seriously. You tell the truth, Ammonia, only as you see it. '"What is truth?" said jesting Pilate, and would not stay for an answer. . . . '"

"You're not afraid of me, are you?" said Ammonia.

"No," I said. "Somewhat to my surprise . . ."

"I can't stand people who aren't afraid of me," said Ammonia.

"It's true," said Peter, staring sadly into his drink. "She can't."

"I'm not hiring you to like me," I said to Ammonia, meeting her gaze steadily. "I'm hiring you to break into our Librarian's head and see if you can put him right. An other-dimensional entity assaulted his mind some years back, and it's still scrambled. You think you can fix that?"

"I do love a challenge," said Ammonia.

"It's true," said Peter. "She does. She really does. . . . Oh. Sorry, dear. Sorry, everyone. I've had too much to drink. Or not nearly enough. It's so hard to tell. . . . But you will help them, won't you, old thing? You can do this for them. You can do anything."

Ammonia ignored him, all her attention fixed on me. "If I can put William Drood right, repair what damage has been done and put his personality back together again . . . will the family agree to pay my price?"

"What do you want?" I said.

"I want your Armourer to make something for me," said Ammonia. "I want a crown like the one Molly is wearing right now. Only much stronger. I want something strong enough to keep the whole world out, so I don't have to. So I can rest."

"Agreed," I said.

"Could I try yours?" Ammonia said to Molly. "Just for a moment, to see what it feels like?"

"No, Molly," I said immediately. Molly's hands were already rising to the crown on her head, but when I spoke she snatched them back down again. I smiled at Ammonia. "You're very . . . persuasive in person, Ammonia. But try anything like that again and the deal is off. Forever."

"What?" said Molly. "What happened there?"

"You know a lot of Drood secrets," I said. "And if you had taken your crown off, only for a second . . ."

"You sneaky cow," Molly said to Ammonia.

"You have no idea what it's like, never to be trusted even for a moment," said Ammonia. "What makes you think I care about your stupid little secrets?"

"Well, you would say that, wouldn't you?" I said.

Ammonia made us both wait outside in the garden while she said her good-byes to her husband. Or perhaps she wanted to lock up all the drinks cabinets before she left. Though Peter had the look of a man who would gnaw through a wooden cabinet to get to his favourite tipple. Molly and I wandered back up the garden path, stopping to smell the roses along the way. It really was a very peaceful setting.

"You know you can't go back with us," I said to Molly. "This is private, and very personal, Drood business."

"Oh, don't worry about me," said Molly, in that special, casual tone of voice she uses only when she wants me to know that I'll have to do something really special to make up for it later. "I'll make my own way back. See you again, lover."

She snapped her fingers and was gone. I sighed. She was going to go off and sulk now. She hated not being included in things. And it was going to take more than a double-layer box of Thorntons dark chocolate assortment to win her round this time.

Ammonia finally came out of the cottage, slamming the front door shut behind her. She stomped over to me, looked round her garden as though she wasn't sure she would ever see it again, then looked at me standing on my own, and sniffed loudly.

"Let's do this, if we're going to. I don't like to leave Peter on his own for too long. Get a move on, Drood; you're the one with the Merlin Glass."

I removed the mirror from its pocket dimension, but before I could even activate it, Ammonia stepped back sharply, as though I'd tried to shove a poisonous snake in her face. I looked quickly at the Merlin Glass, but for the moment it still looked like an ordinary hand mirror.

"There's something in there!" said Ammonia, glaring into the Glass. "Something, or someone. I can't see it, but it can see me. I can tell. It's looking at me right now."

I looked into the Glass, but all I could see was my own somewhat puzzled reflection. I shook the Glass a few times, on general principle, but the reflection stayed the same. I looked at Ammonia.

"Friendly . . . or unfriendly?"

Ammonia shrugged. "I could find out for you. But that would cost extra."

"Then it can wait," I said. "Let's see what you can do with the Librarian first."

I shook the Merlin Glass out to full size and opened a doorway directly to the Old Library. Ammonia peered interestedly at the new view on the other side of the mirror. Rows and rows of bookshelves, under a pleasant golden glow, stretching away in all directions for as far as the eye could follow. I went through the Glass first, to reassure Ammonia, but she didn't hold back a moment in following me through. I shut down the Glass and put it away, turned to Ammonia and found the most dangerous telepath in the world was trembling visibly.

"It's the memories," she said. "Every book in this place still carries the traces of everyone who ever read it. It's like millions of voices, all shouting in my head at once. It's taking everything I've got to keep them out. Your Old Library is a lot older than you realise. It doesn't belong to your family. Droods didn't put the Library together; you inherited it. And then you brought it here with you from the Hall before this, and the Hall before that."

"Okay," I said, "you're getting into family business and family secrets you don't need to know about. Look away, Ammonia."

She wasn't even listening to me, her gaze fixed on something only she could see. "So many have passed through this place, and left footprints in the sands of Time. Not all of them were human. Gods and monsters have walked these dusty ways in search of lost and forbidden knowledge."

"Okay," I said, "you're pushing it now. I don't need the dramatics."

Ammonia shrugged easily. "All part of the service. All part of what you're paying for. I'm fine now. I've got your Library's measure. It's really quite pleasant, now that I've shut out the books. I can work here. Well away from your family, I'm happy to say, off in the Hall proper."

I looked at her. "How do you know we're not actually in the Hall?"

"Because it's my job to know things like that. This is some kind of pocket dimension. The Hall itself is . . . that way."

And she pointed up and to the left with complete certainty. Given that the Old Library is only lightly connected to the real world, I decided not to push the point. She might be right.

"Hello!" Ammonia said suddenly. "I'm picking up something . . . odd. There's you and me, and your Librarian, and his assistant; but I'm also picking up another presence . . . definitely not human."

"That's probably Ethel," I said. "The other-dimensional entity who lives with us. She's always looking in."

"The source of your family's power, and your new armour," said Ammonia. "I know all about Ethel. And it's not her. I can sense her watching us from back in Drood Hall. Behind quite extraordinarily powerful shields. I have to wonder what it is she's so desperate to hide from me . . . and you. I could find out; but that would cost you extra. But never mind about strange presences. That's not why I'm here. Where's the patient?"

Ioreth appeared suddenly from out of the nearest stacks, glaring at Ammonia from what he probably believed was a safe distance. He was wearing a monk's habit, with the hood pushed back to reveal a shaved head, on which was jammed a crown very similar to the one the Armourer had given Molly. Ioreth was doing his best to stand tall and proud, but couldn't quite bring it off. He looked more like someone desperately in need of a toilet.

"Hello! I'm Ioreth! I'm fine, thank you! I'm not thinking about anything. I'm definitely not thinking about that. Or that. I'm fine! Really."

"Ioreth, if you don't calm the fuck down right now, I am going to hose you from head to foot with Ritalin," I said. "You've had plenty of warning about this. And I know I'm going to regret asking, but why are you dressed like a monk?"

"William says he finds it soothing," said Ioreth. "You wouldn't believe the number of outfits we had to go through to find one he could live with. I can tell you for a fact that he really doesn't like sneakers. Or ties. Found that out the hard way. It was either this or a kilt, and this was less draughty. You haven't seen my dignity, have you? I'm sure I left it around here somewhere. I'm fine! Thanks for asking."

"And why are you wearing one of the Armourer's brand-new psychic protection units?" I asked, gesturing at his crown. "Your torc is all you need."

"The council insisted," Ioreth said stiffly. "In your absence. The telepath cannot be allowed access to

Drood secrets. Especially the kind you learn from reading the books in the Old Library. I know things even I don't think I should know."

"Like I care," said Ammonia. "I have enough secrets. I am stuffed full of secrets. I crap secrets and piss mysteries. And as for your blessed books . . ."

She ran her fingertips roughly along the spines of the books nearest her, and I swear they winced back from her. Ioreth almost jumped out of his habit.

"Don't touch the books! Don't touch anything in here! We have a large number of really dangerous books here in the Old Library, and by dangerous I mean violent, possessive and occasionally homicidal. This is not a petting zoo! I use special gloves to take some of these books off the shelves, and they're knitted personally for me by cloistered nuns from the Salvation Army sisterhood. Gloves that are actually holier than I will ever be. And even then I cross my fingers for luck."

"You're babbling, Ioreth," I said.

"I know! I'm fine, very fine; I'm really very nervous. I really don't think this is a good idea, Eddie, and I especially don't like the way that woman is looking at me; why is she looking at me like that? Eddie, make her stop looking at me like that! William . . . is not in a good mood. And yes, I know, he rarely is, but I would have to say that today he is even more not in a good mood than usual. He doesn't like visitors, he doesn't like telepaths, and he very definitely doesn't like Ammonia Vom Acht, though of course who does—sorry, I said that out loud, didn't I? Perhaps you could bring her back some other day, Eddie, when William's feeling more . . . receptive."

"Neither of us is going to live that long," I said. "It has to be now. It's for his own good, Ioreth."

He sniffed. "That's what they told Joan of Arc, poor girl. All right, follow me; I'll take you to him. But try not to make any loud noises or sudden moves. I don't want to have to get him down from the high stacks with the boat hook again."

He scurried off down the nearest aisle, and Ammonia and I went after him. William wasn't far. We found him standing straight backed and stiff necked, with his back to a display of Very Restricted Books. all passes must be shown, said a polite sign. and a list of your next of kin. William had clearly made an effort to improve his appearance, or perhaps Ioreth had, on his behalf. His grey hair and beard had been neatly trimmed, and he was wearing a brand-new and very clean dressing gown. He was still wearing his favourite white bunny slippers, which still disturbed me, for no good reason I could put my finger on. He looked a lot older than his years, and spiritually as well as physically tired. But he held himself well, and his face was calm, if a little distracted. He looked at Ammonia with his lost eyes, as though expecting the worst but holding up bravely nonetheless.

"I'm not sure I want to be healed," he said, speaking directly to Ammonia. "I think I prefer this me to the me I used to be. I'm not sure the old me was a very nice person."

"Lot of my patients say that," Ammonia said briskly. "It's avoidance and displacement at work. Like when your toothache disappears on the way to the dentist."

"But if I was a bad person . . ."

"Of course you were!" said Ammonia. "You were a Drood!"

"Ammonia," I murmured. "Not really helping . . ."

"William," said Ioreth, standing protectively close to the Librarian, "if she can help, you might not be so frightened all the time. . . ."

Ammonia moved forward to stand before William, and to his credit he didn't flinch. She looked into his eyes.

"Interesting. I'm getting . . . absolutely nothing from him. As though he were a psychic null, like my Peter. And it's not only his torc protecting him. Someone has placed very powerful blocks inside this man's mind."

"Can you break through them without damaging him?" I said.

"Can you stop talking about him as though he wasn't here!" said William.

"No problem," said Ammonia. "Easy-peasy, lemon squeezy. That's why you hired me." She looked back at William and gave him what she probably thought of as a reassuring smile. "I need you calm and relaxed. Sitting in your favourite chair, perhaps. Do you have a favourite chair?"

"Of course," said Ioreth. "I'll go and get it, shall I? Yes. Don't talk about me while I'm gone. I'm really very nervous."

He hurried off and quickly came back with a sagging overstuffed armchair so heavy he couldn't pick it up, but had to push it along in front of him as fast as the squealing and protesting castors would allow. He pushed it into place, and then leaned on the back breathing heavily, to show how much effort he was making on our behalf. William sank into the chair and arranged himself until he was as comfortable as he was going to get. Ammonia was surprisingly patient with him, until it became clear he was never going to stop wriggling about.

"Will you bloody well relax!" said Ammonia. "I am not the bloody dentist!"

"Don't like him either," said William. "Is this going to hurt?"

"Probably not physically," said Ammonia.

William started to get back up out of his chair, and Ioreth and I had to step forward and push him back into it. William subsided and scowled at Ammonia.

"I demand a second opinion!"

"All right," said Ammonia. "You're a Drood and I despise everything you stand for. Now shut up and let me concentrate."

I was expecting her to go into some kind of trance, or wave her hands about, or at least have her eyes light up; but there was nothing of the dramatic about what she did. She stood there before the Librarian, frowning thoughtfully, holding his gaze with hers. He stared back at her blankly, as though waiting for the real scanning to begin. Suddenly, I realised that the temperature in the Old Library was dropping. It's mostly maintained at a little more than comfortably warm, for the sake of the books; but now it was growing distinctly chilly. As though something were sucking all the heat out of the Library. Even the light seemed dimmer than before. Shadows slowly filled the stacks around us, until we were all standing in the only real pool of light left. Everything was still and silent, the whole Library's attention focused in one place. William's face was entirely blank now, his gaze unblinking and far away.

"I'm past the the shields," said Ammonia. Her voice was quite calm and matter-of-fact. She might have been talking about her shopping. "A lot of really nasty protections here . . . Nothing I couldn't handle. I'm inside his head now. His thoughts are a mess. His memories have been heavily interfered with; whole chunks are missing, destroyed. Quite deliberately. There are things he discovered, truths he was never meant to know, that someone didn't want him to ever be able to think about again. But there's more to it than that. Whole sections of his mind have been placed off-limits; he doesn't even know they're there. More shields, more protections . . . high walls with barbed wire on the top . . . What are you trying to hide from me, William? Or what has someone been hiding from you all these years? What's hiding inside your head?"

William's face suddenly exploded with emotion, contorting with rage and hatred and a vicious malevolence. He didn't look like William anymore. It was as though someone else were using his face for a mask, looking out through his eyes and hating everyone it saw. It glared threateningly at Ammonia, who stared calmly back at him.

"Well, well, what have I woken up? Who are you?"

"Get out! You don't belong here! You have no business being here! Get out or I'll kill you! I'll kill all of you!"

But for all the evil in that face, and the venom in the voice, William didn't move a muscle in his chair.

"That . . . doesn't sound like William," said Ioreth.

"It isn't," said Ammonia, still apparently entirely

calm. "There's someone else living inside this man's head, inside his mind, his thoughts. Not a complete person or personality, as such; more like a residue . . . left behind by whatever assaulted his mind all those years ago. Something implanted, left to grow . . . A seed! Yes, a psychic seed! Hidden so deep within him he didn't even know it was there. The seed has been infiltrating his mind slowly but surely, like a parasite. Eating him up a little at a time, replacing him with itself."

"It's the Heart," I said. My stomach was churning painfully, and my hands were clenched into fists. "It's the Heart, isn't it? I always knew it had done something awful to him."

"Yes," said Ammonia, nodding slowly. "William didn't run away from the Hall and his family; he was driven out. Sent into exile, commanded to hide himself where no one else would look, so his family would never discover what had been done to him. It made William its last-chance bolt-hole, hiding the smallest part of itself deep within this man's mind. So that if anything should ever happen to the Heart, it could grow back again. From the safety of William's mind."

"Like a witch, hiding her heart somewhere safe?" I said.

"Same principle, yes," said Ammonia. "William would have returned to the Hall at some point. He'd been programmed to do everything necessary to bring about the rebirth of the Heart. Eventually it would have burst out of him like some evil moth from its human cocoon, and your family would never have seen it coming." She looked thoughtfully at William, spitting and snarling at her from his chair. "The Heart . . . must have had some kind of premonition. Extradimensional entities often don't perceive time in our limited, linear fashion. Either that or it was warned by the traitor in your family. Still sure you don't want me to look into that?"

"Stick to William," I said. "Look, the Heart is dead. I saw it die. I killed it!"

"Not all of it," said Ammonia. "You destroyed its

physical form . . . destroyed its power over you and your family. I'm impressed. Really. But given enough time, the seed inside this man's mind would have grown into a new Heart. Probably not in William's lifetime, or yours. It would have gone on hopping from mind to mind and digging in deep, concealing itself like an invisible parasite, growing stronger with every generation. Reaching out with its increasing mental skills, influencing your family's thoughts, affecting their decisions, pushing them in the right direction . . . and they'd never even know it was happening. Until the Heart was finally ready to manifest in the material world again, and retake control of the Drood family."

"Why didn't Ethel detect this?" I said. My mouth was dry, and my voice wasn't as steady as I would have liked.

"Good question," said Ammonia. "Presumably the Heart knows how to hide itself from its own kind. Probably it intended to attack your Ethel from ambush, destroy her and take her place. A very clever plan. Might well have worked, if you hadn't called me in. But then, you never met a mind like me."

William stood up suddenly, and then kept rising up until he was levitating in midair, above his chair. He hung there unsupported, completely at ease, glaring down at Ammonia with a terrible cold malice. His face didn't look human anymore, as though what was on the other side were pushing through. Strange energies formed out of nowhere, swirling in the air in thick black blotches, spitting and crackling as they discharged on the material plane. Bits of the dark world called through to keep their master company. I started to armour up, and then stopped as I looked at Ammonia. She was staring up at the levitating man, entirely unperturbed. She seemed to know what she was doing, and this was her show, so . . . I decided to wait and see what she could do. I gestured to Ioreth not to armour up, and he nodded reluctantly.

"You're showing off now," said Ammonia. She hadn't

budged an inch. "Come down from there, and get back into that chair. Don't make me come up there and get you."

Their eyes locked. Nothing obvious happened, but the air seemed colder than ever. There was a growing tension in the Old Library. It felt like . . . there were a lot more than four people present. It felt like the four of us were standing on a great dark plain, while two massive forces clashed together, battling savagely without restraint or mercy. And then, very slowly, inch by inch, William dropped back down into his chair. The dark energies slowly dissipated, while long trails of static ran up and down the bookshelves. William was so stiff, so motionless now, he barely seemed alive. His face was flushed red with rage, his eyes glaring malignantly. His mouth was stretched wide in an almost animal snarl as the thing inside him fought for every inch of psychic ground.

"Don't be too impressed," said Ammonia. "All of that was sound and fury, preprogrammed defence routines. Just mental attack dogs. Bad dogs!"

Oily black smoke burst out of William's mouth and nostrils, forming into thick clouds and streamers in the air before us. It twisted and shuddered like some horrible black ectoplasm, taking on the shape of a vast demonic face hanging in the air between William and Ammonia. It had horns and teeth, and it wept thick black tears that fell to steam and hiss on the bare floorboards. Ammonia laughed right into the demonic face, and inhaled sharply. The face abruptly lost all shape and structure as Ammonia breathed it in, every last bit of it. When it was all gone, she smacked her lips briefly.

"Tasty . . ." said Ammonia Vom Acht.

"I can't help feeling I should be contributing something," I said.

"You are," said Ammonia. "If I look like I'm losing, kill me."

And then we all retreated a step, even Ammonia, as a brilliant light flared up before us, incandescent, blinding. And when the light fell back to a bearable level, a huge diamond shape had formed around William and his chair, encasing the Librarian completely. He was only a vague image now, inside a huge multifaceted diamond. The Heart had taken on its true form again. Nowhere near as big as it had once been, when it dominated the Sanctity in Drood Hall. When we all worshipped and adored it, because most of us didn't know any better. The diamond blazed with a fierce cold light that chilled my flesh and shuddered in my soul. My new torc tingled sharply at my throat, warning me. I moved forward, very cautiously, and rapped one shining facet with a knuckle. It felt very real, and very cold.

"It's the Heart!" I said to Ammonia. "It's back!"

"No, it isn't!" Ammonia said immediately. "This is just a memory, a projection, given shape and form by the sheer power locked within the seed. This is good, Drood! We're forcing it to use up that power, to fight us and defend itself. Manifesting in the material world like this, to defend its host from me, takes a hell of a lot of energy. It'll eat itself up . . . if we can last long enough."

"Should I armour up?" I said. "Try to smash the diamond so we can free William?"

"Don't be a fool, Drood! At this stage, an attack on the physical diamond would be an attack on the host. The seed's still a part of your Librarian. The psychic feedback would almost certainly kill him!"

"Then give me another option!" I said. "But don't take too long. We can't risk letting the Heart seize control of the family again. William would rather die than let that happen. Anything for the family."

"You Droods are always so keen to die for your precious causes," said Ammonia. "Why don't you try finding one to live for?"

The light from the diamond was pulsing fiercely now, like a heartbeat, filling the Old Library with its unnatural glare. It seemed to be growing stronger. Ioreth and I were both shielding our eyes with our arms. Ammonia narrowed her eyes, but didn't look away. She stood still, glaring into the light, bristling with her own fierce energy.

"This is a psychic attack," she said. "Not material. I can hear the seed. It's trying to talk to me, now that it knows it's been detected. It's offering me things, promising me all kinds of things, but that's a distraction. It's trying to sneak past my defences so it can invade my mind and take control of my powers. Smart little seed . . . And the really bad news is, I'm not sure I can stop it without attacking it head-on. Which could kill William. The Heart is powerful. So inhumanly powerful. I'm good, but I'm still only human; and the Heart isn't bound by human limitations."

"Neither is my armour," I said.

I subvocalised the activating Words, and my golden armour swept over me in a moment. I felt stronger, sharper and ready to rock. The diamond's fiercely glowing light was nothing to my armoured mask. Ioreth followed my lead, and another gleaming golden figure appeared in the Old Library. Ammonia actually fell back a step. It is not an easy thing to see a Drood take on his armour and his power. A great cry of rage filled the Old Library as the Heart saw Droods in armour not of its making. I stepped forward and placed a golden hand flat on the shimmering facets of the diamond, and Ioreth quickly followed suit. Even through the strange matter covering my hand, I could feel the terrible strength of the Heart, pulsing like a living thing. I reached out with my mind, trying to contact William through his torc, but the diamond blocked me. I could feel Ioreth trying, too, and together we slowly forced our way in, until we could feel William's presence inside the diamond. Ioreth and I said the activating Words together, and William said them along with us.

The Heart cried out again as golden strange matter welled out of William's torc and encased him from head to toe: a golden figure inside the shining diamond. The light flared up again, almost unbearable now even through my mask, as the Heart seed fought to hold on to its host. William fought to move, and we fought to reach him, but even linked together the three of us weren't strong enough to shatter the diamond. We were strong enough to keep the seed from jumping out of William and into Ammonia, but nowhere near strong enough to destroy it. Because in the end we were only three men in armour, and it was an other-dimensional entity from someplace we couldn't even imagine. We'd fought the seed to a standstill; but even that wouldn't last for long.

"Kill me," said Ammonia.

"What?" I said, not taking my eyes off the diamond.

"Kill me! I'm the catalyst here. My presence, my power, has activated the Heart seed. It won't give up now that it sees a superior host in me. I'd rather die while I'm still human than have this thing use me as a cocoon. I told you that you might have to do this. It's why I let you stick around. You Droods aren't the only ones who understand duty and responsibility. Now do what you have to. Without my power to draw on, the seed will go back to sleep inside your Librarian. And then you can take as many years as you need to find a way to destroy the bloody thing."

"We don't kill innocents, Ammonia," I said. "That's not the Drood way. We save people."

"We're barely holding the Heart off!" said Ioreth. "And William's weakening! What are we going to do?"

"Call for help," I said. The idea came to me quite spontaneously, but it was as though I'd always known what to do. "You said it yourself, Ammonia; we're not alone in here." I raised my voice. "I know you're here! You're always here! You protected William from the Immortal posing as Rafe! Help us protect him now! Because if you don't, there's a fate far worse than death waiting for him and all the people he cares for!"

"All right," said a calm and amused voice from out of the nearby stacks. "No need to shout. I'm here."

Suddenly, a ten-foot-tall giant white rabbit stepped out into the light to join us. It was a huge, overbearing creature, muscular rather than fat, with tall, floppy ears over a wide, intelligent face. It wore a pale blue dressing gown, elegantly styled, with the Playboy logo prominent on one lapel. It moved like a man, but with animal grace. And for all the clear intelligence, there was still a wildness to it, an almost feral charm, dangerous and untamed. It smiled at the diamond, showing sharp, pointed teeth. The tips of its long ears brushed against the ceiling as it moved forward to join us, and its presence beat on the air like a roll of thunder. Or perhaps a roll on the drums.

It wasn't hiding anymore.

It nodded easily to Ioreth and me, winked at Ammonia, and then laid one great furry white paw on top of the diamond, right over William's head. The diamond cracked, and cracked again, and the Heart seed screamed. William's mind leapt out and joined with mine and Ioreth's, and together we smashed the diamond with our golden fists, until there was nothing left but a few shimmering motes of light drifting in the air, winking out one by one.

I armoured down, and so did Ioreth and William, and we all turned to look at the giant white rabbit. It leaned easily against the nearest bookshelf, which groaned slightly under its weight, and looked us over with calm, cheerful eyes. Ammonia made a big deal of ignoring the rabbit, and leaned in close to study William's face. A single shimmering tear ran down his cheek, and Ammonia reached out to catch it on the end of one fingertip. She held the single tear up before her, studied it for a long moment and then flicked it away. It snapped out of existence and was gone.

"That's it," Ammonia said loudly. "All done. The seed has been destroyed. With its malign influence removed, this man should be able to recover most of what he's lost. In time. Another triumph for Ammonia Vom Acht!"

"Is it really gone?" I said. "I mean, all the way gone?"

"Gone, and good riddance," said Ammonia. "Bloody other-dimensional creatures, always more trouble than they're worth."

"I feel so much better," said William, and immediately collapsed back into his chair. Ammonia snorted loudly.

"Hardly surprising, carrying that bloody thing around in your head all these years. But I had a good look around inside; there's nothing in there but you now. Anything you still can't cope with is therefore very definitely your problem, not mine."

I considered Ammonia thoughtfully. "That does leave us with the problem of whatever Drood secrets you might have seen in there while you were working."

"Couldn't see a damned thing," Ammonia said briskly. "His torc protected him; only let me see what I needed to see. Your Ethel is very protective. I do have to wonder what it is she's so keen to hide from me . . . and perhaps you. Could it be she has plans of her own for the Droods, like the Heart did? I could find out for you, see exactly what it is she has on her other-dimensional mind. . . . But that would cost extra."

"We'll think about it," I said.

"If Ethel lets you think about it," Ammonia said cheerfully. "Never trust anything from Outside. And speaking of which . . ." She turned abruptly to look at the giant white rabbit now standing behind William with one fluffy white paw resting protectively on his shoulder. Ammonia glowered at the rabbit, entirely unimpressed. "What the hell are you?"

"I'm Pook," the rabbit said easily, in a deep, cultured voice. "I am that merry wanderer, travelling the world, being mischievous. I am the laughter in the woods and the lightning in the sky, and you never had a friend like me. Your Molly would know of me, Eddie Drood; many's the time we danced together in the early morning mists in the wood at the end of the world. But now I'm here. I took a liking to William when I happened to be passing through the asylum where he was staying, and I followed him here. Just because. Do not question me; I am beyond answers. Accept that I'm here, and I'm marvellous."

"It was you who protected William from the fake Rafe?" I said.

"Yes," said Pook. "That was me."

"You frightened the bastard half out of his mind."

"No one messes with my friends," said Pook.

"But . . . what are you?" said Ioreth.

"Perhaps I'm a figment of someone's imagination," said Pook. "Perhaps I'm the last survivor of the world before this one. Perhaps I'm all that remains of an old god, fallen low. And perhaps I'm just a giant white rabbit. I'm Pook, and I'm a good friend. Be grateful."

"I remember you from the asylum," William said slowly. "You kept me company. Comforted me. We had such marvellous long talks together. I'm glad you are real, after all. Why didn't I remember you till now?"

"Because it wasn't safe for you to do so," said Pook. "The seed knew me as a danger, and I wasn't strong enough to rip it out of your head on my own. I had to wait for the right time and the right kind of help. That's why I summoned Ammonia Vom Acht here."

"You didn't summon me!" Ammonia said immediately. "No one summons me anywhere!"

"I put your name into the council's heads," said Pook. "And then I persuaded you to come all the way here to help the Droods, even though you despise everything they stand for. Or perhaps I didn't. Who can tell? I am wise and wonderful and know many things, some of them true."

Ammonia glared at the rabbit, but couldn't find anything to say.

"Is that it?" said William. "Are we all done now? Is this what sanity feels like? It's been such a long time. . . . What do I do now?"

"Put the Old Library in order," said Ioreth. "You're the Librarian."

"Of course," said William. "Come along, Ioreth. Lots of work to do . . ." He got up out of his chair, and then stopped to look at the rabbit. "You will still be . . . around, won't you?"

"Of course," said Pook. "We still have so much to talk about."

"I'm going to have to discuss this with the family council," I said.

Pook inclined his great white head to me, grinning

broadly. "You really want to tell them there's a possibly imaginary giant white rabbit haunting the Old Library? Good luck with that one. Especially since I guarantee I won't be around if they come looking. I'm very choosy about whom I reveal myself to. Even Ethel can't see me, not least because I am of this world, and she isn't. Let me become a rumour, a whisper, a family legend. One final family secret, and a last line of defence."

He walked off into the Old Library and disappeared between the tall stacks with William on one side and Ioreth on the other. They all seemed very happy together. And I . . . was left alone with Ammonia Vom Acht.

"Take me to the Armourer," she said. "I want the crown we talked about. The one strong enough to keep out the whole damned world."

"You can wait here," I said. "I'll have someone bring it down to you." I considered her thoughtfully for a long moment. "You know, there is something else you might be able to help us with. . . ."

Ammonia grinned at me nastily. "The true name and identity of the traitor hiding inside your family? Oh, yes, I could find him for you. No problem. But you'd have to give me access to every living mind in Drood Hall. And your family would never allow that, even though it's clearly in your best interests, and those of all Humanity."

"You don't get to decide what's in Humanity's best interests," I told Ammonia. "Only Droods get to do that."

CHAPTER SEVEN

The One True Thing

t was all happening at Drood Hall. I was saying good-
bye to Ammonia Vom Acht when the next great
steaming pile of ordure hit the fan. Or at least, I was
trying to say good-bye. For someone who hadn't
wanted to come to Drood Hall in the first place, Ammonia was displaying a marked reluctance to leave.
She stuck both fists on her hips, stuck out her chin, tilted
her head back and did her best to glare right into my
face.

"I am not leaving here without the psychic protection
crown I was promised! I know all about you Droods;
promise me the world and everything in it to get what
you want, but the moment I've done your dirty work, it's
all, 'Thank you kindly; we'll be in touch!'"

"Let me contact the Armourer again," I said, as patiently and politely as I could manage through gritted
teeth. "See what he has to say."

I used the Merlin Glass to contact my uncle Jack in
the Armoury. His face appeared immediately, filling
the hand mirror. "Eddie! Listen . . ."

"I've still got Ammonia here," I said loudly, overrid-
ing him. "She's saying she won't leave without her crown."

"She'll have to wait," said the Armourer. "We have an emergency on our hands, Eddie, and I mean a first-class, fire-in-the-hole, circle-the-wagons-and-call-in-the-reserves type emergency. Kick her out, and get your arse down here to the War Room."

His face disappeared from the mirror, and I shut it down. I looked at Ammonia. She was opening her mouth to say something I knew I didn't want to hear it, so I shook the Merlin Glass out to full size, locked it onto her house in Cornwall, grabbed her by the scruff of the neck and tossed her through. Some days you don't have the time to be diplomatic. Ammonia spun round and glared back at me through the Glass, sputtering with rage and offended dignity.

"I want my crown!"

"We'll mail it to you when it's ready," I said.

"You can't just throw me out! I know things you need to know!"

"Thank you," I said quickly. "Good-bye; write if you get work."

"We'll meet again! I've seen it!"

"Don't you threaten me," I said, and shut down the Merlin Glass.

I never like working with psychics. The trouble with telepaths is that they always want to tell you what's going on in other people's minds, and it's nearly always things you're better off not knowing. I certainly wouldn't want anyone else knowing what was going on in my mind most of the time. Especially if it involved Helen Mirren in her prime. I looked at the Glass and frowned. Why did the Armourer want me to join him in the War Room? He never went there. In fact, I was a bit surprised he was able to find it without a sat nav. Must be a real emergency, after all. I opened up the Merlin Glass and stepped through into the Drood family War Room.

All hell seemed to have broken loose, accompanied by every manner of siren, alarm, ringing bells and flashing lights. People were running back and forth like someone had just announced the Second Coming and we'd forgotten to book our seats. Men and women at their workstations were yelling into comm mikes, or bent over their computers, and none of them looked at all happy at the answers they were getting. I spotted the Armourer, turning dazedly from one display screen to another and looking very out of place in his stained lab coat. I put the Glass away and moved over to tap him firmly on the shoulder. He almost jumped out of his skin, and when he turned to face me he looked drawn and tired, even shocked, like someone had hit him.

"What's happened, Uncle Jack?" I said. "What's the big emergency? And why didn't you tell me something bad was happening until it got this out of control?"

"If I took the time to tell you everything I know that you don't, we'd never get anything done," snapped the Armourer, regaining some of his composure. "This is bad, Eddie, really bad. Very nasty, all-hands-to-the-pump kind of bad. The Satanist conspiracy has made its first moves. One indirect but troubling, and one very direct and downright scary."

"Never a moment's peace," I said resignedly. "And the pay's lousy. I'll bet the Satanists offer their people really wicked fringe benefits."

"Will you listen, Eddie! We've lost an entire town! The whole population's . . . gone!"

"You have my undivided attention," I said. "How can the Satanists have taken out an entire town?"

The Armourer shook his head slowly, seemingly lost for words. Which wasn't like him. "The family psychics all went crazy some twenty minutes ago. All of them saying Something Bad had happened. And then the details started coming in. . . . Hold on. Hold on a minute while I check something."

And he was off, moving swiftly along the workstations, his gaze jumping from one monitor screen to another. I took the time to look around me. The War Room had never seemed this busy, not even when we were fighting the Loathly Ones in their nests during the Hungry Gods War.

The family War Room is a vast auditorium carved

out of the solid stone under the north wing of Drood Hall. Normally you have to pass through a heavily reinforced steel door, a retina scan and a very thorough frisking before you're even allowed to descend the old stone stairs that lead down to the vault. Which are in turn guarded by a whole bunch of cloned goblins noted for their utterly vile natures and a complete lack in the sense-of-humour department. The Merlin Glass had allowed me to bypass all that nonsense, which is one of the reasons the rest of the family keeps trying to take it away from me. They think it makes me too powerful. They are, of course, absolutely right. Which is one of the reasons I have no intention of ever giving it up.

All four walls of the War Room, tall and broad as they are, are covered with state-of-the-art display screens showing every country in the world, including a few that aren't supposed to exist, but unfortunately do. All of them dotted with variously coloured lights to indicate trouble spots, ongoing missions, certain individuals on the family's "of interest" list, and the current locations of every Drood field agent, active or not. The War Room was currently packed to bursting with family members of every rank and station, crowding round the workstations, darting back and forth with urgent messages, and shouting at one another with a complete lack of professional calm and composure. Much of the activity and commotion seemed to be gathered around the communication systems and the far-seeing stations. The family has raised remote viewing to something of an art form, using every kind of high tech and old magic the Armourer and his staff could come up with; but I'd never seen it reduce the War Room to such sheer chaos before. A chill ran down my spine. To panic the family this thoroughly, the emergency had to be something really special.

As I looked around I realised the Armourer wasn't the only familiar face in the War Room. Cousin Harry was there, bent over a comm screen and peering intently through his wire-rimmed spectacles. He was discussing the situation with the Sarjeant-at-Arms, who was only half listening as he leafed through a thick handful of urgent memos, more of which were constantly being handed him by hurrying messengers. Both of them were so focussed on the situation they'd apparently forgotten how much they hated having to work together. And the head of the War Room, Callan Drood, stood at the conference table, reading through one important report after another and barking out a series of orders. And yet for all the deafening noise and hurried motion, there was a sense that things were being done. The family trained hard for emergencies, so that everyone would know what to do when the time came. Except me. I still hadn't a clue what I was doing there. And then Molly emerged from the crowd and hurried over to join me. She gave me a quick hug to show all was forgiven, if not actually forgotten, and then she stepped back to look at me with real concern in her face.

"Tell me later," she said. "Tell me everything later. Because you need to concentrate on what's happening right now."

"What is happening?" I said plaintively. "Why is everyone running around like their backsides are on fire?"

"The Satanist conspirators have launched their campaign," said Molly. "Come with me; I'll get you to Callan, and he can bring you up-to-date."

She took me by the arm and led me to the conference table by the quickest route, which basically involved intimidating everyone else into getting out of our way. Molly's always been very good at that. Callan looked up as I arrived and actually seemed glad to see me. Which wasn't like him. He gestured sharply for his people to stand back and give us some room, and beckoned for me to stand next to him, so we wouldn't have to shout to be heard over the general bedlam.

"It all started half an hour ago," he said flatly. "Came out of bloody nowhere. The comm stations began picking up television broadcasts from every country in the world. Government leaders, individual leaders, religious leaders . . . all preempting television time to make a special announcement. Often during prime time, which doesn't come cheap. You can look at the recordings later, if you want, but they're all singing the same tune: all of them talking a lot, but not actually saying much. Talking about the great future that's coming for everyone, and not the usual pie-in-the-sky stuff. They're talking about good times for all by the end of this year . . . as a direct result of the Great Sacrifice that the people of every country are going to make. No details as yet, not even a hint as to who or what is going to have to be sacrificed. Perhaps the conspiracy hasn't told the leaders yet.

"Anyway, all the speeches sounded remarkably similar, once we'd translated them from the original languages. Almost as though they'd been written by the same person. And for all we know, they were. . . . You have to understand, Eddie; this is unprecedented. This kind of agreement and cooperation, from every country in the world, regardless of politics or religion . . . simply doesn't happen. Even we couldn't arrange something like this without years of planning, a hell of a budget and a whole lot of assassination threats. . . . It's hard to believe the conspiracy could have this much influence over so many important people. . . . Hell, we didn't even know the conspiracy existed this time last year. All right, we've been a bit busy, what with the Hungry Gods and the bloody Immortals, but even so . . . Could these bastards really have this much *control* over so many different kinds of government? I'd like to think most of them don't actually know who and what they're dealing with, but these are politicians we're talking about, after all. . . . I have to wonder if it would make any difference if they did. . . . You should never have let them out from under our control, Eddie! The world was a lot safer when we still had our boot on their necks!"

"Except for when we didn't," I said. "Two world wars and an endless cold war; I don't call that being in control. I have to believe that some good will come from giving Humanity their freedom. Or what's the point of going on?"

"No one was at all clear about what this Great Sacrifice might involve," said Molly, tactfully easing us onto a new subject. "Either their leaders think their people aren't ready to be told yet, or their new lords and masters haven't told them yet."

"When we lost control of the world's politicians, it was inevitable that someone would move in to take our place," murmured Harry, casually joining us at the conference table. "So you could say this is all your fault, Eddie."

"That's what you say, Harry," I said. "But then, that's what you always say, isn't it? Learn a new tune; that one's getting old. Now, I can see this is all distinctly worrying, but why was I called here in such a rush? What's the emergency?"

"I'm sure we could have coped without your help," said Harry. "But . . . something else has happened. It would appear that a small country town in the southwest of England has been attacked by the Satanist conspiracy."

"It could be the first part of their Great Sacrifice," said Callan. "The news isn't officially out yet. British authorities have slapped a D Notice on the whole affair. On the grounds of national security. Though God knows how long that will last in this electronic day and age . . ."

"But what's happened, exactly?" I said. "What have the Satanists done?"

"The town of Little Stoke has vanished," said Harry. "The whole population is just . . . gone."

"It all happened so quickly," said Molly. "I was killing some time down here, waiting for you. . . ."

"And pestering the life out of me," said Callan.

"Shut up, Callan," said Molly. "It must have happened pretty much instantaneously. Not a word of warning or a cry for help. There was this . . . massive energy surge that set off every alarm in the War Room, and by the time we'd zeroed in on the exact location, it was all over. There have been no communications in or out of where Little Stoke used to be, ever since."

"We knew about it before the authorities," said Harry. "But then, we're Droods. We know everything. That's our job."

"Don't you have a job you should be doing?" Callan said pointedly. "This is my War Room; I'll do the briefings. Make yourself useful. Get me some tea. Milk, two sugars."

Harry drifted away from the conference table as though he'd remembered somewhere he'd meant to be. Callan glared after him.

"And some Jaffa Cakes!" He sniffed loudly and turned his attention back to me. "Irritating little tit. Thinks he's such a big deal because his dad was your uncle James. I could put together a brigade of the Grey Fox's various bastards. . . . Anyway, as soon as we were sure something bad really had happened, we hacked into a CIA satellite orbiting over the area, and this is what we got. . . ."

He pushed his way through a crowd of messengers shifting impatiently from foot to foot with important-looking messages in their hands, opening up a path by sheer angry presence, and stopped before one particular display screen locked onto a set of coordinates in southwest England. Callan gestured angrily at the screen.

"See that black spot, that circle of impenetrable darkness exactly five miles in diameter . . . ? That's where the small town of Little Stoke used to be. No light gets in or out, no communications in or out. Just . . . that."

"What is it?" I said. "Oh, hell, it's not a black hole, is it?"

"Of course it's not a black hole!" snapped Callan. "Or the sheer gravitational pull would have sucked the whole country in by now. Am I the only one who paid attention during science lessons?"

"Probably," I said. "You always were a science geek."

"Science geeks are in!" Callan said defiantly. "Look at all those CSI television shows. Geek chic!"

"Boys, boys," murmured Molly. "If we could concentrate on the matter at hand . . ."

"Ah . . . yes," said Callan. "Little Stoke. Population under eight thousand. Nothing important or significant about any of them, as far as we can tell. Even the local history is particularly dull. But after the energy surge that caught our attention, and before the darkness set in . . . the entire population of Little Stoke vanished. Eight thousand men, women and children . . . all gone in a moment. The town buildings are still there, under the darkness. Don't ask me how."

"Look at the location," I said. "Little Stoke is only up the road from the far more important and significant town of Bradford-on-Avon. Could the Satanists have been after that, and . . . missed?"

"I don't think so," said Callan. "Even they wouldn't have the stones to attack that town. Not given who lives there."

"I've been there," Molly said brightly. "They do a lovely cream tea. . . ."

"Really?" said Callan. "How very nice. Now shut up; grown-ups are talking. No, Eddie, Little Stoke was quite definitely the target. The black circle covers the town's boundaries exactly. What lies there now . . . is a little bit of Hell on Earth."

I gave him a hard look. "How can you be so sure about what's going on underneath all that darkness?"

Callan gave me a pitying look. "We're not dependent on other people's spy satellites; we've got the best far-seers in the business working right here in this room. They've been keeping an eye on everything that's happened through their scrying pools and crystal balls. Come with me."

He led Molly and me into the heart of the communications section. A harried-looking young man stood in Callan's way and refused to move.

"We've been monitoring world communications for mentions of what's happened in Little Stoke," he said urgently. "And after the first flurry of rumours it's all gone very quiet. No one's talking about it, because word's come down from on high that they're not to talk about it. And there's no sign at all that the British authorities are intending to do anything."

"Well, that's why we're here," I said. "Keep listening."

We moved on, into the far-seeing section. The Armourer was there, building something complicated from the disassembled scraps of several important-looking machines. He nodded brusquely to us, intent on his work.

"They say modern technology won't mix with traditional magics. I say they will, if you bang them together hard enough. Give me time, and I'll give you something that will show you everything that's happening inside that darkness. In high definition, with surround sound."

Callan ignored him, peering over the shoulder of a fey young woman who was staring intently into her scrying pool, or magic mirror: an impossibly flat extrusion of compressed silver ectoplasm spread out on the bench before her. Images came and went in the pool too quickly for me to follow.

"You need the gift to be able to See the world through a magic mirror," said Callan. "I specialised in far-seeing before I became a field agent. . . . Still got my crystal ball somewhere . . . Ah. Yes! There . . . Focus, Amelia, focus. . . ."

He squeezed the shoulder of the far-seer, adding his strength to hers, and they both concentrated. Just like that, I could See what they Saw in the scrying pool. A street, a perfectly normal small-town street. The buildings were all intact, though there were no people anywhere. But there was something subtly *wrong* about the image. It took me a moment to realise that the scene was too still, too sharp, too perfect.

"This is a cover image," said Callan. "Meant to deflect anyone who did get a look in. It's not safe to look underneath, not yet. We found that out the hard way. All the people are quite definitely gone . . . snatched away in a moment, kidnapped by unknown forces. But more than that, the whole area inside the town has been ... changed. Horribly altered. Outside the five-mile radius of the dark circle, everything remains normal, as it should be. The world goes on, untouched, unaffected. But inside Little Stoke ... We've had to put in a whole series of filters and safeguards to protect the far-seers. When they first broke through the circle and got a good look at what was happening, we lost nine good men and women almost immediately. They went mad from what they saw. But ... I think we're ready to try again, yes?"

The young woman, Amelia, nodded stiffly. The Armourer looked up sharply.

"I wouldn't, Callan! Wait till I'm finished here, and I can give you some real protection. . . ."

"We don't have time!" snapped Callan. "Go for it, Amelia."

He beckoned forward a dozen other far-seers who'd been waiting nearby, and they all crowded in around Amelia. Linked together, that many far-seers should be able to See through anything. We've always had the best remote viewers in the world. The problem's been to keep them out of the bedrooms of the rich and famous. They leaned in together, shoulder-to-shoulder, peering intently into the scrying pool. And then Amelia's head exploded. Her skull shattered, blown outwards as though someone had buried a grenade inside her brain. Bone fragments and spatters of pink and grey meat shot across the scrying pool, and her headless body slumped forward, spouting blood in thick jets. Two more far-seers screamed shrilly as their eyes exploded, splashing the others with thick, viscous, bloody fluids. Another far-seer reached up and tore his own eyes out so he wouldn't have to See what he was Seeing. Two more spontaneously combusted, burning fiercely with thick yellow sulphurous flames. They didn't move; just stood where they were, burning right down to the bone. Another far-seer started laughing and couldn't stop.

"Shut down the far-seers!" shouted the Sarjeant-at-Arms, running forward. "I told you to shut down the whole section!"

"Armour up!" Ethel's voice said suddenly, out of no-where. "Everyone armour up! My strange matter will protect you!"

We all put our armour on, and the whole War Room was full of gleaming golden figures. The golden man who had been the Sarjeant-at-Arms moved forward, pushing others out of his way, and smashed the scrying pool with one armoured fist. The silver ectoplasm lost coherence immediately and ran away down the legs of the workstation. We all waited a moment, but nothing else happened. The Sarjeant grabbed up a fire extin-guisher and put out the two burning far-seers. Their charred and blackened bodies just stood there. Callan gestured for some of his people to come and take them away and escort the surviving far-seers out of the War Room to the nearest hospital ward. The Sarjeant-at-Arms glared around him.

"All right, everyone armour down! The danger's over. But stay cautious! Callan, you and Eddie stay in your armour, with me. You're always boasting about your old scrying skills, Callan; use that magic mirror on the next bench, and See what you can See."

Callan nodded stiffly, and then glanced at Molly. "You'd better stay back. You won't have armour to pro-tect you."

"Please," said Molly. "Remember whom you're talk-ing to."

"Ah. Yes . . . quite," said Callan. "On your own head be it." He nodded to the Sarjeant and me. "Let's do this."

He moved over to the next bench, still covered with its shimmering screen. The Sarjeant and I moved in on either side of him, and Molly leaned in. At first all I could see was a dark bloodred light, shining from some new and terrible kind of sun. The town buildings stood as they always had, but the air in the streets shook and trembled like some unearthly heat wave. There were great cracks and rents the whole length of the road, as though earthquakes had torn through the underlying strata. As I watched, some of the rents slammed back together again, and then reappeared, like doors opening and closing. Waiting for something to come through them. And there was something *wrong* about the buildings. In slow and subtle ways they seemed to slump, to seep, to fall in on themselves, as though they couldn't quite be bothered to keep up the facade of normality. Some of the shop signs were misspelt, or garbled, or just plain gibberish. Or perhaps words from unknown languages. Doors and windows were set in the wrong places, or in the wrong proportions, or tilted at crazy angles. As though the madness in this place were infecting the very structure of the buildings.

"Have you ever seen anything like this?" I said quietly to Molly.

"Not on this earth," she said.

I looked to Callan, and he shrugged uneasily. "We're getting some information as to what's happening inside the dark circle, but there's no telling how dependable the readings are. . . . The very building blocks of reality have been compromised. No linear time, no cause and effect, everything changing for no purpose, from moment to moment. . . ."

"The Satanists have blown apart the very rules that hold everything together," said Molly. "Dropped a whole town into chaos. That's some bomb. . . ."

"We can't be sure they're behind this," said Callan. "Not yet. More important, we haven't a clue how they did this. That's why I called in the Armourer."

He looked hopefully at my uncle Jack, but the Armourer shrugged without looking up from whatever he was working on.

"Would even Drood armour be enough to protect me in such an environment?" I asked him.

Molly looked at me sharply. "You're not thinking of going in there, are you?"

"There could be survivors," I said. "People trapped in there. What do you think, Ethel? It's your armour."

"I don't know!" Ethel's voice sounded definitely troubled, issuing from somewhere above us. "It ought to, but this is all new to me. I can't see inside the dark circle, but from what you're seeing . . . I've never encountered such extreme conditions before; and I've been around. But I designed your armour to survive whatever your reality could throw at it. And since strange matter comes from my domain, not yours . . . Roll the dice, and see what happens! I can't wait to find out!"

"Sometimes her endless enthusiasm can get a bit creepy," murmured Molly.

"I heard that!"

"Somebody's got to go in there," said the Sarjeant-at-Arms, moving forward to glare at the images on the screen. "We have to figure out how this was done, before the conspiracy does it somewhere else. Next time they might go for a city. And yes, Edwin, we do need to check for possible survivors as well."

"You're all heart, Cedric," I said.

"But . . . why pick a nowhere place like Little Stoke?" said Callan.

"To test their new weapon," said the Armourer, looking up from doing something unnatural with a bunch of silicon chips and some mistletoe.

"Then why remove the people before they unleash the weapon?" said Molly.

"Maybe they want them for test subjects for other weapons," said the Sarjeant.

"I don't like the way we're playing catch-up with the conspiracy," I said. "Always one step behind. I say we storm Lightbringer House in force, use every field agent available. Smash through their defences, grab everyone there and ask them a whole bunch of really pointed questions."

"Way ahead of you, as always." The Sarjeant-at-Arms sniffed. "We sent our people in while you and the Armourer were off playing tourist at the Supernatural Arms Faire. But the Satanist conspiracy people were all long gone. Their files with them. And no, they didn't leave a forwarding address. They stripped the place clean and vanished into the undergrowth the moment you and the Metcalf sisters left the premises. Some of our best people are currently tearing the whole building apart, in case they missed something, but right now there's no sign anyone was ever there."

"Hold it," I said. "No booby traps?"

"They left in a really big hurry," said the Sarjeant.

"Something must have frightened them," Molly said artlessly. "But then, Iz and I always did believe in making an impression."

"I'm surprised they didn't leave skid marks," I said solemnly.

"Try to be serious, Edwin," said the Sarjeant. "This is a serious situation."

"I know," I said. "Someone has to go into Little Stoke and see if anyone survived."

"Of course," said the Sarjeant. "I'm sure survivors could provide us with valuable information as to what happened."

"No," I said flatly. "We go in and rescue them, because that's what Droods do. We exist to stand between the innocents and the horrors of the hidden world."

"Ah, Eddie," said Harry, drifting over to join us. "Always intent on the small things, and missing out on the big picture. Anyone who got left behind in that town wouldn't survive long under those conditions. It's already too late for them. Which means we need to concentrate all our resources on working out how this appalling attack was orchestrated. Here's your tea, Callan. They were all out of Jaffa Cakes."

Callan accepted his tea with bad grace and sipped at it suspiciously before grudgingly nodding approval. "Always said you'd make a good tea boy, Harry." And then he looked round sharply as a far-seer farther down the row called out to him urgently. We all hurried down to join the young man at his station, and he goggled for a moment, overwhelmed at having so many important members of the family all staring at him at once. But give the man credit; he recovered quickly and nodded jerkily at the monitor screen before him.

"Virgil Drood, at your service. Don't blame the messenger. I picked this up off the feed we're intercepting from the CIA satellite. What you're looking at is a hill outside the dark circle. Conditions there are completely unaffected by . . . whatever's happened in the town. It seems we have observers, just teleported in. Ten men, three women, some of them . . . familiar faces."

We all crowded in around him, studying the screen. Thirteen people were standing on top of a grassy green hill overlooking what had been Little Stoke, chatting cheerfully among themselves. It was only a visual image—no sound. One of the men was Alexandre Dusk, leader of the Lightbringer House Satanists. And standing right next to him was Roger Morningstar, son of the legendary James Drood and a lust demon out of Hell. The half-breed hellspawn who fought alongside the Droods because he'd fallen in love with one of us. And now there he was, standing quite chummily with Dusk, nodding and smiling as they looked down on the dark circle below. They both seemed quite pleased with what they'd done. Harry turned to Callan.

"We need sound. We need to hear what they're saying."

"I'm sorry," said Virgil. "We're lucky to have visual under these conditions. Getting sound is going to take some time."

"Then get a lip-reader in here! We must have one somewhere. We need to know what they're saying!"

Alexandre Dusk looked round suddenly, and seemed to stare right out of the screen at us. I don't think he could See us, but he knew someone could See him. He smiled a wintry smile, snapped his fingers, and the image disappeared from the screen. Virgil worked his controls fiercely and then sat heavily back in his chair with frustration.

"We've lost the feed."

"Then get it back!" said Harry.

"You don't understand! The feed is gone because the satellite is gone. It isn't there anymore. Something blasted it right out of orbit. And according to my readings, the observers are gone, too. I suppose it's too much to hope that they might have blown up, too."

He tried an uncertain smile on us, but none of us was in the mood for even the slightest of jokes. We all looked at one another, and then we looked at Harry, who'd moved away a little to be on his own. He was rubbing his chin with jerky, shocked movements, thinking hard.

"I didn't even know Roger had left the Hall," he said almost plaintively. "He didn't tell me he was going anywhere. Ethel, when did Roger Morningstar leave Drood Hall?"

"Right after the last council meeting, when you were all together," said Ethel. "He left on his own, through a dimensional door he created on the grounds."

"Didn't you ask him where he was going?" said Harry.

"Not my place," said Ethel. "You people do so value your privacy, even if I still don't understand why."

"Once a hellspawn, always a hellspawn," the Sarjeant-at-Arms said heavily. "I did warn you, Harry. Everyone warned you. Never trust a hellspawn."

"Roger's been . . . different ever since he returned from Hell," said Harry. "The trip you insisted he go on! Maybe they did something to him there. . . ."

"The question is," said the Sarjeant, talking right over Harry as he addressed the rest of us, "how long has the hellspawn been working against us? How long has he been conspiring with our enemies, passing on secret information, including details of our missions?"

"No need to rub it in, Sarjeant," I said.

"He was present at council meetings!" said the Sarjeant. "Because of you, Harry! Think of all the things he knows about this family! I'll have to reset all the security measures, change all the codes and passwords, beef up our defences . . . and recheck every piece of information acquired from every mission he was involved with!"

"He fought alongside us against the Hungry Gods, and the Accelerated Men, and the Immortals!" said

Harry. "He risked his life to fight in our cause, because of me! There must be a reason for this. . . . I have to go to Little Stoke."

And then he stopped and couldn't say any more. His face had gone pale and sweaty, and his hands were shaking. I knew why. We all did. He was remembering his time in the ghoulvilles, towns taken over by the Loathly Ones and removed into a separate reality. Terrible places. Sanity destroying. Soul destroying. We all knew Harry had been affected by what he'd seen there, what he'd had to do there. None of us said anything. A lot of Droods came back spiritually wounded from fighting in the ghoulvilles. Those who did come back.

"Roger's not there anymore," I said, carefully. "You heard Virgil; he and the others teleported out."

"I have to know," said Harry. "I have to be sure. I need to talk to him. . . ."

"Of course you do," I said. "But there'll be another time. I have to go into Little Stoke. You have to stay here. You're needed in the War Room to help Callan and the Armourer work out how this was done. And there's always the chance Roger might return here to the Hall. You need to be here for that."

"Why would Roger come back?" said Callan, to show he was keeping up with the rest of us.

"Because Dusk doesn't know who was watching him on the hilltop," said the Sarjeant. "The hellspawn doesn't know that we know he's a traitor."

"We don't know that!" said Harry. "And Roger would know who was watching him. He's always been very . . . gifted. He won't come back here because he'd know I'd be waiting for him. I wouldn't shoot him on sight, and I wouldn't let anyone else do it. I'd want to talk to him. Hear his side. But if he really has joined the conspiracy . . . he hasn't betrayed just me; he's betrayed my family. His family, as much as mine."

"No one would expect you to go up against Roger," I said.

"I would," said Harry. "If he has turned traitor . . . I will kill him. Anything for the family."

Hell hath no fury like a lover scorned, I thought, but had enough sense not to say out loud.

"I'm going to Little Stoke," I said. Because it needed doing, and because I knew a trip into that disturbed place would destroy Harry. So, tired as I was after the arms fair and Ammonia Vom Acht, it was all down to me. Again.

"You are not going in on your own," Molly said firmly. "I'm going with you."

"Not a good idea . . ." I said carefully.

"You never take me anywhere," Molly said cheerfully. "You wouldn't last ten minutes in that place without me to watch your back, and you know it."

"We do have other field agents in the family," said the Sarjeant. "You don't have to do this, Edwin."

"I'm the only field agent who's right here, right now, with experience operating inside ghoulvilles," I said. "Who else is there?"

The Sarjeant-at-Arms looked at Callan, who shrugged uncomfortably. "We have five field agents currently operating in England, but none of them could get back to the Hall inside three or four hours."

"And even then, you'd still have to wait for the Armourer to find a way into the dark circle," I said. "Whereas I . . . have the Merlin Glass."

"Hold hard," said the Armourer, looking up from his work. "There's always the chance that if you use the Glass to open a door between here and there, what's inside the town might burst through into Drood Hall!"

"I would never let that happen," said Ethel, a touch haughtily. "I guarantee the integrity of Drood Hall against any and all threats. Trust me. I'm a doctor."

"I still think you should rest, Eddie," said the Armourer. "Let me design something to protect you, give you an edge. . . ."

"There isn't time, Uncle Jack," I said. "We have to sort this mess out before it starts spreading."

"You're right," said the Armourer. "Get us all the information you can. And, Molly, don't let him do anything too dumb in there."

"Damn right," said Molly.

"I don't have anything useful to offer you," said the Armourer. "And this bloody thing is taking a lot longer than I thought it would. . . . Remember your armour is equipped to study your surroundings and record everything it encounters. Knowledge can be ammunition in a situation like this. So bring back as much data as you can."

I looked at him for a moment. "Do you have anything, any weapon that could do what the Satanists did in Little Stoke?"

"No," said the Armourer. "Not a damned thing. Not even in the Armageddon Codex. What has been done in that town is a crime against reality itself."

"How long before you could come up with some kind of defence?" said the Sarjeant.

"Depends on what kind of information Eddie brings back," said the Armourer. "So let's stop wasting his time with unnecessary chatter. Eddie, go."

"Got it, Uncle Jack," I said. But I still hesitated and looked at Molly. "You've seen what's happening in the town. There's no guarantee that Drood armour will be enough to protect me. And you don't even have that."

"I have been to Heaven and Hell and Limbo," said Molly. "And a whole bunch of other really extreme places not even dreamt of in your limited philosophies. I can survive this."

"Of course you can," I said. "I'd bet on you against the whole damned universe."

"You say the sweetest things sometimes," said Molly.

I activated the Merlin Glass and opened up a doorway into what remained of Little Stoke, while everyone else retreated to what they hoped was a safe distance. A lot of people hid behind things. Like that would make any difference. A series of violent images swept across the full-size Glass, flashing by so fast I couldn't keep up with them. Stars and flames and blindingly bright lights; dark, monstrous shapes rearing up to look in my direction; the whole physical world grown hideously soft and leprous; all of it under a sky the colour of dried blood. I looked away for a moment, to rest my eyes, and found Harry hadn't retreated with the others.

"You don't have to do this, Eddie."

"Yes, I do, Harry," I said. "It's the job."

He nodded briefly. I turned to Molly, who was peering into the Merlin Glass, fascinated.

"You ready, girl?"

"I came out of the womb ready."

"I can believe that. Probably demanding a stiff drink and a harsh word with the midwife. Let's do this, before one of us gets a rush of common sense to the head."

"When has that ever happened?"

We laughed briefly, I armoured up and we both stepped through the Merlin Glass. Out of the sane and sensible world into a place where reality had been broken. With malice aforethought, the bastards.

Stepping into what was left of Little Stoke was like being clubbed around the head with a baseball bat soaked in LSD. Everything was wrong, different, corrupted . . . and constantly changing. The ground surged and rocked under my feet, rising and falling like a ship at sea. I glared about me, but it was hard to see anything clearly through the disturbed air. My armour was doing its best to protect and insulate me from my surroundings, swiftly adapting to cope with this new, ever-changing world. I could actually feel my armour straining as it thickened and improved itself, moment by moment. My second skin was under constant assault from a world that hated it.

Gravity came and went, fluctuating wildly, so that I felt light as air one moment, and as though I had a mountain on my back the next. Nothing was constant or dependable. Except my armour. It pushed back at the world, refusing to be affected or altered in any part, and I stood straight and tall under a bloody sky, safe and solid and untouched by anything Little Stoke could throw at me.

I looked around for Molly and found she was standing right beside me, but now floating quite happily in midair. She stood on nothing, defying the uncertain ground, surrounded by a shimmering field of unnatural forces. She looked down at me and I nodded briefly. She gave me a thumbs-up, and I went back to studying the surroundings. It was hard to get a hold on anything. Whichever way I looked, nothing made sense. Directions seemed to snap back and forth, so that left and right changed places or swirled around, and even up and down weren't always where I thought they should be. Little Stoke did remind me of a ghoulville, as I'd expected; but this town was worse, much worse. Someone had studied ghoulvilles, and learned from them, improved on them. The sheer psychic pressure of not being able to depend on anything was almost overwhelming. All I could feel was loss, and horror, and growing hysteria. My sanity was taking a real beating. Part of me wanted to fall to the ground, curl up in a foetal ball and pray for it all to go away. But I couldn't do that. I was a Drood, and I had a job to do.

I looked up. "Molly, is this Hell?"

"Not even close," she said flatly. "Hell is worse. This is chaos. Hell has purpose."

"You'd know," I said. "Hello, War Room? Hello? Callan? Edith? Can anyone hear me? Anyone?"

"Well?" said Molly, after a moment.

"Apparently not," I said. "I'm reaching out through my armour, but no one's answering. We're on our own, Molly."

"Best way," she said briskly. "We know what we're doing."

"Since when?"

"Hush, lover; think positive. Okay, this is a seriously nasty place. I'm not sure we're even on Earth anymore."

"Technically, I suppose we're not," I said. "Local conditions have been . . . rewritten."

"I'm not picking up any traces of major magical workings," said Molly. "You couldn't do something this big without leaving serious handprints all over everything."

I remembered the Armourer's advice, and had my

armour probe and investigate my immediate surroundings. I concentrated in a certain way, and the armour's findings appeared on the inside of my mask, floating before my eyes. All kinds of readings and graphs and scales, half of which meant nothing to me. My uncle Jack is the scientist. It's all I can do to program my TiVo. But . . .

"No radiation," I said to Molly. "No toxins, none of the usual dangerous energies . . . Everything else . . . doesn't make sense. I've never encountered anything quite like this."

"Your armour is smoking," said Molly.

"What?"

"Smoking! There's steam or something boiling right off your armour. Is everything all right inside there?"

I felt fine. I felt great. I felt sharp and strong and totally alive, as I always did when wearing my armour. It was all that was keeping me sane. I looked down at myself, and sure enough thick curls of smoke were rising up off my golden torso and arms.

"I think my armour is reacting to the new environment," I said to Molly. "Or possibly . . . the other way round. The town is trying to break through my armour to get to me, and my armour is fighting it off. You could say there's a war going on between the stability of the strange matter and the changing conditions of the town. And so far, my armour is kicking the town's arse. I think strange matter is too weird even for here. I think . . . reality here is breaking up on contact with my armour. How cool is that? The one true thing in this crazy new world. Though how long it will last is anybody's guess. I say we get this job done as quickly as possible, and then get the hell out of here."

"Best idea you've had so far," said Molly.

I looked up at her. "Are you okay inside that spangly bubble of yours?"

"This is a spiritual force shield," Molly said firmly. "I am maintaining Earth-normal conditions around me by sheer effort of will. Anyone else would have the sense to be impressed."

"Sorry," I said. "I don't do impressed."

"I know. It's one of your better qualities."

"How long can you maintain that bubble?"

"I think we should get moving. Right now."

But still, something held me in place as I looked around me. "Why did the Satanists do this? What's the point?"

"A demonstration, probably," said Molly. "A show of power. 'Look what we can do. We can smash reality. Break all the rules and let chaos thrive. Better not stand against us, or else . . .' Standard Satanist bullying. This is as much a psychological weapon as anything else. They're saying, 'We can destroy everything you believe in and depend on.'"

I had my armour scan the town for life signs, for any traces of human survivors, but my armour's sensors were overloaded and confused by the weird conditions. I was picking up life signs all over the place, but none of them made any sense. I said as much to Molly, and she nodded thoughtfully, concentrating. She pointed in one direction, hesitated, and then pointed in another.

"People. Definitely people. Unaffected, unharmed. I can See them in a safe place, shining like diamonds in the dark. Maybe . . . fifty of them. They're protected by something I can't quite get a handle on. I think perhaps they were overlooked, or left behind. . . ."

"Fifty people?" I said. "Out of a town of some eight thousand? Left behind, abandoned, trapped in this horror . . ." I could feel the anger building within me, cold and raging. "I will not stand for this. I won't see innocent people treated like this! Lead the way, Molly. We are going to find these people, get them out of this bloody mess and take them home. . . . And when I find the bastards who did this to them, I will put the fear of God and Droods into them!"

Molly smiled fondly at me. "I think that's what I like

best about you, Eddie. You always get really angry about the right things."

I nodded. I was too angry to speak.

Molly headed deeper into what remained of the small country town of Little Stoke. She strode along, her feet hammering on the disturbed air like the drumbeats of an approaching army. I followed her, trusting to her witchy Sight to guide us, even though every direction felt the same to me. It was hard to make progress in a place where streets had no beginning and no ending, as though the world moved under our feet and we stayed put. We walked down one street several times before we realised what was happening: that its far end was attached to its beginning, like an endless Möbius strip. I lost my patience and my temper and applied a lateral thinking solution to the problem by turning abruptly sideways and smashing my way through one of the buildings. Bricks broke and shattered stickily under my hammering golden fists, some of them cracking into moist fragments, like exploded fruit. I broke through the wall and strode through the house, bludgeoning my way through room after room, rubble raining down on my armoured shoulders, until finally I burst out the other side and into a new street. Molly followed close behind me. We set off down the street, one that had sense enough not to piss me off, and Molly quickly picked up the trail again.

I couldn't trust anything I saw, even through all the filters and protections built into my golden mask. Not everything I saw was actually there, or acted the way it should act, and things became other things became things I had no name for. I kept slogging doggedly on after Molly, trusting her to guide me through the ever-shifting chaos, kept on slamming my heavy feet down, forcing my way through anything the town could send at me, fuelled by willpower and a stubborn refusal to be beaten. There were people depending on me.

Often it seemed to me that Molly was changing direction again and again, choosing ways that made no sense at all, going up and down and back and forth and not getting anywhere. But I trusted her, and I didn't trust the world, so I kept going.

My armour was still smoking and steaming as the rotten world fought to get through the strange matter and get at me.

Cars parked in the street were now strangely alive: no longer metal, but made up of meat and bone and cartilage. Ghastly red striations of muscle all along their length, with eyes instead of lights and snapping fanged mouths where radiator grilles should have been. The tyres were pink and sweaty, like internal organs pushed out into the light. The cars made sounds like children crying as they lurched up and down the streets, attacking one another, tearing and rending, their glistening hides oozing sweat and blood and musk. One of the cars came right at us, howling like some jungle creature, and I stood my ground and let it crash into me. For all its speed and weight it slammed to a halt immediately, its fleshy hood crumpled against my armour, torn meat leaking blood and pus. It backed away, crying miserably, hawking up blood, and every other car fell on it and ate it alive. Molly and I kept going and didn't look back.

Time couldn't be trusted in this broken place any more than space. Linear time, cause and effect, past and present and future came and went, following strange new patterns and connections. Sometimes it seemed like I was leading Molly, or that we were already on the way back from wherever we were going, so that even talking became difficult.

"Still heading for the survivors," said Molly.

"How should I know?" I said.

"I don't think *before* means what it used to."

"I'm sure we've been this way before."

"Where are we going?"

"Is any of this making sense to you?"

"Are we nearly there yet?"

"I think time is out of joint."

"What?" said Molly.

"What?" I said.

After that, Molly dropped down so that she drifted along only a few inches above the uncertain ground, and I held her hand firmly in mine. I could feel it even through my armour. With our hands held tight together, we couldn't be separated.

Buildings seemed to crawl and seep and run away like slow liquids, surging out across the street like plastic tides. I fought my way through them, tearing horrid sticky substances apart with my armoured hands. Molly followed after me, one of her hands resting on my golden shoulder, until I had a hand free for her to take hold of again. Several buildings all melted away in a moment and surged along the street towards us like a creeping tidal wave, with bits of brick and broken window and shattered doors still protruding. I ran straight at the wave, golden fists clenched. I wouldn't be slowed and I wouldn't be stopped, not while people here still needed my help. Molly blasted the creeping wall with lightning bolts from her outstretched fingertips, and the tidal wave soaked them up. I hit the wave hard, smashing my way through by brute strength. The wave tried to cling to my armour, but couldn't get a hold. I burst out the other side and kept going, while Molly rose majestically over the wave and then dropped gracefully down to join me again.

We both felt safer, saner, more real . . . when we could feel each other's hand.

I had no idea how long we'd been in the town. Hours, days, years . . . It was like one of those dreams that seem to go on forever, one thing after another, until you know you're dreaming and struggle to wake up, and can't.

Sometimes the houses on either side of the road changed into things. Living things. Molly and I stuck to the middle of the road to avoid them. Brick and stone became plant and fungus, windows were eyes, and doors swung slowly open to reveal sweaty organic passageways, pulsing throats lined with teeth like rotating knives. Some of the changed houses roared like dinosaurs, or howled like souls newly damned to Hell. Some slumped together, becoming bigger, greater creatures, with alien shapes and impossible angles that hurt to look at with merely human eyes. They didn't bother with Molly or me. They had their own unknowable concerns.

Bright lights went streaking up and down the street like living comets, shooting this way and that and bouncing off buildings, laughing shrilly. Low voices boomed deep under the ground, saying terrible things. The sky was red and purple, like clotting blood, and the sun was a dark cinder giving off unnatural light. Awful shapes came and went, monstrous things, big and small. Some of them walked through the shifting world as though only they were real and everything else mere phantoms. Molly and I gave them plenty of room. When the Satanist conspiracy broke reality in this place, they blasted doors open that had been closed for millennia. Things from Outside had found a way in; things that would still have to be tracked down and dealt with even after this particular mess had been cleaned up. The family would have to keep an eye on this area for centuries to come.

In one place we encountered things like mutated children, with insect eyes and bulging foreheads, scrabbling through the streets in packs. Naked, vicious, feral. I studied them carefully through my mask to be sure they weren't in any way human and never had been. Molly wasn't fooled for a moment. She threw fireballs at them, and they scuttled away, spitting and snarling at us. After them came horrid shapes made up of shimmering phosphorescence, as though burned onto the surface of the world. Passing through walls like smoke, leaving dark stains behind them on the brickwork. A great clump of bottle green maggots crusted around a huge alien eye sailed silently down one street, watching everything with a terrible malevolent joy. Great balloon shapes of rotting leather stalked the streets on long, spindly legs like stilts, slamming into one another endlessly, like stags in rut, trampling the fallen underfoot. And a storm wind full of razor blades swept down the street with vicious speed, the razors clattering harmlessly against my armour, and unable to pierce Molly's shields.

I was starting to take such things for granted. You can't be shocked and horrified and appalled all the time. It wears you out. So you become numb to the atrocities, untouched by the horror shows. Maybe that's how you know when you're going mad: when such sights no longer bother you. Madness is when all your nightmares have come true and you just don't care anymore. I clung to Molly's hand, and she held on to mine. As long as we still had each other and wouldn't give up . . . the town hadn't won.

Sometimes it seemed to me that I was someone else, a whole different person with a new purpose. And sometimes it seemed to me that Molly was someone else, someone I'd always known. There were times when we looked at each other and didn't recognise the person looking back. Sometimes I walked alone, had come in alone, had always been alone in this awful place. And sometimes it seemed to Molly and to me that there was someone else with us. That there were three of us walking down the street together. He walked between us, his face always turned away, and I was afraid that if ever that face turned to look at me, I would see someone or something too horrible to bear.

But that didn't last.

Whatever happened, the armour kept pulling me back to reality. The one truly solid thing in this place, it would not change and would not allow me to be changed. And Molly . . . was probably too stubborn to accept any reality other than her own for long. I don't know if she experienced all the things I did. I didn't ask.

Living cobwebs fell on us from above, crawling all over my armour, trying to hold me down and eat their way in. I pulled them off me in handfuls, crushing them in my hands and throwing them down to trample underfoot. My sanity was starting to get its second wind. Though I had to wonder what state the town's survivors would be in when we finally got to them. The human mind was never meant to endure under conditions like these. The shattered reality of Little Stoke didn't even have dream logic to hold it together. Being in the town now was like suffering an endless series of hammer blows to the mind. But Molly had said they were safe, protected for the moment, and I trusted Molly.

When there was nothing else left in the world to depend on, I would still trust my Molly.

Finally, despite everything the broken world could do to stop us, we came at last to the Old Market Hall. It was set right in the middle of the town, I was told afterwards, though such spatial references had become meaningless in Little Stoke. Molly and I had no trouble spotting the old hall; it was the only building that still looked like an ordinary, everyday building. It stood tall and proud, firm in all its details, inside a circle of normality: a sharply defined circle of normal conditions, surrounded by madness. The moment Molly and I crossed that boundary, it was as though a great spiritual weight had been lifted off us. I stopped and sighed heavily, stretching as luxuriously as any cat, enveloped in a palpable sense of pure relief. Molly laughed out loud and hugged me tightly. I hadn't realised how much of a struggle it had been, how much strength it had taken to keep going and stay sane, until I didn't have to fight any longer. My mind cleared in a moment, as though someone had thrown a bucket of ice-cold water in my mental face.

"I think this is the place," said Molly.

"I think you're right," I said.

We both looked back the way we'd come, but the way we'd come wasn't there anymore. The town had devolved into utter chaos, with nothing holding sure or certain even for a moment. We both shuddered at the thought of how long we'd spent fighting our way through madness. And then I drew a deep breath, and so did she, and we straightened our backs and held up our heads and marched right up to the Old Market Hall. The front door was wonderfully, reassuringly ordinary. I knocked politely, and we waited.

"There are quite definitely people in there," Molly said quietly. "I can hear them. They sound like . . . people. That's a good thing, isn't it?"

"It's a bloody miracle in this place," I said. I knocked again, a little louder. "Hello? People inside? We are people, too. We're here to help."

I could hear raised voices inside the old building, but the door remained closed. I was pretty sure I could kick it in if I had to, but that wouldn't make the kind of first impression I was hoping for. So I moved away from the door and peered in through a window.

"A face! A golden face!"

"Don't let it in! Monsters!"

"Don't be silly; monsters wouldn't bother to knock, would they?"

"He's got a point."

"Oh, you always agree with him! We can't risk opening the door. We can't risk letting the outside in!"

"We can't hide in here forever, either!"

There was a long pause, and then I heard the sounds of heavy bolts being drawn back, and a lock turning. I moved back to stand beside Molly, and the moment the door opened we hurried forward into the old hall. The door immediately slammed shut behind us, and people busied themselves with the bolts again. The inside of the old building looked perfectly normal. The floor was solid wood that hadn't had a decent waxing in quite a while; the walls were reassuringly straight and upright; and the high ceiling stayed where it was supposed to be. A perfectly ordinary, very human last resort. Packed full of people staring at Molly and me with wide eyes. They huddled together, looking very uncertain, as though they half expected Molly and me to turn into monsters at any moment. A lot of them didn't look too happy at the sight of me in my armour. They knew nothing of Droods. Since the hall seemed such an ordinary place, I armoured down so everyone could see I was human. Molly dropped her force shield and beamed around her.

"The worst is over now," she said to the crowd of survivors. "We're here to get you out of this mess."

They all cried out in relief or simple joy. Many hugged one another. Several came forward to shake me by the hand, smiling widely as my hand remained an ordinary, everyday hand. But a lot of them still looked shocked, hanging on by only their mental fingernails, not quite daring to believe the nightmare could finally be over. A spokesman came forward, a bluff, hearty type in a battered tweed suit. He smiled at Molly and me and shook our hands, the beginnings of hope in his eyes.

"I'm Geoffrey Earl, local vicar. Good to see you! Welcome to the Old Market Hall. You really are very welcome, oh, yes! We are the last survivors of . . . whatever it is that's happened here."

"Hi," I said. "I'm Eddie Drood; this is Molly Metcalf; we're the rescue party."

"I wasn't sure there'd be one," said the vicar. "Do you know what's happened here?"

"Tell us the truth! Are we in Hell?" said a large, red-faced woman who'd pushed her way to the front of the crowd. She looked like she'd been crying a lot.

"No," Molly said immediately. "You're all still in the land of the living. So to speak. What you see out there is . . . local conditions. Outside the town, everything is still as it should be. The world goes on as it always has. We were rather hoping you could tell us what happened here."

The vicar shook his head. "It was just another day; we were in here planning the next harvest Sunday, and then . . . we heard this great sound outside, and when we went to the windows to look, we found the world had gone mad."

"What kind of sound?" I said.

"A great scream," said the vicar. "As though something had wounded the world. A few of us went outside to see what was going on; we saw what happened to them through the windows. None of us dared leave after that. We stuck close together. Praying. Waiting to be rescued. Hoping to be rescued . . . We were beginning to think we'd been forgotten. Can you tell us anything about what's happened?"

"We believe this town was made the target of some appalling new weapon," I said carefully. "Terrorists. We're still working on the details. Do you have any idea why you survived, when so many didn't? Why this building is . . . protected?"

"We believe it to be God's will," the vicar said steadily. "We all have faith in Him."

Molly looked like she was about to say something unwise, so I quickly cut in. "As good an answer as any, I suppose."

"Did you encounter any other . . . survivors, on your way here?" said the vicar, trying not to sound too hopeful.

"I'm sorry," I said. "You're all that's left."

"Dear God," said the red-faced woman. "Everyone's gone? Everyone?"

"Hush, Margaret," said the vicar. "Are you sure, Mr. Drood? There couldn't be another refuge like this somewhere else?"

"I'm sorry," I said. I looked around the hall. "There's some kind of protection operating here. . . ."

"And a pretty damned powerful one, at that," said Molly.

"Don't use such language here!" said Margaret. Molly looked at her, and Margaret faded back into the crowd. Molly looked slowly round the hall, and people gave way before her. She stopped abruptly, bent over and stared hard at the floor.

"Got it!" she said. "I can See it! There's an object of power, really old and incredibly powerful, laid down under the floorboards. Eddie, we need to take a close look at it."

"I really don't think we should disturb it," the vicar said quickly. "We are protected here; we can all feel it."

"It's got to be done," I said. "We need to know what's

kept the madness out of here, in case this happens somewhere else."

"Of course," said the vicar. "I'm sorry. We're all a bit . . . shell-shocked. Do what you have to."

The crowd started to mutter, and a few protested, so I put on my armour again, and they all went very quiet. I flexed my golden arms, and some of the crowd gasped, and said prayers, and even crossed themselves. I moved over to where Molly indicated, and then smashed a hole through the floorboards with one golden fist. The old wood cracked and splintered as my fist drove through, and my arm followed it down as far as the elbow. I yanked my hand back, and that part of the floor exploded outwards, leaving a jagged great hole. And there, lying revealed in the dark earth, was a single stone tablet, some four feet long by three. I armoured down and hauled it up into the light, and then laid it carefully on a nearby table. Molly was immediately there by my side, crowding in for a good look. The vicar moved diffidently in on my other side. The tablet was covered with long lines of writing in half a dozen languages, carved deep into the surface of the stone.

"Do something, Vicar!" said a familiar voice. "Make them put it back! You're putting all our lives at risk!"

"Hush, Margaret!" said the vicar.

"I will not hush! I have a right to be heard!"

"We're here to help," I said.

"But who are you?" said Margaret, pushing her way to the front of the crowd again. She glared at me, and especially at Molly. "We don't know you! You're not from around here. And that metal suit of yours isn't natural! You walked through Hell to get here, and expect us to believe that you emerged untouched? No. You're part of the Devil's work. You're here to give us false hopes, and then steal our only protection!" She drew herself up and looked around her for support. "I say we take the stone back from them, and then throw them out, back into the Hell they came from!"

"Like to see you try," said Molly.

"We can get you out of here," I said, in my most reasonable voice. "Anyone else want to shove your only hope for an escape out the door, and hope someone else will turn up to rescue you?"

There was a bit of muttering, but that was all. Margaret realised she was on her own and shut up, still glaring daggers at Molly and me.

"We've all been under a lot of strain," said the vicar.

"Understood," I said. "Hang on a bit longer. It's almost over."

"Can we please concentrate on these writings?" said Molly. "Before the natives start getting restless again?"

There were dozens of lines of writing, still perfectly clear after who knew how many years buried in the earth. The stone itself could have been any age, but there was something about it that made the hairs on my neck stand up. Somehow I knew this stone was *ancient*. . . .

"Latin," said Molly. "Greek, old but not classical, and I'm pretty sure *that* . . . is Aramaic."

"That's a very significant combination of languages," I said. "Put them all together and they suggest Roman Britain. Some two thousand years ago."

"Can you read any of this?" said Molly. "I can probably bluff my way through the Latin, but the rest . . ."

"This is another of those occasions when I really wish I'd paid more attention at school," I said.

"So you can't read it either," said Molly. "Typical."

"Perhaps I can help," the vicar said diffidently. "It's been a long time since I studied ancient languages at Cambridge, but . . ."

"Who said the age of miracles is over?" said Molly.

The vicar smiled at her. "Get us all out of here and I'll look it up for you. Now, then . . . Yes. Yes. Most of this is pretty obscure, but one name stands out. Joseph of Arimathea. Well, bless me. . . ."

"'And did those feet in ancient times . . .'" I murmured. "The man who was supposed to have brought Jesus to visit Britain, during his gap year. But why would he have placed such a powerful protection stone here? Did he know something bad would happen, in this place, eventually?"

"Maybe a certain other personage told him," said Molly. "I think we're treading on dangerous ground, Eddie. All that matters is that we now know how, if not necessarily why, this place is protected. But I am telling you, the power contained in this stone is not limitless. Maintaining normal conditions against the pressure from outside is using up a lot of power and draining the stone dry. If we don't get these people out of here soon . . ."

"What?" said the vicar. "What will happen?"

"Absolutely nothing," I said. "Because we are leaving right now."

Something banged on the locked and bolted door. A loud, aggressive sound. The door shuddered in its frame, but the lock and the bolts held. Everyone stood still and silent, staring at the door.

"Nothing's ever been able to get that close before," the vicar said quietly.

Something went running back and forth up on the roof: something heavy, with too many legs. It ran up and down, never pausing, never stopping. Something hit the door again, hard. The light outside was changing, the normal daylight darkening as though suffused with blood. The survivors cried out and huddled together again as strange, distorted shapes peered in through the windows.

"The circle of normality is shrinking as the stone uses up its power," said Molly.

"I told you not to let them disturb it!" shrieked Margaret, her voice thick with imminent hysteria.

"I don't think the conspiracy knew about the stone," I said quietly to Molly.

"Seems likely, if even your family didn't know," said Molly.

"Conspiracy?" said the vicar. "Your people? What is going on here? Exactly who are your people, Mr. Drood?"

"We're the good guys," I said briskly. "Now hush—there's a good vicar; we're talking. I think the stone is a rogue element, Molly. No one knew it was here, because it didn't activate until it was needed. The conspiracy didn't mean to leave any survivors behind. The stone hid these people from the chaos, and the conspiracy . . . overlooked them."

"How are we going to get all these people out of here, Eddie?" said Molly. "I can't generate a field big enough to protect everyone if we have to walk them all the way back to the town boundary. And I sure as hell can't teleport this many people out. So what are we going to do?"

"When in doubt," I said cheerfully, "cheat! Or improvise, with extreme prejudice. The Merlin Glass got us in; with the stone's power to draw on, I don't see why it shouldn't get us all out."

Molly looked at me, and then at the stone. "Genius. You're a genius! Have I told you lately that you're a genius, Eddie? But . . . punching a doorway through all that chaos, and keeping it open, is going to take one hell of a lot of power. You could drain that stone really quickly. The hall would lose its protection, and the chaos would break in. . . ."

"Let's not go there just yet," I said. "Let us not even discuss it until we have to. Don't want to panic the nice survivors, do we? Because there isn't any other way to get everyone out of here. We could, of course, sneak off on our own and abandon all these good people. . . ."

"Well, I could," said Molly, "but you couldn't. You're not made that way. Another of the things I love about you."

"How do I love you?" I said. "Let me count the ways. . . ."

"Later," said Molly.

She kissed me with sudden passion, and I hugged her to me, ignoring the scandalised mutterings from all sides. Then I sent her to watch the door and windows while I took out the Merlin Glass and activated it. It quickly sprang up to full size, to appreciative noises from the survivors, and I locked the doorway onto the grassy hill outside town. The image flickered unsteadily, coming and going in a very dangerous way. Not at all what you want to see in a teleport device. I took the Arimathea stone and placed it carefully under the Glass, and the image cleared and settled. The Glass had tapped into the stone's power.

The vicar stepped forward and peered at what was on the other side of the Glass. His eyes were wide with simple wonder, and he smiled like a child.

"It's real . . ." he said. "I can feel the wind blowing through, smell the grass. . . . What is this?"

"Your ticket home," I said. "Gather your flock together, and let's get the flock out of here. Molly and I will be right behind you."

The vicar nodded quickly, rounded up his people and drove them through the Merlin Glass with encouragement, discipline and the occasional burst of harsh language. There's no one like a vicar when it comes to organising people. He chivvied them from one side, inspired them from another and drove the rest through the Glass like a collie dog with a flock of sheep. A lot of people were nervous about the Glass and didn't want to be rushed, but no one wanted to be left behind. I made several circuits of the hall as they filed through, checking for weak spots and the sound of anything breaking in. But it wasn't until the last few survivors were queuing up that something large and bulky smashed the door in.

There was no warning. One moment the door was securely closed, and the next it was flying across the hall, blasted right off its hinges. The broken bolts flew through the air like shrapnel. Something dark and twisted filled the doorway, light glowing from sickly yellow eyes. I stepped quickly forward, armouring up as I went, and punched it in the head. I put all my strength into the blow, and I felt bone shatter under the impact. My golden hand drove on deep into its misshapen head. And something inside the head closed around my fist and held it there. I struggled to pull my hand free and couldn't. Arms with too many joints unfolded from the creature's sides, and clawed hands slammed against my armour, scrabbling against the strange matter as they tried to force their way in.

Since I couldn't pull my hand out, I steadied myself and pushed it deeper in, until it burst out the back of the creature's head. It squealed once, a high tremolo that pained my ears, and thick purple blood jetted from the back of the head. I put my other hand on its face, golden fingers thrusting deep into the yellow eyes, braced myself and yanked the other hand out. Then I shoved the creature hard on the chest, driving it backwards, and moved forward to fill the doorway, so nothing could get past me. Outside, the circle of normality was gone. The stone's protection had retreated right back to the walls of the Old Market Hall, and soon it wouldn't even reach them. I yelled for Molly to get the last of the survivors through the Glass.

Something smashed a hole in the roof and dropped down into the Hall. It hit the floor hard, old floorboards shattering under its weight, and then it turned on the last few survivors. Molly hit it with a lightning bolt, and the dark-haired creature burst into flames. It ran round and round in circles, the flames leaping higher and higher as the thing screamed in a disturbingly human way. Something else thrust up through the floorboards, sending splinters flying in all directions. It was white and wet and segmented, springing up out of the hole it'd made like a malignant, alien jack-in-the-box. Molly threw a fireball at it, and the blunt head snapped round and caught the fireball in its clacking multipart mouth. The flames didn't seem to bother it in the least. Molly advanced on the thing, throwing shaped curses at it, and the segmented horror cracked and shattered under the impact of her Words, spouting a thick, creamy blood. I didn't dare leave the doorway to help. A lot of things were heading my way, all of them really bad, and while the sight of my armour was giving them pause for the moment, I had no idea how long that would last. They'd seen the collapse of the protective field, and they wanted in.

"How many left?" I yelled to Molly. "How many more to go?"

"Last ones going through right now!" she yelled back. "It's just you and me! Leave the doorway and let's blow this joint! Eddie! Eddie . . . why are you still there?"

"Because you can't see what I'm seeing," I said steadily. "There's a whole army of really unpleasant things out here, and I'm all that's stopping them from storming the Hall. I can't go. You go, Molly. Go through the Glass, and then shut it down from your side. So none of this madness can follow you through to infect the sane and normal world."

"Hell with that," said Molly. "I'm not leaving you! I'll never leave you. I went all the way to Limbo to bring you back and I'm damned if I'll give up on you now."

By this time she was standing right beside me, looking out. She made a shocked, disgusted sound. I nodded.

"Nasty, aren't they? And dangerous with it. We can't risk their getting through the Merlin Glass."

"Are you suggesting we shut the Glass now?" said Molly. "You are, aren't you? You're prepared to sacrifice both our lives to save a bunch of nobodies. Because they're innocents."

"It's the job," I said.

"That's why I love you," said Molly. "Because you're the one true thing in my life."

"No," I said. "Together we're one true thing. Hold everything."

"What now?" said Molly.

"I mean, hold on; I have an idea."

"I love it!" Molly said immediately. "It's a wonderful idea and I want to have its babies. What is it?"

"If we can't go to the Merlin Glass, we'll bring the Glass to us."

I concentrated, reaching out to the Glass through my armour. And the Glass surged forward and enveloped Molly and me in the doorway I'd opened; and then we were standing on the grassy hill outside town. Through the doorway I could see horrible things charging into the Hall, and I slammed the Glass shut in their awful faces. And finally it was over.

I shook the Merlin Glass down to normal size and put it away, and armoured down. A gusting breeze swept past me, smelling of grass and earth and flowers. I'd never smelt anything so deliciously normal. I sat down suddenly as the last of my strength went out of me. I hadn't realised I'd been running on adrenaline for so long. Molly sat down beside me and cuddled up against me.

We were sitting on top of a pretty steep hill, looking down at the great dark circle where Little Stoke used to be. The rescued survivors were sitting or standing in small groups on the hillside below us, talking animatedly about what they'd been through. Several were lying on their backs on the grass, staring up at the perfectly normal sky with ecstatic faces. Happy to be in a world that made sense again. The vicar sat not far away from us, running his hands through the thick, tufty grass as though he'd never seen anything so wonderful.

And as Molly and I looked down the hillside at the dark circle, it suddenly began to shrink. It fell in upon itself, the sides rushing in faster and faster, until finally the whole thing collapsed and disappeared. The town was back, or at least the buildings were, looking for the most part untouched and untransformed. Made me wonder how much of what we'd experienced inside the town had been "real" in any sense.

"Such a bad place had to be inherently unstable," said Molly. "It was always going to collapse in on itself, eventually. That was probably what the conspiracy intended all along. Leave nothing behind to show what they'd done. Only the Arimathea stone prevented that from happening: the one true thing in all that chaos. Once we removed that . . ."

"Excuse me," said the vicar, moving diffidently forward to join us. "But can you tell me what just happened?"

"Sorry," I said. "I could tell you, but then I'd have to excommunicate you. All details are classified. National security. You know how it is."

"Ah," said the vicar. "Yes . . ."

He turned away to round up the survivors and lead them off. Though hopefully not straight down into the returned town buildings. I wanted my family to check the place over thoroughly before we let people back in. No telling how much psychic contamination remained. . . . The survivors made it clear to the vicar that they weren't ready to be moved yet. They were talking excitedly among themselves. Already the worst of their memories were fading. The untrained human mind isn't equipped to deal with such things. Soon enough they'd be arguing over what they'd seen, or thought they'd seen, or experienced. In the end . . . all they'd be left with were some bad dreams.

Hopefully.

"They're going to talk, some of them," said Molly. "I would."

"Let them," I said. "See who believes them. With the dark circle gone and the buildings returned, they have no proof, no evidence. The rest of the townspeople are still missing . . . but the usual authorities will never find them."

"You think they're dead, don't you?" said Molly.

"It seems likely," I said. "The family will do everything it can to find them, but . . . the conspiracy is too far ahead of us. By the time we catch up . . . it'll be too late for the poor people of Little Stoke."

"What if the survivors go to the media?" said Molly.

"Let them," I said. "It is, after all, a very cynical and disbelieving world. They might get a briefly bestselling paperback out of it, maybe a television movie, but that's it. The best we can do for them . . . is make sure this never happens again. Ethel? Can you hear me now?"

"Of course," her voice said, right in my ear. "I'm receiving all kinds of fascinating recorded information from your torc. Come home now, Eddie, Molly. You need some rest, both of you."

"Rest," I said. "That does sound good."

"Time for bed," said Molly.

"She said rest."

"Eventually," said Molly.

CHAPTER EIGHT

Getting Down with the Damned

There's a lot to be said for saying to hell with it all and hiding in your bedroom until everything's calmed down again. Molly and I stepped through the Merlin Glass directly into my room at Drood Hall. Partly because we were both exhausted and running on fumes, but mostly because neither of us was in the mood to make a formal report to the Drood Council. I barely had time to shut down the Glass and put it away before Molly was sprawled on her back on my bed, stretching luxuriously as she sank slowly into the deep goose-feather mattress. I dropped down beside her, groaning out loud as my muscles were finally able to relax. We lay there side by side for a long time, snuggled together, enjoying the luxury of not having to worry about anything for a while. It felt good to be back in my own room, among familiar things, with no more duties or responsibilities.

"I like it here," said Molly, after a while.

"Really?" I said, after another while. "I thought you preferred your own private woods."

"It's nice there, too," said Molly. "But mostly . . . I like it wherever you are." She turned her head on the pillow to look at me. "Are you sure someone from your family isn't going to come charging in here, demanding we make a full report on everything that happened inside the dark circle?"

"Ethel will have told them that I'm back," I said calmly. "But she'll also have told them that I am more than ready to punch out anyone who pesters me, and then Riverdance on their head. And no one would even think of barging into another Drood's room. It isn't done. When you've got this many people all living together under one roof, privacy is nonnegotiable. They wouldn't even knock unless there was a major emergency. We're safe. Anyway, Ethel has all the readings and information my armour picked up and stored in my torc. She'll have passed that on to the Armourer."

"I didn't know your armour could do that," said Molly.

"The old armour couldn't," I said. "This new strange-matter armour is far more sophisticated. We're still learning all the things it can do. The Armourer keeps bugging Ethel for an operator's manual, but she says it's important we learn these things for ourselves. Enough about my family, sweetie. Let them take care of the world for a while, while we take care of each other."

Molly smiled. "Help me with this zipper, would you?"

Quite a while later, Molly and I were drowsing quietly, lying naked on top of the sheets, entwined in each other's arms and legs, when Isabella Metcalf appeared very suddenly out of nowhere to stand at the foot of the bed. I was half-asleep, and half-convinced I was dreaming, until Molly sat up abruptly and said something very rude. I realised there actually was someone else in the room and sat bolt upright, moving instinctively to put my body between Molly and the intruder. She slapped me on the shoulder and pushed me firmly to one side.

"Sweet of you, dear, but a bit patronising. I am quite capable of defending myself."

"What is your sister doing in my bedroom?" I said

loudly. "Does she have any idea of what time it is and oh shit I'm naked."

"Never mind that . . ." said Isabella.

"I do mind!" I said loudly. "Did you invite her here, Molly?" And then a thought occurred to me, and I looked thoughtfully from Molly to Isabella. "Oh . . . is this about a threesome?"

"Not why I'm here," said Isabella, very definitely.

Molly elbowed me in the ribs. "In your dreams, stud."

"Then I still want to know what she's doing here while we've got no clothes on," I said firmly.

"Oh, don't be so conservative, Eddie," said Molly, leaning back against the headboard quite unself-consciously. "Being naked is nothing to a witch. I've danced skyclad among the standing stones of Stonehenge, and in the snows of the Himalayas, and up and down Wall Street under a full moon. It comes with the territory."

"Not with my territory it doesn't," I said. "I am not big on sharing." I wanted to grab a pillow and hide certain parts of me behind it, but I knew they'd laugh at me. So I sat up straight, pulled in my stomach and did my best to hang on to what was left of my dignity. And still almost lost it when Molly scratched at her left tit reflectively.

"Calm down, Eddie," said Isabella. "I've seen it all before."

"Not mine, you haven't," I said. "We are now going to change the subject. How is it you keep getting in and out of Drood Hall so easily, despite all of our more than state-of-the-art defences and protections expressly designed to keep out people like you?"

Isbaella sniggered. "When you let Molly in, you let all of us in. The Metcalf sisters come as a package deal. One for all, all against the world."

"You mean Louisa could turn up here anytime, without warning?" I said. "Oh, bloody hell . . . Someone's going to have to break the news to the Sarjeant-at-Arms, and please, God, let it not be me."

"Why are you here, Iz?" said Molly.

Isabella folded her arms across her chest, and her bloodred biker leathers creaked loudly. She gave us both a severe look. "I am here to report what I've discovered about the new Satanist conspiracy. And no, it couldn't wait. This is important and significant stuff, and urgent with it. I've been talking with certain friends and associates, along with others who owe me money and favours, and I have learned something you need to know, right now."

"Iz has contacts on every side of the fence," Molly said proudly. "She knows people in places most people don't even want to admit exist. They tell her things. If they know what's good for them."

"People . . ." I said dubiously. "What kind of people are we talking about here? I'm not going to place much trust in information that comes from anonymous sources. And neither will my family. I need names, Isabella."

She sighed loudly, in a put-upon kind of way. "Oh, very well, if you're going to be stuffy about it . . . John Taylor, from the Nightside. Razor Eddie, punk god of the straight razor. A ghost called Ash, from Shadows Fall. Jimmy Thunder, god for hire. The Grey Eidolon, the Lord of Thorns, and the Regent of Shadows."

"Don't mention that last one around here, dear," said Molly. "I never knew a man to be so thoroughly persona non grata. Droods really know how to bear a grudge."

"Centuries of practice," I said proudly.

"I trust you find some of those names acceptable?" said Isabella.

"Oh, sure," I said. "I've worked with most of them at one time or another. Not the most reputable bunch, or the most tightly wrapped, but they usually know what they're talking about."

Molly looked at me. "I thought Droods weren't allowed in the Nightside?"

"We're not," I said.

"Then how . . . ?"

"Ask me no questions and I'll tell you no lies."

"You want a slap?"

"The important thing," Isabella said loudly, "is that all of them agree on one thing: where you need to go next. It seems that most of the higher echelons in the conspiracy will be attending a very important meeting very soon now. Alexandre Dusk won't be there, but there is to be a special surprise guest who will have a good deal to say about the details of this Great Sacrifice they're planning."

"Okay," I said. "That is pretty important. But I still don't see why you had to bring it straight to my bedroom! Why couldn't this have waited till the morning, so we could have discussed it with the full council?"

"Because I don't trust them," said Isabella.

"Why not?"

"Because they're Droods!"

"Ah," I said. "Fair enough."

"I'm not entirely sure I trust you," said Isabella. "Even if Molly does vouch for you."

I turned to smile at Molly. "You do? That is so sweet of you."

"Well," said Molly, "I am the sweet one."

"Young people in love," said Isabella. "The horror, the horror . . ."

I gave her my best serious stare. "All right, where do we have to go to crash this vital satanic get-together? Am I going to have to dress up formal?"

"Have I got time to buy a new dress?" said Molly.

Isabella smiled unpleasantly. "You're going back to your old stomping grounds, Eddie. They're meeting in London, in the Under Parliament."

That stopped me dead, and I hugged my knees to my chest while I had a good think. Under Parliament is part of the old Roman catacombs set deep under the Houses of Parliament, the Commons and the Lords. The ancient catacombs are part of an extensive labyrinth of tunnels, caverns and stone galleries that stretch back and forth under the entire city, holding all the secrets and secret people too dark even for that ancient and knowledgeable city, London. The labyrinth itself is known as London Undertowen. And most people cross themselves when they say it.

The Romans built the original catacombs under what was then called Londinium, so they could go down there and do things in private they knew their gods wouldn't approve of. The Romans believed that if their gods couldn't see what they were doing, it didn't count. Very practical people, the Romans.

After the Romans declined and fell and got the hell out of Britain, other people moved in and used the tunnels for their own purposes, extending them as they went along. London Undertowen has been greatly expanded and added to, down the centuries, by many hands, for many reasons. It's sunk deep in the bedrock, well below the underground trains, and used by all kinds. These days the dark tunnels and galleries are home to everyone from the Sleeping Tygers of Stepney to the Slow Subterraneans. From the Dark Fae to the Night Gaunts to the Sons of the Old Serpent. You can find aliens, kobolds, dream-walkers and downbound souls, and even the deformed children of celebrities and lust demons. Abandoned and forgotten by their parents, they thrive in the dark and the cold and plot terrible revenges on the world that should have been theirs. And no, they don't ride around on giant albino alligators that were flushed down toilets when they got too big to be pets. That's only an urban legend. The Lost Children eat alligators, and wear their teeth as crowns on their bulging, misshapen heads.

London Undertowen: home to any who have good reason to prefer the dark to the light. The lost and the fallen, the cursed and the corrupt. Neutral ground for all the groups and individuals who wouldn't be tolerated anywhere else. The kind who play too rough for the Nightside, or are too sick, or sickening, for the World Beneath. It's where the underpeople go to hide and scheme and do awful things, far from the sight of man.

Just the place for Satanists to party.

"I've been down there a few times," I said slowly. "The ambience is awful, and the company is worse."

"Louisa loves it there," said Isabella.

"She would," said Molly.

"Is she . . . ?" I said.

"No," said Isabella. "She's still excavating the Martian Tombs."

"Still?" said Molly. "What the hell is she up to there?"

"Last I heard, trying to raise up something that would talk to her."

"Oh, this can only end badly," said Molly.

"That's Louisa for you," said Isabella.

"Look," I said firmly, "I am still waiting to hear what makes this so urgent that you had to come bursting in here to interrupt our quality time."

"The Satanists' meeting is scheduled for one a.m. tomorrow morning," said Isabella. "Some three hours from now."

"The thirteenth hour," said Molly. "Satanists can be terribly sentimental about some things."

"Three hours from now?" I said.

"Give or take," said Isabella. "I'd get moving, if I were you."

"Just once, I'd like some downtime between emergences," I said wistfully. "A weekend off in a nice hotel, with room service . . . I need my beauty sleep."

"Getting old," said Molly, prodding me somewhere indelicate.

"I'll meet you both there, in Under Parliament," said Isabella, averting her gaze from such a blatant display of fondness. She snapped her fingers and disappeared from my bedroom.

"I thought she'd never go," said Molly. She leaned companionably against me and trailed the fingertips of one hand across my bare chest. "Now, where were we?"

"You never told me that granting you access to the Hall also allowed your sisters access," I said sternly.

"Do you expect me to tell you everything?" said Molly.

"When it involves Drood security, yes!"

"You can be very stuffy sometimes, Eddie Drood," said Molly.

She turned abruptly away from me, got up from the bed and gave her full attention to getting dressed, with her back to me.

"I've killed the moment, haven't I?" I said.

Molly said nothing—very loudly. I sighed, rolled regretfully off the side of the bed and wandered round the room, picking up bits of my clothing from where I'd flung them earlier.

"Don't you dare put those back on," said Molly, without looking round. "They've been through a lot, and little of it good. Dump it all in the laundry basket, and pick out some fresh ones."

"They were fresh yesterday. . . ."

"That was yesterday!"

We got dressed. Molly chose an impressive backless, shoulderless creation from the pocket dimension she kept in the back of my cupboard. I was never allowed to look into it, which made me suspect she kept other things there as well, apart from dresses, but I never asked. I chose a smart but nondescript three-piece suit, because I was going to have to enter the House of Commons in order to reach Under Parliament, and I didn't want to stand out. Or be in any way memorable. I put on an old Etonian tie. Might come in handy. I waited until Molly was putting the last touches to her makeup in the dressing table mirror, and then tried a hopefully innocuous question.

It's hard to keep a relationship going when there's an argument in the room.

"We've got a good three hours until the Satanists' little bash gets under way. Do we have to leave now?"

"I do," said Molly. "You can hang around here if you want. I have somewhere to go first."

"Where?"

"The Wulfshead Club. You are, of course, perfectly free to go and wake up all your council members, and make a full report, and listen to them discuss everything in great detail before finally authorising you to investigate the situation, but I am off. Right now. Things to see, people to do. It's not that I don't trust Isabella, you understand, or her fascinating friends and allies . . . but I'll feel a lot better once I've confirmed their information through some friends and allies of my own. And that means a short, sharp visit to the Wulfshead." She finally turned to look at me. "You can tag along if you like, while I pin people to the wall and ask them pointed questions; just don't embarrass me. You can usually trust Isabella to tell you the truth, but you can't always trust her to tell you everything. Forewarned is forearmed, and since we won't be able to take any weapons into Under Parliament for fear of setting off all their alarms . . ."

"I'll go as Shaman Bond," I said, when she finally paused for breath. "He won't seem out of place, either in the club or London Undertowen. People expect him to turn up anywhere. I've put a lot of work into establishing that reputation, for times like this. And people will say things to Shaman that they wouldn't dream of discussing in front of a Drood."

"Good," said Molly, smiling for the first time. "I like Shaman. He's good company."

"But he's me. . . ."

"Not always."

"I can be good company. . . ."

"Stuffy," said Molly airily. "Definitely stuffy."

The Merlin Glass couldn't take us directly to the infamous Wulfshead Club, semilegendary watering hole for all the really interesting and dangerous people on the fringes of reality . . . because the club's defences wouldn't allow it. So instead it dropped us off in a garbage-strewn back alley somewhere in the grubbier part of London's Soho. Access points to the club are always changing, drifting back and forth across the seedier parts of London. The Wulfshead isn't actually in the city; in fact, there are those who claim it isn't even on Earth. As such. But you can access the club from selected very secret locations in every major city in the world. As long as you're a member in good standing, of course.

The alley was full of uncertain shadows, a flat amber light sprawling across black garbage bags and the nastier sort of litter from the single streetlamp at the mouth of the alley. A cold wind was gusting, picking up a few leaves and playing with them, but not strong enough to move anything else. The tang of fresh urine was sharp in the air. Molly ignored it all, staring intently at one particular part of the bare brick wall that seemed no different from any other. She ignored the obscene graffiti, nodding slowly as her witchy Sight showed her the signs beneath the signs. She said the current passWord, and a great door of solid silver appeared in the wall before us. As though it had always been there, and we hadn't noticed it till now. The dully gleaming metal was deeply etched with threats and warnings in angelic and demonic script, the disturbing characters sharp and clear, actually painful to merely human eyes. I stepped forward and pressed my left hand flat against the unnervingly warm metal, and the door swung slowly inwards. Attempting entry to the Wulfshead Club is never going to be easy, because if for any reason, good or bad, your name is no longer on the approved list, the door will bite your hand off. One of the many reasons the Wulfshead has never felt the need for a bouncer at the door.

Molly and I stepped quickly through the opening into dazzlingly bright light, pounding music, aggressively modernistic furniture and more good times and hard living than can usually be crammed into such limited time and space. The joint was jumping, and the place was packed. Let the good times roll, and the Devil take the hindmost. I eased my way through the crowd, Molly at my side, smiling and nodding. A lot of people smiled and nodded back; Shaman Bond and Molly Metcalf were familiar faces on the scene. Giant plasma screens covered the walls, showing intimate secrets of the rich and famous, while impossibly pretty girls wearing hardly any clothing danced madly on spotlit stages, and a group of seriously high bright young things danced on the ceiling.

Molly and I took up casual but watchful positions leaning against the bar at the far end of the club. They'll serve you anything you ask for at the Wulfshead, from an atomic cocktail with a strontium 90 Perrier chaser, to a bracing glass of medicinal absinthe with a little parasol in it. I've seen people order drinks so volatile they had to be served in depleted uranium cups, and alcohol so potent it was served by a miniature tap-dancing pink elephant. Though admittedly, the night I saw that I'd had a few. . . . I ordered my usual bottle of Beck's, and a Buck's Fizz for Molly. She thinks the orange juice makes it healthy. There are always a dozen or so bartenders stationed up and down the length of the bar, all with the same face. I've never asked.

The usual crowd was in. Larry Oblivion, the dead detective, looking to make useful contacts and touting for business. He was drinking neat formaldehyde, with a crème de violette chaser to take the edge off his breath. He was quite happy to tell Molly that he didn't know anything about a new satanic conspiracy, and didn't want to. Having been murdered by his ex-partner, and then brought back to life as a zombie, he had more reason than most to be careful about the state of his soul. There's nothing like having died to make you very thoughtful about the afterlife.

A fat, middle-aged and disturbingly hearty fellow in a Hawaiian shirt and grubby shorts waved cheerfully to Molly. He was drinking from a whiskey bottle with a nipple on the end, and scratching himself in an entirely too unself-conscious way. Molly moved over to join him, and I followed after. Neither of us wanted to get too close to him. He leered at Molly, and nodded briskly to me.

"Hail fellows well met, and all that crap. Trash, sir, at your service. It's not my given name, you understand; I chose it. It's real, it's romantic, it's . . . me. Trash: child prodigy, eccentric dancer, and necromancer-in-waiting to the court of St. James, the bastards. I understand you're hot on the trail of a new satanic conspiracy. . . . Whatever happened to the old one, I wonder? People can't be bothered to look after their conspiracies anymore. In my young day, you could expect a decent conspiracy to give you a good run for your money; be something you could hand down to your children and grandchildren. Not that I've ever been cursed with such. I would love to be of assistance, Molly, dear, but these days if it isn't directly concerned with death and dying, I'm really not interested. Sex and death, you see; it's all down to sex and death. Or if it isn't, I don't want to know. I could ask some recently departed if they know anything, but frankly I wouldn't trust anything they have to say. The dead have their own strange ideas about what's real and what isn't. Either that, or they have a really weird sense of humour, and lie a lot. And they always have their own agenda."

We moved on, leaving Trash to chat up an emo ghoul with far too many piercings. I spotted Jeremy Diego wistfully waving a folded banknote in the air as he tried to attract a bartender's attention. Some people can't get served. Jeremy was a ghost finder from the Carnacki Institute, and it showed in his prematurely aged face and otherworldly eyes. A short and stocky chap in a battered suit and a jaunty fedora, and what appeared to be half his breakfast all down his front. He seemed pleased enough to see me, and nodded politely to Molly, but as always, if it didn't involve ghosts, he didn't have a clue.

"The word is," he said, peering at us owlishly over the drink I'd bought him, "things are stirring in the afterworlds. Very powerful things. An awful lot of our psychics are looking into the future and coming back with spiritual shell shock. Something Bad is heading our way. Can't get any of them to agree on what it might be, but then, that's psychics for you. The one thing you can be sure of is that when we do find out what it is, we're really not going to like it. Mark my word, young Shaman, there'll be tears before bedtime. . . ."

And then there was Monkton Farley, the famous consulting detective, leaning very casually against the bar in his immaculately cut suit, elegant cuffs and brightly polished brogues. He had the usual small crowd of admirers set out before him, listening eagerly to his tale of the Case of the Unnatural Progression. Luckily he'd almost finished, because we'd never get anything out of him until he had. We waited for the crowd to finish applauding, and then pushed our way through to the front. He looked down his long nose at me, over his flute of pink champagne, but had better sense than to try that with Molly, and so gave her a wintry smile.

"Satanic conspiracy?" he drawled, in that aristocratic tone I knew for a fact he wasn't entitled to. "Haven't heard a thing. Been very busy, you know. Nothing succeeds like success, and all that. Only just got back from the wilds of rural Somerset. God, I despise the countryside. It's so . . . uncivilised."

Molly and I split up after that, so we could cover more ground. I worked the club with my usual practiced charm, asking a discreet question or two here and there, and reading between the lines of what I was told; but when I joined up with Molly again neither of us had much to show for our efforts. There was a general feeling among the club regulars that there was definitely Something in the air, but no one knew anything for sure. And when I did come right out with it, and asked if anyone had heard anything about a new satanic conspiracy, most people laughed at me. *A satanic conspiracy? Oh, my dear, that's so last century. . . .*

And then, while Molly and I were refreshing ourselves with several new drinks, I spotted a familiar if somewhat unexpected face. Philip MacAlpine was one of the old-time spies, who spent his whole adult life in the treacherous trenches of espionage and double-dealing. He was supposed to have done good work with my uncle James and uncle Jack back in the day, but now, at the end of his career, he was only a minor functionary at MI-13, helping to keep the lid on things the public wasn't supposed to know about. He'd tried to kill me on more than one occasion, but I did my best not to take it personally.

He was looking old and tired, so I decided to cheer him up with my company. He took one look at me advancing on him and tried to run. But I'd already sent Molly ahead of me to block his way. He looked back and forth, and his shoulders slumped. I smiled at him, and he grunted back. Anyone would have thought he wasn't pleased to see me.

"Not pleased to see me, Philip?" I said brightly.

"I used to have a career!" he snapped. "I used to have prospects, and an office with a window! And then you happened to me."

"Shouldn't have tried to kill me then," I said reasonably.

"I shouldn't have failed," said MacAlpine, pouting. "I told them there was no point in trying to go head-to-head with a Drood field agent, but no; no one ever listens to me. Even though I've got more field experience than half my superiors put together, these days. The departments aren't what they were. I used to swan around Eastern Europe in a cool car, with all the latest weaponry, making trouble in all the right places . . . and now I have to fill in forms in triplicate just to go to the toilet. I blame the end of the Cold War. They knew how to play the game. . . . Now it's all fanatics and religious head cases with no sense of humour, who wouldn't understand the rules of the game if you tattooed them on their foreheads."

"I heard you'd found a new niche for yourself at MI-13," said Molly. "Cracking down on unregistered aliens from other dimensions . . ."

"MI-13 is still a force to be reckoned with," MacAlpine said quickly. "Droods don't have all the answers. There's still plenty for us to do."

I nodded, only half listening to what he was saying. A strange sense of déjà vu was raising all the hairs on the back of my neck. The last time I'd talked with Philip MacAlpine, it had been at the Winter Hall, in Limbo. I still remembered that conversation, but he didn't, because he wasn't really there. Or was he? It was hard to be sure about anything that had happened in that strange other place. I wondered, if I were to remind him of what he said there, would he remember? I decided it was better not to ask. I cut into his ramblings about how his life hadn't worked out the way it should have, and fixed him with a hard stare.

"You owe me, MacAlpine. You, MI-13 and this whole country. I saved the crown jewels from being stolen."

MacAlpine sniffed moistly. "All right. Say you did. Even though officially that never happened, and don't you forget it. What do you want, a medal? I could probably get you a nice illuminated scroll, signed by Her Majesty."

"You owe me," I said, and something in my voice made him look away for a moment. "You owe me, and I want a favour. Right now, with a ribbon on it. Nothing too difficult. I need to get into Under Parliament, and for that I need access to the outer lobby of the House of Commons. Now, I could force my way in, but that would make more trouble than it was worth, for both of us. So I want you to supply Molly and me with two MI-13 security passes. One day only, of course. Do it now, Philip. Or watch me turn seriously crotchety."

He growled and muttered for a while, but his heart wasn't in it. He took out his mobile phone and moved away so he could talk in private. Though he needn't have bothered; over the blasting music and the sheer bedlam of raised voices, we'd had to shout at each other to be heard anyway. Molly glared after him.

"Never trusted him. Shifty little scrote. You really think he's going to help us? He hates your guts!"

"Possibly," I said calmly. "But he's far too much the professional to let that get in the way of doing business. He may not want to help me now, but his superiors will. They owe the Droods, and they know it, and they'll be glad to get off this easily. What are a couple of passes to them? They hand the things out like party favours these days."

MacAlpine put his phone away and came back to join us, looking even more sour than before, if that was possible. "All right, it's arranged. Two security passes will be waiting for you at the entrance to the House of Commons: a full pass for Shaman Bond, and a backup pass for one other."

"One other?" Molly said ominously. "The powerful and legendary wild witch of the woods is *one other*?"

"If I put your real name on the pass, they'd never let you in," said MacAlpine. "Your reputation precedes you."

"Yes," said Molly, not displeased. "It does tend to."

MacAlpine made a point of turning his full attention to me. "The passes will get you into the outer lobby, but no farther. Don't push your luck. And getting into Under Parliament is strictly your business."

"No problem," I said cheerfully.

"I really didn't like the way you said that," MacAlpine said sadly.

"Good," I said.

"It's not supposed to be easy to get into Under Parliament!" snapped MacAlpine. "Or London Undertowen! Because that's where you're really going, isn't it?"

I considered him thoughtfully. There had been something in his voice. . . . "What have you heard, Philip?"

He smiled at me for the first time. "That maybe . . . there's something worse than Droods in the world now."

Molly and I left the Wulfshead Club by the back door, and emerged into a shabby side street in Westminster. The streetlights were sharp and bright, there was hardly anyone about, and only the very best kinds of cars rolled smoothly past. Molly and I strolled along arm in arm, allowing our hearing to recover from the deafening noise of the club. It wasn't a long walk to the House of Commons. I didn't even bother trying the Merlin Glass; both Houses of Parliament are all but buried under overlapping layers of defences and protections, laid down over the centuries. The establishment has always looked after itself, first and foremost. Bring an object of power like the Merlin Glass anywhere near Parliament, and every SAS combat sorcerer in the army would teleport in, loaded for bear and ready to commit extreme violence against anything that moved. So Molly and I strolled along, taking the pretty route, killing time till one a.m.

We stopped off along the way at a pub called the Floating Voter. The pub sign showed the actual voter, floating facedown in the Thames. They're not exactly subtle around Westminster. It was definitely downmarket, as pubs went, and this one went pretty far, but it had the benefit of being the local watering hole for all the political hacks, all the reporters and researchers and hangers-on that accumulate around Parliament like flies round a dead dog. Print reporters, of course; the television people were a more refined breed, with their own upmarket dives to hang around in. And the researchers here were really only glorified runners, making sure their respective MPs had all the information they needed, so they wouldn't disgrace themselves every time they opened their mouths. Heaven forfend that they might have an opinion of their own, not thoroughly tested in advance by market research. It was a hard, thankless and never-ending job, but it was often the only way into the game for people who didn't have the right family or party connections. And there's never been any shortage of people who want to get close to power without the trial of actually getting elected. The Floating Voter was where all these people came to vent their anger as they wet their whistles, and let off steam about what idiots their masters were, and all the other people who were holding them back.

Molly knew a whole bunch of these people from her time in Manifest Destiny, back when that organisation was still pretending to be a part of the political process. We strolled casually into the main bar, and a number of heads came up to smile and nod in our direction. Molly isn't someone you easily forget, and as always, people expected Shaman Bond to turn up anywhere. A bunch of tabloid hacks waved us over to join them at the bar.

"Welcome back to the din of iniquity, Molly dearest!" said an overstuffed gentleman in a long, grubby coat. "Still plotting character assassinations and general insurrection?"

"Ah, happy days," said Molly. "Hello, Brian. Stand me a drink, and I'll tell you where a few bodies are buried."

Everyone laughed, though a bit uneasily. You never knew with Molly. . . .

The pub itself gave every indication of being a bit dodgy, a place where quiet deals could be made, and expensive items purchased cheaply out the back when no one was looking. It was also more than a little old-fashioned, with political cartoons from the fifties and sixties in framed cases on the walls. No one sat alone. People came here to talk. Secrets were currency, and gossip was gold. And everyone had something to sell or, more hopefully, swap. Reputations could be made or destroyed here, and old slights avenged by nudging the right person in the right direction.

There were a lot of sideways glances and muttered conversations, as the regular clientele wondered what Molly Metcalf and Shaman Bond were doing here. Because no one ever came to the Floating Voter by accident, or dropped in for a quiet drink. We must want something; and they were all wondering how best to sell it to us. A lot of them seemed to remember Molly; but then, she always did make an impression. A political journalist from one of the more upmarket tabloids, one Linda Van Paulus, remembered Shaman Bond, and made a point of drifting casually in my direction. She bought me a drink, which was decent of her, and we propped up the bar together for a while, as Molly reestablished old connections and pumped them ruthlessly for information.

"Shaman, darling," said Linda, peering at me sharply over her glass of neat gin, "surprised to see you and the infamous Molly Metcalf together. Business or pleasure?"

"Bit of both," I said.

"Did I hear right, that you two are an item now?"

"Can't keep anything from you, Linda."

"How the hell did that happen?"

"I don't know," I said. "Just lucky, I guess."

Linda was tall and overbearing, with a long, horsey face and a mouth with too many teeth in it, dressed so casually it bordered on downright careless. But she had a mind, when she cared to use it. She looked over at Molly and the people she was talking with, and I could almost hear the wheels turning in her head as she realised what they had in common. I moved in quickly, to distract her.

"So, Linda," I said. "What story are you working on? Anything interesting?"

"The prime minister and his whole cabinet are up to something," Linda said immediately. She never could resist showing just how in-the-know she was. "Bit of a surprise there, because normally they can't agree on anything. They say the new cabinet table is round, so they can all stab one another in the back simultaneously. But whatever it is they're up to, it must be really important, because I can't get even a sniff of it. All my usual sources have either gone into hiding or are holding out for more money than my editors are prepared to pay. Fools. I keep telling them you have to spend money to make money, but the boards are all run by bean counters these days. Penny wise, pound foolish. Not one of them's got printer's blood in their veins." She looked at me suddenly, and put her glass down on the bar. "You know something. You do, don't you? Come on, Shaman; share the goodies, for old times' sake. I'll see you don't go short."

"Well," I said carefully, "you're probably not going to believe this, but I have been hearing very solid rumours that the prime minister and his people are in bed with a new satanic conspiracy."

And the interesting thing was, she didn't immediately laugh in my face. She looked at me thoughtfully and drummed her fingers on the bar. "So, that's what you've been hearing, is it? Wouldn't have anything to do with this Great Sacrifice that our glorious leader was on about? Oh, yes, darling, Auntie Linda has been

244 • Simon R. Green

hearing things, too. My regular sources might be fading into the woodwork, or pricing themselves out of the market, but there are still people willing to talk, if you know where to listen. No one's got any details about this Great Sacrifice yet, but you can bet that the likes of you and I will be the ones who end up making it. And the PM and his lot who end up profiting. See that quiet little chap over there, brooding into his rum and Coke? He's the one you want to talk to. Dear little Adrian Toomey, works for the *Times*, and occasionally as a researcher for the BBC's only decent documentary programme, *Panorama*. Talk to him. See what you can get out of him." She gripped me firmly by the arm, her long fingers digging deep into the flesh. "And be sure you share anything you find out. Yes ... dear, dear Adrian. He's deeper in this than anyone else. Or so he likes to claim ..."

I thanked her, made a few promises I had no intention of keeping and moved over to join Adrian Toomey, who was sitting on the edge of a conversation and paying it no attention at all. His pale blue eyes were far away. He was a stocky, wistful type in a chubby pullover and a shapeless blazer, and his old-school tie was almost certainly more genuine than mine. He blinked mildly at me as I pulled up a chair and sat down beside him, and then he shifted uncomfortably on his chair as I explained what I wanted to know. He leaned forward so he could talk confidentially, his soft, clear voice almost lost in the general noise of the pub.

"All my usual sources have disappeared, Mr. Bond. No one seems to know what's happened to them. And of the few who are left, the official spokespeople, the briefers and the leakers ... they're still talking as much as ever, without actually saying anything. And not because they've been leaned on or scared off; they genuinely don't seem to know what's going on. And these are people who are used to being in the loop, in the know. Everyone's talking about this Great Sacrifice, and the wonderful new future it's supposed to usher in for all of us; but no one knows what it is, or what it involves. Except our current lords and masters. And they only ever talk about it behind closed doors, and with major levels of security, with no record kept of what's said. Someone said . . . they saw the prime minister crying yesterday.

"The farther in I go, the less people have to say. There's an atmosphere in the corridors of power, Mr. Bond. People are scared. Genuinely terrified of something that's coming. They know enough to know that they don't want to know any more. I've never seen anything like it."

"Pardon me for being blunt," I said. "But have you heard anything about a new satanic conspiracy?"

Adrian Toomey looked at me sadly. "Oh, Mr. Bond. I took you for a serious researcher. I don't do that tabloid nonsense."

Molly and I left the Floating Voter not much wiser than we'd arrived. Molly had quizzed all her old contacts, to no effect. The prime minister and his cabinet were definitely planning something, and probably up to no good; everyone was certain of that. . . . But no one knew what. Molly was quite annoyed, and a little mystified, that she hadn't been able to get anything more specific. Westminster isn't usually that good at keeping secrets. Someone always knows, and can't wait to tell . . . for politics, or principle, or money. But it seemed the few people who were in the know weren't talking. Because they were too scared.

Though, interestingly enough, few people were ready to believe in a new satanic conspiracy, except for those who worked on the more downmarket tabloids, for whom such things were their everyday meat and drink. I couldn't help thinking of the boy who cried wolf. . . .

Still, it was a nice enough night, only just past midnight, so we enjoyed a pleasant stroll through the brightly lit streets of Westminster, and happily discussed all the truly appalling things we were going to do to the Satanists at the meeting, once we got our hands on them.

We reached the House of Commons with a good half hour to spare, and one of Philip MacAlpine's people was already there waiting for us. I recognised him immediately, having done business with him before, back when I was only another field agent in London, and still learning my craft. No one ever sent a minor functionary like Alan Diment out on anything important. Alan was a middle-aged, lower-rank courier, as quietly anonymous as any secret messenger should be. He was blond and blue eyed in a minor aristocratic sort of way, the kind that drifts into intelligence work because that was what Daddy did. He would clearly have liked to be mysterious, but didn't have the poise to carry it off. I've no idea what he does at MI-13 when he isn't running errands, but he's trustworthy enough. If only because he doesn't have the ambition to be treacherous.

He was actually walking up and down outside the House of Commons quite openly, looking very much like he didn't want to be there. He nodded quickly to me as I approached, and managed a small but punctiliously polite nod to Molly.

"I can't believe I'm doing this," he said. "But orders are orders, and all that, needs must. . . . So here are two MI-13 security passes: one made out to Shaman Bond, and the other to . . . well, one other. Is she really . . . Yes, thought she was. Best not put her name down on a pass, eh? Don't want to give the chaps inside a coronary. . . . The passes will give you access to the outer lobby, but *no farther*. I was instructed to say that in a very definite voice, and I think you'll agree I gave it my best shot. Anyone bothers you, show them the passes and look mean, and they'll leave you alone. Please don't break anything, *please* don't kill anybody and above all, please don't do anything that might embarrass the department. We're up for a budget review next month, and this is no time to be making enemies, so try not to make any trouble. . . ."

"Trouble?" I said innocently. "Us?"

"If you should be arrested, the department has never heard of you," said Diment. "We'll deny all knowledge of you, and swear blind the passes are forged. Would you like to sign for your passes?"

"What do you think?" said Molly.

"Oh, here," said Diment. "Take the bloody things, so I can go home."

He thrust two small laminated passes into my hand. Very official-looking, but carefully bland. No photo ID, because MI-13 agents don't like to be remembered, and the official signatures were just scrawls. Perfect.

"Right. That's it. I'm off," said Diment. "I am going home to a warm bed and a hot wife, and if you should need any further assistance, feel free to phone anyone except me. Phone MacAlpine. He never liked me. Good-bye."

And he strode off into the night, still muttering to himself. Molly looked at me.

"If I'd known it was this easy to break into Parliament, I'd have done it years ago. You know, I could get you a really good deal on several gallons of napalm. . . ."

"Another time," I said.

Getting into the House of Commons was easy: Flash the passes around and look confident. The police on duty nodded to us. The security guards inside insisted on a close look at the passes, but bowed down to the implied might of MI-13. The outer lobby was exactly like it looks on television: very old, steeped in history and tradition. Full of people with vaguely familiar faces coming and going with an important air about them, even at this early hour of the morning. The business of government never sleeps, which is sometimes a good thing, and sometimes not. Occasionally someone very dignified and important would come striding through the outer lobby, on very important business, smiling graciously at the television crews waiting about, because you never knew when a camera might be rolling. The television reporters showed no interest in Molly or me. They didn't recognise us, so we couldn't be important.

A uniformed security guard with a large sniffer dog felt quite the opposite, and came forward to check us out. So I immediately knelt down and made a big fuss over the dog, rubbing his head and scratching behind his ears, and he wagged his tail happily as I spoke cheerful nonsense to him. The guard looked pained.

"Please don't do that, sir; he's working."

"Oh . . . is he working, then? Is he?" I said to the dog. "Is he working then!"

"Soppy," said Molly.

I showed the guard our passes, and he reluctantly dragged his dog away, only to be replaced almost immediately by a plain-clothed security man who seemed to take it as a personal insult that he hadn't been briefed about an MI-I3 presence in advance. He looked down his nose at me, and then at Molly, and studied our passes very thoroughly, obviously just itching to find something he could say was wrong with them.

"MI-13," he said sniffily. "I am Peregrine Le Behan." And he looked down his nose again, clearly expecting the name to mean something to us. I think we were both supposed to bow down and offer him our firstborn, to appease his wrath. When we looked back at him blankly, he glared at both of us. "No one from your department cleared this with me! Or anyone from Drood Hall. Oh, yes, Eddie Drood and Molly Metcalf . . . I've read your files. You're trouble, both of you, and I want to know what you're doing here with MI-13 passes!"

"At least I'm not one other anymore," said Molly.

"The fact that we're using the passes should tell you that we're not here as ourselves," I said. "As far as you're concerned, as far as anyone's concerned, there's no need to make a big deal of this. We're just two MI-13 people having a quiet look round. No need to panic anyone, is there?"

Le Behan sniffed loudly. "These passes have no validity, since they weren't cleared with me. So I'm confiscating them. And you will both have to come with me while I make further enquiries. I'm sure we can find somewhere suitably depressing to hold you while I find out what's really going on. You should never have been allowed in here in the first place."

"Allowed?" I said, and something in my voice made him fall back a step. I smiled coldly. "No one allows Droods to do anything. We do what needs doing, and minor functionaries like you get the hell out of the way, if they don't want to be trampled underfoot."

Le Behan started to splutter something officious and suitably outraged, so I armoured up my right fist and held it up in front of his face. He stopped talking immediately, his wide eyes fixed on the golden spikes rising up from my knuckles. He actually whimpered a little. He jerked his gaze away and looked at Molly. She smiled unpleasantly, snapped her fingers and turned his expensive shoes into a pair of dead fish. Le Behan looked like he was going to burst into tears.

"Now be a good little functionary, Peregrine, and piss off," I said. "Or we'll get cranky."

"Seriously cranky," said Molly.

"And give me back the bloody passes," I said. He thrust them into my hand, and I gave him a hard look. "Remember: We were never here. Or we'll fix it so you were never here."

"Ever," said Molly.

Le Behan squelched mournfully away in his dead fish, and I made my armoured fist disappear. No one noticed. No alarms. No one was paying us any attention at all. The television people were still waiting for someone important to show up. Security in the outer lobby was seriously rubbish. I'd have to have a word with someone about that later.

Molly and I wandered around the outer lobby, looking the place over. The old walls looked solid enough, but my torc-backed Sight led me immediately to one particular section tucked away in a corner. As we approached, several quite powerful *move along; nothing to see here* avoidance spells kicked in, more than enough to divert normal attention. Molly brushed them aside with a sweep of her hand, like clinging cobwebs. As we drew closer, my Sight showed me a massive door set into the wall, made of solid gold. Molly made admiring noises.

"Is that really solid gold . . . ? It is, it is! Tons of it! Well, one up on the Wulfshead's silver door . . ."

"Don't get any ideas," I said. "The door is fused to the wall; you couldn't pry that loose with an enchanted crowbar." I ran my fingertips across the gleaming gold. It was unnaturally warm to the touch, and subtly unpleasant. As though there were something really nasty on the other side. "This isn't just gold, Molly. It feels . . . inhabited."

"Could this be the same material as your armour?" said Molly.

"Good question," I said. "Obviously not the strange matter of my current armour, but . . . the Heart got up to a lot of stuff that most of the family never got to hear about. No . . . No. I don't think so. London Undertowen had already been in existence for centuries before the Heart crashed into our reality. This is probably a coincidence."

But I couldn't seem to make myself feel comfortable about that, even as I said it.

"How do we get in?" Molly said briskly. "Without our having to do something urgent, violent and attention-gathering?"

"We use the passWord," I said; and I said it. The golden door swung smoothly and silently open before us.

"How did you know that?" said Molly.

"Because Droods know everything," I said.

"Not always," she said sweetly. "Or we wouldn't need to be here, would we?"

"True," I said.

Inside the door, a narrow stairway of very old, very smooth and worn-down stone steps led away into darkness. They looked old enough to have actually been Roman. I looked back, but no one was paying us any attention. The door's avoidance spells were protecting us. I led the way down the steps, Molly following close behind. She wanted to go first, but I wouldn't let her, and then she wanted to walk beside me, but the steps weren't wide enough; so she settled for walking close behind and sulking. There was no handrail, so we had to press our shoulders hard against the rough stone of the adjoining wall to be sure we didn't accidentally get too close to the edge of the steps, and the apparently bottomless drop beyond.

We went down and down and down for quite some time. When I looked back the way we'd come, the light at the top was already gone, shut off by the closing door. The only light came from floating balls of pale green fluorescence, bobbing along on the air before us, leading the way down, like more than usually dependable will-o'-the-wisps. They paused when we paused, but were always careful to maintain a respectful distance, no matter how much I tried to close the gap. The shadows were deep and dark, and the long drop to our side still showed no sign of having any bottom. We descended, following the lights, until I lost all track of how deep we were.

"How deep do you think it goes?" said Molly.

"All the way," I said.

"I hate answers like that," said Molly.

The rough stone wall boasted many overlapping layers of graffiti, laid down over centuries, in many different languages and dialects, including a few traces of Latin. I pointed out one of the clearer sections to Molly.

"Any idea what that says?"

"Sorry," she said. "That is in no way classical Latin. It could be saying, 'Biggus Dickus will make your eyes water,' for all I know."

Some of the writing became clearer as we descended, though many were of ambiguous intent. *The Juwes Are the Men Who Will Not Be Blamed for Nothing. King Mob Leads the Way. We Are All Lilith's Children. Dagon Has Returned!* That last one looked very recent.

My legs began to cramp up, from the strain of the continuing descent, and my back was killing me. Molly had to be feeling it, too, but she didn't complain, so I couldn't. I gritted my teeth against the pain and kept going.

"You'd think they'd have an elevator put in, in this day and age," I said.

"Whom would you trust to run it?" said Molly.

"Good point," I said. "Is it just me, or is the air getting seriously cold . . . ?"

"We're a long way from the sun down here."

"That's probably the point."

"Have you ever visited London Undertowen before?" said Molly. "I mean, you have the passWord. Even I don't know the passWord."

"I'm a Drood field agent in London," I said. "I get to know all the passWords. But no, I've never been down here before. This was always more Matthew's province than mine. He mixed with the authorities, the movers and shakers; worked all the important cases and knew all the important people. I knew about London Undertowen . . . heard all the stories. This is the shadow world, the distorted mirror image of the world above, where the tail wags the dog. As below, so above. They say that all new members of Parliament are brought here after they're elected, dragged down into Under Parliament to be shown where true power lies. And those who won't kneel or bow their head are driven mad or killed."

"I've heard those stories as well," said Molly. "And for once, I really hope they aren't true."

Sometime later, and by then I had no idea at all how much later, we reached the foot of the stairs. Molly and I stopped and leaned on each other, breathing hard. We took it in turn to massage some feeling back into our legs and rub each other's backs, and when we were ready we looked around. We were standing in a narrow stone tunnel lit by a few of the green lights bobbing up by the ceiling. The stone walls gave every indication of being authentically ancient, with the original tool marks still plain to the eye. We followed the corridor for a while, took a sharp left turn, and found ourselves in a large but surprisingly pleasant stone grotto. Bright electric lights pushed back the darkness, which still filled a number of empty doorways leading off. Thick rugs and carpets covered the floor, comfortable furniture was scattered around, and there was even a bar. People stood around chatting cheerfully. Quite a lot of people. If not for the setting, it could have been any party, anywhere. A few people glanced in our direction as we arrived, but no one seemed particularly interested. Because if we were here, it could only be because we were expected.

"It looks like someone's living room," said Molly. "And the people look so . . . ordinary."

"I see a bar," I said. "When in doubt, head for the bar."

Molly looked at some of the empty doorways, full of impenetrable darkness, and actually shivered. "You can't trust anything down here. They say you can find anything, or anyone, somewhere in the catacombs of London Undertowen. Evocations of every place or period, every style and culture. Because nothing's ever lost or forgotten down here. But this . . . this looks like a seventies swingers' party."

"As long as we're not expected to throw our car keys into a bowl," I said.

"Watch your back," said Molly. "Here there be monsters."

I headed for the bar, with Molly striding right at my side. And that was when Isabella Metcalf emerged suddenly from the crowd to confront us. I almost didn't recognise her. She'd abandoned her usual bloodred biker leathers for a city business power suit of navy blue, dark stockings and some shoes that were no doubt very fashionable.

"Are those . . . padded shoulders?" I said innocently.

"Shut up, Eddie," said Isabella.

"No, really, I've heard they're coming back."

"*Shut up*, Eddie."

"Please," I said. "It's, 'Shut up, Shaman Bond,' if you don't mind. I have a secret identity to maintain."

Isabella moved in close, so she could speak clearly without having to raise her voice. "And my name here is Felicity. I killed a conspiracy agent and disposed of the body so I could use her invitation to get in here. How did you . . . ? No. I don't want to know. They all think I'm one of them, for the moment. Luckily I've never been as well-known as you, Molly. No one will be too surprised to see you here, or Shaman; but watch yourselves. This is an even bigger meeting than I'd expected, for people pretty high up in the conspiracy."

I looked around me. "I have to say this really isn't what I was expecting, for a Satanist gathering. I mean, where are all the goats, and the naked women sprawled over altars?"

"You sweet old-fashioned thing, you," said Molly. "Try to keep up with the times. This isn't a religious ceremony; it's a meet-and-greet for the conspiracy faithful. A chance for the upper echelons to get to know one another and show off how well they've all done. A taste of the good life, of rewards yet to come, with probably a few inspirational speeches, and perhaps a minor celebrity from among the higher-ups. And no goats. You've been watching those Hammer horror moves again, haven't you?"

"We need to separate," said Isabella. "Wander around, mingle, talk to people. See what we can learn."

She moved determinedly off, and Molly gave me a quick smile before drifting away in another direction. I went straight to the bar and ordered a Beck's. With a nice cold bottle in my hand and a happy taste in my mouth, I felt much more at ease. The bartender gave me a bit of an odd look when I gave him my order, but I stared him down. I like what I like. I wandered around the huge stone grotto, nodding and smiling at the faces around me. Some of them I knew; a surprising number seemed to know me. But then, Shaman Bond has a reputation for turning up anywhere.

At first, everything seemed normal enough. Just another party, with expensively dressed men and women standing around, drinking from expensive crystal and snacking on expensive party nibbles carried around on expensive silver trays by underpaid tuxedoed waiters. But there was something . . . off about the whole affair. I stopped one of the waiters, who bowed courteously to me.

"Tell me," I said, "what's good in the food department? What are people eating and drinking?"

"Ah, sir," said the waiter unctuously, "only the very best for our honoured guests. The most popular drink is menstrual blood from possessed nuns, and tonight's most requested delicacies are lightly spiced cancers, baby's hearts with cardamom seeds, and pickled eyeballs. Might I offer you—"

"Maybe later," I said.

I dismissed him with a curt wave of the hand, because he seemed to expect it, and he carried on circulating with his tray of satanic delights. Proof, if proof were needed, that some people will eat absolutely anything if they think they're not supposed to. And that nothing here was necessarily what it seemed. The expensively dressed men and women were not here to enjoy themselves. Even though they all displayed that easy smugness that comes from wealth and power and station, they were all working the room with quiet desperation, endlessly circulating, trying to sort out the really important people from the upstarts and wannabes, so they could make a Good Impression with the Right People, and maybe even make that Important Connection. This wasn't a party; it was survival of the fittest. A high-strung woman with darting eyes and far too much makeup planted herself in front of me, and addressed me with practised charm.

"I don't know you, do I?"

"I don't think so," I said. "I'm Shaman Bond. Don't mind me. I'm not anyone important."

"Then why am I wasting time talking to you?" she snapped, and strode off.

"Nice to meet you," I murmured. "I do hope you get dysentery soon."

"You always did know how to make an impression on the ladies," said Molly, easing in beside me.

"Don't touch any of the food or drink," I said.

"Oh, I know all about these dos. You should see what they serve up at witches' sabbats. Some of it would make a goat gag."

"They might be Satanists, but they really don't know how to throw a party," I said. "I've never seen so many people absolutely failing to have a good time. I have also never seen so many faces I would dearly love to punch, on general principle. Everywhere I go, they're all trying to impress me, and one another, with lengthy tales of how horrible they can be, and all the awful things they've done. 'Oh, it's so liberating being a Satanist,' is all I hear, as they talk oh, so casually about rape and torture and murder, and spiritual atrocities of all kinds. 'We might be evil, but at least we're smug about it.'"

"What else did you expect?" Molly said reasonably.

"I could kill every single person here and feel good about it, without a second thought," I said; and there must have been something extra cold in my voice, because Molly looked at me sharply.

"That isn't like you, Eddie, and you know it. Don't let them get to you. We're here to get information—this time."

I shrugged uncomfortably, and took a long drink from my bottle. "I think these people are a bad influence on me."

"Hello, Molly!" said a short, chubby redhead in a silver evening dress that didn't suit her. She and Molly kissed the air near each other's faces, and made *mwah-mwah* sounds, and then the redhead looked me over like I was on sale in a catalogue. Her face was flushed, and she didn't look too steady on her feet.

"This is Jodie Harper," said Molly. "Jodie, Shaman Bond."

"Oh, yes, darling, I've heard about you," said Jodie. "Had enough of being a lone operator at last, eh? Ready to join a winning team?" She didn't give me a chance to answer, turning straight back to Molly. "Been such a while, darling, since the old Danse Academie in the Black Forest, hasn't it? I should have known you'd be here, Molly; you never could bear to be left out of anything." And then she turned back to me. "So, coming up in the world, eh, Shaman? Or, more properly, down!"

She laughed loudly at her own joke, and for the first time I realised how frightened she was. The glass in her hand looked like it contained good old-fashioned booze, and whatever was coming, she'd clearly felt the need to knock back a lot of the stuff in order to face it. Which made me wonder what could be coming that was so bad it scared even hardened Satanists. Jodie realised she was laughing on her own, and stopped abruptly. She swore almost absently, turned her back on us and headed for the bar.

Molly looked coolly after her. "Nothing worse than a superficial Satanist. Jodie never could commit to anything all the way. I don't think she'll last long in this company. Have you noticed, Eddie, all the rugs on the floor come from furs of endangered species? The candles in the candelabra are made from human fat, derived from the bodies of prisoners of conscience and ebola plague victims. Even the air we're breathing has been scented with the essence of suffering, distilled from the tears of innocents."

"How can you possibly know all that?" I said.

"Because it's standard for satanic gatherings," said Molly. "I have been to this kind of do before."

"We will discuss that later," I said.

"The point is," said Molly, "most of this is laid on to impress the guests, to shock and awe them into a proper state of respect for the forces they've sworn to serve. It's not enough for them to break the laws of this Earth; they have to sin in their hearts in everything they do, and glory in it. Everything is permitted, every horror is encouraged, and trampling the weaker underfoot is their duty and delight. There's no room here for the weak of conviction or intent. The atrocities on offer are deliberately designed to weed out the wannabes and impostors."

"Ordinarily, probably," I said. "But I think . . . there's

more to it than that this time. Can't you feel it? In the air, in the faces, in the conversations? There's something coming, and they're all scared shitless of it. Even beyond all the nasty trappings, there's a palpable sense of evil, of spiritual corruption. Like fingernails down the blackboard of my soul. Makes me sick to my stomach . . . makes me want to lash out at everyone. This isn't a party for people, Molly; there's something else here. Something touched by the Pit."

"You don't think they've actually called something up?" said Molly. "Something from Hell, just for this gathering? No . . . No. I would have felt that. I'm sure I would have felt something like that."

"But you do feel something?" I said.

"Yes," said Molly. "Something bad . . . something familiar . . ."

We both stopped talking as another guest homed in on us. Tall, pale, hard faced under long, flat blond hair, wrapped in an apple green cocktail dress, she bestowed an icy smile on me, and nodded quickly to Molly. She looked stringy enough that a strong breeze might blow her away, but fierce nervous energy burned in her eyes and in every bird-quick movement.

"I'm Mother Shipton," she said, in a sharp, clipped voice. "Not my given name, of course. I chose it. Names have power, old names especially so. Thought I recognised you, Shaman; we met at Barty's party, a few years back. While you . . . must be the infamous Molly Metcalf. Yes . . . How sweet. Glad to see such an important witch as yourself finally committing to the Left-hand Path. That Wiccan nonsense was never going to catch on. Far too wishy-washy. You know where you are with Satan. I take it you're both here for the special event? Of course you are. We all are. He is going to tell us the truth at last. All about the Great Sacrifice. I can't wait. He'll be speaking from that special pulpit over there." She gestured at an old-fashioned wooden pulpit wedged awkwardly into one corner of the grotto. Mother Shipton smiled happily. "It's been quite thoroughly debased, of course. In fact, we made quite a party of it. The girls all drank gallons of holy water and then pissed all over it . . . and the boys finished it off with a wicked bukkake session." She giggled briefly. A flat, unpleasant sound. "If that pulpit were any more debased, it would bleed brimstone. A suitable setting for our special guest to enlighten us as to the final stages of the great plan."

"Who is this special guest?" I said.

She looked at me. "You don't know?"

"I've heard several names mentioned," I said carefully. "But I've been disappointed before, so I'll believe it's him when I see him, and not till then."

"Oh, it's him, all right," said Molly. "Look . . ."

The whole party fell silent as everyone turned to watch Roger Morningstar ascend into the debased pulpit. I hadn't seen him arrive, and from the look on the faces of everyone else, they hadn't either. Roger was wearing a blindingly white three-piece suit liberally splashed with fresh bloodstains, like some great Rorschach card from Hell. He wasn't bothering to suppress his demonic side anymore. Two great curling horns sprouted from his forehead, his easy smile showed pointed teeth, his eyes glowed a sullen crimson, and I had no doubt that behind the debased pulpit he now had cloven hooves instead of feet. Roger had embraced his infernal inheritance. And as he took up his position in the debased pulpit and smiled down on his congregation, his presence seemed to fill the whole grotto like a hot and ash-filled wind blowing out of Hell. You only had to look at him to know he was evil, in every sense of the word.

There were startled gasps, and mutterings. And a whole lot of backing away. Suddenly, no one wanted to be noticed. One woman dropped to her knees and vomited. A man started bleeding from his eyes. But most people there looked at him adoringly, as though he were the answer to every vicious prayer they'd ever had.

Roger Morningstar seemed very pleased with himself, looking down at the happy, upturned faces. They

were his before he ever said a word. Because Roger was
a hellspawn, born of man and succubus: the real thing,
the real deal. They all envied him his power and position and wanted it for themselves. He was a prince of
the world to come, and they all wanted to be exactly like
him.

When he leaned forward and rested his hands on the
pulpit, the old wood scorched and blackened and
steamed at his touch.

He didn't bother with opening remarks, or introduc-
tions, or pleasantries to the crowd. He didn't bother
with flattering words or inspirational speeches. He had
come to this place, to these people, to tell them something important. To tell them of Hell's plans for mankind. I could feel my heart pounding in my chest, my
hands clenching into fists. This was about the Great
Sacrifice; had to be. I was finally about to find out what
the hell this was all about.

"Soon it will be time for the Great Sacrifice," said
Roger, his steady ordinary voice still managing to command everyone's attention. "Soon enough, we will have
persuaded all the governments of the world to persuade
all the people of the world to do our work for us. They
will be persuaded to sacrifice their children, at their own
hands, in the cause of a greater good. It's always easier
to persuade people to do terrible things in a good cause.
At the same time all over the world, parents will murder
their children, from teenagers to toddlers to babes in
arms. In all the towns, in all the cities, in all the coun-
tries . . . they will kill their children to gain a better life
for themselves. One generation shall utterly wipe out
another, for the promise of better times to come.

"It shouldn't be too difficult to persuade them. The
old have always distrusted and been jealous of the
young. And the media has been demonising youth for
decades. Blaming them for everything, mocking their
beliefs, presenting them as a menace . . . Parents have
become frightened of their own children. All the leaders of the world will persuade their adult populations
that the current generation of children is rotten, cor-

rupt, beyond saving . . . and a threat to civilisation itself. How much better, how much safer the world will be when they are all gone! They must die so that everyone else can live safely. They can always have more children, better children, in the future. . . . Once the adult population has been properly bombarded with propaganda and whipped into a suitable hysteria, the governments will put weapons into the hands of the adults, step back . . . and let nature take its course.

"Blood shall run in rivers, and all that can be heard will be the screaming of children as the whole world takes part in the greatest mass sacrifice Humanity has ever known. It has to be done willingly; it has to be their choice or it won't be a sin. Managed properly, the whole adult population of the world will damn themselves to Hell.

"We can't intervene directly, but we can influence things, nudge them along. We have people working on a mind-influencing machine of great power, currently being updated by the weapons makers we so recently abducted from the Supernatural Arms Faire. Amazing how fast some people can work, once properly . . . motivated. Soon enough this machine will be completed, and then its influence will spread across the world. Not strong enough to change a mind in itself; that's no use to us. But the machine will help people recognise the good sense of what's being explained to them. We've been using the townspeople we abducted from Little Stoke as test subjects, with most encouraging results. Soon enough we'll have the whole world dancing to a tune only we can hear; and oh, what a merry dance we'll lead them. . . ."

He paused, and the whole crowd burst into ecstatic applause, cheering and clapping and stamping their feet. Molly joined in, to avoid standing out, but I couldn't. I thought I'd been sick to my stomach before, but this . . . I had never heard anything so simply evil, so utterly appalling, so . . . inhuman, in my life. Parents killing their own children? A whole generation betrayed and slaughtered by the very ones supposed to love and protect them? I looked at Roger, and I'd never wanted to kill anyone so much in my life. I clamped down on my emotions and made myself think coolly, so I could work out what best to do next. First I had to get this information back to Drood Hall. The family had to know what was being planned: nothing less than the destruction and damnation of the whole human race. And then Roger started speaking again.

"I know, I know," he said, holding up his hands, and the whole grotto went deathly still and silent again, hanging on his every word. "How does any of this benefit us? What do we get out of it? The purpose of this Great Sacrifice is to make a whole generation guilty of an unforgiveable sin. A despicable act that can never be taken back or atoned for. A whole generation lost to Heaven forever. It won't be enough on its own to release our lord Satan from Hell; he can't break the doors from his side. But with the power the Great Sacrifice will give us, we will smash all the Gates of Hell from this side and let Hell out. Satan shall come forth and rise up, and with him all the fallen and all the damned that have ever been. There will be Hell on Earth; governments shall be cast down, leaders butchered in their seats of power when we no longer need them; and all the populations of the Earth shall be subdued and made slaves, punished for their sins for all time. And all of you who have assisted in this great conspiracy shall be made kings of the Earth, to do with Humanity as you please. They shall suffer at your hands, for your pleasure, forever and ever and ever."

The applause to that was truly deafening. It took a long time to die down, and when it finally did, someone else spoke out before Roger could. I knew it immediately. Isabella. She must have thought she could speak freely from the anonymity of the crowd.

"We've heard all this before, Morningstar. *When* will it happen?"

Roger Morningstar looked down from his debased pulpit and knew Isabella immediately. His glowing crimson eyes snapped back and forth and found Molly and me. He stabbed an accusing finger in our direction.

"A Drood!" he said loudly. "A Drood has come among us! And those treacherous Metcalf witches Isabella and Molly! Seize them! Drag them down!"

The assembled Satanists turned on us like a pack of wild dogs, driven out of their minds with rage at having been infiltrated so easily and having their great moment spoiled. They had been offered a taste of everything they'd ever dreamed of, and they were ready to kill anyone who might thwart that. They threw themselves at Isabella and Molly, howling and spitting, reaching for them with clawed fingers. But the two witches had already moved back-to-back, calling their magics around them. Wild energies sparked and sizzled round Molly's upraised hands, and swirling magics stained the air around Isabella. Powerful magical shields slammed down around both of them, sealing them off, and the Satanists couldn't get to them. There were witches and psychics and sorcerers in the crowd, but none of them were a match for the legendary Metcalf sisters.

Everyone else was looking for the Drood, but none of them were looking at me. They were expecting a figure in golden armour, because that's what a Drood meant to them. They didn't realise Roger Morningstar had pointed at Shaman Bond; why should they? Everyone knew Shaman. . . .

"Get out of here, Drood!" yelled Isabella, lightning crackling round her fists. "We'll keep these bastards occupied!"

Molly threw fireballs into the packed crowd, and suits and dresses and hair immediately caught alight. Men and women screamed shrilly, banging into one another and spreading the flames around. Isabella threw lightning bolts this way and that, blasting men and woman into blackened corpses and throwing jerking bodies in all directions. Molly threw something that spit and fizzled at the debased pulpit, which exploded immediately, throwing Roger through the air and sending jagged wooden shrapnel into the crowd. Screams filled the grotto: shock and pain, horror and rage.

But Roger landed easily, unhurt, and there were so many in the crowd, too many for Molly's and Isabella's attacks to make any real difference.

In the confusion of so much happening at once, it was easy enough for me to armour up while no one was paying any attention to Shaman Bond. As far as the crowd was concerned, a golden-armoured Drood appeared among them out of nowhere. There were shouts and screams, and everyone around me backed hastily away. The Satanists looked at one another, not sure what to do, but perfectly ready for someone else to do it first. A sudden quiet fell over the grotto, broken only by the crackling of flames from burning bodies as Roger Morningstar walked forward to face me, and the whole crowd fell back to give him room.

Roger smiled at me and gestured grandly, raising his voice so everyone could hear. "Full protections are now in place, Drood! You can't get out of here. All the entrances and exits have been sealed, and your precious Merlin Glass can't make contact with the outside world anymore. You're trapped in here with us."

I laughed, and those Satanists near me fell back even farther. I turned my featureless golden mask on Roger. "Well, yes, that's one way of looking at it. Another would be to say that you're all trapped in here with me and the infamous Metcalf sisters. Come to me, Roger. I've never wanted to kill anyone as much as you."

"Typical Drood arrogance," said Roger, not moving. "You have no idea how much power there is in this place for us to draw on. In Under Parliament, in London Undertowen. This is our place, not yours, and you should not have come here, little Drood, little witches."

Molly threw a fireball right at him. Flames spattered all over him and then ran away like so much fiery liquid to pool unnoticed at his feet. He looked at Molly and raised an eyebrow.

"Please, Molly, remember who and what I am. Fire holds no fear for me. You're embarrassing yourself." He turned his attention back to me. "Fight all you want, Drood. It'll make it so much more satisfying when we finally drag you down. And when we eventually send your broken bodies back to Drood Hall, even the most hardened members of your family will weep and vomit at the sight of all the awful things we did to you before we finally let you die."

The Satanists laughed: a low, mean, ugly sound. More animal than human. The sound of people lowering themselves to beasts and glorying in it. I was still separated from Molly and Isabella, the press of the crowd keeping us apart. The Satanists stood very still, watching with hot, eager eyes for any sign of weakness, for any opening they could exploit. There were an awful lot of them, but for the moment they seemed happy enough to follow Roger's authority.

"Really don't like the odds, Iz," said Molly.

"Time to go," said Isabella. "I think we've worn out our welcome. I had the foresight to set up a teleport spell in advance, before I came down here. Roger's shields can't block that, because technically it's already happened. I have only to say the activating Word and we're out of here. But . . ."

"I knew there was going to be a *but*," said Molly. "But what?"

"The spell isn't strong enough to take the Drood with us. It's the armour. . . ."

"No!" Molly said immediately. "I won't leave here without him!"

"Go," I said. "I have armour. You don't. I'll catch up with you later."

"I won't leave you!"

"You have to! Get her out of here, Iz!"

And Isabella grabbed Molly, holding her tightly in her arms as she yelled the activating Word; and they were gone, air rushing in like a miniature thunderclap to fill the place where they'd been.

The crowd of Satanists made a loud, savage, hateful sound and turned all their attention on me. But I was already off and running. I lowered my golden shoulder and ploughed right through them, sending broken bodies flying to either side of me as I pressed on. I struck about me with spiked golden fists, tearing flesh and sending blood spraying through the air. I wanted to kill them all, wanted it so badly I could taste it; but I knew bad odds and a worse situation when I saw one. What mattered now was getting the information out. The family had to know about the Great Sacrifice.

Shrieking and howling men and women threw themselves at me, trying to block my way and drag me down, but they were no match for my armour. Bones broke and people fell as I slammed through the crowd, heading for the way I'd come in. I tried to reach Drood Hall through my armour, or even Ethel; but no one heard me. Roger's shields saw to that. I was on my own. And then a voice came to me through my armour: Roger Morningstar's voice, saying, "You can't get out. You can't get away. You belong to us now."

I forced the voice out of my head and burst through the crowd, only to find the stone tunnel that led from the stairs to the grotto was no longer there; the exit had been sealed off with solid stone. I hit the wall with my golden fist, and the stone broke and fell apart, but there was only more stone beyond. I hit it again and again, but there was always more stone, as though the whole tunnel had been filled in. I spun round to face the waiting crowd. I'd seen other exits on the far side of the grotto, but I'd have to fight my way through the crowd to reach them. With no guarantee Roger hadn't sealed them off, too.

The Satanists took their time closing in, jeering and taunting me in thick, spiteful voices. I'd spoiled their fun, their special event, and they meant to make me pay for that in blood and horror. They showed me their weapons, the awful things they'd brought down into London Undertowen with them. Some had Aboriginal pointing bones; some had glowing witch daggers; some had bone amulets. One had a Hand of Glory made from a mummy's paw: a forbidden weapon. Some had black-

magic charms, made from the bones and skin of sui-
cides. One of them even had what looked very like a
variation of my own Colt repeater. Which I hadn't
brought with me for fear of setting off the security
alarms. I kept a watchful eye on the gun; it didn't seem
likely the Satanists would have access to strange-matter
bullets, but you never knew. . . . The Immortals had
them.

The crowd hit me with everything they had, unleash-
ing all their weapons at once. Terrible energies crawled
all over me, dancing on my armour, discharging in the
air, unable to pierce strange matter. Magics fell away;
curses failed, unable to get a hold. My armour rang like
a gong and sounded like a bell from all the many impacts and concussions, but I felt none of it, safe from
harm.

The armour absorbed bullets and shook off everything else. I stood firm, defying them all, letting them
exhaust their weapons. The crowd quickly grew tired of
that, and the braver of them surged forward to attack
me directly. Glowing blades shattered on my armour,
and magical weapons glanced aside harmlessly. I
laughed behind my featureless mask, waiting for them
to come within reach of my armoured hands. A part of
me wanted to run wild and kill them all. To smash their
hated faces with my spiked gloves, to kill and kill, sinking myself in rage. But I couldn't do that. Wouldn't do
that. Partly because . . . that would make me just like
them. But mostly because I still knew my duty: to wait
for a chance to escape and get the information out.

And then suddenly, it all stopped. No more weapons,
no more attacks, no more shouted threats and insults.
The crowd was silent, backing away to allow Roger to
walk through them to face me again. They didn't want to,
but Roger's air of authority, and his sheer infernal presence, overpowered them. He stood before me, careful
to stay out of arm's reach. I studied him carefully from
behind my mask. He knew I was Shaman Bond. Was he
about to reveal and destroy my other identity? Because

he could? I didn't think so. . . . More likely he'd keep
that knowledge for himself, for some future occasion of
pressure or blackmail.

He looked more demonic than ever. Crimson flames
curled around his cloven hooves, and he'd left a trail of
burning hoofprints behind him in the expensive rugs
and carpets. He carried with him a stench of blood and
sulphur and sour milk: the scent of Hell. A circle of
buzzing flies surrounded his horned head like a halo.

"Sorry about all that," he said easily. "Have to let
them have their fun now and again."

"Why?" I said.

He nodded slowly, knowing I wasn't talking about the
crowd. "Why am I here? Why am I on Hell's team? Oh,
Eddie, it's really very simple. When I last went down into
Hell, as an emissary for your family, it was made very
clear to me in the Houses of Pain that I was persona non
grata. For letting the side down, for embracing my human nature over my infernal inheritance, for siding with
the Droods. But most of all for showing love and compassion to Harry. That's not allowed for my kind. I was given
a choice: Show which side I was truly on by leading this
new Satanist conspiracy, betraying the Droods in general
and Harry in particular . . . or be hauled down into Hell
again at the first opportunity, dragged screaming and
kicking into the Pit, to know torment and horror forever.
Not a difficult choice, really.

"And now, the end is nigh. There's enough power in
this place and in these people to allow me to peel that
armour right off you. If you won't see sense and surrender."

I laughed right into his face. "You could try, hellspawn."

"The time of the Droods is over. This is Hell's time,
come round at last. You heard what's coming. You can't
stop it."

"This isn't you, Roger," I said. "Not really. You were
with us when we fought the Hungry Gods, and the Accelerated Men, and the Immortals."

"That was then," said Roger. "This is now. And this, truly, is me."

"Do you really think this pathetic bunch of losers and wannabes will ever be a match for my family?"

The crowd made ugly noises, only to fall silent again the moment Roger glanced at them. Roger smiled calmly. "We have something you don't."

"Like what?"

"You'll find out. The whole point of a secret weapon is to keep it secret right up until you finally use it."

"So," I said. "What now? Are you really going to try to kill me, cousin?"

"No," said Roger. "I'm going to let you go."

"What?" I said.

But my voice was drowned out by the crowd's. They turned on Roger, yelling and protesting in a hundred voices at once. A Drood, helpless before them? They'd dreamed of an opportunity like this. Some of them had been at Lightbringer House when Alexandre Dusk had let me go, and they weren't at all happy about my escaping their anger again. But Roger glared about him, not even deigning to speak to them, and where his gaze fell the Satanists grew silent and looked away. And slowly, like a man surrounded by a pack of half-trained dogs, Roger brought them under control again.

"I want you to go back to your family, Edwin, and tell them of your failure." Roger smiled slowly, letting me see his pointed teeth. "I want you to make your report to the council and tell them everything you learned here."

"Tell Harry?" I said.

"Tell them all. I want the Droods to know what's coming, what I've put together to send against you. There's nothing you can do to stop it. Because you're one oversize and overextended family, while the conspiracy is a worldwide organisation with governments at our beck and call."

"What should I tell Harry?" I said.

"Tell him . . . it was fun while it lasted." He made a

brusque gesture with one hand. "There. The shields are down. Go. While you still can."

Molly and Isabella appeared immediately behind me, grabbed me in their arms and teleported me out. And the last thing I heard was Roger Morningstar's infernal laughter.

CHAPTER NINE

For a Moment There, I Thought We Might Be in Trouble

Glad as I was to be waving good-bye to the Satanists' little get-together, of all the places Molly and Isabella might have teleported me to, a Drood Council meeting in the Sanctity... wouldn't even have made my top ten. But still, when the glare of the teleport died down, there Molly and I were, standing right in front of the council table, facing a somewhat startled Sarjeant-at-Arms, the Armourer, Harry and... William the Librarian. The Sarjeant went from startled to shocked to a state of utter outrage, where his face went a shade of purple not normally seen in nature. Unless you're thinking of a baboon's arse, which mostly I try not to. The Armourer cracked a big smile, and actually dropped me a brief wink. Harry looked at me disapprovingly, but then, he always did. While William... considered me thoughtfully, his expression surprisingly cool and collected. He was also a whole lot better dressed than usual, in that he looked like he might actually have dressed himself, for once. The Sarjeant glared at Molly and me.

"Just once, I would appreciate it if you could find the common courtesy to use the bloody door, like everyone else!"

"Boring," said Molly. "I don't do ordinary, and I have never been like everyone else."

"One of your many charms," I said. "And thanks for the rescue."

"Rescue?" said the Armourer. "Are we to take it something went wrong with your infiltration of the Satanists' meeting?"

"Pretty much everything that could go wrong did," I said.

"Hold it," said Molly, looking quickly around her. "Where's Isabella?"

"She was right there with you when you arrived to grab me," I said. "Was she supposed to appear here with you?"

"Well, I assumed . . . We were both hovering nearby in London Undertowen, waiting for the Satanists' shields to drop long enough for us to jump in and haul you away. . . . We didn't bother to discuss things. I suppose she must have decided she wouldn't be welcome here." She scowled at the Sarjeant. "Wonder where she could have got that idea."

"I'm sure she'll turn up," I said soothingly. "Whether we like it or not."

"Yeah, that's Isabella for you." Molly beamed at me suddenly. "Hey, I rescued you!"

I sighed. "You're never going to let me forget that, are you?"

"Never," Molly said happily.

"He was letting me go, you know."

She snorted loudly. "That's what he *said*. . . ."

"Enough!" said the Sarjeant-at-Arms, slamming one huge fist on the table. "I want your report, Edwin! I want to know everything that happened at the Satanists' meeting, everything that went wrong, and why a Drood in full armour needed to be rescued!"

There are some things you can't put off indefinitely, and one of them is the breaking of bad news. I armoured down, and then Molly and I drew up chairs and sat down at the table, and I filled the council in on all that I'd learned in Under Parliament. Including Roger Morningstar's presence, his important position in the conspiracy, and his explanation of the true nature of the coming Great Sacrifice. No one on the council said anything, but all of them listened intently. They couldn't keep the emotions out of their faces. They were appalled, disgusted, outraged; but in the end they all showed nothing but a cold determination. Because we are Droods, and we know our duty: to seek out the evil forces that threaten Humanity and put a stop to them. Whatever it takes; whatever it costs us.

"But who's behind all this?" the Armourer said finally. "Alexandre Dusk was the front man at Lightbringer House, but bad as he is, he's not top rank and never has been. And while Roger was the main speaker at Under Parliament, there's no way he could be in charge of the conspiracy. So who's running things? Who came up with the idea of the Great Sacrifice, and then arranged the necessary threats and pressures to make all the governments of the world go along with it?"

"No one at the meeting knew," said Molly. "And it wasn't for lack of trying to find out."

"I still can't believe Roger could have betrayed us all," said Harry. He was trying to sound calm and professional, like everyone else, but his heart wasn't in it. He took off his wire-rimmed spectacles and rubbed at his forehead tiredly. He was sitting slumped in his chair, as though he'd taken a hit. "He couldn't do this to us. He wouldn't! He must be working undercover, trying to bring them down from inside. . . ."

"I'm sorry, Harry," I said, and I really was. "I don't think so."

"You never liked him!" Harry yelled at me, his face flushed with anger and something else. "You were one of those who wanted to split us up because . . . just because he was what he was. . . ."

He stopped, on the edge of tears he refused to shed in front of us. No one said anything. In the end, surprisingly, it was Molly who tried to comfort him.

"I cared for him, too, once. He did have . . . admirable qualities. But we always knew what he was, what he really was. . . ."

"Once a hellspawn," said the Sarjeant-at-Arms.

"Shut up!" said Harry. "I don't want to hear it! You didn't know him! You never even tried to understand him!"

He jumped to his feet, turned his back on us all and stormed out of the Sanctity, slamming the door behind him. We all looked at one another, but there was nothing we could usefully say, so we returned to the more pressing business at hand. Harry would come around. Or he wouldn't. Either way, we'd deal with it.

"The truly disturbing part of all this is how far and how deep the conspiracy's control goes," said the Sarjeant. "All the governments, all the leaders in the world? Not one holdout? How long has this been going on? How could we have missed this?"

"In our defence, we have been rather busy of late," said the Armourer. "And it is the nature of conspiracies to go unnoticed."

"The question we have to consider," said the Sarjeant, scowling harshly, "is how far does the corruption go?"

"Anyone can be bought," said William, in a surprisingly reasonable voice. "Anyone can be persuaded, bribed, threatened. Even possessed, I suppose, in this case. We are facing an enemy with no restraint and no moral convictions, who will do absolutely anything to get what they want. You can't trust anyone anymore. . . ."

"Am I going to have to scan the whole family again?" said the Armourer.

"I think we can see Roger as a separate case," I said. "Given who and what his mother was. And anyway, how could you scan a mind for evil intentions?"

"Hmmm. Yes," said the Armourer. "Tricky. Not impossible, necessarily, but definitely tricky . . ." And he sat back to think about it.

Sometimes I think my uncle Jack is the scariest Drood of all.

"Roger mentioned a new machine that could directly influence people's thoughts," I said. "Apparently they've already carried out basic testing, with encouraging results. Roger implied this new machine could quite definitely give people's minds a good solid nudge in the wanted direction. On a worldwide basis. Do we have anything like that, Uncle Jack?"

"Of course not," said the Sarjeant-at-Arms. "Or we'd be using it on a daily basis."

"Can I mention free will and individual freedom?" said William.

"Of course," said the Sarjeant. "Feel free to mention it, and I'll feel free to use anything that would prevent a horror like the Great Sacrifice."

"If the machine really doesn't exist," I said, "Roger could have been blowing smoke up their arses to impress the faithful. But if it does . . . could we perhaps come up with something to block the effect: some kind of counterbroadcast?"

"Without knowing what this machine is?" said the Armourer. "Without knowing how it works, or how it does what it does? You want me to set up a counterbroadcast that would cover the whole world? Hmmm. Tricky. I'll have to think about it."

I raised my voice to address the rosy red glow suffusing the Sanctity. "Ethel?"

"I'm here, Eddie. I'm glad you got back safely. I could see what was happening in Under Parliament, but I couldn't reach you. Such a tacky gathering, confusing bad taste with spiritual evil."

"Can you do anything to stop this?" I said bluntly. "Could you prevent this Great Sacrifice from taking place?"

"You're asking me to intervene directly?" said Ethel.

"I don't like to," I said. "But with so much at stake . . ."

"The children," said the Sarjeant-at-Arms. "We have to save the children. We can't let our pride get in the way of that. I'll beg if I have to."

"Right," said William. "This is more important than us."

"And that's precisely why I can't intervene," said Ethel. "I'm your guardian angel, not your god. This is your world, your reality. I have given you weapons with which to fight evil. But I won't fight your fights for you. Or that would be the end of free will for your whole species. I have made a great effort to stay out of your affairs, to be an observer and adviser, for fear of upsetting the natural balance of your reality. I will not save you. You must save yourselves."

"And if we fail?" said William.

There was a long pause, and then Ethel said, "I will mourn your passing."

Everyone at the table looked at everyone else, but no one felt like saying anything. I cleared my throat.

"So, how can we best take the fight to these bastards? I've had enough of tiptoeing around the conspiracy, gathering information. We know all we need to know. We have to hit these evil little shits hard, before they can set up the necessary conditions for the Great Sacrifice!"

"Know thy enemy," said William.

"Fine," I said. "Go do your research in the Old Library. Find out things we can use against them. Sarjeant, how can we hurt them?"

"Give me a target," said the Sarjeant, "and I'll throw Droods at them till every single member of the conspiracy is dead. The problem with Satanists is that they can be anyone, anywhere, hiding within respectable institutions, using innocents as human shields."

"Isabella did a lot of thinking about that," said Molly. "She said . . . she thought she knew someone who might be able to at least point her in the direction of the conspiracy's headquarters."

"Did she mention a name?" I said.

"No. But then, Iz has contacts everywhere."

"Call her," I said. "Contact her. Now."

But before any of us could do anything, Isabella was suddenly right there in the room with us, standing at the end of the table. She was a mental sending, not a physical presence. Her image was vague and unstable, semi-transparent, trembling as though bothered by some harsh-blowing aetheric wind.

The Sarjeant slammed his fist on the table again and looked seriously upset.

"How the hell do you keep appearing inside Drood Hall, despite all the defences and protections I have put in place precisely to keep out persons like you?"

Isabella looked at me. "Haven't you told him yet?"

The Sarjeant looked at me suspiciously. "Told me? Told me *what*, Eddie?"

"Later," I said. "Iz, where have you been?"

"Going back and forth in the world, and walking up and down in it," Isabella said calmly. "Talking to people. Making them talk to me. I found a certain person who was only too willing to tell me what I wanted to hear, after a certain amount of physical persuasion. A charming little rogue called Charlatan Joe."

"I know him," I said immediately. "Not sure I'd agree with the description. Joe's a city slicker, a confidence trickster. A sleazy adventurer who never met a mark he couldn't shaft. But it's surprising how often he's in the right place to overhear things that matter. . . ."

"Exactly," said Isabella. Her sending shifted and trembled, as see-through as any ghost for a moment, and her mouth moved with no sound reaching us, until she suddenly snapped back into focus again. "By being somewhere he really shouldn't have been, while doing something anyone could have told him was a bad idea, dear Joe overheard something so big, so important and so shocking that it scared the crap out of him. So he dropped into a deep hole and pulled it in after him, determined to disappear until what he knew wouldn't matter anymore. Except I can find anyone when I put my mind to it. And I know more about the darker magics than he ever dreamed of. I found him and made him cry, and after I'd wiped his nose for him he couldn't wait to tell me everything he knew. To be exact: where the next big meeting of the satanic conspiracy leaders will be taking place. Not the upper echelons, like Alexandre Dusk and Roger Morningstar, but the guys at the very top.

"You haven't got much time, Molly, Eddie. . . . It's three hours from now, and they won't be there for long. According to Charlatan Joe, they're there to witness the first wide-range test of the mind-influencing machine on a city full of unsuspecting people."

"Okay, that's it," I said. "We have to go right now. A full-on preemptive strike, a whole army of Droods led by all the field agents we can round up at such short notice. Hit the bastards hard when they're not expecting it, stamp them into the ground, take out the machine and capture all the conspiracy leaders in one go."

"Sounds like a plan to me," said the Sarjeant-at-Arms. "Three hours . . . Give me one hour, Eddie, to put a strike force together. It'll have to be a really good size; we can't know how many ground troops there'll be, or what kind of weapons they might have. But we can do this. We can stop the conspiracy dead before they even get a chance to start the Great Sacrifice. Where are they, Isabella? Where are they meeting?"

"The setting is a deconsecrated cathedral at Glastonbury," said Isabella. "Apparently it was turned into a hotel decades ago. It's been completely refurbished as the Cathedral Hotel; runs business courses, that sort of thing. The conspiracy's booked the whole hotel under different names, so you don't have to worry about any innocents being involved."

"Sounding better all the time," said the Sarjeant.

"A deconsecrated cathedral," said the Armourer. "These old-time Satanists do love their traditional touches. For masters of evil they can be surprisingly sentimental about such things."

"Let's not get ahead of ourselves," said William. "And for the record—I can't believe I'm being the calm voice of reason here—can I remind you, Eddie, the last times you went head-to-head with the Satanists didn't go too well, did they? You were run out of Lightbringer House, and you had to be rescued from Under Parliament. You were lucky to get out alive even with your Drood armour. We need to talk about this. And yes, I know that phrase is dripping with irony where I'm concerned, but . . ."

"We don't have time for academic discussions," said the Sarjeant. "Three hours, remember? You think; we'll organise."

"Don't worry, William," I said. "This time we'll be going in mob-handed, at the head of an army of armoured Droods. Like we did with the Immortals at Castle Frankenstein. The Satanists won't know what's hit them till it's far too late."

"I still don't like it," the Librarian said stubbornly. "Violence is playing their game."

"Then we'll have to play it better than them," said the Sarjeant. "Isabella, what else can you tell us . . . ?"

But she was gone, not even a wisp of presence left at the end of the table. Molly tried to reach her, to regain contact, but couldn't. She frowned unhappily.

"It's not like she's blocking me out; it's as though she isn't even there. Something's wrong."

"Maybe she thought someone else might be listening in," I said. "She wouldn't want to risk giving the game away."

"Yes," said Molly. "That makes sense." But she didn't sound happy about it.

The Sarjeant hurried off to organise the troops. The Armourer wandered off to go think destructive thoughts in the Armoury. William waited till they were gone, and then took me to one side for a few private words.

"I've been feeling a lot better since Ammonia Vom Acht's . . . intervention," he said. "My thoughts are clearer than they've been in . . . well, I don't know how long."

"I had noticed," I said.

"I wanted to ask you about her. Ammonia." The Librarian gave me a look I wasn't sure I understood. "A most remarkable woman."

"Remarkable," I said.

"Excellent mind. There was a certain amount of . . . transfer, you see, when she made contact with my thoughts. She really was very impressive."

"Impressive," I said.

"So, you see, I was wondering . . ."

"She's married," I said.

"Ah. Of course she is." He nodded slowly. "The best ones always are, aren't they?"

He strode off, back to the Old Library, and I genuinely didn't know what to think.

Over the next hour, the Sarjeant-at-Arms ran himself ragged all over Drood Hall, gathering up volunteers from every section and department, putting together a small army of more than a hundred Droods for his strike force. It was all I could do to keep up with him. Give the man his due: He's good at his job. And if there's a big fight on, there's no one else in the family you'd rather follow into danger and sudden death, because you know he'll move Heaven and Earth not only to get the job done, but to bring you back safely as well. All Droods are trained to fight from an early age, but few ever realistically expect to see action. Recent events—in the Hungry Gods war, and with the Accelerated Men attack—had changed all that. A lot of previously purely academic Droods had had to go out and fight, and much to everyone's surprise they found they had a taste for direct intervention. So when the Sarjeant went looking for volunteers, he found them everywhere.

He assembled his strike force on the grounds outside the Hall and put them through their paces to see who was actually up to the job. He strode up and down, barking orders, watching closely as Droods duelled in their armour. I stood well back and let him get on with it. The Sarjeant had always been better at the military side of things than I ever had.

We had nine active field agents: all that had been present in the Hall, reporting in from completed missions. They should have been resting, recovering, but once they heard what the job was, we couldn't keep them out. A dozen more were on their way in, but the odds were it would all be over before they could get here. We also had five ex–field agents retired from active duty for various physical and psychological reasons. They were just as determined not to be left out. They had things to prove, to the family and themselves. One of them was Callan.

"My deputy can run the War Room till I get back," he said defiantly, standing beside me as we watched the Sarjeant run the strike force.

"You don't have to do this, Callan," I said.

"Yes, I do." Callan stared out at the organised mayhem before him, so he wouldn't have to look at me. "Last time I was out in the field, I had my torc ripped right off me by that bastard traitor the Blue Fairy. You have no idea what that felt like. I haven't left the Hall since, even after Ethel gave me a new torc. I need to get out there, beat some Satanist brains in, prove to myself that I can still do this. That I'm still a Drood. Or I'll end up back in my room again, refusing to come out, afraid of everything. I can't go back to that, Eddie. I won't go back to that. I'm going with you. You need the numbers. And besides . . . I've got a bad feeling about this."

"You've always got a bad feeling about everything," I said. "That's why we put you in charge of the War Room."

"I went out to fight the Accelerated Men," said Callan. "Along with everyone else. I'm not like you, Eddie. I never enjoyed the violence of being a field agent. But I enjoyed it well enough that day. Sometimes . . . it does you good to strike back at the world that's hurt you."

And he went off to get involved in the mayhem.

We'd also found twelve retired field agents, the youngest being fifty-two, the oldest sixty-four. They all looked older than their years; life in the field does that to you. Most field agents don't live long enough to retire; the great game chews most of us up long before that. So for these old men to still be around meant they had proved themselves very hard to kill. I had a hunch that could come in handy.

Everyone in the strike force was a volunteer; not one pressed or pressured man. News of the nature of the Great Sacrifice had spread quickly through the Hall, and the general feeling of outrage was so thick in the air you could practically taste it. So there was no shortage of people willing and eager to go and fight the Satanists, to prevent such an obscenity from taking place. And yet . . . even though I would be going out with over a hundred armoured Droods to back me up, I still had a terrible cold, sick feeling in the pit of my stomach. As though I'd missed something—something important, even obvious . . .

On top of that, the last time I'd led an army of Droods out against an enemy, against the Loathly Ones on the Nazca Plains . . . it had all gone horribly wrong. We'd been ambushed, taken by surprise, outnumbered by hidden forces, and a lot of good men and women died badly that day. I went out at the head of an army, but all I brought home were body bags. . . .

Still, this time I had an ace in the hole. The Merlin Glass. It could drop us right on the Satanists, appearing out of nowhere, without warning. As long as I left it open, I'd always have a way out. If it was needed. If everything went wrong again.

At the last moment, Molly and Harry came out of the Hall to join us. I had wondered where she'd been. The two of them had clearly been talking together, because they were almost comfortable in each other's company. Molly moved in close beside me, linked her arm through mine and leaned her head against my shoulder. She'd been talking with Harry about the time she and Roger were lovers, long ago. I knew that, and she knew that I knew. And we both knew this wasn't the time to be concentrating on the past.

"I'm going with you," said Harry, in a way that made it very clear there was no point in arguing with him. "Roger's going to be there."

"Probably," I said. "You really think you can talk him out of this? Bring him back to the side of the angels?"

"Before you left Under Parliament," said Harry, looking out across the grounds so he wouldn't have to look at me, "before Roger let you go . . . you said you asked him if there was anything he wanted to say to me. Any message. He could have said any number of things: told me it was all over, told me he never really loved me, told me to go to Hell. . . . But he didn't. I can still reach him; I know I can. . . . So I have to go, Eddie. I have to try."

"Fair enough," I said. "But don't get in the way once the killing starts. This is war. And given what's at stake . . ."

"I know," said Harry.

The Sarjeant-at-Arms finally called a halt to his martial exercises, assembled his army before him and took the opportunity to bore the arses off them with what he probably thought was an inspirational speech. I looked the Droods over, and was quietly pleased with what I saw. They looked like soldiers ready to go into battle. They looked like an army. I put up with as much of the Sarjeant's speech as I could stand, and then took out the Merlin Glass and activated it. The Sarjeant stopped talking as he realised no one was listening to him any longer. I shook the Glass out to full size, and then opened it up even further, pushing it to a greater size than I'd ever attempted before, finally ending up with a gateway some twenty feet square. I hadn't been sure that would work, but it seemed stable enough.

I looked through the opening, and there was the Cathedral Hotel, right where the coordinates said it should be. A large building, clearly much rebuilt, with a slick modern facade. The sign said simply, cathedral hotel. Four stars. The only remaining vestige of the building's original nature was an old bell tower stuck right on the end, presumably retained as a historical touch. Something for the tourists to take photographs of.

A massive car park sprawled out before the hotel, with neatly marked bays but only a handful of parked cars. No one about, no signs of Satanists anywhere. The whole place was quiet and peaceful on a warm sunny day. So far, so good. I decided it was time for a quick inspirational speech of my own. I turned to address the Drood army, and they looked at me expectantly.

"You look like you're ready for a fight," I said. "Good. I'll lead you through the Merlin Glass. No armour—not yet. We don't want to freak any innocent passersby. Straight across the car park and into the hotel. Armour up then. The Satanists have block-booked the hotel, to ensure their privacy. So once you're in there, if they're not clearly hotel staff, stamp them into the ground. No warnings, no mercy. They won't be taking prisoners and neither will we. Except for their leaders: Alexandre Dusk, Roger Morningstar and anyone with them. Take them alive, if you can. We have questions."

"Kill them if they stand; kill them if they run," the Sarjeant said bluntly. "Don't hold back. For everything these bastards have done, and everything they plan to do . . . death is the only answer, the only justice."

"The mind-influencing machine should be on the premises somewhere," I said. "Take it intact, if you can. Just to make the Armourer's day. But if it looks like someone's trying to run it, kill them and smash the machine. Your armour should protect you from all outside influences, but we're not taking any chances on this mission. All right, that's it. Good hunting."

I strode through the Merlin Glass, Molly at my side, Harry and the Sarjeant all but treading on my heels. The Drood army filed through after us. In a few moments we were all through the Glass and spreading out across the empty car park. And that was when it all changed. The calm and quiet scene before us disappeared, gone in a moment, swept away like the illusion it always was. Between us and the hotel stood a massive army, thousands of heavily armed Satanists, with Alexandre Dusk standing at their head . . . smiling complacently at me.

"It's a trap!" yelled the Sarjeant. "Defend the Glass! It's our way home!"

But when we all turned to look, the Merlin Glass was only a twenty-foot-square mirror reflecting our shocked faces. I tried half a dozen different control Words, but the Glass was just a glass. The Satanists had blocked it again, like they had in Under Parliament. I was getting really tired of that. I turned to Molly.

"It was all false information, designed to lure us into a trap. Could Isabella have been turned? Could she have been one of them all along?"

"No!" Molly said immediately. "She couldn't hide something like that from me. She never had any time for Satanists. They must have captured her. No wonder we saw only a sending in the Sanctity. It was an illusion, never her at all. What have you done with my sister, Dusk, you Satanist scumbag?"

Alexandre Dusk smiled easily at Molly and me. He looked very relaxed, very at his ease, as though he were out to enjoy the sunny day, not standing at the head of an army ten times the size of mine. He nodded easily to me, the condescending bastard.

"Why do you think Roger let you go?" he said, in an infuriatingly reasonable tone of voice. "We knew Molly and Isabella were still hanging around, waiting for a chance to jump in and rescue you, so we made that possible. When they teleported you out, we were waiting, and it was a simple task for a few of our more accomplished sorcerers to reach in and grab Isabella and materialise her in one of our places of power. She never even saw it coming. And while she is a very talented young lady, we have some very powerful people of our own these days. People who can tell which way the wind is blowing.

"Then all we had to do was send you the image of her, and have her say our words with her mouth. Present you with an urgent deadline so you didn't have time to think about it, and an opportunity too good to resist. So you'd charge right in, Eddie, like you always do. And here we all are! Ah ... so many Droods in one place. Unprecedented! So many torcs for us to take from your dead bodies and make our own."

"Yeah, right," I said. "Like that's going to happen."

Dusk's smile didn't falter in the least. "I'm really

looking forward to this, Eddie. There are still those in the world waiting for you to save them from us; I shall make a point of sending a severed Drood's head to each and every one of them, to stamp out that last trace of hope."

"Arrogant little prick," I said. "You're facing an army of Droods. A sane man would be running by now. Not that it would do any good."

"One hundred and seven Droods, by my count," said Dusk, still entirely unruffled, and I was beginning to wonder why. "Whereas I have one thousand three hundred highly motivated men and women, armed with all the very latest weapons. Your precious and much-vaunted armour is a thing of the past. You are yesterday's men. We are cutting-edge."

I had to smile. "You didn't keep up with the memos, did you? We've upgraded."

Dusk made an annoyed, frustrated gesture, upset that we weren't properly impressed and taking his threats seriously. "You're all going to die, Droods! And your pathetic antiquated morality with you!"

"Not going to happen," said the Sarjeant-at-Arms briskly. "A battle can go either way; any good soldier knows that. But even if you should destroy all of us, it wouldn't make any difference. Whatever happens, the family goes on. Droods maintain."

"You don't know what you're facing," said Dusk, his voice cold though his face was flushed. He wasn't finding this as much fun as he'd thought he would. He kept giving us the right feed lines, and we kept refusing our cues. We were supposed to realise we were already beaten and shiver in our shoes, try to surrender, maybe even beg for mercy so he could laugh in our faces as he turned us down. We shouldn't only be staring defiantly back at him and laughing in his face. He gestured at the ranks and ranks lined up behind him. "Allow me to present our very latest acquisition, courtesy of one of those brilliant minds we abducted from the Supernatural Arms Faire. We have our own armour now. Modern armour. He really was ready to present Drood-equivalent armour at the fair this year, only we got to him first. Step forward, boys."

A dozen men stepped forward to show themselves off. At least, I assumed they were men. It was hard to tell.

"This new armour is state-of-the-art living superplastic, preprogrammed to follow direct instructions from its wearer via a cybernetic mind-link," Dusk said proudly. "Indestructible, endlessly adaptable, capable of taking on any shape or function the mind of the wearer can conceive. A thousand weapons in one, combined with an absolute defence. Every wearer an army in his own right."

And then he stopped, because there was a certain amount of quiet sniggering going on in the Drood ranks. Dusk glared back and forth.

"Sorry," I said. "Terribly rude, I know, but . . . is that it? Really? *That*'s your modern armour?"

"They look like toy soldiers," said the Sarjeant-at-Arms.

He had a point. They did. Covered from head to toe in a dull grey plastic, smooth and featureless, like grown men dipped in liquid plastic and allowed to harden. I kept wanting to look at their feet for the bases they should be standing on. Some of them were holding plastic rifles, the material of the guns blending seamlessly into their plastic hands. Their faces were rough and blurred versions of the features under the plastic, like any toy soldier.

"Go!" Dusk said angrily to his plastic men. "Show them what you can do! A special bonus to the first man to bring me a Drood head!"

The plastic men surged forward inhumanly quickly, followed by more than fifty others from the ranks. The plastic armour stretched smoothly with every movement. Those without guns extruded swords and axes from their plastic hands, with fiercely sharp edges. Some had rifles; some had handguns; some had machine guns, though I still hadn't worked out what they were going to fire. Plastic bullets? Against Drood armour?

And then . . . it all started to go wrong. The plastic armour began to change, the basic grey flushing with bursts of swirling colours. Dark, angry shades of red and blue and green, feverish purples and sick yellows. Swirling on the surface of the plastic armour like infected oil slicks.

The wearers stumbled to a halt and looked at one another confusedly. Strange bulges and eruptions rose and fell in the armour, the surface bubbling and seething as it burst out in new shapes. Some hunched over; some sprouted wings; some grew extra arms. Shocked and startled voices cried out from inside the armour. Some blossomed into strange new shapes, violent and aggressive and increasingly inhuman, reflecting the thoughts and wishes and inner needs of the wearers. Some became medieval demons, complete with horned heads and cloven hooves and clawed hands. Roger Morningstar had clearly made an impression.

But the changes didn't stop there. The men inside the armour were screaming now, in pain and horror and anguish, begging for help. Some of them became living gargoyles, twisted and misshapen. Some expanded jerkily, in bursts and spurts, till they were ten, twenty feet tall, wavering uncertainly as they struggled to support their own weight. Others became warped, monstrous things, horribly inhuman, the kind of things that chase us in nightmares. Dusk's army was crying out in shock and alarm, and beginning to back away, shouting that something had gone wrong. And it had. The changes continued, the plastic armour forming horrid abstract shapes from the depths of the unconscious mind. Things that hurt the human eye to look at, impossible for the conscious mind to deal with.

I knew what was happening. The living superplastic was linked directly to the wearer's mind through a cybernetic implant. Similar to how Droods operate our armour. But these new armoured men hadn't had

Drood training. In the family, we are taught from an early age how to control what we think about our armour, so we always have full conscious control. These unfortunate men had lost control to their subconscious minds, and were producing shapes from the under-mind, reflecting hidden needs and desires. Monsters from the id. Evil shapes, monstrous forms, nightmare impulses never meant to escape into the waking world. Without the mental discipline drilled into every Drood from childhood, the armour was giving each wearer what he really wanted. . . .

The plastic shapes were constantly changing now, flickering from one thing to another in the blink of an eye, directed by long-buried needs and unacknowl-edged motivations. Clashing appetites and raw jealou-sies and sexual hungers ran loose, given form and purpose in the ever-adaptable superplastic. Until fi-nally they turned on one another, the Drood enemy forgotten in their instinctive need to pay off old hurts and envies. No discipline, no direction, just every man for himself. Except that what was left inside the plastic armour wasn't really men at all.

I turned to the Sarjeant-at-Arms. "I've had enough of this. They're Satanists. Hit them hard, Sarjeant."

"Like I need you to tell me that," he said, and charged forward, yelling for his men to follow him. And we did.

We all surged forward, glorious in our gleaming golden armour, and slammed into the front ranks of the enemy. The plastic shapes didn't stand a chance against our strange-matter weapons. The men and women be-yond them had weapons of all kinds, scientific and mag-ical, most of it strictly forbidden. And none of it was worth a damn against Drood armour. When the bullets and energy blasts and attack magics broke and shat-tered and ran harmlessly away from our armour, their confidence broke. They had no discipline, had no idea what to do; they'd been told to expect a weakened, de-moralised enemy, and they'd believed it, the fools. We moved swiftly among them, striking them down with spiked gloved fists and golden swords and axes. Bones broke and shattered, flesh pulped and blood flew on the air. We had no mercy in us. Not for them. Not after what they'd done, and what they planned to do. We were fighting to save a whole generation of children from slaughter and horror. We struck the Satanists down and trampled them underfoot in our eagerness to get to the next target, a wild and vicious exhilaration in our hearts.

We were born to fight evil, but we rarely get our hands on the real thing.

We slammed through the enemy ranks, and they shattered and fell apart before us. Some fought; most turned to run; none escaped. The Sarjeant saw to that. He sent his people off to surround the enemy and block their escape routes, driving them back to their deaths. Some threw down their weapons, tried to surrender, begged and cried for their lives. But we had no time for that. They gave up every right to civilised treatment when they joined the Satanists. They had sworn their lives and souls to evil, given up everything that made them human.

You can't simply join the Satanists. You have to buy your way in with blood and murder, horror and the suffering of innocents. You have to do things from which there can be no coming back, no chance of atonement or redemption. You don't just sell your soul; you spit on it and throw it away.

They belonged to Hell, and that's where we sent them.

I moved steadily through the ranks of the enemy, smashing in chests and crushing skulls, moved by an implacable cold rage. I have always thought of myself as an agent, not an assassin, but if ever I have felt justified in what I do and what I am, it was on that day. Some evils are so great all you can do is stamp them out to keep them from contaminating Humanity. But even as I fought I never lost control, because it wasn't enough to just strike down the rank and file. Dusk was still out there somewhere. And if he got to the mind-influencing machine . . . I fought on through the ranks, my spiked golden fists rising and falling tirelessly while blood ran endlessly down my armour . . . heading for the Cathedral Hotel.

Molly was right there with me, grabbing Satanists by their shirtfronts, hauling them in close and screaming, "Where's my sister? Where's Isabella? What have you done with her?" right into their faces. But no one even knew what she was talking about, so she threw them aside and moved on, searching for someone who would know. Now and again someone would make the mistake of attacking her, and Molly would strike them down with some swift and nasty magic and keep going.

I'd almost reached the far edge of the conflict when Harry suddenly ran past me, leaving the fighting behind and heading for the hotel. The Sarjeant yelled angrily after him, thinking he was abandoning the battle, but I knew where he was going. I hadn't seen Roger Morningstar anywhere in the ranks of the army, which meant that if he was here he was inside the hotel. Harry was going to find him. So I went after him. The fight was already won; it didn't need either of us. And if Roger was there, I wanted to be there when he met Harry.

I burst into the hotel lobby almost on Harry's heels. It looked bright and open, modern and efficient, and completely deserted. Harry spun round, ready to fight, and I quickly stopped and raised my hands to show they were empty.

"I'm not here to stop you, Harry. I'm here to help."

His featureless golden mask looked back at me. "Why would you do that, Eddie?"

"Because I don't want to believe that Roger is totally lost to us."

"You never liked him."

"He never liked me. So what? He's family."

Harry shook his head slowly. "I don't want you here. This is private."

"Roger's not going to be here alone," I said, lowering my hands. "He'll have guards. Protections. Layers of security. You're going to need someone to watch your back, or you'll never get to him."

Harry nodded stiffly, reluctantly, and then we both broke off and looked around sharply, as we heard rapidly approaching footsteps. We moved quickly together, side by side, and a whole bunch of heavily armed security guards came running in from a side corridor. They all had automatic weapons, and they all opened up on Harry and me the moment they saw us. We stood our ground, not flinching in the least at the roar of automatic fire, and our armour soaked up every single bullet. The sheer impact would have knocked over a horse, but we didn't budge an inch. More guards arrived, firing strange-energy weapons. Violent forces crawled and crackled all over our armour, trying to force a way in. They failed and fell away.

Harry and I waited to be sure they'd thrown everything they had at us, and then we strode purposefully forward. Heavy blades erupted out of Harry's hands, while terrible spikes rose up from his arms and shoulders. He moved among the security guards like a living scythe, cutting down everyone who stood before him. I grew a long golden sword from one hand and moved alongside him, hacking and cutting. There was no room for mercy in either of us. All I had to do was think of the Great Sacrifice and mountains of dead children, and my heart was a cold and terrible thing.

It didn't take long. It was a slaughter, not a battle. Soon enough, the lobby was full of bodies and soaked in blood. More blood ran down our gleaming armour in streams, to pool around our feet.

"Well," said Harry. "I think we can safely assume they know we're here. Let's go introduce ourselves."

He strode down the corridor the guards had come from, and I went with him. The corridor led to another corridor, and then we stopped again. There was a low, ominous growling from somewhere up ahead.

"Oh, bloody hell," I said. "They've summoned up a demon dog. I hate those."

"Any way round it?" said Harry.

"Beats me," I said. "I don't see any side corridors. But whatever that is, it has to be here to guard something. Or someone. So we have to go through it. . . . Okay, I'll handle it. You go on. Find Roger."

"Getting cocky, Eddie? No Drood's ever managed to take down a demon dog on his own before."

"You haven't been keeping up with my reports, have you, Harry? I took one down at Lightbringer House."

"I did read your report; you had Molly and Isabella there to help you."

"You read my reports?" I said. "I'm flattered. Look, I can keep the thing at bay while you go talk with Roger. That's what matters."

"I can't let you do that."

"Yes, you can. You can't stand me, remember?"

"Oh, yes. There is that. Anything for the family?"

"For family, Harry."

We strode down the corridor together, took the sharp left turn, and found it wasn't a demon dog after all. The whole of the corridor before us had been changed, transformed, possessed by a spirit out of Hell. The corridor was alive, its every surface organic, fleshy, corrupt. Like the living throat that had replaced the elevator shaft back at Lightbringer House. The walls were flesh: scarlet and purple meat, with dark rotting patches and networks of heavy, pulsing veins. The floor was a long, rippling, shocking pink tongue, slick with digestive juices. The whole of the ceiling was one long elongated eye, watching us unblinkingly with mad, fascinated intent. Huge, jagged teeth protruded from the meat of the walls in regular rows; and as we watched, they began to revolve slowly, like a meat grinder, or a living chain saw. The whole thing stank of blood and sulphur and sour milk; it was alive and it was hungry and it was waiting for us. I looked at Harry.

"After you."

"It's only meat and teeth," said Harry. "You really think that could get through our armour?"

"That . . . is a demon out of Hell," I said. "A major power and a major presence, to be able to overwrite our reality so completely. I have absolutely no idea what that thing could do to our armour."

"It was put there to stop our getting to Roger," said Harry.

"Almost certainly," I said. "Still, when in doubt, cheat. If we can't go through it, maybe we can go around it."

I turned away from the possessed corridor and punched a hole through the ordinary wall next to me. My golden fist slammed through it with no problem at all. I pulled my hand back, and broken bricks and brick dust fell to the floor. I hit the wall again and again, making an opening big enough to step through, but when I stopped to look, all I could see on the other side was the possessed corridor, looking back at me.

"Damn," I said. "It's written over the whole hotel, mapping itself to every corridor at once. It's everywhere it needs to be, all at the same time. Whichever way we go to try to reach Roger, this thing will always be there to block our way."

"You understood all that from looking through one hole?" said Harry.

"Of course not. I accessed my armour's sensors."

"We should have brought an exorcist with us."

"Well, next time we'll know, won't we?" I said. "You can't think of everything when you're in a hurry. Why don't you wish for a tactical nuke as well, while you're at it?"

"Don't get tetchy," said Harry. "Let me try something."

He concentrated and brought both his arms together before him. Swift ripples ran along his golden armour, which then shifted and fused together, forming itself into a huge machine gun. The kind you see in action movies when the hero wants to bring down a whole house at once. I moved quickly to get out of the way, and Harry opened fire on the possessed corridor. Strangematter bullets exploded from the long golden barrel with incredible speed and fury, chewing up the demonic flesh of the floor and walls. Purple meat exploded under the impact, dark blood spattering everywhere, and sustained firepower ripped the long pink tongue apart from one end to the other. Something screamed horribly: a vast, harsh and utterly malignant sound. Harry shifted his aim, tearing the corridor apart and devastating the elongated eye from end to end. The long split pupil exploded, and thick fluids rained down into the churned-up flesh of the corridor. Harry stopped firing, and the gun sank back into his armour again. And as he stood there, considering his work and finding it good, every single strange-matter bullet he'd fired jerked free of the demonic meat and flew back to him, to be absorbed into his armour.

"All right," I said. "That's impressive. Terribly destructive, but neat with it. I didn't know our armour could do that."

"I've been practicing," said Harry. "Roger gave me the idea. His favourite film was always *The Wild Bunch*. I don't know how many times he's made me watch it with him."

"The fiend," I said.

And then we both broke off and stared blankly as the ripped and torn-up flesh of the possessed corridor repaired itself, rebuilding and reestablishing itself, demonic flesh fusing back together until the corridor looked exactly as it had before. Rotting walls, pulsing tongue, watching eye.

"*Damn*," said Harry.

"Well, quite," I said. "*Major* demonic presence . . ."

"Now what do we do? Send out for a tanker full of holy water?"

"Take too long," I said. "Let me think. This is more Molly's territory than mine." I thought hard. This had to be a delaying tactic, to hold us off while Roger and Dusk got the hell out of Dodge, probably taking the mind-influencing machine with them. We had to find a way through. . . . A thought occurred to me.

"Are you religious, Harry?"

"What? Not as such . . . not in any organised way. Hard to find an organised church that wants anything to do with the likes of Roger and me. You?"

"In my own way. We know Heaven and Hell are real; the family has regular dealings with them. But we don't know much about either; only enough to know we don't want to know more."

"How is this helping us?" said Harry. "What do you want me to do, shape my armour into a big golden crucifix?"

"Might come in handy if we come up against a nest of vampires," I said. "But no, I have something else in mind. And you're really not going to like it, Harry."

"What else is new?"

"How brave are you feeling?" I said. "And how much do you really love Roger?"

"What kind of a question is that?" said Harry angrily.

"A relevant one. You're not here for duty or vengeance, like me. Or even to fight Satanists. You're here to find, and hopefully rescue, the hellspawn Roger Morningstar. You're the only one who came here just for him. Because you love him. And there's no place for love in any place possessed by Hell. So I think you should armour down and walk into that corridor, and trust to your love to protect you."

"Are you crazy?"

"Maybe. But I think it'll work. If you're up for it."

"I knew it," said Harry. "You want to get rid of me!"

"You're here for Roger! That's what matters to you! So is he your love true or not? Because if he isn't, this is where you get to find out the hard way. If he is, Hell itself won't be able to stand in your way."

"Love conquers all?" said Harry. "Aren't you a little old to be believing in that?"

"I believe in evil because I've seen it," I said. "And I believe in good because I've seen it. And I believe in love. My Molly went into Limbo, into the shadow of death itself, to find me and bring me back. Do you dare do less for your love? Whenever Hell intrudes on Earth, Heaven is also there. What we do in Heaven's gaze has Heaven's strength."

"You are so full of it," said Harry. He looked down

the possessed corridor standing between him and Roger. He looked back at me. "You really want me to do this?"

"I'll be right there with you," I said.

"I'm not sure I believe in this," said Harry. "So you'd better believe enough for both of us."

He armoured down, and so did I; and then he walked slowly forward into the living corridor, an ordinary-looking man, in his smart suit and wire-rimmed spectacles, with a face trying hard to be brave and determined. I walked behind him, but he didn't look back once. He walked steadily forward into the foul and stinking air and the bloodred light. His foot came down on the thick, pulpy tongue that had replaced the floor, and it shrank back from him. Where Harry's foot came down it was suddenly ordinary corridor floor again. He didn't hesitate, or look down after the first incredulous glance; he kept walking forward . . . and Hell retreated before him. The tongue fell back, and the rotting flesh of the walls retracted in sudden jerks, revealing patches of ordinary wall. Jagged teeth fell out of the walls, disappearing before they hit the floor.

About halfway down the corridor, the decaying flesh still on the walls bunched up, thickened and threw itself at Harry, trying to engulf him; but it couldn't reach him. It dissipated and fell apart, made mist and dust and less than dust. Harry walked down the corridor, all the way to the end, with me right behind him. And when he finally stopped and turned around and looked back the way he'd come, there was nothing left to show that Hell had ever had a place on Earth there.

Harry looked at me. He was trying to smile, but he was too shaken. I was trembling a bit myself.

"I wasn't altogether sure that would work," I said.

"Now you tell me." Harry took a deep breath and let it out. "I . . . am going to have to consider the implications of what just happened. And when I get to Roger, maybe I'll sing him a quick chorus of 'The Power of Love.' Roger always did love Frankie Goes to Hollywood."

"I've always had a soft spot for 'Welcome to the Plea-suredome,'" I said. "Great video."

Harry looked at me. "You're full of surprises, aren't you, Eddie?"

"You have no idea," I said cheerfully.

"You really think Heaven's watching?" said Harry.

"Maybe."

"Well, I didn't do this for Heaven. I did it for Roger."

"Then let's go tell him," I said.

We started off, and then Harry stopped abruptly and looked at me. "What would you have done if it hadn't worked?"

"Oh, I'm sure I'd have thought of something else. . . ."

"I could have died!"

"Every plan has its drawbacks, Harry."

"I hate you."

"Careful," I said. "You never know who may be lis-tening."

We moved on, deeper into the building. Harry seemed to know where he was going, so I followed him. And soon enough we reached the conspiracy's control centre. It was a function room at the back of the hotel, right next to the old bell tower, presumably chosen because it was closest to the last remnant of the deconsecrated cathe-dral. The door was not only not locked or guarded; it was standing half-open so those inside could get a breath of fresh air on such a hot, sunny day. Harry and I ar-moured up and strode right in, and there was Roger Morningstar, looking perfectly human, along with half a dozen assistants, and two armed guards having a quiet sit-down on a smoke break. They were all watching what was happening outside on a series of large display screens. It was pretty obvious the fight was over. The Sarjeant-at-Arms was directing mopping-up operations on the few surviving Satanists in the car park.

Roger looked round suddenly and saw Harry and me. He nodded slowly. His assistants and the two guards looked round. The guards went for their guns, and Harry and I killed them quickly. The assistants bolted out the back door, and I let them go. I could have caught them, but I'd had enough of killing. Let the Sarjeant deal with them. They weren't what we'd come here for. Harry advanced on Roger. I stayed back by the doorway.

"You did come," Roger said to Harry. "I wondered if you would. Hello, Harry."

"Hello, Roger," said Harry. "I think we need to have a serious talk about where our relationship is going."

Roger looked at me, and I looked back. I wasn't ready to leave Harry and Roger on their own together, not yet. Roger got up from his chair before the display screens to stand before Harry. The two men looked at each other for a long moment.

"I've missed you, Harry," said Roger.

"I've missed you, Roger. Now tell me what the hell this has all been about."

"A test," said Roger. "I'm afraid, in the end, this has all been about me. I knew you'd come here with the Drood army, and so did my superiors. This is my final test of my loyalty to Hell. I have to kill you, Harry, here and now, to prove to them and to me that the emotions of this world no longer have any hold over me. That my only allegiance is to the forces of Hell." He held up one hand to show off a small device. "Our new weapon designers made this for me. A simple toy, based on something the Armourer once used. A clicker that can temporarily force Drood armour back into its torc, against the wearer's wishes. Leaving the wearer helpless and vulnerable. All I have to do is use this and then kill you, Harry. And you, too, Eddie; I wouldn't want you to feel left out. And then . . . I will finally have proved which side I'm on. I will be made one of the generals of Hell, and when the Gates of Hell are finally thrown open, and all the damned come forth to tread the Earth and all its peoples under our cloven hooves, I shall be a prince of the Earth and have dominion over mankind. Everything I ever wanted, in return for killing you, Harry. It's not much of a choice, is it?"

"But you never wanted any of those things, Roger," said Harry.

I wasn't so sure about that, but I said nothing and stayed where I was. I wanted to see how this was going to work out. The forces of Hell had retreated before Harry's conviction; that had to mean something. And I . . . had faith in Harry and Roger.

Roger looked at the simple device in his hand, and then back at Harry. He held the clicker up and all my stomach muscles tightened, and then Roger opened his hand and let the clicker fall to the floor. He stepped on it hard, and I heard it break and breathed a lot more easily.

"How about that?" said Roger. He seemed honestly shaken. "I couldn't do it. I thought I could, but I couldn't. I thought I wanted power, and prestige, and to take my revenge on a world that's always rejected me . . . but in the end, all I wanted was the only thing I've ever really wanted. And that's you, Harry."

He moved forward, and Harry took him in his arms, and they stood together, holding each other.

"I do so love a happy ending," I said after a while. "If Molly was here, she'd be in tears. Really. You're not listening, are you?"

They finally turned to face me, standing casually arm in arm. Harry was smiling broadly, while Roger favoured me with a small, only slightly sardonic smile.

"Thank you for not interfering," he said. "Now do me a favour and get Harry out of here. Get back to Drood Hall with the rest of your people. While you still can."

"I'm not going without you," Harry said immediately.

"You don't get it," said Roger. "This is still a trap for all of you. The army outside was only the beginning—expendable troops to hold your attention. And a chance to try out their precious new plastic armour. The real army is on its way. Thousands of them, armed with powerful new weapons. Strong enough to blow the armour right off you. They will kill you all and tear the torcs from your agonised corpses. The only reason they aren't already here is because they wanted to watch you fighting, see what you're capable of. Now that they know, they'll be here any minute. So you have to go now. I'll shut down the blocks on the Merlin Glass, and you can retreat back to Drood Hall."

"Come with us," said Harry.

"I'm sorry," said Roger, and I could see he meant it. "I can't. Someone has to stay here with the machines, prevent the conspiracy from reestablishing the blocks and shutting down the Glass again. My superiors already know I'm not going to be what they wanted me to be." He glanced at the display screens. "They're watching now. Everyone watches everyone in the conspiracy. They know by now that I've betrayed them. By choosing you, Harry, I've signed my own death warrant. So you have to go; you have to live, or everything I've done will have been for nothing."

"I'm not going," Harry said stubbornly. "I'm staying here with you. Eddie, go tell the Droods what's happening, and get them all safely home. Then put together a real army and come back here and save the day."

"Sounds like a plan to me," I said.

"You're not ready to face the army that's coming!" said Roger. "They have weapons beyond your worst nightmares! Harry, you have to go!"

"You think I'd leave you here to die alone?" said Harry.

"I'm going," I said. "I have to get my people out of here. Harry, link your torc to the Drood War Room, so it can broadcast real-time images of what's happening here. Hold the fort, boys; I'll be back with reinforcements before you know it."

"Of course you will," said Harry. "That's what you do, Eddie."

I ran back through the hotel corridors as fast as my armoured strength could drive me. The walls blurred, the floor cracked and shattered under the pounding of my feet, and the world became just so many smearing colours until I burst out of the hotel and into the car park and slammed on the brakes. The Sarjeant-at-Arms looked up sharply as I seemed to materialise right in front of him. I had to pause for a moment to get my breath back, and the Sarjeant gestured easily at the dead bodies piled around him, broken and bloody.

"All dead," he said. "Poor bastards never stood a chance. Good training for the troops, though."

"They were expendable," I said. "The real army's on its way."

I ran quickly through the situation, and the Sarjeant got the implications immediately. We both looked at the Merlin Glass, and a sharp sense of relief ran through me as I saw a clear view of Drood Hall and its grounds on the other side of the mirror.

"Get everyone back to the Hall," I said. "Then make me an army so big it won't matter what the conspiracy is sending."

"For Harry and Roger?" said the Sarjeant.

"They're Droods," I said.

"Of course they are," said the Sarjeant. "Anything for family."

He rounded his people up and drove them through the Merlin Glass with barked orders and harsh language. I waited right till the end, hoping I'd come up with some last-minute desperate plan, but I didn't. Sometimes there isn't anything you can do. Molly stayed with me, and in the end I had to go, because she wouldn't go without me. We passed through the Merlin Glass, and I shut it down so nothing could follow us through.

I ran through the Hall to the War Room, leaving raising the army to the Sarjeant. I needed to see what was happening with Harry and Roger. When I got there, they already had the transmissions from Harry's torc up on the biggest display screen. We could see them in the hotel function room, hear every word they said, but there was nothing we could do to help. We could only watch, and wait for the Sarjeant to tell us the army was ready.

*   *   *

Harry Drood and Roger Morningstar sat quietly together, watching their own display screens showing endless scenes of an empty car park. They seemed easy, comfortable in each other's company.

"We'll see Hell's army when they teleport in," said Roger. "Actually, it'll be pretty hard to miss them."

"Thousands of them?" said Harry. "Really?"

"Oh, yes. No shortage of soldiers in the satanic conspiracy. It does tend to attract people who like obeying orders. And killing people."

"With terrible new weapons? More powerful than Drood armour?"

"Unfortunately, yes. It had to happen eventually. The Droods couldn't stay cutting-edge forever."

"Can't you . . . do something, with your infernal powers?"

"No," said Roger. "Everything I had was stripped from me the moment I chose to side with you and embrace my human heritage."

"I still have my armour," said Harry.

"It won't help you," said Roger. "The army that's coming will strip it off you like an old coat. I told you: They've been planning this for a long time."

"Isn't there anything we can do?" said Harry.

"The hotel still has all its protections, provided by these machines," said Roger. "And as long as I'm here to keep changing the passwords, they can't override the defences from outside. If we can hold them off long enough, maybe Eddie will get here with reinforcements. Though he'd have to bring the whole family with him, and every weapon in the Armoury. I hope you're listening to this, Eddie."

"So we do have a chance?" said Harry.

"No," said Roger. "I was being optimistic. It's a human thing."

Harry thought for a while. "The conspiracy can't stay here long—not with an army that big. They'd be noticed by the authorities."

"Harry, dear, they own the authorities," said Roger.

"They could perform a mass slaughter of the innocents, right here, with flamethrowers, and it would all be covered up."

Harry made a brief frustrated sound. "Talk to me, Roger. What have your leaders promised the world governments to get them to go along with the Great Sacrifice?"

"What Hell always promises: power. And the indulgence of secret needs and pleasures. Everything you think you want. They have been promised they will be kings of the world to come. The fools."

"So," said Harry, "answer me this, at least. Who are the leaders of this new satanic conspiracy? Who's in charge?"

"Just one man, really," said Roger. "And it's a name you'd know. And, I think, one that would surprise you. It's always the little men, the quietly resentful, secretly ambitious little men you have to look out for. But I can't say his name. Not even now. I'm under a geas, a compulsion laid down by Hell itself, never to use his name outside the conspiracy."

"I'd know the name . . ." Harry said thoughtfully. "It's not a Drood, is it?"

"No," said Roger. "That much I can say."

Harry looked about him. "Can't say I feel very secure in here. Couldn't we barricade the room?"

"Yes, if you like," said Roger.

"You think that would help?"

"No. But it's something we could do while we're waiting."

"Hell with that," said Harry. He folded his arms, tapped one foot on the floor and thought hard. "As Eddie is entirely too fond of saying, when in doubt, cheat. Or at least improvise with style. If I were to armour up and smash a hole in the floor . . . maybe I could excavate a tunnel and burrow past the conspiracy—Why are you shaking your head, Roger?"

"Because the hotel's protections are still in place," said Roger. "And I daren't let them fall, even for a moment. We are sitting inside a bubble around and above and below. . . . Nice idea, though."

They sat together side by side, happy in each other's company. Waiting.

"I used to love walking with you through the Hall grounds," said Roger. "All those endless lawns, and the woods, and the lake . . . I missed out on all that, growing up apart from the family. I felt at peace there. Like maybe I could belong, if I tried hard enough . . ."

"When did you first go rogue?" said Harry. "Turn against us, the Droods, Humanity?"

"Before Eddie was attacked and stabbed," said Roger. "How else do you think that disguised Immortal got into the Hall so easily?"

"Were you happy as a Satanist?"

"Actually, yes," said Roger. "It's a very self-indulgent lifestyle. You really do get to do everything you ever wanted, indulge every sin, wallow in every pleasure, satisfy every need. . . . But self-indulgence gets very boring after a while. Because if you can do *anything*, then nothing really matters anymore. It's all so . . . superficial."

And then he broke off, leaned forward and looked at the display screens. Harry looked, too, and all the colour drained from his face.

"They're here," said Roger.

"How many of them?" said Harry.

"All of them."

"Dear God . . ." Harry's face was white with shock now. "I didn't know there could be an army that big. Men and monsters and . . . Eddie! Listen to me! Don't come! You wouldn't stand a chance!"

"No one ever realises how powerful Hell can be, until it's too late," said Roger.

"What are we going to do?" said Harry. "We can't fight that!"

"I was never planning on fighting," said Roger. "I was planning on hiding out here long enough for the army to get bored and leave."

"Eddie could still come," said Harry, slowly recovering some of his composure. "There's still the forbidden weapons in the Armageddon Codex."

"Yes," said Roger. "Do you see Alexandre Dusk out there anywhere?"

Harry looked hard, moving from screen to screen. "No."

"Oh, good," said Roger. "For a moment I thought we might be in trouble."

And that was when all the machines exploded at once. The conspiracy had found it couldn't override the passwords and protections, so they hit the self-destruct. The blast filled the War Room's display screen, and for a long time all we could see was smoke, slowly clearing, to reveal rubble and wreckage and blazing fires. I saw Harry, on his hands and knees in his golden armour, digging frantically through the rubble. He hauled heavy pieces of broken machinery aside as though they were nothing, until finally he uncovered what was left of Roger Morningstar. The hellspawn was a mess. The man who had defied Hell itself for the man he loved had been torn apart by the explosion. Both his legs were missing, and his torso and half his face were burned and blackened by flames. Only one eye was still open; the other was seared shut. Somehow, he clung to life with more than human energy. He looked up at Harry with his one eye, and managed something like a smile with scorched and blackened lips.

Harry made a space amid the rubble and sat down beside Roger, holding his body in his arms. He said Roger's name several times. And then Roger closed his eye, blood bubbled briefly at his mouth and he stopped breathing.

Harry armoured down. He was only a man now, sitting amid destruction, holding his dead love in his arms.

"No," he said. "You can't be dead. I fought my way through Hell to be here, scared off a demon with my love for you; you can't be dead! It isn't fair! God damn you! God, this isn't fair!"

There were sounds from outside, people and perhaps

things not people, digging their way through the rubble, trying to get in, to get to Harry. He laid Roger's dead body down and smiled briefly, bitterly.

"You won't get me," he said. "Anything for the family."

He raised one golden hand, grew a blade out of it and stabbed himself cleanly through the heart.

CHAPTER TEN

The Things We Do for Revenge

The display screen went blank. And in the War Room at Drood Hall, there was a long, terrible silence. I looked slowly around me. Molly, Callan and the Sarjeant-at-Arms had joined me in time for the end. In time to see Roger and Harry die. Everyone in the War Room was shocked, stunned. Death in the field was nothing new to Droods; but we don't usually get to see our own murdered in cold blood right in front of us. And I think we were all perhaps a little more than usually upset because Roger and Harry had died so very bravely, serving the family, even though most of us had never particularly liked or trusted either of them. Some of the comm technicians were quietly holding and comforting one another. A few of the far-seers were crying quietly. Nobody seemed to know what to do or say.

"Ethel?" I said.

"I'm here, Eddie," said the calm, quiet voice from out of nowhere. "I'm sorry. They're gone. I can't See what's happening there anymore. There are powerful shields in place. There's nothing I can do."

I turned to the Sarjeant-at-Arms standing beside me.

"Raise your army. Raise the whole damned family, if that's what it takes. We're going back."

"There's no point," said the Sarjeant. "Roger and Harry are dead, Eddie. There's nothing any of us can do for them."

"They'll have taken Harry's torc," said Callan. One of his hands rose unconsciously to the torc at his throat, replacement for the one ripped off him by the Blue Fairy, to reassure himself it was still there.

"We have to go back!" I said. "We have to make those bastards pay!"

"Eddie," said Molly, moving in close beside me. "You're shouting."

"We are not going back," said the Sarjeant, his voice very cold and very steady. "That's what they want, Eddie. Given the size of the conspiracy's army they could have taken Harry and Roger alive, if they'd wanted to. They could have found a way. Hell, they could have entered the hotel in force and overwhelmed them. They could have taken the two of them prisoner, held them for ransom, threatened them to put pressure on us. . . . But instead they blew up the room, quite deliberately, knowing we were watching, to make us so mad we'd go charging back in, and to hell with how outnumbered we were. And then . . . they would slaughter us, Eddie. We're not prepared for all-out war, not yet, and they are.

"Give me time, Eddie. Give me time to raise a properly trained and equipped army, with some of the nastier forbidden weapons from the Armageddon Codex, and I will set that army against anything the conspiracy can put up. But we're not ready. Not now."

"They won't wait," I said. I felt numb and cold, and my voice seemed to be coming from a long way away. "As soon as they realise we're not taking the bait, they'll leave."

"We'll find them," said the Sarjeant. "And then we'll take the fight to them." He looked at the empty display screen. "They died well. Like men. Like Droods. I was wrong about them."

"We have to do something," I said. "We left them there on their own. We have to do something!"

"You do something," said Callan. "But do it somewhere else. I have a War Room to run."

He moved off among his people, murmuring reassuring words and occasional sarcasm, ordering fresh pots of tea and more Jaffa Cakes, and quietly but firmly encouraging everyone back to work. The technicians turned back to their comm stations, the far-seers to their scrying pools, and the War Room went back to watching the world again.

"Isabella Metcalf's information was false," the Sarjeant-at-Arms said carefully. "Designed to lead us into a trap."

"The conspiracy has her," I said. "They snatched her right out of her own teleport, just as we left Under Parliament."

"She'd never help them willingly," said Molly.

"Isabella does have a . . . certain reputation," said the Sarjeant, still very carefully.

"Can you ever see a free spirit like Iz bowing down to those circle-jerk Satanists?" snapped Molly. "God knows what they've done to her. . . . We have to rescue her!"

"We have to find her first," I said.

"What about the source of Isabella's information?" said the Sarjeant. "The sending mentioned one Charlatan Joe."

"Dusk said the sending was only an image of Iz," I said. "Their words, through her image . . ."

"Yeah, right, and Satanist conspiracy leaders are so well-known for telling the truth," said Molly. "Come on, Eddie! Dusk was messing with our heads, trying to demoralise us. That's what they do. . . . No. The sending was real. I know my own sister. She was trying to get information to us, despite being held captive."

"And they let her, because they wanted us to know," I said.

"I will make them suffer," said Molly. "Every damned one of them."

Her voice wasn't unusually cold or threatening. It was just Molly being Molly. The Sarjeant and I looked at each other, and I decided to change the subject.

"Charlatan Joe is the only real lead we have," I said. "I know him. Confidence trickster, merry prankster, thief and rogue and treacherous little shit. He and Shaman Bond have been friends for years."

"Is he a usually reliable source?" said the Sarjeant.

"He knows his stuff," I said. "He's an honest enough villain: always gives good value for money."

"So how could he have been so wrong this time?" said Molly.

"He couldn't," I said. "If he really did put Isabella onto the Cathedral Hotel, it can only be because someone paid and/or persuaded him into saying what they wanted him to say."

"I think we need to go talk to this man," said Molly. "I think we need to have a few firm words with him."

"He'll have gone to ground by now," I said. "But the Merlin Glass will find him."

I reached out to the Glass through my torc. It was still standing out in the grounds, a twenty-foot-square gateway, going nowhere now. I called it to me, and it shrank back down to its usual size and reappeared in my hand, in the War Room. Everyone jumped a little, looking at the Glass suddenly in my hand.

"I didn't know it could do that," said the Sarjeant.

"I've been practicing," I said.

"I didn't know the Merlin Glass could jump around inside the Hall, appearing anywhere it liked, without setting off any of my very sensitive alarms," said the Sarjeant.

"Well, now you do," I said. I held the hand mirror up before me. I hardly recognised the face I saw before me in the mirror. I hadn't known I could look that angry, that cold. "You're supposed to be able to locate anyone I know," I said to the Glass. "So find me Charlatan Joe. Wherever he's hidden himself, whatever's hiding him. Do it."

My face disappeared from the mirror, replaced by a

series of blurred images as the Merlin Glass fought its way through any number of defensive screens and distracting measures, until finally it cleared to show a crystal clear image of a very familiar scene. Molly pressed in close beside me for a better look.

"But . . . that's the Wulfshead Club! What's he doing there?"

"Drinking with a few old friends, by the look of it," I said. "And, presumably, hiding in plain sight. The Wulfshead is, after all, supposed to be neutral ground."

"Look at him," said Molly. "Standing there at the bar, knocking back the drinks like he doesn't have a care in the world . . . I'll make him care. Who are those people with him? Do you know them, Eddie?"

"Of course," I said. "Shaman Bond knows everyone. That's what he's for. The tall, scary woman is Lady Damnation. Born, or perhaps created, in one of those places where the walls of the world have worn thin, and influences from outside have seeped through. There are those who say she eats a little death every day to make herself immune to it. And there are those who say she's nothing more than a jumped-up Gothette with delusions of deity. Doesn't make her any less dangerous, though.

"Standing beside her, in the heavy scarlet robes and cape, is the biggest and certainly the heaviest priest in the world: Bishop Beastly. Who refuses to belong to any organised church that would accept the likes of him as a member. He loudly proclaims that delighting in all the pleasures of the flesh is the best way to worship God, who gave them to us. He claims to have eaten one representative of every living species on this planet, so he can contain their souls within him and thereby strengthen his contact with the living world. He is very strong. Winner of the Vatican Pro-Am Exorcism Tournament for seven years running. The nuns of sixty-three different nunneries pray for his soul every day. No one knows why.

"And finally, we have the Indigo Spirit, standing tall and proud in his midnight blue leathers, cowl and cape.

An old-fashioned costumed crime fighter and adventurer. A man who became his own fantasy, because he thought someone should. Surprisingly effective. The real deal, in an increasingly fake world."

"What's a bottom-feeding scumbag like Charlatan Joe doing hanging out with people like that?" said Molly.

"Buying them drinks, by the look of it," I said. "And looking for protection. The Wulfshead is famously neutral ground for anyone and everyone. But not today. I can't go there as Shaman Bond, not with what I need to do. I'll have to go in armoured up, as a Drood. And no, you can't come with me, Molly. You might need the club's protections someday."

She nodded slowly, reluctantly. "Eddie, find out what happened to my sister. Whatever it takes."

"Don't worry," I said. "Joe is going to tell me everything I need to know."

I armoured up, shook the Merlin Glass out to door size and stepped through into the Wulfshead Club. Then I shook the Glass down, put it away and looked unhurriedly about me.

Everyone in the club had stopped what they were doing to stare at the armoured Drood who had appeared in their midst out of nowhere. That wasn't supposed to be possible. That was why you came to the Wulfshead: to be safe from people like me. No alarms sounded, but the pounding music cut off abruptly, and one by one the massive display screens shut down. The dancers stopped dancing, and everyone in the club stood very still, hoping not to be noticed. Sudden puffs of displaced air marked the sudden disappearance of certain particularly nervous individuals as they teleported out. Others started edging nonchalantly towards various exits. It's surprising how many people can find something to feel guilty about when a Drood turns up. The club's much-vaunted security was supposed to protect everyone from everyone, but sensible people didn't take chances.

I headed straight for Charlatan Joe, standing at the bar with his new friends, and everyone else looked relieved and got out of my way. Joe looked immediately at the thirteen bartenders with the same face.

"I'm supposed to be safe here! I'm supposed to be protected! Even from the high-and-mighty bloody Droods!"

The bartenders were the club's first line of defence, in that between them they could gang up on pretty much any troublemaker. But they took one look at my golden armour and decided they were outgunned and outnumbered, and that this was way above their pay scale. They all hunkered down behind the bar, out of sight. A very sensible attitude, I thought.

Charlatan Joe swore bitterly at the deserted bar, and sank back behind his new friends. "You promised me I'd be safe here, you bastards! What do I pay my membership dues for?"

"You don't," said a voice from behind the bar.

"Do you take plastic?"

Everyone fell back to give me plenty of room. I recognised friends and enemies and allies to every side of me, but they were all people Shaman Bond knew, not me. I didn't acknowledge any of them. I couldn't risk any of them recognising me. I didn't want them looking at Shaman Bond the way they were looking at me now: with a combination of awe, fear and not entirely hidden hatred. We Droods protect the world, but no one ever said the world would love us for it.

I'd almost reached Charlatan Joe when the Indigo Spirit stepped suddenly forward to block my way. He looked firm and determined and very impressive, the way costumed heroes are supposed to look. And the thing was, I knew he'd never practised that stance in front of a mirror, or even thought about doing so. It came naturally to him, because he was the real deal. Out of respect for his reputation, I stopped and considered him thoughtfully. If my featureless and forbidding golden mask disturbed him at all, he did a really good job of hiding it.

"Sorry," said Indigo. "Joe may be a crook and a swindler and a general pain in the arse, but even he's entitled to protection in this place. The club is sanctuary for all of us: good and bad and in between. And if the bar staff are too gutless to do their job, I'm not."

"You don't know what he's done," I said.

"It really doesn't matter, dear boy," said Bishop Beastly, surging forward in a splendid swirl of his scarlet robe and cape. I swear I heard the floor creak loudly as it bore his massive weight. The bishop smiled easily at me, his pursed rosebud mouth almost lost in his huge, fat face. His deep-sunk eyes were kind, but unwavering. "Sanctuary is for everyone, or it's for no one. How can a small thing like Charlatan Joe be worth all this upset? Sit down, dear boy; have a drink and a nibble on one of the more palatable bar snacks, and we will discuss the situation in a civilised manner."

"Anywhen else, I might have," I said. "Anyone else, perhaps. But not him, and not today. I can't let you interfere, Bishop; and if you knew what he'd done, whom he's done business with and what he's responsible for . . . you'd let me have him."

"I rather doubt that," murmured the bishop. "Come, let us reason together. . . ."

"He doesn't do reasonable," snapped Lady Damnation. "He doesn't have to. He's a Drood."

She stalked forward to confront me, sneering right into my golden mask. Her corpse-pale skin stood out starkly against her brightly coloured Gypsy dress and shawl. Thick curls of long, dark hair spilled down around her pointed face, with its fierce green eyes and dark lips. She put her hands on her hips and tilted back her head, the better to sneer down her long nose at me.

"Talk to me, Drood. Give me one good reason not to go Romany on your golden arse, and curse you and yours down to the seventh generation."

"I'm here for Joe," I said. "He's going to talk to me."

"I don't know anything!" Joe said immediately. "You've got to stop him! He's going to kill me!"

"You probably earned it," said the Indigo Spirit. "But . . . you can't have him, Drood. It's the principle of the thing."

"I'm sorry," I said. And I really was. "But I don't have time for this."

Lady Damnation came dancing forward, every step graceful and focussed and quite deadly. She can kill with a touch, they say, wither your heart in your breast, draw your soul out through your eyes. But she'd never met armour like mine. She stamped and pirouetted around me, chanting loudly in the old Rom style, her hands darting out at me . . . but always drawing back at the very last moment, unable to make contact with my armour. She made sudden clutching movements with both hands, but my heart never missed a beat. In the end she lunged forward and thrust her face right into my featureless golden mask. Her eyes blazed fiercely, huge in her pale face, but all she saw in my mask was her own reflection.

The power in her eyes rebounded, and the psychic feedback threw her backwards, howling with shock and horror. She turned and staggered off into the crowd, shaking and shuddering, and the crowd let her hide herself among them.

Bishop Beastly sighed heavily, shook his great bald head slowly and waddled forward to take up the fight. His great form was vast as a wall, and almost as solid. There was a lot of muscle under that fat. He thrust a large bone crucifix at me, almost lost in his huge hand. Up close, I could see the cross had been made by lashing two Aboriginal pointing bones together. A good use of horrific materials. It would probably have worked on anyone else. The bishop thrust the bone crucifix into my mask, and the cross exploded in his hand, driving vicious splinters deep into his pudgy flesh.

Blood dripped thickly from his hand, but he didn't flinch. He shook his injured hand once, to dislodge the worst of the splinters, and then held up his other hand. Massive rings showed on every fat finger, each with its own magically glowing crystal. He cursed me then, in loud, ringing tones, and I stood there and let him do it. He had a fine voice and a lot of faith, but the confidence went out of him as one by one the light faded from the rings' crystals, their energies exhausted against my armour. The bishop surged forward, his robes billowing like a scarlet sail, hitting me with an old-school exorcism in classical Latin, and I punched him out. His massive head snapped back, his eyes rolled up and he measured his length and considerable girth on the floor. I swear the whole floor shuddered out of respect.

The Indigo Spirit looked at me expressionlessly, and then he moved unhurriedly forward to stand before me. He did look like the real thing: lithely muscular under the costume, every calculated movement showing extensive training and hard-won skill. A man who became what he believed in, and made it real, because he believed it was the right thing to do. He did much of his work in the Nightside, because this world has become too cynical to believe in good dreams.

He'd have made a good Drood.

"Whatever Joe's done," said Indigo, "there must be some way to put it right. . . ."

"No," I said. "Not this time."

"It can't be that bad," said Indigo. "I mean, come on: This is Charlatan Joe we're talking about! What did he do? Stiff a Drood on a deal? Try to sell your family some Florida swampland?"

"Droods are dead," I said. "Because of him."

"Oh, God," said Joe miserably. "I didn't know! I swear I didn't!"

Indigo looked back at him sharply, and he must have seen something of the truth in Joe's face. But give Indigo his due; it didn't alter his determination in the least. There was a principle at stake—sanctuary for the needy—and he would not stand aside. I knew there was a reason we were friends. He looked at me steadily.

"I can't let you have him, Drood."

"He doesn't have to die," I said. "Just tell me what I need to know."

"He's lying!" Joe said immediately. "I don't know anything! Don't let him hurt me!"

"Your reputation does precede you, Drood," said Indigo. "And I really can't stand by and let a shark like you chew on a small fish like him."

Charlatan Joe and the Indigo Spirit had both been friends of Shaman Bond for years. I'd worked cons with Joe, fought bad guys with Indigo. Spent more time in their company than I had with most of my family. But this . . . was more important than friendship.

Indigo must have sensed that the time for words was over. His gloved hand moved too swiftly to follow, and a razor-edged shuriken flashed through the air towards me. I snatched it out of midair and crumpled the solid steel in my golden hand. But Indigo had planned for that. The shuriken was a distraction, something to hold my attention while he grabbed a handful of useful items from his utility belt.

Of course he has a utility belt. What's the point of embracing a fantasy if you don't go all the way?

He threw a capsule onto the floor before me, and a thick grey fluid splashed everywhere, lapping against my golden feet. I knew what it was; I'd seen Indigo use it before: a specially engineered frictionless fluid, designed to cut off all contact between a bad guy and the floor he was standing on. I'd seen whole crowds of villains lose their footing and crash to the floor and not be able to get up again. Very useful stuff. Indigo gets it from some military source. I walked right through it and didn't miss a step. Indigo backed away, startled. The frictionless fluid had never failed him before. But strange matter follows its own rules. Or imposes its own rules on the material universe. Just like a Drood, really.

Indigo threw another capsule at me, and it smashed against my golden chest. Thick, steaming fluid ran down my golden armour, and again I recognised it. Acid strong enough to eat through steel. It ran harmlessly down my armour and pooled around my feet, hissing and spitting as it ate holes in the floor.

The Indigo Spirit was still backing away, but he

hadn't given up yet. He held up a large, blocky piece of tech in one hand. There was a loud, uneasy murmur from the crowd, as many of them recognised it. I knew what it was, because I'd had the Armourer make it for Indigo as a Christmas present: a handheld EMP device. Indigo made sure I got a good look at it and, when I still didn't stop, activated the thing with a dramatic gesture. The electromagnetic pulse swept out across the Wulfshead in under a second, and all the lights went out at once as every piece of technology stopped working. In the sudden darkness there were brief flashes of light from small explosions in the crowd, hidden bits and pieces going bang. A few fires broke out. Dull amber lighting came on as the emergency generators kicked in. The new subdued lighting made the club look like a cave with far too many shadows in it.

"Sorry," I said to Indigo. "But my armour isn't technology. As such."

The Indigo Spirit had stopped backing away. He stood defiantly between Charlatan Joe and me, his leather gloves creaking as he clenched his fists. "Sorry, Drood," he said calmly. "But you'll have to strike me down to get to him. And I don't think you can do that without killing me. And I don't think you're the kind of man who could do that to a man who's only doing what's right."

"On any other day you'd be right," I said. "But not today."

"Then let's dance," said the Indigo Spirit.

I did try to take him down easily and relatively painlessly, but Indigo wasn't having any of it. He attacked me with every skilled move, practiced blow and dirty trick he knew, moving faster than I could, even in my armour. He struck at me again and again, searching for weak spots in my armour, trying to turn my own strength against me. But he only damaged his hands against the hard, unyielding strange matter. I tried to take him down, but somehow he was never there when my fists sailed through the air. He was so very skilled. I kept speeding up, drawing more and more on my armour, until finally . . . his skill didn't matter anymore.

I crowded him up against the bar so he had nowhere to go, and then he took a terrible beating from my golden fists. I hit him again and again, but he wouldn't fall. I beat him horribly, saw his blood fly and heard his bones break; but he wouldn't cry out and he wouldn't stop fighting. There were no spikes on my gloves, no extruded blades. I didn't want to kill him. But in the end, because he wouldn't give in, I ran out of patience. I moved in close, broke his ribs and his collarbone and then both his arms. And as his arms hung uselessly at his sides, I clubbed him to the ground with blow after blow to the head. His cowl protected him from the worst. At least, I hoped it did.

He made one hell of a good showing, like the hero he was. But he never should have got between a Drood and his prey.

I looked at him, sitting slumped on the floor with his back to the bar, his chin resting on his chest, blood streaming from his crushed nose and mouth. Blood bubbles formed from one nostril, and I hoped a rib hadn't pierced his lung. He was my friend, but I was too angry, too coldly determined, to be stopped. I'd apologise to him later. I'd care about what I'd done later. I had to have some measure of revenge for what had been done to Harry and Roger. Because I'd left them there to die. Because I hadn't gone back to rescue them, like I promised. Because I'd never liked them. And because revenge was all that was left. All I could do for them. I had to do *something*. . . . If you can't hurt the ones you hate, hurt the ones you can reach.

I looked around at the remaining patrons of the Wulfshead Club, huddled together in tight little groups, staring at me as though I were the monster.

"Go," I said. "Leave. I'm not here for you."

They left as fast as they could. Charlatan Joe called pitifully after them, but no one even looked back. They'd seen a Drood in his anger, the monster was loose, and they wanted nothing to do with him. Joe made a small move toward the nearest exit, but I was already there, blocking his way. He cringed back against the bar. I looked over the bar, at the staff hiding there.

"Don't interfere," I said.

"No danger of that," said the nearest bartender. "But you'd better be quick. The management knows what's happening here. They'll have already put in a call to the real security people. And you know who they are."

I nodded. I knew. "The Roaring Boys."

I turned to face Charlatan Joe, so close now I could reach out and touch him whenever I felt like it. He was so close his breath could have fogged up my mask. He was a pitiful sight: terrified, trembling, his features white and pinched, his eyes huge and rolling like those of a panicked animal. When I placed one golden hand on his shoulder, he cried out sharply and wet himself. The sudden smell of urine was shockingly clear on the still air. His legs started to buckle, and I had to hold his shoulder more firmly to keep him from collapsing.

He'd been my friend for years. We'd known good times together. And I had reduced him to this.

"Who gave you the information about the satanic conspiracy gathering at the Cathedral Hotel?" I said. "And who told you to pass it on to Isabella Metcalf?"

"Oh, God," Charlatan Joe said miserably. "You know I can't talk about that. They'd kill me!"

"What do you think I'll do if you don't?" I said. "Good Droods, good men, are dead because of you."

"I didn't know!" said Joe. "I just did what I was told! That's what people like me do. I can't tell you. . . ."

"I can make you tell me," I said.

"You're going to beat the information out of me? Torture me? Is that what Droods do these days?"

I'd had enough. I placed the tip of one golden finger in his left ear.

"Talk to me, Joe," I said. "Or I will send razor-sharp filaments of my armour through your eardrum and into your brain and tear the truth right out of you. You'll still be alive afterwards, but what's left inside your head won't be much use to you."

I was bluffing, but Charlatan Joe didn't know that. After everything he'd seen me do, he believed me. He started crying, great, shuddering sobs that racked his whole body. Snot ran out of his nose. I told myself I'd make it up to him later. Shaman Bond would make it up to him. But I think I knew, even then, that some things can never be undone.

"The source for the information was Sir Terrence Ashtree," said Charlatan Joe, in between crying and gasping for breath. "Big man in the city. He's part of this new satanic conspiracy. Because it's good for business. He told me what to say to Isabella Metcalf when she came around. And how to tell it to her in such a way that she wouldn't remember it until the conspiracy wanted her to remember. Ashtree. He's your man. He's the man you want. Not me . . ."

I didn't ask him whether he'd been paid, or pressured, or even threatened into doing it. It didn't matter.

I knew Terrence Ashtree. Part of an old business family, all of them leading lights in the establishment. Except that Terrence had never been all that successful in his own right. I didn't know much about the man himself. That had always been Matthew's territory, back when he was the main field agent in London, and I mopped up the crumbs that fell from his table. But then Matthew betrayed the family, and was killed by the family, and I became the main London agent. Which I thought was what I'd always wanted. Our dreams betray us by coming true.

I always meant to do a tour of all the big city names, and put the fear of God into them. But I'd barely made a start, only got as far as Ashtree, when the Hungry Gods war kicked off . . . and then there were the Immortals, and I was so busy. . . . City cases, business cases, seemed such small fry compared to the end of the world. Of course, that was before we found out what the bankers were really up to. . . .

Sir Terrence Ashtree, also known as Terry the Toad

because of his complete willingness to screw over anybody in pursuit of a deal or because they were in his
way. Not that his ruthlessness had ever done him much
good, as such. Until recently . . . Word was, Terry the
Toad was on the way up, a man to be reckoned with,
which, at his middle age, was something of a surprise.
Cutthroat business is a young man's game. I'd been
vaguely aware of changes in the city recently, but hadn't
paid it much attention. I hadn't known about the satanic conspiracy then.

I turned my attention back to Charlatan Joe. He'd
almost stopped crying. His eyes were red and puffy, his
mouth loose and trembling.

"Where's Isabella Metcalf right now?" I said.

"I don't know! I don't know! I swear, I don't! The
conspiracy has her; everyone knows that . . . but I don't
know anything! They don't tell people like me things
like that. If only so people like you can't beat it out of
people like me."

He had a point. I stepped away from him, lowering
my hand, and he almost collapsed in sheer relief. He
smiled and nodded at me, eager to show his gratitude,
and I almost wanted to hit him for being so pathetic.
For making me feel like such a monster.

"Why?" I said. "Why did a small-time con artist like
you get in bed with the Satanists in the first place?"

"For the money," said Charlatan Joe. "That's what I
do. And the money was really good. . . ."

Yes, I thought. *That is what you do, what you've always done. The clue is in the name. I always knew what
kind of man you were, all those years we were friends.
What right have I to feel angry now?*

"Vanish," I said. "Go on; get out of here. Lose yourself somewhere in the great wide world where no one
will think to look for you. Until the Droods and the
Metcalf sisters finally forgive you."

"But . . . that could take forever!" said Charlatan
Joe.

"Yes," I said. "But that's all the mercy I have in me
today."

I took him to the nearest exit. Forced the door open with my armoured strength, so that it opened onto some back alley somewhere. Joe gaped at me.

"That isn't supposed to be possible," he said. "No one can open those doors, except the club owners. Everyone knows that."

"You'd be surprised what a Drood can do when he's mad enough," I said.

Charlatan Joe hurried through the open door, and I forced it shut behind him. I never saw him again.

I took out the Merlin Glass, activated it and opened up a doorway between the club and Drood Hall. Molly came straight through and I shut the Glass down. I didn't want anyone else to see what I'd done. What I'd become. Molly looked quickly about her as I put the Glass away, taking in the dimly lit club, the wreckage, the bloody, unconscious forms of Bishop Beastly and the Indigo Spirit.

"Well," she said. "You can always tell where a Drood's been. . . . Eddie, what happened here?"

"I did," I said. "You wanted answers, remember?"

Molly came forward to stand before me, and I armoured down. She put a hand to my face, and her fingers came away wet. I hadn't realised I'd been crying.

"Oh, Eddie, what have you done?"

"Bad things," I said. "Necessary things."

"You did this to them? I thought they were your friends."

"I'm not always a very good friend. Comes with the job."

"Eddie," said Molly, "this isn't like you. I don't like you like this."

I looked at her, a sudden anger flushing my face. "I did this for you! You want your sister back, don't you?"

"I want my Eddie back!"

"When it's over," I said. "I'll be back when it's over. Until then . . . it's all about the conspiracy. I will do what I have to do to stop them. To save Humanity. To save the children."

"You can't fight evil with evil methods," said Molly.

"I should know. Fighting evil is supposed to bring out the best in us, not the worst."

I managed a small smile. "Shouldn't we be on opposite sides of this argument? Shouldn't I be lecturing you on excessive behaviour?"

She came into my arms and hugged me tightly, and I hugged her back like a drowning man clinging to a straw. Molly finally pushed me away.

"We've been through a lot," she said. "We need drinks. We need really big drinks." She leaned over the bar and scowled down at the hiding bartenders. "You! Serial face! I want the finest wines in creation, all mixed together in one bloody big glass, shaken not stirred, with two curly-wurly straws."

The bartender she was addressing shrugged helplessly. "If it were up to me, you could have one of everything, on the house, with a little parasol. But when the electromagnetic pulse went off, it shut down all the machinery. Management keeps all the booze in a pocket dimension attached to the bar, and with the systems down we can't reach it. We can't serve anything until management turns up and hits the reset button."

"I hate you," said Molly.

To take her mind off that, I filled her in on everything I'd learned from Charlatan Joe. It didn't take long.

"That's it?" said Molly. "Just one name? What about Isabella? Where are they holding her?"

"He said he didn't know anything about that," I said.

"And you believed him?"

"After what I did to him? Yes. You can't make people tell you what they don't know."

"I can come bloody close," Molly growled. "I can't believe you let the little creep go."

"We've got a new name," I said. "A new lead, a new way into the conspiracy. Terry the Toad was an important member of the business establishment, even before he joined the conspiracy. Odds are he knows all kinds of important things. And names. Want to go have a word with him?"

"Try to stop me," said Molly.

And then her head snapped round as she tried to look in every direction at once. "Did you feel that? What the hell was that? The whole atmosphere in this place changed. The temperature's dropped; something's sucking all the energy out of the room. . . . Something's coming. Something bad."

"The Wulfhead's security," I said. "The Roaring Boys."

"Oh, shit," said Molly. "Eddie, get the Glass working. Get it working right now, because I really don't want to be here when they arrive. Even I have enough sense to be scared of the Roaring Boys."

I already had the Merlin Glass out and activated. "I'm pretty sure I could take them," I said. "But I think I've probably done enough damage here for one day."

"This is no time to be getting cocky, Eddie! Get us the hell out of here!"

I opened a door between the club and a certain office deep in the city, and we both stepped quickly through into the outer office of Sir Terrence Ashtree. A terrible roaring sound filled the club on the other side of the mirror, wild and awful and full of fury, as something awful downloaded into the Wulfshead. I shut down the Glass. It almost seemed to fight me for a moment, as though something were trying to force it open from the other side; but the connection was quickly broken, and the Glass was only a hand mirror again. I put it away and joined Molly in checking out where we'd arrived.

My family would make apologies to the Wulfshead management. And they would accept, because we all have to do business together sometime.

We'd arrived in Ashtree's outer office: fairly old, maybe even Victorian originally, with lots of heavy wood panelling on the walls, and really quite ugly furniture. The only modern touch was the highly efficient computer on the secretary's desk. There was no one around. It was all very peaceful and quiet, and therefore worrying.

"I've been here before," I said to Molly. "I'm sure Sir Terrence will remember me. Still . . . this is odd."

"Odd?" Molly said immediately. "How odd?"

"This is the outer office, where the secretary makes you wait till Terry the Toad is ready to see you," I said. "And like all bosses' secretaries, she's there to guard his privacy and her territory like an attack dog. So . . . where is she?"

We both looked at the empty desk. The computer was turned off; everything was neat and tidy, not even a half-finished cup of coffee.

"Let's go see if Terry the Toad is in," said Molly. "Since we've come all this way."

"Yes," I said. "Let's do that. I'm sure we've got lots to talk about."

The heavy door that led into Ashtree's very private office wasn't locked. I tried the handle carefully, mindful of booby traps, but it turned easily in my hand. I slammed the door all the way open with my shoulder, and Molly and I strode in. Ashtree was sitting quietly behind his desk, a tired old man in a crumpled suit, his face drawn, haggard. He didn't so much as flinch when Molly and I made our entrance. He nodded to both of us slowly.

"I've been waiting for someone," he said. "I knew somebody would come eventually. But I can't say I recognise either of you."

"Edwin Drood," I said. "And Molly Metcalf."

"Ah. Yes. Isabella's sister. Please come in; make yourselves comfortable. I have so many things to say to you."

I had a good look round his office, but there didn't seem to be any hidden assassins crouching in the corners, so I pulled out a chair for Molly and then dropped easily into one beside her. Ashtree didn't move at all, looking us over with tired curiosity.

"Edwin . . . Yes. I do remember you. . . . I was actually pleased to see you, you know. I never did get on with Matthew."

"Not many did," I said. "Do you know why we're here?"

"Of course. I'm surprised it's taken you this long. I left a clear enough trail. I'm glad you're here, so I can get this over with. I never wanted any of this, you know. It was . . . I'd struggled so long, trying to be the success in business I was supposed to be, even though I never had any taste for it. . . . But it was what my family wanted, so I went along. . . . You'd know all about that, Edwin. But I never got anywhere that mattered, or achieved anything of note, no matter how hard I tried. So when this new satanic conspiracy came looking for me, headhunted me . . . I jumped at the chance. You do know about the . . . Of course you do. I didn't think they were *real*, you see. . . . I mean, who believes in satanic conspiracies in this day and age? I thought it was like the old Hellfire Club, a chance to dress up and play games. . . .

"Suddenly everything I touched was golden. I was the big man in the city my family had always wanted me to be. I had everything I'd ever wanted. I was happy, you see. Such a long time since I'd been happy . . . So when they told me to pass some information on to Charlatan Joe, I thought . . . Why not? Who's Isabella Metcalf to me? I had to do it in a certain way, using some rather unpleasant magics, but . . . it was all playing the game; you see? I should have known better. Nothing's ever simple or straightforward in the conspiracy. It's all plans within plans, traps within traps. . . .

"I was there when the conspiracy kidnapped Isabella. Snatched her right out of her own teleport spell. They have very powerful people working for them. She put up one hell of a fight. I was impressed. But the conspiracy people had all kinds of weapons and dirty tricks at their command, and they . . . wore her down. And when she was helpless, stripped of all her magics, they . . . did things to her. They hurt her horribly, broke her spirit, defiled and abused her . . . and laughed while they did it. They let me watch. It was their idea of a reward. They thought I'd enjoy it.

"It sickened me.

"I couldn't wait to get out of there. I thought I was a hard man, up for anything . . . but to my surprise, it seems there was a good man inside all along, struggling to get out. There was a line I wouldn't cross. I couldn't help Isabella, but I couldn't stand by and watch. They saw the weakness in me; they *knew* I wasn't one of them anymore. So I came here to wait for whoever found me first. I could have run, could have hidden, but . . . I think I need to be punished for what I've done."

"Is she alive?" Molly said harshly. "My sister? Is Isabella still alive?"

"As far as I know," said Ashtree. "They took her away with them. Dragged her off . . . So much blood. I'd never seen so much blood before. They said they had a use for her, you see. I didn't know any of that was going to happen! You must believe me; I didn't know. . . . I never understood what I was getting into. Or maybe . . . I didn't want to understand, because I was having such a good time. . . . I didn't believe in Devil worshippers. Didn't believe in the Devil. But it turns out he believed in me. . . . I'm not a bad person, Eddie, Molly. . . . Not really. I've done bad things, I know, things I'm not proud of, but it was just to get on. . . . Nobody ever really got hurt."

"If you want to atone," I said, "help us find Isabella. And the mind-influencing machine. And the leaders of the conspiracy."

"You don't understand," said Ashtree. "I never dealt with people on that level, never worked with anyone that high up. I was never that important to the conspiracy."

"Did you know about the Great Sacrifice?" I said.

"No!" said Ashtree. "I never dreamed . . . I had no idea. I was just in charge of raising money! Moving numbers around . . ."

"You must know something," I said. "Something that can help us. That's why you stayed, isn't it?"

"Of course," said Ashtree. "That's why I'm glad you found me first. I was at Lightbringer House, you see, to make a report, and I happened to pass by a door that was a little ajar. Curiosity got the better of me, and I peeked. And there he was, the great leader of the satanic conspiracy, holding a private meeting. I couldn't believe it. I couldn't believe it was *him*! I knew him; I'd had dealings with him in the past. I couldn't believe such a small man could be the leader of the conspiracy. But then, I suppose it's always the small men with big ambitions. . . ."

"Who?" I said. "Tell us his name!"

"I can't," said Ashtree. "I can't say his name to anyone outside the conspiracy. No one can. They found me listening, you see, and they put a geas on me, a binding burned right into my soul. . . . It hurts even to think the name. . . . But I can tell you where to find Isabella Metcalf. I wasn't supposed to know that either; but people will talk in front of me, you see. Because I'm not important. They've taken her to the conspiracy's most secret place, their hidden fortress, where the leader sits and gloats among his treasures and his prisoners and makes all the decisions that matter. I can't tell you how to get there. But that's where you have to go."

"Where?" said Molly. "Where do we have to go? Where is my sister?"

"They're holding her in the Timeless Moment," said Sir Terrence Ashtree, never again to be Terry the Toad.

And then he screamed horribly, convulsing in his chair as his flesh began to rot and corrupt. Roger said, *They're always listening. . . .* I pushed the heavy desk out of the way to get to Ashtree, but it was already too late. The conspiracy was taking its revenge on him for having dared betray them. Ashtree screamed and screamed again, whipping back and forth in his seat as his flesh melted and ran away in thick streams of putrescent liquids. He should have died from the shock of it, but the same dark magic that was killing him kept him alive to suffer, to know horror . . . to be punished. His head snapped back and forth in agony, and thick gobbets of suppurating flesh flew off to spatter and stain the floor. I heard his bones snap and break and splinter inside him, torn apart by savage forces. There was nothing I could do to save him. I looked at Molly, but she shook her head helplessly. I looked at Ashtree, with his melting face and empty eye sockets. The timbre of his screams was changing as his vocal cords rotted and ran away down his throat.

I armoured up, extended a golden blade from my hand and cut his head off. It was the only mercy I could give him. The head fell away as the body collapsed in upon itself, and in a few moments he was gone, leaving nothing behind but thick, greasy stains on and around his desk. The stench was so bad it drove Molly and me from the room, and I slammed the door shut to contain it. Molly glared at me.

"Where the hell is the Timeless Moment? You know, don't you?"

"Yes," I said.

"Well, what is it?"

"Just what you'd think," I said. "The perfect hiding place."

CHAPTER ELEVEN

What We Do in Heaven's Gaze

Sometimes even the strangest of journeys begins with a single step. Molly and I stepped through the Merlin Glass and passed instantly from the dead man's office to the Armoury at Drood Hall. It was the usual chaos of lab assistants running wild, explosions, transformations and brief outbreaks of spontaneous combustion. Strange machines doing things the laws of physics never allowed for, and even stranger contraptions doing things nature never intended. And one lab assistant with two heads, arguing furiously with himself as to whose fault it was. And, indeed, which was the original head, and which needed pruning. Business as usual, in the Drood family Armoury. Molly looked at me darkly as I shut the Merlin Glass down and put it away.

"Okay, what are we doing here? Why aren't we in the War Room, which is where I thought we were going? You know I don't like surprises. And there had better be a really good reason for this. . . . Why are we in the far more dangerous and unnervingly arbitrary science lab from hell?"

"Because you want to know what the Timeless Moment is," I said. "And I know enough to know I don't know nearly enough about it. So we are here to talk with my uncle Jack, because as the Armourer he understands six impossible things before breakfast. This is, after all, the man who invented a time machine to go back in time and tell himself not to build time machines, because they're far more trouble than they're worth. You have to be impressed by lateral thinking like that. Ah, here he is."

I led Molly through the bedlam of unrestrained genius at work, to where the Armourer was sitting unusually quietly in his favourite chair. The one with all the chemical stains and blast marks, and the sign on the back saying, sudden experiments make god jump. The Armourer was sitting pensively, his eyes far away, completely untroubled by loud noises and the occasional outburst of harsh language. He had a fresh cup of hot, steaming tea to hand, along with a plate full of Jaffa Cakes and a packet of chocolate HobNobs. Brain food, if ever there was. He ignored Molly and me, completely lost in thought. There are those who have been known to say that the Armourer is never more dangerous than when he's thinking. I had to say his name several times, increasingly loudly, before he looked up.

"Ah, Eddie," he said vaguely. "And Molly, too. How nice. Yes. I was thinking about the best way to counter the satanic conspiracy's new influence machine. It seems to me the best way to do it would be to build one of my own, and then figure out how to stop that."

"We have had this talk before, Uncle Jack," I said carefully. "The family exists to serve Humanity, not rule them. And most especially, we are not here to make up their minds for them."

"I'm not talking about direct mind control," said the Armourer. "Not as such . . . But would it really be such a bad thing to nudge Humanity in the right direction now and again? Whisper in their ear things like, 'Make war no more'? 'Feed the hungry, house the homeless, bring back proper Coke in the original bottles and stop making crap film versions of perfectly good television shows'?"

"You see?" I said. "It's not where you start, but where you end up. It's all too tempting to stop helping and start meddling. Put the whole idea out of your mind, Uncle Jack."

"Oh, all right, all right," said the Armourer, pouting. "Consider it done. You young people today don't know how to have fun. . . . So, what are you doing down here, Eddie? I know I'm your favourite uncle, and I do enjoy our little chats. . . . Oh, would you like a biscuit? That's real chocolate, you know."

"Not right now," I said.

"But the fact is, you only ever come down here when you want something," said the Armourer, fixing me with a hard gaze from under his bristling white eyebrows. "What is it, having trouble with your TiVo again?"

"If we could return to the subject at hand," I said patiently. "Why have you given up on trying to block the influence machine? You don't usually give up so quickly. What's wrong? Something's wrong; I can tell."

The Armourer sighed briefly and nodded reluctantly. "Sit down, both of you."

Molly and I looked around. There weren't any other chairs. So we stole a couple from some lab assistants who weren't actually using them, and sat down facing the Armourer. He made a big deal of pouring some tea into his saucer to cool it, and then sipping it loudly, but we all knew he was putting off the moment, so he put the tea down and gave us his full attention.

"It's Harry and Roger," he said heavily. "Their deaths . . . hit me hard. Harder than I expected, given that I couldn't stand the pair of them half the time. My poor nephews . . . They tried so hard to do the right thing. Old men shouldn't have to see young men die before them. Uncles shouldn't have to bury nephews. My generation hasn't done too well with its children. Harry was James's only legitimate child. And yes, I know there are many other bastards like Roger . . . some good, some bad, most somewhere in between, scattered across the world. All of them thrust outside the family because we didn't approve of their mothers. Many of them have made names for themselves, but I can't help wondering how much more they might have achieved if only we'd embraced them, brought them up and trained them as Droods. There will have to be a funeral after this mess is over. And I think we should invite all of James's numerous progeny. Bring them all home. We've left them out in the world alone for far too long. Open to too many bad influences and temptations. They must feel as though we abandoned them, as though we didn't care, and they'd be right. So bring them all home, because they're family and we owe them."

"Harry and Roger came back to the Hall," I said carefully. "And it didn't work out too well for them. We kept sending them out on missions until it killed them."

The Armourer looked at me sharply. "That's not how it was, Eddie, and you know it."

"Do I?" I said. "That's how it feels. . . ."

"Timothy was my only child," said the Armourer. "I can't help wondering whether, if I'd spent more time with him, he might not have grown up to become Tiger Tim. But I always had so much work to do, so many responsibilities . . . and I never was any good with children. Never knew what to say to them . . . I only got to know you, Eddie, because you were a teenage troublemaker, cutting lessons to sneak down here and badger me with endless questions about life out in the field. . . . Because you were already plotting on how best to get the hell out of the Hall, and as far away from the family as you could."

"And here I am, back where I belong," I said. "Funny how life works out sometimes."

The Armourer nodded slowly. "Charles and Emily's only child. The only surviving descendent of my generation. Only you and me left now of the Matriarch's direct line."

He scowled brusquely and looked away, his gaze the thousand-yard stare of a soldier who's seen too many die in too many wars. I wondered if I should tell him what Walker had said to me during my time in Limbo.

That my parents might not be dead after all . . . But there were already too many important things happening at once, and I couldn't afford for him to become distracted. Not when there were still so many things I needed him to do. His attention snapped back to me as though it had never been away.

"What are you doing here, Eddie?"

I gave him a quick rundown on what had happened at the Wulfshead, and then at Sir Terrence Ashtree's office. Leaving out all the bits that made me look like a monster. I told him that the upper echelons, and possibly even the leader himself, of the new satanic conspiracy were probably holed up in the Timeless Moment, and he nodded thoughtfully.

"Yes . . . Yes, that would make sense, actually."

"Why?" Molly said loudly, unable to hold her peace any longer. "Why does it make sense, and what is the Timeless bloody Moment?"

"The headquarters, hideout and last retreat of the previous satanic conspiracy, back in the nineteen forties," said the Armourer, leaning back in his chair and lacing his fingers together in his lap as he slid effortlessly into lecture mode. "My uncle Laurence was a field agent back then—your great-uncle, Eddie, Grandmother Martha's elder brother—and he told me all kinds of yarns about battling Satanists in occupied France. They were at the peak of their influence back in 1943, and plotting all kinds of black-magic attacks against England, from what they foolishly thought were safe bases along the French coastline. Safe and secure . . . Uncle Laurence showed them! Moving from city to city and town to town, arranging all kinds of unfortunate accidents to screw up their progress. You couldn't blow everything up, or kill all the people who needed killing, because the Nazis would take reprisals on the local populations. Always very keen on executions, the Nazis. It must have felt so fine to be out in the field in those days, fighting the last good war. . . . I couldn't wait to be a field agent, but all I got for my troubles was the Cold War. . . .

"Sorry, drifting . . . 1943. October. Uncle Laurence was checking out a particularly nasty coven down in Nantes when he stumbled over information about the Satanists' secret bolt-hole and weapons depository, tucked away in the Timeless Moment. I'm not sure whether the Satanists created the place, or discovered it, or moved in and took it away from someone else. . . . Either way, it was the perfect hiding place. The Satanists established their main headquarters there, where none of their enemies could reach them. All right, Molly, don't be so impatient; I'm getting there. The Timeless Moment was, and presumably still is, a pocket dimension of a kind, outside time and space as we know them. A strange alternate dimension tucked away between the tick and tock of linear time. Very hard to locate, and even harder to get into. Uncle Laurence led the mission to destroy the dimensional doorway the Satanists used to access the Timeless Moment, cutting the rank and file off from their headquarters, their leader and all the secret superweapons they'd been hoarding there to present to Hitler to help him win the war. Without all this, the rank and file were fatally weakened. Most of them legged it for the nearest horizon and disappeared. The few who stuck it out lost all their influence with Nazi High Command once it became clear they couldn't deliver all the marvellous things they'd promised. That was the end for them as a vital force in the war. Which helped us win the war, no doubt about it."

"This must be what rejuvenated the conspiracy again!" said Molly. "Someone must have regained access to the Timeless Moment!"

"Seems likely," said the Armourer.

"Presumably this mysterious new leader of theirs," I said. "Whose name we still don't know. Why are all his people put under a geas, never to use his name outside the conspiracy? What's the big deal about his name? Why make it such a secret?"

Molly looked at the Armourer. "Apparently because we'd recognise it. Apparently we know him."

"Oh, bloody hell," said the Armourer. "Not a Drood?"

"No," I said quickly and very definitely.

"Good," said the Armourer. "I suppose that's something. If I have to announce I'm scanning everyone in the family *again*, I think we can expect some very unfortunate responses."

"The influence machine must be inside the Timeless Moment," I said. "It's the only safe place for it until it's needed. The one place we couldn't hope to find it. They need only to wheel it out when it's time to prepare people for the Great Sacrifice."

"Same for the kidnapped townspeople of Little Stoke," said Molly. "And the abducted weapons makers from the Supernatural Arms Faire. And Isabella! The one place they could hold her from which even she couldn't escape!"

"If she's still alive," I said carefully.

"Of course she's still alive!" Molly glared at me, her hands clenched unknowingly into fists. "She has to be alive. I'd know if she were dead."

I considered her thoughtfully. "You once said to me ... that the Metcalf sisters come as a package. Which is why Isabella can keep getting in and out of the Hall so easily."

"It is?" said the Armourer.

"Molly," I said, "could you use that link to find your sister, and establish a connection between this reality and the Timeless Moment?"

"It's not as simple as that," Molly said reluctantly. "The conspiracy wouldn't be able to detect the link, so they couldn't block it; but even so, the best I could do would be to point you in the right direction. Metaphorically speaking."

"I have an idea on how to take it from there," I said. "Not a very safe or even particularly sane idea, but ... Uncle Jack."

"This is going to be really bad, isn't it?" said the Armourer. "I always know it's going to be something really bad when you start calling me Uncle Jack instead of Armourer. What do you have in mind, Eddie?"

"Back when the Hall was under attack by the Accelerated Men," I said carefully, "the Sarjeant-at-Arms mentioned a last-resort defence called Alpha Red Alpha."

"What's that?" Molly said immediately. "I've never heard of it before. And from the way you said it, it sounds like something I very definitely ought to have been told about."

"Alpha Red Alpha," the Armourer said heavily, "is Drood Hall's very last and scariest line of defence. A powerful dimensional engine buried deep under the Hall. Most of the family don't even know it's there, on the grounds that if they knew there was a very powerful and largely untested dimensional engine right under where they lived, they wouldn't want to live here anymore. And quite rightly, too. Powered up, Alpha Red Alpha can rotate the entire Hall and everyone in it out of this reality and into another one. The idea being that we could escape a real catastrophe by disappearing into another dimension, and staying there until the danger was past. The engine would bring everyone back when it was safe. However . . ."

"I just knew there was going to be a *however*," Molly said to me. "Didn't you just know there was going to be a *however*?"

"The engine has never been properly tested," said the Armourer. "Most of us aren't even sure it will work. It was only ever activated once; and after what happened on the trial run . . ."

"Did you build this engine?" said Molly.

"No! No . . . that was the Armourer before me. Your great-uncle Francis, Eddie. Grandfather Arthur's younger brother. A brilliant mind, but I think he must have been dropped on his head as a baby. Repeatedly. Francis Drood was an excellent designer and weapons maker, no doubt about it. But unfortunately, he was what these days we would call an extreme lateral thinker. . . . Or completely off his bloody head, as we said at the time. He produced a lot of really useful equipment, which field agents still use today; and he designed three of the forbidden weapons locked away in the Armageddon Codex. Weapons so powerful and potentially destructive that we've never dared use them. Simply reading the instruction manual is enough to bring you out in a cold sweat. . . . I'll say this for the man: He never had any problems thinking big. Thinking rationally and responsibly, yes, major problems there . . .

"He created Alpha Red Alpha after the Chinese tried to nuke the Hall back in 1964. Bit of an overreaction, I always thought. . . . Anyway, Francis talked the then Matriarch into setting the engine up for a trial run. We moved most of the family out into the grounds, just in case. . . . We were all very interested to see what would happen, but preferably from a safe distance. Your uncle James came home specially from East Germany, I came back from Nepal and your parents came back from Peru. Then the Matriarch asked for volunteers from among the field agents to accompany and protect the Hall wherever it went, just in case. We tended to use those three words quite a lot, whenever Francis was involved. . . . So the four of us, and four more, volunteered, and we were all there inside the Hall when Francis fired up Alpha Red Alpha for the first time. We had no idea where we were going, where we'd end up. All Francis had was a whole bunch of mathematics that made sense only to him, and assurance that his engine would most definitely send the Hall *away*. . . .

"At first, everything seemed to go fine. The actual transition was a bit . . . disturbing when the Hall dropped out of the world, but it did very definitely reappear Somewhere Else. Not an alternate Earth, or even another reality, but an entirely alien world. Once we came up from the basement and looked out the front windows, the first thing we saw was two suns, blazing impossibly bright in a sick green sky, and when we opened the front door, the air was so packed with excess oxygen and really nasty trace gases that we couldn't breathe it. We had to armour up to survive in the strange new world that Francis's engine had brought us to. We'd been dropped right into the middle of an alien jungle full of plants and animals and . . . creatures we'd never seen before. Some of them so different and disturbing they hurt your head to look at them. Everything was *wrong* . . . a living nightmare packed with horrible things everywhere we looked.

"And while we were still getting our heads round that, the whole jungle rose up at once and attacked us. Not only the awful things that lived in the jungle, but the plants themselves. Raging, thrashing, whipping long tendrils at us . . . Everything was alive and angry and utterly antagonistic. Thousands of creatures hit the Hall at once, from every direction, smashing through the windows, hammering against the closed doors, rising up to try to break in through the roof. We fought them off as best we could, sending Francis back down to fire up the engine and get us all home again. It couldn't have taken him long, but it seemed to take forever. It was like fighting in a nightmare against horrible things that keep coming at you, no matter how hard you fight. I saw young Alice fall with a hundred thorns blasted through her armour. I saw Oliver pulled down and ripped apart by thrashing plants that crawled all him, his armour no more protection than tinfoil. I saw plants eat them both, and drink their blood.

"I still have nightmares sometimes. . . .

"But finally Alpha Red Alpha kicked in again and we came home. The Hall was a mess: battered and broken and infested with all kinds of alien life-forms that had forced their way in. Luckily they couldn't live in our air, so we stood well back and watched them die. They didn't understand what was happening to them, but they still tried to kill the few Droods who tried to help. There're always a few who do the 'if only we can communicate with them' thing. . . . I would have taken a flamethrower to the lot of them. We waited till we were sure everything was dead, and then Droods in their armour dragged them all out of the Hall, chopped them up fine, to make sure, burned them in great piles and then buried what was left in a far corner of the grounds. To this day nothing else will grow there.

"It took weeks to reopen the Hall. And fumigate it, because some of the little bastards had left spores to be breathed in by the unsuspecting. . . . After the Matriarch got a good look at what had come back with us, and listened to our story, she told Francis to his face that he was never to use the engine again until he could be sure of where he was sending the Hall. And that Alpha Red Alpha was only ever to be used as a very last resort, after we'd tried everything else, including prayer and closing our eyes and hoping it would all go away. Francis spent the rest of his life, as Armourer and after, in retirement, trying to figure out how to control what he'd created, but he never did. The family buried the engine deep under the Hall, called it Francis's Folly and wiped it from the official records.

"For everyone's peace of mind."

"But," I said, "could it get us into the Timeless Moment?"

"Somehow I knew you were going to say that," said the Armourer. "I tell you the most cautionary story I know that doesn't involve sex, and it didn't even slow you down. Technically, yes, I suppose it's possible. But . . . all I could do would be to turn the bloody thing on. And hopefully off again. I have absolutely no idea of how to steer the damned thing, and neither does anyone else."

"But I can help with that!" said Molly. "My link with Isabella will point us in the right direction. . . ."

"And I can focus that link through the Merlin Glass to take us where we need to go!" I said. "You start the engine up, Uncle Jack; Molly will aim it, and I will steer it. Right into the Timeless Moment."

The Armourer smiled suddenly. "You know, it's a crazy idea, but it just might work!"

I looked at Molly. "It always sounds so much worse when he says it."

The Armourer looked at Molly. "If all you Metcalf sisters are linked to one another . . . does that mean the dreaded Louisa knows what's happening?"

"Almost certainly," said Molly. "But don't worry; it'll take even her a long time to get back from Mars."

The Armourer's face twitched. "I'm not even going to ask what she's doing on Mars."

"Best not to," I said. "Now, where is Alpha Red Alpha, exactly? You said you *buried* it under the Hall?"

The Armourer's mouth winced, as though he'd tasted something bitter. "I had hoped I'd never have to go down there again. Or at the very least, that I'd be very old and safely retired before some other poor bastard had to do it . . . Come with me."

He got up out of his chair with a certain amount of effort and the usual pained noises, and led Molly and me to the very back of the Armoury, out beyond the firing range and the corrupt-spell dumps. Three lab assistants were standing around the sparkling watercooler, commenting excitedly on the miniature mermaid they'd dropped into it. The Armourer drove them back to their workstations with barked commands and harsh language. He finally stopped before a large, hulking piece of machinery of no immediate significance. It didn't even have a nameplate.

"Armour up, Eddie," said the Armourer. "I need you to move this machine two feet to the left. My left, not yours. And be careful. It's heavier than it looks."

"What is it?" I asked after I'd armoured up. Molly was already poking and prodding and kicking at the machine's solid steel sides in an experimental sort of way.

"It was supposed to be a food synthesiser," said the Armourer. "The idea was all the rage back in the seventies. And it would have helped to take the strain off feeding a family of our size. But we never could get it to work right. Francis tried, I tried, and now and again one of the more than usually ambitious lab assistants will take a crack at it, but even though the theory works out to a thousand decimal places . . . no matter what settings we try, all the machine ever produces is a kind of glowing green porridge that looks bad and smells worse."

"What did it taste like?" said Molly, ever the practical one.

"We never found out, because if you got too close to the stuff, it ate you," said the Armourer. "And once we had the stuff, we couldn't get rid of it. We tried everything, including fire and acid and beating it with sticks, but it was a stubborn little organism. . . . In the end, we teleported every last bit of it to the bottom of the Pacific Ocean. Where for all I know it still is, crawling across the ocean floor and scaring the crap out of the giant squids that live down there." He paused for a moment. "The numbers do seem to be dropping off of late. . . ."

"Then . . . why haven't you destroyed the machine?" I said.

"Oh, really, Eddie, you should know the answer to that. Because someday the family might have a need for really vicious green porridge that eats people," the Armourer said. "The family never wastes anything. And the machine does serve a useful purpose in itself, as you'll discover when you stop arguing and move the bloody thing two feet to the left. My left, not yours."

I put my golden shoulder to the huge machine and applied a steady pressure. The machine didn't budge an inch. I settled myself, dug my feet in and threw the whole of the armour's strength against the damned thing. For a long moment nothing happened, except that the steel section under my shoulder began to buckle from the pressure; and then the machine jerked a few inches to the left. Reluctantly, and fighting me all the way, the stubborn machine moved two feet to the left, revealing a solid wooden trapdoor in the rough stone floor. I stood up slowly, stretching my aching back, while Molly crouched down to take a good look at the trapdoor.

"I'm not sensing any protections or defences," she said.

"Of course not," said the Armourer. "They would

only have drawn attention. And besides, if we ever do need to get to the engine we'll probably need to do it in a hurry."

He knelt down beside the trapdoor, his knees complaining loudly. He picked up a solid steel padlock and hefted it in his hand for a moment before concentrating and armouring up his left hand. He then extended a complex golden key from his index finger and inserted it carefully into the padlock. The key turned easily, and the padlock opened. The Armourer removed the padlock, placed it carefully to one side and retracted the golden key into his fingertip. Then he hauled the heavy trapdoor open, the great wooden slab swinging back easily and silently, as though its massive brass hinges had been oiled only the day before. We all stared down into the dark hole in the floor.

All I could see was darkness, and the first few rungs of an iron ladder heading down into it. Even the overbright lighting of the Armoury couldn't penetrate the darkness more than a few inches. I studied the opening through my armoured mask, using infrared and ultraviolet, and finally my Sight, and none of it helped. The darkness remained absolute, holding secrets within. I checked for electromagnetic radiation, and half a dozen other warning signs, but still, nothing. My armour couldn't detect a single thing about what was down there. Which should have been impossible.

"I know the details of the key," the Armourer said quietly. "So does the Sarjeant-at-Arms. No one else. Not even the Matriarch knew how to access Alpha Red Alpha, by her own command. It's too dangerous. Eddie, you're always complaining the family keeps secrets from you . . . this should cure you of that. Follow me down the ladder. Mind your step, don't crowd me and when we get to the bottom don't wander off and *don't touch anything.*"

He went down the iron steps with an ease and agility that belied his years. The show-off. I followed him down more cautiously, and Molly brought up the rear, sticking so close to me she practically trod on my fingers. The trapdoor slammed shut over us the moment we were all inside. I was still in my armour. I have a tendency to do that when descending into complete darkness containing unknown threats. The steps seemed to fall and fall away below me, going down and down until my leg and back muscles began to cramp from the strain. The only sounds were the clanging of our feet on the iron steps, and the Armourer's loud breathing below.

"It's all right!" he yelled back up cheerfully. "The trapdoor's supposed to do that! Safety feature. Not so much to keep lab assistants out as to keep anything here from coming up into the Hall."

"Like what?" Molly said immediately.

"No idea," said the Armourer. "But it's best not to take chances."

After enough descending that I was getting really fed up with it, I finally reached the end of the ladder, and my armoured feet found a rough stone floor. I stepped away from the ladder to get out of Molly's way, and lights suddenly flared up, dazzling me for a moment. My mask quickly compensated for the glare, and I looked round a massive stone cavern stretching away in all directions. My first impression was that the cavern had to be bigger than the Hall itself, but that couldn't be right, or the Hall would have collapsed into it long ago. Even so, it was really big. . . . The stone walls were covered with line after line of carefully delineated mathematical symbols, none of which meant anything to me. I looked at Molly, and she shrugged.

"Mathemagics," the Armourer said cheerfully. "Designer theory, only supercharged. Don't look at them too long, or your eyes will start to bleed."

He had more to say on the subject, but I wasn't listening. I was looking at what the huge cave contained, packing it from wall to wall and from floor to ceiling, with only narrow walkways between: strange machines and intricate technology, and weird objects that might have been really high-tech or particularly worrying examples of abstract art. No flashing lights, no obvious control panels; often one piece would seem to slide or evolve into the next. Some parts were actually blurred or indistinct, as though my eyes couldn't properly understand what they were seeing. Mile upon mile of colour-coded cables stretched back and forth across the cavern, linking everything together, and hung in a complicated web between the upper heights and the ceiling. I moved slowly forward into what I reluctantly recognised as one big machine. It was like walking through a technological jungle. Molly stuck close by my side. The Armourer was, of course, already ahead of us, bumbling along with his hands in his coat pockets, muttering happily to himself.

Things were constantly moving, rising and falling, or turning this way and that. Other parts leaned and slumped and sort of merged into one another. Some were slowly changing shape, as though unable to settle, humming loudly to themselves in an important sort of way. There were even things that seemed to be watching me thoughtfully. I couldn't make sense of any of it. Except that for a machine that hadn't been used in years, an awful lot of it seemed to be very busy. . . . All I knew for sure was that being down here creeped the hell out of me. It didn't feel like a place where people should be, where anything as limited and fragile as people had any business being.

All my instincts were yelling at me to get the hell out while I still could, or at the very least give the machine a good kicking to make sure it knew its place.

"Armour down, Eddie," the Armourer said quietly. "We don't want to start anything."

I did so, reluctantly. The first thing that hit me was how warm the cavern was, almost uncomfortably hot and humid. There was bristling static in the air, which smelt of iron filings and something burning. Molly slipped her arm through mine, and I patted her hand absently.

"Try not to be so impressed," the Armourer said dryly. "It's only a machine. All right, there's a lot here I don't understand as yet, but that doesn't mean it can't still be useful to the family. Your great-uncle Francis was a brilliant man, Eddie, and only occasionally seriously disturbed. Yes . . . I can handle this. Turn it on. And off. Everything else should run itself, I think."

"Given how seriously wrong your first little trip went," said Molly, "why keep this around? I know something really potentially dangerous when I see it, and I'm looking at it right now."

"Because Francis always had a reason for everything he did," the Armourer said patiently. "Not always an obvious reason . . . Alpha Red Alpha was never intended to be just a bolt-hole for us to hide in; he had all sorts of ideas for it. He wrote them down in his workbooks, and one day we're going to break that code, and then, my word, we'll know a thing or two. No, Molly, Droods never throw anything away that might be useful someday. And this would appear to be Alpha Red Alpha's day. I do see what you mean, though. To be honest, being down here after all these years is disturbing the piss out of me."

He came to a sudden halt before one huge machine as big as a house, rising all the way up to the high ceiling. It was like a plunging waterfall frozen into solid crystal, with glowing wires running through it like multicoloured veins, etched with row upon row of strange symbols and studded with pieces of clearly alien-derived technology. It all surrounded a massive hourglass some twenty feet tall, fashioned from solid silver and glass so perfect you could barely see it was there. The top section of the hourglass was full of shimmering golden sand, all of it in place, with not one golden mote falling down into the chamber below.

"When I activate Alpha Red Alpha," said the Armourer, "the golden sands will start to fall. And the engine will rotate us out of this reality and into another. When the bottom section is full, it means we've arrived. Upon return, the golden sands will fly back up again. As I recall, it's really quite . . . unnatural to look at."

"All of this?" I said. "Built around an hourglass?"

The Armourer nodded unhappily. "Your great-uncle Francis was a seriously weird person."

*   *   *

Molly and I went back up into the Armoury, leaving Uncle Jack with the dimensional engine. He said he needed some quality time with it. The trip back up the iron ladder didn't seem to take nearly as long as the trip down; perhaps that was a safety feature, too. Once we were both back in the Armoury, I shut the trapdoor and contacted Ethel to ask where the Sarjeant-at-Arms was.

"He's in the ops room, Eddie, being very in charge. And can I just say, whatever it is you've got down in that hole, I don't like it. It's far too complicated for its own good, and it puts my teeth on edge. And I don't even have teeth."

There didn't really seem to be any answer to that, so Molly and I stepped through the Merlin Glass into the operations room. We could have walked, but the ops room is all the way across the Hall, in the south wing, and I didn't think we had the time. Besides, people would have wanted to stop me and ask questions, and I wasn't in the mood. The guards on duty in the operations room nodded brusquely to Molly and me as we appeared out of nowhere, which was a sign of how much things had changed. The leader of the ops room is Howard, a buttoned-down man in a buttoned-down suit that doesn't suit him. He nodded quickly to me and went back to studying his display screens. Howard has incredible organisational skills and a very real sense of passion where the family's security is concerned. He used to be one of the Armourer's finest lab assistants, but he turned out a bit too serious for that, so the Matriarch kicked him upstairs, where he could work out his basic vindictiveness against the family's enemies in a more useful way.

The operations room is our really high-tech centre, designed to oversee all the Hall's defences, from force shields to weapons systems to really powerful long-range sensors. The surprisingly reasonably sized room was always packed full of the very latest equipment and the best-trained technicians to run it all. But there was none of the hustle-bustle and basic urgency that always characterise the War Room. These people knew their job and performed their various tasks calmly and expertly, standing between the family and all the outside forces that would threaten us. They sat in comfortable chairs before technology they knew better than the backs of their own hands, and everything they might need was always within reach. There was a really long waiting list to work in the ops room.

The Sarjeant-at-Arms turned away from the communications people to talk briefly with Howard, and then moved over to join Molly and me.

"I've put together the army you wanted, Edwin. Nearly eighty percent of the family are ready to go to war. Those too young or too old to fight will make up a skeleton staff, to run all the necessary systems in our absence. No one wanted to be left out."

"Maybe we should leave some behind," I said. "In case we don't make it back."

The Sarjeant shook his head firmly. "They all know what's at stake, and they all want to be a part of the fight. The Satanists can't be allowed to win, or there'd be no point in coming back. Everyone's ready; we're waiting for you to provide us with a target."

So I told him about the Timeless Moment, and Alpha Red Alpha, and the Sarjeant took it all in his stride. Right up to the point where William the Librarian suddenly appeared in the ops room wearing a flak jacket and jeans and a Rambo-style headband, demanding loudly to be allowed to join the attack force. I couldn't help noticing he was still wearing his bunny slippers. He strode up to us, looking awkward but determined, and the technicians he passed stopped what they were doing to look at him with surprise and something very like awe. They'd all heard of the Librarian, and his story had only grown in the telling. None of them had ever seen him before. In fact, this was the first time that I knew of that he'd left the Old Library, except to appear very reluctantly for the occasional council meeting. I was surprised he could even find operations without a ball of string to follow. I nodded easily to the Sarjeant as the Librarian joined us.

"Oh, yes, I forgot to mention. The Librarian says he wants to go into battle, too."

"No, Uncle William," the Sarjeant said very firmly. "You can't join the actual fighting. You're far too valuable to the family."

"Flattery will get you nowhere, young Cedric," said the Librarian. "I have to do this. Those Satanist arsewipes are holding Ammonia prisoner, and I have to rescue her. I have to. I owe her."

The Sarjeant looked at me. "Is he . . . ?"

"Apparently," I said. "When she made contact with his mind, it seems she made quite an impression on him."

"But she looks like . . ."

"Looks aren't everything, Cedric," I said sternly.

"She has a magnificent mind," said William dreamily. "Really. You have no idea. I'm sure we've got a lot in common."

We all looked at one another, but none of us felt like saying anything. There was always the chance that Ammonia had put something inside the Librarian's head, something to make herself attractive to him . . . but would William's friend Pook have stood for that? I didn't think so. Still, Ammonia and the Librarian . . . I hadn't seen that one coming. Maybe it was the meeting of two minds. . . .

And, of course, she was already married. But then, the course of true love never did run smooth. I didn't say any of this out loud. I didn't want Molly laughing at me. She always says I'm far too romantic for my own good. And this from a woman who reads one bodice ripper after another.

"You have to let me in on this," William said stubbornly, "because I know where we're going—into the Timeless Moment. Laurence wrote a whole book about what he found inside that unnatural place. Ah, you didn't know he'd actually gone in there, did you? He led a team of local resistance fighters in, to attack the satanic conspiracy in their headquarters. Seems the Satanists built themselves a very special home away from home inside the Timeless Moment. A castle, Schloss Shreck—or, more properly, Castle Horror. He had a lot to say about it, and I've read every word of it. So I'm going with you, Cedric. Because you're going to need what I know."

I looked at the Sarjeant, leaving it up to him, and he sighed quietly. "You're going to have to look after him, Edwin. I am going to be too busy killing Satanists."

"Hold hard," I said. "Back up and go previous. You need to understand we're not just going in there to kill everything that moves that isn't us. There are people in this castle who need rescuing. The townspeople of Little Stoke, Molly's sister Isabella and, most probably, Ammonia Vom Acht. Maybe even some of the abducted weapons makers from the Supernatural Arms Faire. Some of them might have refused to work for Satanists, and some of them are old friends of the Armourer. This can't be only an extermination run, Sarjeant; it's a rescue mission, too."

"We'll do what we can for those people," said the Sarjeant. "Bring them all safely home if we can. But our first priority has to be putting the conspiracy out of business before they can start the Great Sacrifice. All the children in all the world are depending on us. The Satanists aren't going to surrender or negotiate; either we kill all of them or they'll kill all of us. They have to be wiped out to the last man, very definitely including this mysterious leader of theirs, or it could all start up again. This is war, Edwin, to the last man, or the last Drood, if need be."

"Understood, Sarjeant," I said. "When will your army be ready to go?"

The Sarjeant looked at Howard, who nodded quickly. The Sarjeant smiled. "Ready when you are, Eddie. Everyone's in place; everyone knows what to do. Callan's ready in the War Room. All defences are on high alert."

"Then let's do it," I said.

I contacted the Armourer through my torc and told him to fire up Alpha Red Alpha. He agreed immediately, with a little too much enthusiasm for my liking.

He does so love a new toy. I took out the Merlin Glass and instructed it to lock onto the Timeless Moment. Molly put one hand on mine and the other on the Glass, and added her link to Isabella to the mix. A slow, steady vibration ran through the floor. Heads came up all over operations as everyone felt it. My skin began to crawl.

"I'm not sure what will happen once the dimensional engine has done its stuff," Ethel murmured quietly in my ear. "I might get to go with you, or I might not. This is all new territory to me."

"But you're a dimensional traveller," I said.

"Yes, but I do it naturally. What your Alpha Red Alpha does is, quite frankly, an abomination, and wouldn't be allowed in a sane universe. If I'm not there with you, in the Timeless Moment, I'll be waiting for you here when you get back."

"And if we don't get back?" I said.

"Then I'll go home," said Ethel. "I wouldn't want to stay here if you weren't here, too. It was nice knowing you, Eddie, you and all your family. I will remember you. It's all been such fun."

The vibrations had grown strong enough to shake the whole room. Equipment was jumping and rattling, and the technicians hung onto their workstations with both hands. The lights flickered and flared, and shadows leapt all over the place. Strange sensations crawled across my skin, and my teeth chattered. I hung on grimly to the Merlin Glass, whose mirror was utterly blank, and Molly hung onto the Glass and to me with a grip so strong I knew nothing in this world would ever shake it loose. Everything around me seemed vague and uncertain, the people around me ghostly. The vibrations shook my bones and shuddered in my flesh, and it felt like I was being torn apart and put back together again, over and over. It reminded me of my time in Limbo, neither living nor dead, and I couldn't trust anything. I concentrated on Molly, and something like a hand gripped firmly onto what I thought was my hand. And then everything snapped back into focus, as though the whole Hall had been picked up and slammed down again somewhere else. Molly and I relaxed our grip and laughed aloud, glorying in being alive.

I looked into the Merlin Glass. The image was still only a blur. I carefully didn't shut it down, but put it away for the time being. Howard was already moving among his people, talking to them quietly, getting them over the shock and back to work. Display screens everywhere were blank, showing nothing but a shimmering silver void all around the Hall.

"There's nothing out there," said one of the technicians, his voice rising. "Nothing! No matter, no energy; that's not even light as we understand it. This is what the end of the universe will look like, when the game's finally over and the doors have been shut and the chairs piled up on the tables. . . ."

"Somebody give that man a stiff drink," said Howard. "And a slap round the head. This is no time to be going to pieces, people. Which part of 'we are going to a whole different reality' did you not understand? Now get working; there has to be something out there. Even if it's only this Castle Horror the Satanists are hiding out in. Come on, people; how can you miss a whole castle?"

The technicians busied themselves at their work, and a certain calm fell across the ops room as they concentrated on familiar tasks. The Sarjeant moved in beside Howard.

"No matter, no energy?" he said quietly. "What about gravity, and heat and . . . things like that? Everything seems normal enough in here."

"The Hall's many defences and protections are still running," said Howard, just as quietly. "I made sure of that before the Armourer activated that bloody machine. I had to be sure we would survive under whatever conditions, or lack of them, we ended up in. The shields preserve our reality inside the Hall. Of course, what happens to us when we go outside . . ."

"Hold everything," said the no-longer-panicking technician. "New readings coming in. We seem to have stabilised. I'm getting . . . no damage reports from anywhere in the Hall. According to the long-range sensors, conditions outside the Hall are ... surprisingly Earth normal. Air, gravity, temperature ... all within acceptable limits. That can't be a coincidence. I don't think this place just happened. . . . I think somebody built it."

"I don't know whether that's more or less worrying," I said.

"Could it be the conspiracy?" said Molly. "The original one, I mean, back in the nineteen forties."

"No way in hell," said the technician. "This is far beyond their abilities. Far beyond ours ... More likely they found it, somehow, and then moved in. And built their castle. This isn't just a pocket dimension; it's a whole *other* reality."

"Could we survive outside the Hall without our armour?" said the Sarjeant.

"Probably," said Howard, moving quickly from workstation to workstation, studying display screens over his people's shoulders. "But I wouldn't try it. Armour up and stay armoured up until we're all safely out of here. Ah! Castle, ho! The Hall appears to be calmly floating in this silver void, and roughly half a mile below us is a castle floating in the void! Put it up on the main display screen."

The big screen flashed a few times, ghosting in and out as though having trouble doing what it was being asked to do, and then the view cleared to show a massive medieval castle hanging in the silver-grey. It was hard to judge the scale with nothing to compare it to, so a stream of sensor information flowed along the bottom of the screen. The castle was huge, some twenty times larger than Castle Frankenstein, home to the now defunct Immortals. Massive stone walls, huge towers, long crenellated battlements, and everywhere, flags and banners of a familiar black and red, dominated by the swastika. Nazi flags. All of them stiff and still, untroubled by any breeze.

"I read all the books," said William, and I jumped a little to find him standing right beside me. "But I never expected ... You couldn't build a castle that big on

Earth; it would collapse under its own weight. The old conspiracy must have brought all its requirements through a bit at a time, and then assembled them here. But why did they need a castle that big? What was it built to hold, to contain? Or is there something else here, in this void that isn't a void, that they had to defend themselves against? There was nothing about that in Laurence's account. . . . And why did they name it Schloss Shreck? Castle Horror?"

The Sarjeant leaned over the comm systems and called down to the Armourer: "Is Alpha Red Alpha okay? Can you get us home safely? Answer the second question first."

"Everything's fine," said the Armourer. "As far as I can tell. I did everything the way I was supposed to, and the engine did everything it was supposed to. If not exactly in the manner I expected . . . So do what you have to do, Sarjeant, and then let's go home again. Because the sooner we're out of this unnatural place, the better."

"Can you get us safely home again?" said the Sarjeant.

"Ah," said the Armourer. "Now you're asking. Technically speaking, yes. Settle for that. I would."

"I think we should get out of here as soon as possible, too," said Howard. "I don't care if the conditions are as near Earth normal as makes no difference; there's no telling what long-term exposure could do to us. All my sensors are telling me this is a really bad place to be. I don't think people are supposed to exist here. I'd almost say the Timeless Moment is straining itself to tolerate our presence. The Hall's shields are holding steady . . . but the energy drain is enormous, far higher than it should be. Which means we have a deadline, Sarjeant. I'd say we've got twelve hours, tops, before the generators go down and the shields fall."

"What are your scanners telling us about Schloss Shreck?" said William. "Can you tell if there's anybody in there?"

"They've got heavy-duty protections of their own," said Howard. "We've no way of telling what's going on in there. I'm not seeing any signs of force shields, as such. . . . Nothing to stop us from walking right in. But I don't like it."

"Why would they need force shields?" I said. "What is there here that they would need to defend themselves against?"

"A really interesting question, and one that we should definitely look into *somewhen else*," said Molly. "Look at the castle. There're lights on in some of those windows. Somebody's home. So let's go pay them a visit and bash some Satanist heads in."

"To the point, as usual," I said. "Enough talking. We're going in."

"Damn right," said the Sarjeant-at-Arms.

Up on the roof of the Hall, the Drood army gathered. Hundreds of golden figures gleaming bright as they scrambled across the slanting tiles, forming groups around gables and cupolas and preparing the flying machines on the landing pads. As more and more of us came up onto the roof, it became increasingly crowded, until it was a wonder we didn't end up pushing one another off the edges to test the water, like penguins on an ice floe. Molly and I hung off both sides of an outcropping gable, me in my armour and her in her best let's-go-arse-kicking white dress, looking down at Schloss Shreck, floating in the silver void some distance below. It really was huge, like a medieval city carved in stone and wrapped in Nazi flags and banners. Lighted windows stared back at us like watchful eyes.

"Good thing they're down there, and we're up here," said Molly, after a while. "We can just drop in on them. Death from above!"

"They must know we're here," I said. "Must know who we are. Must know we're coming . . ."

"Good," said Molly. "Let them panic."

"There's no telling how many of the bastards there are," I said. "Could be a whole army . . . Could be the army we never got to face at Cathedral Hall."

"You have got to stop obsessing over that," said Molly. "None of it was your fault."

"I have unfinished business."

"You know more ways to feel guilty about things that you're not responsible for than anyone I know," said Molly. "I've never felt guilty about anything. You should try it. It's remarkably liberating."

More and more golden figures spilled up onto the roof, emerging from attics and trapdoors and other less official openings, and were quickly harangued into groups by the Sarjeant-at-Arms. I'd never seen so many armoured Droods in one place before, not even when we were defending ourselves against the invading Accelerated Men. A lot of them were carrying weapons, courtesy of the Armourer. Normally the golden armour is all the weapon a Drood needs in the field, but this was different. We were going to war.

One by one the various flying machines powered up, their cheerful roar and clatter a reassuring presence in the uncanny quiet of the Timeless Moment. There were skeletal autogyros, coughing out black clouds of smoke and steam; carefully preserved Spitfires from the 1940s, with supercharged engines, really nasty guns and their own personal force shields (the Armourer got the idea from some television show); and dozens of different kinds of flying saucers. Not actual alien craft; rather reverse-engineered alien tech made into saucers . . . simply for the fun of it. Some Droods have the strangest hobbies. . . . All of which are encouraged, because you never know when they might lead to something useful.

The Sarjeant-at-Arms came over to join me, striding across the rising and falling tiles with calm assurance. You can always recognise the Sarjeant in his armour; he's modified it to look as blunt and businesslike as a golden bullet.

"The flying machines are ready to go," he said. "I've ordered them to take a first look at the castle, sound out any defences and maybe even try a few strafing runs to put the wind up whoever's at home. I'd feel happier if I knew how many we were facing; could be anything in there from a skeleton staff to a full army."

"Eddie said that," said Molly.

"Really?" said the Sarjeant. "Some of me must be rubbing off on you, Eddie."

"What a terrible thought," I said.

"And a mental image I could really have done without," said Molly.

"It doesn't matter how many there are," I said. "We're going in. We have people to rescue, and punishments to hand out. Send in the first wave, Sarjeant."

He turned and waved one golden hand at the landing pads, and all the flying machines rose up. The autogyros sprang into the air like startled birds, banking away from the Hall and then plunging down towards the castle. The Spitfires threw themselves off the edge of the roof and curved smoothly round to swoop down on the castle like angry eagles, force shields shimmering and sparking where their edges made contact with the void. The flying saucers rose up in ones and twos, silent and serene, glowing all kinds of colours, some of them never meant for human eyes. They dropped down towards the castle like so many gaudy ghosts.

They all took it in turns to overfly the castle and then buzz it again and again, increasingly close each time, trying to provoke a response. They hit it from every side at once, pulling away only at the last moment, but the castle didn't react. The lights were still very definitely on in many of the windows, but no force shields sprang up, and no weapons appeared. One Spitfire flew in so close its passing actually rippled one of the Nazi banners hanging down from the battlements. Another Spitfire roared right across the castle roof, opening up with all its guns. A loud series of explosions rocked the castle battlements as bullets chewed up old stone and sent heavy fragments flying . . . but still no response. I looked at the Sarjeant.

"Give the signal. We're going in."

And I let go of the gable and jumped off the Hall. My

armoured legs pushed me out and away, and I dropped into the silver void like a stone, aiming for the castle below. Even inside the protection of my armour, I seemed to feel a chill wind caressing my flesh and shuddering in my bones. Air and light and gravity be damned; there was nothing Earth-like about this place. I plummeted towards the castle, arms and legs stretched out wide, and then I concentrated and great golden wings erupted out of my back. They slowed my fall appreciably, and I soon got the hang of tilting them this way and that to steer me in towards the castle roof. More golden figures appeared beside me as we fell on Schloss Shreck like avenging angels.

This would never have worked on Earth, of course, but we were all a long way from home.

Molly swooped in to join me, flying under her own power, her long white dress rippling around her. She was laughing and whooping with glee, her face alive with uncomplicated joy. She always was a great one for being in the moment, and also clearly happy to finally be doing something. She moved in close beside me, grinning widely, and then rolled over onto her back and crossed her legs casually.

"Show-off," I said.

I glanced to my left and to my right. Droods filled the silver void all around me, falling at increasing speed on their various wings. Some had golden support struts like living biplanes, while others had formed actual birds' wings with sculptured golden feathers. Some hadn't bothered with wings at all; they streamlined their armour and threw themselves at the castle like projectiles. They were already far ahead of the rest of us, and at the speed they were going it seemed to me there was a good chance they'd punch right through the roof, through the castle and out the other side. I admired their ambition, but I was determined to be more cautious. If only because I couldn't believe the castle was utterly without defences.

The flying machines were all over Schloss Shreck now, sweeping back and forth and opening up with every weapon they had, blowing holes in the outer walls and whole chunks off the battlements. They buzzed the castle like angry wasps while the golden Drood army closed inexorably in on its target. We got in really close . . . before gun emplacements opened up the length of every wall, and huge guns with terrible long barrels took aim on us, all of them blasting away in a massive broadside, slamming into the targets laid out before them. They'd been waiting for enough of us to come within range. Droods in their armour were protected; but the flying machines weren't.

The autogyros went first, blown out of the void. Their engines exploded in clouds of black smoke and steam, and lovingly maintained fuselages were raked with bullets. Many of them burst into flames. Golden pilots were flung from their doomed craft, clutching helplessly at nothing as they fell into a void without end. They were still alive, but we had no way of reaching them. I wondered how long they'd fall, and how long they'd live. . . .

The Spitfires banked and rolled at incredible speed, blasting away at the gun emplacements, but they were too few against too many guns. The bullets couldn't broach the planes' force shields, so the castle produced guns that fired strange energies that crawled all over the Spitfires, opening up holes in the shields for the guns to fire through. Some exploded, some lost power and some spiralled away into the void like wounded birds. The remaining Spitfires saw there was no point in pressing the fight any longer and turned away, plunging into the void to rescue the fallen. Strictly speaking, they shouldn't have done that, but family looks after family.

The energy guns then targeted the flying saucers, and they exploded silently one after another in sudden outbursts of unnatural colours.

The rest of us fell on Castle Horror, drawing in our wings to add more speed, but bullets and vicious energies still found us, beating against our armoured breasts, unable to break through. We fell like Furies and hit the castle roof like a rain of golden ammunition. Solid stone shattered under the impact of our golden feet, and many of us ploughed right through to whatever lay below. Some manoeuvred sideways at the last moment and swung round to hit the castle walls dead-on. There were huge stone gargoyles and stylised stone eagles everywhere, and they made good handholds. Soon we were swarming all over Schloss Shreck, opening up holes in the roof with our golden fists, scrambling over the walls like golden beetles, ripping guns out of their emplacements and throwing them into the void.

New weapons fired up through the roof, hitting us with unfamiliar energies. Some were blasted up into the air by the impact; others were knocked off their feet. Droods staggered this way and that as vicious energies crawled all over us, fighting to get in. But our armour held.

I smashed a hole through the roof until I had an opening big enough to drop through. I jumped down into the dark, and I was inside Schloss Shreck. Molly dropped down beside me. None of the attacks had even come close to touching her. We'd arrived in an attic full of junk, most of which I kicked out of the way as I hurried through it, looking for a way down into the castle proper. I could hear more Droods forcing their way in. Molly grinned at me like a naughty child trespassing somewhere she knew she wasn't allowed. Behind my mask, I couldn't help smiling, too. It felt good to be striking back at the enemy at last.

I found a trapdoor and a ladder that led down into a wide stone corridor, and soon we were moving swiftly along the castle's upper floor. Solid stone walls, marble floors, all on a big enough scale to make mere humans feel small. A heavy quiet hung over everything like a shroud. Everywhere I looked there was Nazi regalia: huge flags and hanging banners, blocky black swastikas, eagles with grasping clawed feet, even giant portraits of stylised Aryan youth and soldiers from the 1940s. It was like moving through a museum to history's worst nightmare, a paean of praise to Hitler's Nazi Germany: the centre for a celebration that never happened. Molly sniffed loudly.

"Been a while since anyone redecorated here."

"Nothing's changed, because this is when the Satanists were a real power in the world," I said. "This has all been preserved from when they last had a chance of winning. Satanists have always been strangely sentimental. They love the past because that's when they were what they think they should be. Do me a favour, Molly. All this Nazi shit is getting on my nerves. Do something destructive about it."

"Love to," said Molly.

She snapped her fingers, and every single flag and banner burst into flames. The sound of crackling fires was pleasantly loud in the quiet as Molly and I strode cheerfully down the burning corridor.

We descended through stone galleries, wide passageways and long, curving stairs, until finally we found ourselves in a great open hall. Still no sign of anyone. We moved slowly forward, my golden feet hammering on the marble floor. In the middle of the hall lay a large circular table surrounded by what could only be described as thrones. The walls were hung with idealised portraits of men in medieval armour, in symbolic settings. All of them bore swastikas on their breastplates and shields.

"Hitler and his inner circle always did have this strange fascination with tales of King Arthur and his knights," I said. "Surprising, really, given they had absolutely no understanding of chivalry. Der Führer was supposed to have a layout like this somewhere under the Berchtesgaden . . . like a twisted Camelot. Which would actually be a really cool name for a new indie band."

"We need to keep moving," said Molly. "I can feel Isabella's presence not too far from here . . . but I'm starting to feel something is terribly wrong."

"Then let's go find her," I said. "Lead the way, Molly."

She turned back the way we'd come, leaving the hall behind us, chose a new direction without hesitation and started down it. She set off at a fierce pace, her face creased with worry, and soon she was running down the corridor, her arms pumping at her sides. Driven on by an urgency only she could feel. I ran alongside her, my armoured feet scarring the marble floor. It occurred to me that I hadn't seen another Drood since I entered the castle, and I couldn't even hear any sound of fighting or destruction. I reached out to the Sarjeant-at-Arms through my torc, but couldn't get an answer. Presumably the castle was jamming our communications. I tried Ethel, but I hadn't heard a word from her since we entered the Timeless Moment. Presumably she was still back on Earth, haunting the place where the Hall had been, waiting for our return. I wondered how long she'd wait. . . .

We went down and down, from floor to floor, until we were forced to a sudden stop by two massive solid-steel doors that blocked our way, twenty feet high if they were an inch, and almost as wide. I pulled at one of the doors, and it didn't budge at all. There were three separate locks, each the size of my head. I grinned behind my mask, placed both golden hands flat against the doors and pushed hard, till my golden fingers sank deep into the steel. And then I pulled. . . . The three locks exploded, one after another, and Molly had to duck behind me to avoid the pieces that flew through the air like shrapnel. The doors surged outwards under my implacable strength, and when I finally had a big enough gap I let go and walked between them into a hall greater than any I'd seen so far, overwhelmingly huge, hundreds of feet long, full of the strangest collection of weapons and machines of war I'd ever seen.

"I thought we'd come across something like this," said the Armourer.

I spun around, startled. Molly jumped and made a loud squeak of surprise, and then tried terribly hard to pretend she hadn't. The Armourer was standing there, in his armour shaped like a lab coat, of all things, looking around the hall with great interest. I slapped him hard across the shoulder, and the sound echoed loudly.

"Sorry," said the Armourer. "Impossible to communicate in this unnatural place. Still, you have to admit this is really impressive. This is where the Nazis stored all their secret superweapons that were going to win the war for them. All the things they never got a chance to use, because Laurence shut the place down and trapped it here. Look at it all. . . . I've read about some of this, but never expected to see it with my own eyes. Prototype flying saucers, massive drilling machines to enter a city from underneath, tanks the size of railway engines, and look at that! A lightweight wooden airplane, to cross the Atlantic and drop their crude nuclear bombs on New York and Washington."

"A balsa-wood airplane?" said Molly. "Oh, come on . . ."

"Howard Hughes built something similar for the Americans," I said. "The Spruce Goose. Never put into production, but it did fly. . . ."

"All right, I'll give you a wooden plane," said Molly. "But Nazi flying saucers, in the forties?"

"Word was the Nazis had access to a crashed alien starship," said the Armourer. "Some of the best Nazi minds broke their hearts trying to reverse-engineer it. Imagine trying to build a stardrive with vacuum tubes and slave labour. . . . Still, who knows what they might have achieved, given time? They nearly had the atomic bomb before we did. They were getting desperate enough to try anything towards the end. I don't even recognise some of the things they've got here. Oh, Eddie, we have got to take this back with us! This is all of major historical importance!"

"First things first, Uncle Jack," I said.

"I have to find Isabella!" said Molly. "She's in trouble; I know she is. . . ."

"Of course you must," the Armourer said immediately. "Lead the way, my dear."

And so off we set again, hurrying through one oversize passageway after another, all of them built to impress or at least intimidate, until finally we found ourselves facing another closed door. More solid steel, with the word *Verboten* etched deeply into the metal. I kicked it open and we hurried in . . . to find ourselves standing at one end of a long, narrow hallway full of strange equipment, all of it covered in a thick layer of ice. Row upon row of tall glass cylinders stretched away before us, disappearing into the gloom, each thickly crusted with frost. The overhead lights came on one by one as we stood there, revealing more and more cylinders fading off into the distance. Each one had a blocky equipment panel at its base, sparkling with its own layer of hoarfrost. I moved in close for a better look. It was all blinking lights and heavy levers, and handwritten labels in German. The Armourer moved slowly down the centre aisle, trying to look at everything at once. Molly stayed with me, shivering and hugging herself.

"It's freezing cold in here. Even after all these years. What were they doing?"

"Storing something," the Armourer said cheerfully. "I wonder what. . . ."

"Specimens of some kind?" said Molly, fascinated despite herself.

"Cryogenics chambers!" said the Armourer. "Crude, but functional." He leaned in close to one cylinder, brushing the ice away with his forearm. "Animal species . . . of a kind." He looked at the control panel. "My German's a bit rusty, but if I'm translating these labels correctly, what we have in these cylinders are . . . werewolves, Nosferatu, dragonkind, changelings . . . and a whole row of cylinders marked 'Alien.' I think this was some crude first attempt at bioengineering, presumably inspired by whatever they discovered in that crashed alien starship."

"Can you tell what species the aliens belong to?" I said. "We may need to contact someone's embassy."

The Armourer cleared more ice from a cylinder and took a good look at what was inside. "No," he said finally. "I don't recognise this. Which is interesting . . . because I could have sworn I knew all the aliens allowed access to this world."

"They were creating monsters in here," I said. "Typical Nazis. Were they trying to create some new form of shock troops, perhaps?"

"Maybe," said the Armourer. "Or perhaps they were . . . experimenting. They did so love to experiment. On things, and people . . . Welcome to the House of Pain, Dr. Moreau."

"Can you make any sense of the control panels?" I said.

"No," said the Armourer regretfully. "Too technical."

"Hold it," said Molly. "You want to wake these things up?"

"I was thinking more about putting them out of their misery," I said.

And that was when the whole place shook, and the lights flared up brilliantly as though hit by a power surge. All the cylinders began to moan and vibrate in place, humming loudly like so many glass tuning forks. Whole chunks of ice fell away to shatter noisily on the floor. Frost on the instrument panels began to steam and melt and run away. It became increasingly possible to see what was inside the cylinders, and I soon wished I couldn't. Too many things that should never have existed, made from pain and horror. This was nothing natural about any of them; they were patchwork things, horrible combinations of man and animal, shaped into living nightmares. All slowly waking up. Mouths opened, revealing jagged teeth. Fingers opened and closed, clutching at nothing, or tapped and clattered against the inside of the cylinders. Eyes opened, full of pain and rage and madness.

"They're all coming back to life!" said Molly. "Armourer, what did you do?"

"I didn't do anything!" said the Armourer, looking wildly about him. "I didn't touch anything! We have must have restarted the systems when we walked in here."

"We don't have time for this," I said.

I smashed the nearest equipment panel with one blow of my golden fist. The light inside the cylinder snapped off, and the contents stopped moving. I made my way steadily up and down the rows, smashing each control panel in turn, until my arm ached even inside

my armour. There was a series of small explosions, a
few fires, some drifting smoke . . . and one by one the
systems shut down. The ice was still melting and running away in streams, but inside the cylinders, eyes
closed, mouths closed, fingers stopped moving.

"Are they all back to sleep now?" said Molly, when I
finally finished my work and returned to her.

"They're all dead, Molly," the Armourer said quietly. "We put them out of their suffering. Sometimes
that's the only mercy we have to offer."

Molly put a comforting hand on my golden arm.
"You did what you had to, Eddie."

"I know," I said. "Lot of that happening recently."

I looked round suddenly. Off in the distance, I could
hear sounds of fighting, conflict, gunfire and explosions.
It seemed the Droods had come to grips with the enemy
at last. But whom were they fighting? I moved back to
the open door to find out, and that was when one of the
largest cylinders suddenly exploded, shooting vicious
glass shards through the air.

The Armourer and I moved quickly to shelter Molly,
and when we looked round it was to see freezing gases
boiling out of the shattered cylinder, falling to crawl
along the floor like heavy ground fog. And out of the remains of the cylinder stepped a massive apelike creature.
I have to say apelike, because it was another patchwork
creature, roughly stitched together from a dozen different species, not all of them apes. It was huge, a giant, nine
to ten feet tall and broadly built, its piebald skin stretched
tautly over bulging muscles. Its fur had fallen out in great
patches. So much time and effort, just so Nazi scientists
could create the killer ape of myth and legend. Its head
had been shaved, and jagged scars ran across the bulging
augmented forehead. Steel bolts circled the skull, sparking static electricity. Its eyes were wild, full of suffering
and the knowledge of what had been done to it.

It advanced slowly towards us, as though uncertain
whether to walk upright or lower its huge knuckles to
the floor. The oversize muscles swelled with every
movement, threatening to split the overtaut skin. I didn't

want to hurt it. Poor bastard had already been hurt so much. And even the biggest ape was no match for Drood armour, after all. So I moved forward to meet it, my arms stretched wide in a gesture of welcome. The ape grabbed one golden forearm and threw me the length of the hall with one snap of its overlong arm. I tumbled through the air, smashing through the standing cylinders, and finally slammed to a halt against the far wall. I was quickly back on my feet again, and scrambling through the wreckage. The ape was advancing steadily on Molly, the only one of us without armour.

She tried some basic magics, but none of them could get a hold. The ape had its own built-in protections. It kept advancing on her, shaking its head from side to side as though bothered by some pain it couldn't reach, and Molly kept backing away. The ape growled at her, and there was nothing sane in that low rumbling sound, only rage and pain and horror. And then the Armourer stepped out of the shadows to stand behind the ape and punch it in the back with all his strength. It screamed, loud as any fire siren. The Armourer's golden hand sank deep into the muscled back, and then he ripped its spine out in one swift movement. A great gout of blood splashed across his armour and quickly ran away. The ape crashed to the floor, twitched a few times and lay still. The Armourer looked at the bloody thing in his hand and opened his golden fingers to let it fall to the floor. Molly stared at him. I came over to join them.

"People tend to forget I was once a field agent," the Armourer said calmly.

"You didn't have to kill it," said Molly.

"It would have killed you," said the Armourer.

"You don't know that!" Molly seemed suddenly on the brink of tears. "We could have saved it. . . . Taken it out of here . . ."

"Some things aren't meant to be pets," said the Armourer. "Come on; let's go find your sister."

But first, we went to see what the fighting was, in case we were needed. Didn't take us long to find it. The Satanists had found and closed with the Drood forces, and the war was under way. Not that the Satanists had come in person; instead they sent something they must have found in Schloss Shreck when they first reopened it. Perhaps standing in rows of icy cylinders. A whole army of blond Aryan supermen in Nazi SS uniforms, all of them with the same arrogantly handsome face. Clones. Hundreds and hundreds of perfect soldiers, all made from the same man. Made to fight in a war long past. The Satanists had sent them out against us to see what they could do. And maybe soften us up a little. I wondered what the Satanists had told the clones; wondered whom they'd been told we were. Whatever it was, it seemed to have motivated them; their handsome faces were flushed with rage and fury.

They closed on us with every kind of weapon, moving inhumanly fast. They had everything from standard-issue Lugers to modern machine pistols to strange-energy weapons, none of them any use against Drood armour. Still, the sheer number of them slowed the Drood advance almost to a halt. We had to smash our way through them, striking them down and advancing over the fallen bodies. Two great forces went head-to-head in the massive stone hall, filling it with lunging bodies from end to end and wall to wall. Both sides strove against each other, no mercy sought or shown. Molly, the Armourer and I joined the fight to do our bit. We had no problem killing the clones; they might not be Satanists, but they were quite definitely Nazis.

The Sarjeant-at-Arms urged his people on, leading from the front, as always. I knew he had to be worrying that the clones were a distraction, there only to slow us down while the Satanists made their escape. They must have teleport capability, to get in and out of the Timeless Moment. We'd have to do something about that. . . . The fighting went on and on, golden fists and swords and axes striking down Nazi clones, while bullets and explosives and vicious energies strove in vain to pierce strange-matter armour. Blood spurted and bones shattered, and the same arrogant, hateful face fell before us again and again. Until finally . . . I ran out of Nazis to kill. I stopped and looked around, blood and gore dripping thickly from my spiked golden fists. I was breathing hard inside my armour, but it had felt good, so good to get my hands on the enemy at last. Or at least *an* enemy.

Molly was right there at my side, harsh magics spitting and sparking round her hands. And not one single bloodstain on her long white dress. The Armourer was nowhere to be seen, swept away from us by the tides of battle. There were Droods everywhere, up and down the hall, surrounded by the piled-up bodies of the dead. They might have been Nazis; they might have been hateful, hate-filled, hate-fuelled Nazi clones, urged on by a hateful philosophy . . . but they never stood a chance against us, not really.

A golden figure in smooth traditional armour worked his way over to join Molly and me. I knew it was William. His feet were still encased in golden bunny slippers.

"You have to help me," he said. "Ammonia's not far from here. I can sense her presence."

"Isabella, too," said Molly. "We must be close to where they keep the prisoners."

I nodded. The Sarjeant was already calling his troops back to order, ready to press on. There were enough of them; they didn't need me. And I was the one who'd come here to free prisoners, not get caught up in the killing. So I gestured for Molly and William to lead the way. I needed to feel that I hadn't come here to kill people.

We found Ammonia Vom Acht first, sitting on her own in the middle of a surprisingly sophisticated laboratory dominated by a single huge machine that filled the whole room, spilling out from its central core to crawl across the floor and halfway up the walls. Growing and spreading like some malignant hothouse plant. Ammonia had been made a part of the machine, strapped firmly to a chair in the very centre of the thing, stripped naked so that tubes could be thrust into her mottled flesh, her head shaved so holes could be drilled into her skull to allow a great many wires access to her brain. The wires curled up into the higher parts of the machine, where softly glowing colours came and went like passing thoughts. Ammonia sat perfectly still, her face blank and empty, her eyes staring straight ahead. I don't think she saw anything.

William armoured down and ran forward, forcing his way through the mess of cables and equipment to kneel before her. He put his face right before hers and said her name several times, but she didn't know he was there. Molly and I looked thoughtfully at the single technician in the room, who'd retreated to the far end of the laboratory the moment we forced our way in. He wore the traditional white lab coat, with white latex gloves, and he was doing his best to hide behind the farthest reaches of the machine. He looked like he wanted to run, but we were between him and the only exit. I beckoned for him to come forward, but he wouldn't. William raised his head and looked at the technician, who actually whimpered at what he saw in William's face.

"Come here," said William, and the technician came out from behind the machine and stumbled forward, almost against his will. He stopped behind Ammonia in her chair, trembling in every limb, his face wet with sweat. William nodded slowly.

"Talk to me. Tell me what's happening here. What is this machine? And what have you done to Ammonia Vom Acht?"

"I'm Stefan Klein. I'm in charge of this—"

"I don't care," said William. "What have you done to her?"

"She's been made a part of the great plan," said Klein, swallowing hard. "There never was an influence machine. I can't believe anyone ever believed that we had such a thing. I mean, a single machine that could influence every single mind in the world simultaneously? Hardly likely, was it? If we had such a thing, we wouldn't have needed the Great Sacrifice; we'd have taken over. No, no . . . this is much better. Take the most powerful telepathic brain in the world, wire it up to the most complex mental amplifier ever and then let her do all the heavy lifting. Ammonia Vom Acht was always far more powerful than she ever allowed herself to be. That's what ethics does for you."

"And I led you people right to her," I said, "when I tracked her down to her hiding place in Cornwall."

"Hardly, old thing," said a familiar voice. "That was all down to me."

We all looked round, and there, slouching elegantly in the doorway, with a really big drink in his hand, was Ammonia's husband, Peter. His smile was as vague as ever, but his eyes were clear and sharp. He smiled benevolently on us all, toasted us with his glass and took a long drink, deliberately making us wait to hear what he had to say. When the glass was empty he tossed it casually to one side, and didn't even look round when it smashed on the floor.

"I'm afraid I got rather tired of the old girl," said Peter. "She really was very needy, very clingy, and she was such hard work: always having to comfort her, and look after her and be a shoulder for her to cry on. I never used to drink, you know, before I met Ammonia Vom Acht. And look at me now. . . . It's the only thing that helps, so I'm able to stand her overbearing presence, her never-ending needs. And never any money for me! Oh, no, no . . . Not a penny for poor old Peter.

"She made millions, but I had to remind her to hand over my allowance! And we had to live like hermits, at the end of the world. I used to have friends; I used to go out; I used to have fun! Finally it all got a bit too much. So I contacted the satanic conspiracy. They weren't difficult to find; the Internet is a wonderful thing. . . . And they were very understanding. So I needed to wait for the right moment to set her up—too soon and people like you might figure out what they wanted with her, and try to stop them. But once you'd come sniffing around, it was clear we couldn't wait any longer. So when she came back from Chez Drood, all tired and worn-out, there I was with a very special nice hot drink waiting for her. And once she was safely snoring in her chair, I shut down the defences and told the nasty old Devil worshippers to come and get her.

"She sort of woke up when they were manhandling her out of the house. She looked at me, wondering why I was doing nothing to stop them, and when she understood, she cried and cried and cried. Ah, you have no idea how good it feels to be free of the old bat at last."

"You utter shit," said William, and his voice was cold and collected and quite deadly. He rose to his feet to glare balefully at Peter, who didn't seem to give even the smallest of damns. William headed straight for him. "She had a magnificent mind!"

"Oh, boo-hoo," said Peter. He took a gunmetal flask from inside his jacket. "Sorry, old sport; do I know you? Do I care? No, I don't think I do, actually."

William armoured up, the golden skin sweeping over him in a moment. "You can be made to care, for what you've done."

"No," said Peter. "I don't think so."

He held up his other hand and showed us a simple metal clicker like the one Roger Morningstar had back at the Cathedral Hotel. And before any of us could even react, Peter clicked the thing, a sharp, metallic sound in the quiet, and William's armour disappeared, driven back into his torc by an irresistible command. My armour disappeared, too, and I was suddenly exposed and shivering in the cold of the laboratory. Molly stepped quickly forward, but when she raised her hands to unleash her magics, nothing happened. She tried a few simple chants, but the words fell awkwardly into the quiet, doing nothing. Peter smiled patronisingly at her.

"Magic won't work here, dearie. All such subtle energies had to be suppressed, so the machine could do its work."

"I don't need my armour to beat the crap out of a treacherous little tit like you," said William.

"Just as well I've got a gun, then," said Peter. He shook his gunmetal flask once, and suddenly it was a

Luger. Peter giggled happily. "Now, that's what I call a transformer. Marvellous little toy, isn't it? My new masters have been very generous." For all his studied vagueness, his hand was very steady as he covered the three of us with the Luger. We all stood very still. None of us doubted he'd use it.

"I've already summoned security," said Peter. "Oh, dear, now that my flask is gone I don't have any booze anymore. I should have told them to bring a bottle. . . ." He smiled at us all easily. "We've all got clickers here, you know. Lots and lots of them. The rest of your people are in for a really nasty shock, once they've got past those Nazi bully-boy clones and encountered the real armed forces. And the best part is, we got the formula for the clicker from inside your own family! Isn't that delightful? It's based on the very device your Armourer created all those years ago. One of your own is a traitor, but then, I think you already knew that, didn't you? He's sold you out again, I'm afraid. Or she! Far be it from me to give anything away! Please don't move, Eddie. I really don't think I can allow any of you to get any closer to me. I'm not a physical person. But don't think I won't shoot if I have to. In fact . . . I think I'd quite like to. Could be fun . . . So, whom should I start with?"

I glanced at William, our eyes met briefly, and we were off and moving. There's a lot more to a Drood than his armour. We're trained to fight, with and without weapons, from early childhood, and one of the first things we're taught is what to do if our armour isn't available. I moved abruptly to the left while William dived to the right, and while Peter hesitated, unable to decide which of us to go after . . . Molly stepped smartly forward and kicked him full in the balls. There was an awful lot of strength and vindictiveness in that kick, and Peter bent sharply forward, tears flying from his bulging eyes. He crashed to his knees, shaking and shuddering, trying to get enough air into his lungs for a decent scream. Molly snatched the gun out of his nerveless hand and pressed the barrel to the side of his head. I didn't think he even knew it was there. I took the clicker away from him, threw it on the floor and stamped on it. It shattered, and immediately William and I were both wrapped in our armour again. William moved over to Molly, took the Luger from her hand and shot Peter in the head, twice. The side of his skull exploded, blood and brains and bone fragments flying in the air, and he fell backwards and lay still. William then turned and shot Stefan Klein, once in the heart and once in the head, and the technician fell sprawling across his machine. William gave the gun back to a somewhat startled Molly.

"Some shit I just don't put up with," he explained, before going back to Ammonia. He leaned in close to study the wires connecting her mind to the machine. "I can deal with this. It's not rocket science. You two go and look for Isabella. I'll free Ammonia from this . . . thing and take her back to the Hall."

"Will you be all right here on your own?" I said cautiously.

"I only came here for Ammonia," said William. "She really is a most remarkable lady. That little shit never was worthy of her." He looked back at me. "I saw her mind when she made contact with mine. You should see what she's really like, Eddie. She glows like a star, burns like a brilliant fire. . . ."

"You really think she can come back, after what's been done to her here?" I said.

"Why not?" said William. "I did."

Molly moved in close beside me. "He doesn't need us, Eddie. And I'm getting really worried about Iz."

"Is she far from here?" I said.

"Not far, no."

"Then let's go. Catch you later, William."

But he was already lost in admiration of his Ammonia, murmuring comforting words to her as he removed the wire connections one by one.

We found the Satanists' prisoners, or what was left of them, holed up in a series of small stone cells that were little more than kennels, with stout locks on the doors.

Molly made a sharp gesture with one hand, and all the doors exploded right out of their frames and into the corridor. The smell hit me first: filth and decay and foulness so bad I had to order my mask to fade it out. Molly and I moved forward to check out the cells. No windows, no furniture, not even straw on the floor or a bucket for waste. The prisoners had been thrown into their cells and left there. Half-blinded, half-starved men and women emerged painfully slowly into the corridor, shielding their eyes from the everyday light they were no longer accustomed to, asking pitifully if they were being rescued at last. Of the thousands of townspeople who'd been kidnapped from Little Stoke, it turned out only over a hundred had survived. The rest had been . . . used up in experiments. Over a hundred people crammed into a dozen windowless cells. And twenty-two weapons makers from the Supernatural Arms Faire who'd refused to cooperate with the Satanists. Because sometimes even merchants of war have a line they won't cross. Molly and I reassured them all as best we could, and sent them to William, so he could lead them back to the Hall.

Sounds of conflict were still continuing on the floors above. Cries of rage and pain and horror, gunshots and explosions. How many Nazi clones did the Satanists have? I had to wonder whether my family had encountered Satanists with clickers yet, and whether I should go back to join them. Or whether I should accompany the prisoners, make sure they got out of the castle safely. But Molly still hadn't found Isabella, and I couldn't leave her here on her own. She was growing increasingly disturbed the closer she got to her sister, convinced something terrible had happened to her. So we moved on, deeper into the cell block.

We found her in the very last cell, set round the corner. A single cell with the door already standing open. No number on the door, no identification, nothing to mark it as any different, but Molly knew. She stormed into the cell with her sister's name on her lips, and then she went suddenly quiet. I hurried in after her, and that was when I saw what the Satanists had done to Isabella Metcalf.

They'd crucified her, hung her upside down on an inverted wooden cross suspended from a single coarse rope, her head a few feet from the floor. Cold iron nails had been hammered through her wrists and ankles, and heavy steel bolts had been thrust through her broken arms and legs. One eye had been gouged out of her head, and the ear next to it had been raggedly cut away. Her face had been beaten to such a pulp I barely recognised her. Blood dripped steadily down from her many wounds, forming a great half-dried pool under the inverted cross. Her clothes were tatters, her skin cut and burned and bruised. Because she defied them.

She was still alive, because she was a witch and kept her heart somewhere else. So she couldn't die, no matter how much they hurt her.

It took me a moment to realise there was a man standing next to her. I turned slowly to look at him, and it was Philip MacAlpine, of MI-13. He had both hands on the tied-off rope supporting the inverted cross. He glared at me.

"Well, don't stand there, Drood! Help me get her down! I didn't come all this way to rescue her just to watch her die!"

I moved quickly over to help him untie the rope, and between us we lowered the inverted cross carefully to the floor. Molly was right there with the cross, taking as much of the weight as she could, murmuring comfortingly to her sister. Isabella never opened her remaining eye, never made a sound. I don't think she knew where she was or what was happening to her. Or at least I hoped not. Between the three of us, we got the cross laid out on the floor, and I armoured down so Isabella would know my face if she did wake up. MacAlpine cried out.

"Eddie Drood! I should have known you'd be here."

"Never mind me, Phil; what are you doing here?"

He sniffed haughtily. "You Droods aren't the only ones who've been investigating the new satanic conspiracy. MI-13 has had its best people all over this case for ages, ever since we discovered how badly they'd infested the current British government. You aren't the only ones with your ears to the ground, you know. All that talk about the Great Sacrifice was the last straw; we knew we had to do something. Luckily, we've had agents in deep cover in London Undertowen for years, so it was easy enough to snatch some low-level Satanists and sweat the information out of them. I wondered why you were suddenly so keen to get into Under Parliament, so I had my people keep an eye on you when you crashed that Satanist tea party. Once we found out what went down there, that they'd run you off and snatched Isabella, we decided it was time to get involved. Isabella had done some work for us in her time, and we always pay our debts. So I came in here first, using the teleport system we found in London Undertowen, to spy out the lay of the land and look for Isabella. And pick up any interesting trinkets that happened to be lying around, of course."

"Of course," I said. "Typical MI-13: always an ulterior motive. Still, I'm glad you're here, Phil. Where's your backup?"

"A whole brigade of SAS combat sorcerers, just waiting for my word," Phil said smugly.

"Let's see what my people can do first," I said. I had a strong feeling a whole bunch of SAS roughnecks would come in very handy if the Satanists did use their clickers against my family, but I didn't want to call them in yet. Couldn't have word getting out that the Droods had to yell for help ... I clapped MacAlpine on the shoulder. "Good to see you, Phil. We'll take all the help we can get. We're not proud."

"Not what I've heard," said MacAlpine, and we both laughed briefly. Molly looked round, her pale face empty of all expression.

"Help me. I need help for Isabella."

I crouched down beside her, and MacAlpine moved in closer, frowning at Isabella's wounds.

"How are we going to get all those nails out?" he

said. "And the steel bolts? I haven't got a crowbar, and even if I did, the shock of digging them out would probably finish her off. . . ."

While he was still talking, Molly gestured sharply with one hand, and every single nail and bolt shot up out of Isabella's flesh with such force and velocity they buried themselves in the stone ceiling overhead. Isabella's body jerked once, but she still didn't make a sound. Molly crouched down beside her, stroking her sister's pulped and bloody face with one hand, crooning ancient healing chants. The gaping wounds left by the dislodged nails were already beginning to close. I didn't know how long it would take Molly to repair the major damage, or even if Isabella would be able to move afterwards; I just knew I couldn't wait around while she did it. There was still a lot of work to be done here at Schloss Shreck. Castle Horror.

"I thought witches couldn't handle cold iron?" MacAlpine murmured in my ear.

"Depends how mad they get," I said quietly.

"I'm amazed Isabella's still alive," said MacAlpine. "After everything that's been done to her. Must have the constitution of an ox. No offence."

"Metcalf sisters are very hard to kill," I said. I could have told him about the hidden heart, but he was MI-13, after all, and he had tried to kill me and Molly more than once. Some secrets should stay in the family.

Molly looked up at me. "I can't leave her, Eddie. She needs me. Look what they've done to her. . . ."

"Do what you can," I said. "Get her stable. Then get her out of here and back to the Hall. They've got specialists; they'll know what to do."

"I don't want to leave you here on your own," said Molly.

"You won't be," I said. "I've got Philip MacAlpine with me to watch my back."

"Indeed," MacAlpine said quickly. "I know a common enemy when I see one."

Molly studied MacAlpine. "Thank you. For trying to help my sister. Look after my Eddie."

"Trust me," said MacAlpine. "I wouldn't dare let anything happen to him."

Outside in the corridor, I reached out to the Sarjeant-at-Arms through my torc. And much to my surprise and relief, I managed a brief if variable contact. He sounded very far away, and his voice kept fading in and out, but we could hear each other. I made MacAlpine stand and wait while I brought the Sarjeant up to speed.

"Where are you, Sarjeant?"

"Damned if I know! We've fought our way in from the outside, down through the roof and in through the walls, heading for the centre of the castle, and waded through a whole army of Nazi clones in the process. We've been destroying anything that even looked dangerous along the way, including the conspiracy's teleport gates! The Satanists aren't going anywhere, Eddie. They're trapped in here with us. Where are you?"

"Just leaving the cells, along with an agent of MI-13 I picked up along the way. He says he can call in a whole brigade of SAS combat sorcerers, if you feel the need. . . ."

"Good to hear," said the Sarjeant unexpectedly. "We've taken casualties, Eddie. I'll take all the help we can get."

"I take it you've encountered the clickers, Sarjeant. How are you coping?"

"After a few fairly disastrous close encounters, when it all came down to hand-to-hand fighting and every nasty trick we could spring on them, we learned to scoop up every weapon we came across and shoot the nasty bastards at a distance, before they could even use their clickers. But it's slowing our advance right down, Eddie. I think the leader and his inner circle have run out of clones to throw at us, but we're no nearer to getting our hands on them."

MacAlpine kept crowding me and demanding to know what was going on, so I broke contact with the Sarjeant and filled MacAlpine in on the high spots.

"I think I know where we can find the conspiracy

leader," he said immediately. "We've had one of our people close to him for some time, in really deep cover. He told us a lot about the layout of this place. Follow me."

I let him lead me through the brightly lit stone corridors and passageways, most of them still lined with burning Nazi flags and banners from where Molly had expressed her displeasure earlier. No sprinkler systems in medieval castles. I could still hear signs of fighting, but way off in the distance. The main party of Droods hadn't caught up with me. MacAlpine warned me not to armour up just yet; golden feet make a hell of a racket on marble floors, and he didn't think we should advertise our approach. If the leader thought the Droods were almost upon him, he'd probably run. As we drew closer, small groups of Satanists would run past, heading for the battle, and MacAlpine would give them the proper password and they'd keep going.

"You're a useful person to have around after all, Phil," I said.

"You have no idea," he said. "Really."

I was starting to be seriously impressed with him. It was too easy to forget that this middle-aged, passed-over man had been a pretty decent spy in his day, and had worked with both my uncle Jack and uncle James. The fact that he'd tried to kill me and failed shouldn't be held against him. A lot of people came into that category.

"Droods may be flashy," said MacAlpine, "but MI-13 is thorough. You never even knew we were investigating the conspiracy, did you? I always was a better field agent than you ever gave me credit for."

"Stop fishing for compliments," I said. "I'm impressed, all right?"

"Not yet," he said. "But you will be."

Finally we came to a great oaken door with a huge Nazi swastika carved into it in brutal bas-relief. MacAlpine eased up to the door, listened for a moment and then carefully turned the handle and opened it a crack. He slipped me a quick wink and then pushed the door all the way open. He strode in, and I moved quickly in after him. Beyond the door was a great auditorium packed with people sitting in row upon row of raked seating, facing an open stage. The door closed quietly behind me.

"All the upper echelons of the new satanic conspiracy," MacAlpine murmured. "Safe and protected here behind layer upon layer of defences too strong for even Droods to break through."

I stayed by the door, studying the people in the raked seating, surprised at how many I recognised. Familiar faces from politics, big business, the media, and all kinds of celebrities. And there on the stage was Alexandre Dusk himself, smiling broadly and looking right at me. He made a welcoming gesture in my direction, and everyone in the auditorium turned to look at me and smile. Except they weren't looking at me. They were looking and smiling at Philip MacAlpine. And when I turned to look at him, he smiled at me and held up one hand. With a clicker in it. He snapped it sharply. I tried to call my armour and couldn't. MacAlpine gestured to two waiting guards, big muscular types in SS uniforms, and they moved quickly forward to take me by the arms. I didn't struggle. I had my pride.

"Typical Drood," said MacAlpine. "Always ready to believe the best of people. I thought I'd had it when you burst in and found me with Isabella, but I always could think on my feet. And you couldn't believe a small man like me could put one over on a big man like you."

"I couldn't believe you'd sink this low," I said.

"How does it feel?" he said. "To be alone and helpless, naked without your armour, among your worst enemies? How does it feel to know that all the things we did to Isabella Metcalf are nothing compared to what we're going to do to you?"

I said nothing. Why give him the satisfaction? MacAlpine laughed in my face and walked down the main aisle to take his place on the stage, the guards hustling me along behind him. MacAlpine nodded to Alexandre Dusk, who moved aside to let MacAlpine take centre stage. The guards held me securely to one side, where everyone could get a good look at me. There was no booing or taunts; they looked at me with hot, greedy eyes. MacAlpine smiled out over the assembled Satanists, and then grinned happily at me.

"Yes," he said. "I am the leader of the new satanist conspiracy. I put it all together, arranged the Great Sacrifice and led you poor old Droods around by the nose. You never saw this one coming, did you? Even when you found me tormenting poor Isabella, you couldn't believe what you were seeing. You believed everything I told you, even though it must have been clear I was making it all up as I went along."

He looked out over the auditorium, at his people hanging on his every word. "Let the Droods have Schloss Shreck! Let them waste their time wading through all the defences and booby traps we set in place! We don't need this castle anymore. I've already given the orders to activate the influence machine, powered by dear Ammonia's amazing brain. What was that, Eddie? Did you want to say something? No? Then shut up and listen. You'll find this both interesting and informative." He turned back to the audience. "We'll leave here through the teleport gates, taking the machine and its room with us, and then we'll seal all the entrances to the Timeless Moment. Leave the Droods locked in here. What could be a better revenge? While out in the world we shall set the Great Sacrifice in motion and watch and laugh as the adult populations of the Earth slaughter their own children and damn themselves forever. And then we shall break down the doors of Hell, and our lord Satan shall rise up with all his fallen, and we shall be made kings of the Earth!

"We can always come back here when we feel the need for fresh meat to torment. Why should the Droods miss out on Hell on Earth?"

He broke off then, because I couldn't keep the grin off my face any longer. The guards forced my arms up painfully behind my back, but I laughed at them, and at

Philip MacAlpine, and all the sheeplike faces in the auditorium.

"Typical MacAlpine," I said loudly. "Too busy boasting about the things you're planning to do to concentrate on the job at hand. We've already found Ammonia Vom Acht and freed her from the machine, and smashed all the teleport gates. My family is coming here, and you're not going anywhere. You're trapped in here with us."

There was commotion then amongst the assembled Satanists; famous men and women jumped to their feet, shouting and arguing, yelling to MacAlpine to do something. He turned away to talk quietly with Alexandre Dusk, and then turned back to stare and shout his people down.

"It doesn't matter!" he said. "The influence machine was never necessary; it was something to give us an edge! We don't need it. What we've set in motion in the world can't be stopped now. The Great Sacrifice will go ahead anyway, as planned. And I doubt very much that the Droods have found all our teleport gates. However, I do think that before we take our leave, we should take time out for a little entertainment, and express our displeasure at this poor, helpless Drood in our midst. Because I think we've all had quite enough of his meddling and interference in our affairs!"

The audience cheered. They liked the sound of that.

"Oh, come on," I said. "You know you're dying to tell me. How did a little nobody like you end up leader of the satanic conspiracy?"

"Because of you, Eddie," said MacAlpine. "This is all your fault. None of it would have happened if it hadn't been for you. I was happy in my job, away from the field, coasting along. I'd had a good career, if somewhat unappreciated, and was actually looking forward to an early retirement. Go down to the coast, somewhere quiet, grow roses . . . And then you ruined all that by screwing up what was left of my career and humiliating me in front of my bosses! You made me look old and useless, and that . . . kicked me awake. Made me realise that my life wasn't over until I said it was over, and that if I wanted to be great I'd have to make myself great.

"So I used my old contacts to make a new life for myself, and let my ambitions run wild. I had access to all kinds of information at MI-13, and I used it to hunt down the last vestiges of the old satanic conspiracy. There were still quite a few of them around, deep underground, waiting for someone to provide them with a new vision. Britain's ruling classes have always had a dark side. . . . And so over the past few years, while you and your precious family were busy with the Hungry Gods and the Immortals, I quietly used the contacts I'd made through a long and mostly successful career to put like-minded people together. It was actually remarkably easy to assemble a new satanic conspiracy; I've always known people on every side of the fence. All part of doing business in the spy trade. Of course, I had help. Alexandre Dusk was the last of the old-school Satanists, and a bit wary until I explained my remarkable new scheme to him. And then he couldn't get on board fast enough. He was happy to be the public face of the new conspiracy, while I put everything together beside the scenes. Until I was ready to launch my revenge on a world that never properly appreciated or rewarded me, despite everything I'd done to protect it."

"Molly was right," I said, when he finally paused for breath. "It's always the sad, embittered little men you have to watch out for. . . . I think counselling would probably have helped."

He glared down from the stage at me. "You don't get it, do you? Everything you and your fellow Droods have been put through was done at my command. Planned, designed to push you to the edge, provoke you into more and more extreme reactions, to drive you step by step out of the Light and into the Dark. Everything we did was intended to provoke increasingly extreme reactions from you, until you . . . were as bad as us. Look back at everything you've done since you started fighting us, Eddie; were you ever so vicious, so violent before? I think that's what's pleased me so much about all this: watching the prim and proper Droods become another bunch of thugs."

I remembered Molly saying, *You can't fight evil with evil methods. Fighting evil is supposed to bring out the best in us, not the worst.* And I remembered all the things I'd done to the Indigo Spirit and to Charlatan Joe, two of my oldest friends . . . all in the name of revenge.

"You see?" said MacAlpine. "You've all done questionable things in your quest to stop us. You've used torture and intimidation; you've killed people to make yourselves feel better. You've demeaned yourselves, Drood. Oh, we went to a lot of trouble to work out schemes best suited to bring out your dark side. . . . And do you know why, Eddie? Because only those who stand in Heaven's gaze have Heaven's strength, and can hope to stand against the forces of Darkness. And you and your family aren't qualified anymore."

"You came close," I said steadily. "But not close enough. We didn't come here to fight evil men; we came here to rescue your prisoners. We didn't come here to punish you for what you've done, but to prevent the Great Sacrifice and save a generation of children. It isn't what you do, Phil; it's why you do it."

"You keep telling yourself that, Eddie," said MacAlpine, smiling easily. "And try to remember which particular road is paved with good intentions."

"That really was you in Limbo, wasn't it?" I said. "That's why I was able to hit you, when I couldn't touch anyone else there."

"Oh, yes," said MacAlpine. "That was me. Once we discovered how vulnerable you were, I couldn't resist taking a shot at you. A chance to know all your secrets . . . It would have made this all so much easier."

"How did you get Walker to represent scum like you?" I said. "He spent most of his life shutting down operations like yours."

"Walker?" said MacAlpine. "You saw Walker in there? I did hear he was dead. . . ."

And while he was thinking about that, I broke free from my guards with a few old and very unpleasant tricks every Drood learns from an early age. Both of them went crying and moaning to the floor, and I sprinted for the doorway. A great cry went up from the assembled Satanists as they rose up from their seats and scrambled after me. I could hear MacAlpine yelling at them, driving them on. I got to the door, hauled it open, stepped out into the corridor and then turned and stopped there, inside the doorway, and smiled nastily at the approaching Satanists. They all quickly stumbled to a halt, holding back. I was a Drood, after all. Even with so many of them and only the one of me, none of them wanted to go first. In fact, they all seemed very keen for someone else to have the honour of going first.

"What do you think you can achieve, Eddie?" said MacAlpine from the stage. "One unarmed Drood against an army of us?"

"This is the only way out of here," I said loudly, so they could all hear me and understand. "This is the only exit, and I'm guarding it. Because there might still be some teleport gates my family missed, and I can't risk your getting to them before my family gets here. So you're going to have to get through me to get away, and as long as I'm standing in the doorway, you can come at me only a few at a time. So all I have to do is hold you here until the rest of my family turns up. They can't be that far away; I heard fighting. And once they arrive and see what you've done to me ... Oh, the things they'll do to you ..."

"Will somebody please shoot this arrogant little turd?" said Mac-Alpine.

"Guns won't work in here," said Alexandre Dusk.

MacAlpine looked at him. "What?"

"No guns, no weapons, no magics! It's all part of the defences you had me put in place to keep out the Droods! You said you wanted every possibility covered!"

"Well . . . lower the protections!"

"I can't! Not like that! It'll take two, maybe three hours. . . ."

"You're an idiot, Dusk." MacAlpine looked back at me. "You can't stand against us all, Eddie! Without your armour, you're only one man."

"One very specially trained man," I said. "One Drood is a match for any number of amateur-night bottom-feeding scum like you."

"We'll drag you down and tear you apart!"

"What we do in Heaven's name has Heaven's strength," I said carefully. "I might have strayed from the path, but I think I've found a way back. I choose to stand in Heaven's gaze again, and pay in blood for what I did in blood. I think . . . when you know you're going to die anyway, it's all about being able to look God in the eye. I know you'll drag me down eventually; enough jackals can always pull down a lion. . . . But all I have to do is hold you here long enough and then my family will avenge me. By slaughtering every one of you. Not for revenge or even for justice. But to make sure none of you can ever harm Humanity again. So here I stand. One last chance for atonement. And you're right, Phil; I do have so much to atone for."

Alexandre Dusk had come down from the stage. He pushed his way through the crowd to address me, though he was careful to maintain a safe and respectful distance.

"Don't talk about God and Heaven here, Drood. They have no place in Schloss Shreck, not after all the awful things we've done. This is our place, our game, our rules. Were you perhaps expecting some great beam of light to shine down from above, and empower you, because you stand against us? 'My strength is as the strength of ten because my heart is pure'? It doesn't work that way, Drood."

"Never thought it did," I said. "I don't expect anything. Except to stand and fight, and hold you here, for as long as I can."

"If you stay we'll kill you," said Alexandre Dusk.

"Wouldn't have it any other way," I said.

And I drew the Colt repeater from my back holster and shot Dusk in the head. He fell backwards, blood flying in the air as he crashed into the Satanists behind him. They fell back, making loud shocked noises, and Dusk was dead before he hit the floor. The crowd fell quiet, looking on with startled, disturbed eyes. They looked at the body and then back at me. I smiled easily at them.

"I got caught without my gun earlier on this case," I said. "So I made a point of bringing it with me this time. Had a hunch it might come in handy. And as long as I'm standing here, on the other side of the door, it works fine. You didn't think I was just going to stand here, did you?"

"Take him down!" yelled MacAlpine from the stage, his voice almost hysterical with rage and frustration.

"This is a Colt repeater," I said. "Never misses, never needs reloading. Usually. But with all the protections on this place, it's probably only a gun. With a handful of bullets. Which means I can kill only a limited number of people. So come on! Who's willing to die so others can have the honour of dragging me down?"

I kept trying to reach out to the Sarjeant-at-Arms through my torc, to tell him where I was, and to get a bit of a move on. But if he could hear me, I couldn't hear him. So it was down to me: one man against a horde of Satanists. I looked about me, and they all stared silently back with sullen, snarling faces and hot, hateful eyes. As long as I was careful to stay in the doorway and not let them draw me forward, they could come at me only a few at a time, and none of them wanted to be the first to die. Even though MacAlpine was yelling himself hoarse up on the stage, screaming at them to do something, no one did. A few actually yelled back at him, saying that if he was so damned keen, he should come down there and try something himself.

And then even these few voices fell silent as Alexandre Dusk sat up. A few drops of blood rolled down his face from the great wound in his forehead, and then stopped. He rose slowly to his feet, brushed himself down and then turned to smile at me. A very cold, very knowing smile.

"Witches aren't the only ones with the good sense to hide their hearts somewhere safe," he said. "Like Phil told you: I'm old-school, and I know all the old tricks."

He came straight at me, and I shot him in the chest. He staggered but kept on coming, and I had no choice but to keep on shooting. I used up every bullet in the gun, and he wouldn't go down again. He stopped and smiled at me.

"So," said MacAlpine from the stage. "One man, without a gun."

"One Drood," I said, tossing the empty gun behind me. "And you bottom-feeding scumbags shall not pass."

They came at me then, rushing past the smiling Alexandre Dusk, hands outstretched like claws in their eagerness to get at me. There were a hell of a lot of them, and some of them looked to be really big bastards, but I'd been right: As long as I held my position, they could come at me only two or three at a time. I struck them down with hard, pitiless, practiced moves before they could even lay a hand on me. They crashed to the floor, and those behind trampled right over them to get to me. Their faces were flushed and distorted with rage; they were desperate to drag me down and get away before the rest of my family arrived. But in the end they were amateurs, facing one very well-trained Drood.

I hit them hard and I hit them often, and I hit them with practised skill, not wasting a single movement or using the least bit more energy than I had to. I was in this for the long run. It felt good; it felt really good to punch a Satanist in the face or the throat, to break their ribs and smash their kneecaps, to feel my fists jar on bone and send blood flying. All I had to do was think of the cells, and the prisoners I'd found there. But I was still careful to pace myself. I held my ground, let them get in one another's way and enjoyed the opportunity to dispense some very basic justice to some very bad people.

Of course, that didn't last long. First my hands hurt, and then they began to bleed. I'd got too used to fighting inside my armour. My fists jarred every time I hit bone, and my hands and arms began to ache. I was getting short of breath, and despite myself I was starting to slow down. Then my legs and back began to hurt, because I was constantly moving and couldn't stop even for a moment. Sweat ran down my face, stinging my eyes and leaving salt on my lips. And my lungs began to labour, because I couldn't stop to get my breath.

I fought on, and still they came at me, an endless tide of cruel, vicious faces, flying fists, clawed hands and improvised weapons. Blunt instruments, stiletto heels, even keys jammed between the fingers of a fist. They kept coming at me, scrambling over the bodies of their own fallen to get at me, and I stood my ground and would not back away. Inevitably, the attacks started getting through. Because in the end I was only one man, against so many. They hit me and cut me, desperate to hurt me and drag me down. And all I could do was stand my ground and take it.

Because of Harry and Roger, left to face their enemies and their deaths alone, because I couldn't get reinforcements to them in time. Because of the Indigo Spirit and Charlatan Joe, my old friends, and what I'd done to them in the name of a good cause. And all I could think was, *Payback's a bitch.*

I was deadly tired now, every movement a struggle, every blow an effort. Blood ran down my face and dripped from my nose. I'd never taken a beating like it. Didn't know you could take a beating like it and still stay on your feet. The things we do for guilt's sake . . . And while I might finally be standing in Heaven's gaze, I certainly didn't feel any stronger. My muscles ached; my hands blazed with agony every time I hit someone; my lungs strained with the effort of sucking in air. I felt like shit. More and more of the blows were getting through, and fewer and fewer of mine were doing real damage. Fists jarred against the bones of my face, slammed into my ribs, hammered against a defending arm. Sharp edges cut at me, darting in and out. And still, somehow, I held my ground. Though the floor at my feet was getting slippery with my blood.

Heaven always did have a thing for martyrs. . . .

I didn't have to do this. I could turn and run, let the Satanists follow me. I could lead them to the Sarjeant's forces. No. I couldn't do that. I had no idea where the rest of my family was. And if the Satanists got out of this room . . . I couldn't take the risk that they did have some last hidden teleport gate to let them escape the castle and the Timeless Moment. Let them escape back to Earth, and the Great Sacrifice . . . And all the children in the world. No. I had to hold them here for as long as I could. And hope my family got here in time.

I was reeling on my feet now. I hurt everywhere. One eye was puffed shut, and there was so much blood in my mouth I had to keep spitting it out. The agony in my sides was cracked ribs, maybe broken. It was an effort to raise my arms now. I was a ragged, bloody thing, all out of strength, held up by only a simple determination not to fall to scum like this. I wasn't fighting anymore, just trying to protect myself as best I could, spraying blood into the faces of my enemies with every breath, because my nose was broken. The only reason they weren't landing more punches was because I was swaying so much. I kept my head down and my hands up, and laughed at them with crushed and bloody lips.

They finally got close enough to grab me, fastening onto my arms and shoulders with clawed hands, trying to drag me forcibly from the doorway, and I fought them with all the strength I had left. Making them fight for every inch. Not for pride's sake. Not even for my family's sake, but because I couldn't let them do what they planned. I had to save the children.

Because there was no one there to fight for me when I was a child, and my parents left me in the cold arms of the family.

And then suddenly they all let go of me and backed away. I almost fell without their fierce hands to hold me up. I stood swaying in the doorway, peering at my enemy with my one good eye, and then, dazed as I was, I heard the pounding of golden feet on the marble floor behind me. The Satanists were backing away into the auditorium now, yelling at one another. I watched them numbly, half-blind and half-dead, while Philip MacAlpine screamed instructions from the stage, trying to rally his people. I managed a small smile then. I was having a little trouble accepting the fact that I was still alive, but you couldn't be dead and still hurt this much. I slowly realised that MacAlpine had descended from the stage and was ploughing through his own people to get to me.

"You've spoiled it all!" he screamed at me. "You always have to spoil everything! You've destroyed my career and my life and my wonderful plan, but I'll still see you dead!"

He lunged forward, a small ceremonial dagger in his hand, reaching for my heart. I vaguely remembered something like that happening before, back in the Hall, so I waited till the last moment, till he was almost upon me, and then I spit a mouthful of my blood into his eyes. He cried out, staggering to a halt, suddenly blinded and confused. And it was the easiest thing in the world for me to step forward and take the knife away from him. I could barely feel the smooth bone handle in my swollen hand. MacAlpine fell back into the crowd, fighting his own people as he tried to get away from me. I slowly opened my hand and let the knife fall to the floor. It wasn't like I had enough strength left to use it. I was amazed I was still on my feet. So I stood there and watched the upper echelons of the new satanic conspiracy panic and scream at one another, while from behind me came the sound of my family racing to my rescue.

Golden figures were suddenly all around me, and golden hands held me up, supporting my weight. The relief was so great I almost cried. More golden figures streamed past me into the auditorium, and the Satanists scrambled back through the raked seating, fighting one another in their desperate need to get away. Blank golden faces loomed up before me. I really didn't like the way my reflection looked in those golden masks. I heard the Armourer's voice.

"Dear God . . . Eddie, my boy, what have they done to you?"

One figure armoured down, and there was the familiar face of my uncle Jack, filled with shock and horror and rage at what he saw. His strong engineer's hands took hold of me and supported me. I tried to smile at him, and blood ran down my chin from my ruined mouth.

"They have a clicker," I said, speaking as clearly as I could. "Like yours. Took my armour away. But I still fought them."

"Of course you did," said Uncle Jack. "You're a Drood."

He produced his own clicker and snapped it before me. My armour flowed out of my torc and encased me from head to toe in a moment. I sighed blessedly as all the pain washed away, soothed by the armour. I felt strong and sharp again. My armour couldn't heal me, but it could hold me up. I took a deep breath and straightened up. My head was clear again. I looked quickly round the auditorium.

"Close the door," I said. "And set a guard outside. No one leaves this room."

The Armourer gestured urgently, and half a dozen Droods went back out into the corridor and shut the door firmly. The Sarjeant-at-Arms came over to stand before me.

"We've evacuated all the surviving prisoners back to the Hall. William's there with Ammonia, and Molly's there with her sister. Everyone else in the castle is dead. All the Nazi clones, all the Satanists—though we lost some good people doing it. Their names will be remembered."

"I see you got your armour back," I said.

"You didn't think I'd invent something as important as the clicker and not have something to overrule it if necessary, did you?" said the Armourer.

"Did you get all of the teleport gateways?" I said. "Are you sure you didn't miss any hidden ones?"

"We've got people checking," said the Armourer. "But, Eddie, listen, I have to tell you—"

"No," I said. "This is more important. This room contains the upper echelons of the conspiracy, and their leader. Philip MacAlpine."

"Never liked him," said the Sarjeant, after a pause. "Good at his job, but never for the right reasons."

The Armourer shook his head slowly. "He did good work with James and me. But his heart was never in it."

The Sarjeant-at-Arms looked out over the quiet crowd of Satanists, who were cowed by the presence of so many Droods in their armour. There were still a lot of defiant faces, but none of them was stupid enough to try anything. The Sarjeant nodded once.

"This is the last of them. We have to deal with them, here and now."

"Deal with them?" I said.

The Sarjeant turned his featureless mask back to me. "Kill them, Eddie. Kill every single one of them. Do you have a problem with that?"

"No," I said. "They have to die. Not for justice, or revenge, or even for the awful thing they planned to do. But because if we let them live, they'd try to do it again. That or something worse. They have to die here, and their dreams and plans and bad intentions with them. No mercy. Not for them."

"Couldn't agree more," said the Sarjeant-at-Arms.

He used his gift to call two heavy machine guns into his hands, and then he walked towards the waiting Satanists and opened fire on them. He moved the guns smoothly back and forth, cutting the Satanists down in rows, and stepped calmly over the dead bodies of the fallen to get at the next. Most tried to run, but the golden figures were there to stop them, striking them down with cold armoured fists. There was screaming, pushing and shoving, people trying to use one another as human shields. Cries for mercy, promising to do anything we wanted, make any reparations we wanted, inform on all their contacts, do anything for their lives . . . but mostly they screamed. None of us had anything to say to them. How could they hope to be forgiven, to be shown mercy, after what they'd done and planned to do? Let them go to God, and see if he had any mercy for them.

They had to die, because it was our duty to make sure they could never harm anyone again.

It didn't take all that long. The Sarjeant-at-Arms' guns finally fell silent, and only Droods were left standing. A few armoured figures moved carefully among the fallen bodies, but there were no merely wounded. The Sarjeant was very efficient. He looked round him at all the bodies lying slumped and piled across one another and nodded once, contemplating a job well-done. The guns disappeared from his hands. And then we all turned to look at the only two people left standing in the room who weren't us. Philip MacAlpine and Alexandre Dusk stood together on the stage, looking defiantly back at us. I started toward them, and the Sarjeant and the Armourer came with me. MacAlpine looked quickly around, but there was nowhere for him to go. Alexandre Dusk smiled smugly at me. The bullet wound in his forehead was almost completely healed. He lifted his hands, and dark energies spit and swirled around them.

"I have my power, and I have my shields," he said. "You can't kill me, and you can't stop me."

"Wrong," said the Armourer. He raised his clicker, snapped it once, and the magics surrounding Dusk's hands disappeared. He looked at his hands dumbly for a moment, and then looked back at us. The Armourer smiled. "There are all kinds of clickers. Eddie, would you care to . . . ?"

I stepped forward and jumped up onto the stage. MacAlpine backed quickly away, but Dusk was still too stunned to move. He opened his mouth to say something, and I grew a long golden sword from my right hand and cut off his head. The body slumped to the stage, gouting blood. The head fell to the stage, rolled over the edge and ended up at the Sarjeant's feet. The mouth was still moving, until the Sarjeant stamped on it. And that was the end of Alexandre Dusk.

I looked at Philip MacAlpine and he snarled back at me. "You can't have me!" he said, his voice high and ragged. "I don't care what you've got. I made a deal! It was promised to me that nothing in the world can harm me."

"Hell always lies," I said. "Except when a truth can hurt you more. You should know how deals with the Devil always work out."

"I can't be harmed! My own people tried to kill me in a hundred different ways, hoping to replace me as leader. I have drunk poison, soaked up bullets, laughed at curses! Nothing can touch me anymore. Your armour is worthless against me."

"Yeah, right," said the Sarjeant, behind me. He strode forward across the stage and launched a golden fist at MacAlpine's head with enough force to tear it clean off the man's shoulders. Except suddenly, impossibly, MacAlpine's hand came up to intercept it. The golden fist slammed harmlessly into MacAlpine's palm, stopped dead. And while everyone watched, MacAlpine closed his hand hard and crushed the serjeant's hand inside his armour. He couldn't break the golden strange matter, but he could destroy the hand inside it. We all heard the bones break and shatter. The Sarjeant grunted once. MacAlpine let go, and the Sarjeant fell back a step, nursing his injured hand to his chest. He didn't cry out.

The Armourer looked at MacAlpine thoughtfully. "I wonder what a golden ax would do to his neck?"

"Don't," I said. "He really is protected. Sarjeant, have all the wounded been evacuated? Is there anyone else left in the castle?"

"All gone," said the Sarjeant.

"Then let's get the hell out of Schloss Shreck, and leave MacAlpine here. Sealed inside the Timeless Moment forever."

"Ah," said the Armourer. "We have a slight problem there. As I tried to tell you . . ."

I looked at him. "What?"

"When we smashed the teleport systems, we accidentally set off a self-destruct mechanism," said the Armourer. "Designed to seal off the Timeless Moment so nothing could get in or out. One last dog-in-the-manger stratagem . . . We found the destruct mechanism, but its workings are protected by powerful shields. We can't get at it. The best we can do is keep resetting the timer every sixty seconds. There's a Drood doing that right now. The trouble is . . . the self-destruct mechanism is so powerful it's affecting Alpha Red Alpha. Basically, if the destruct mechanism goes off, our machine will be destroyed, too. And Alpha Red Alpha takes a lot more than sixty seconds to fire up. We'd be stuck in here forever. Which means . . ."

"One of us has to stay here," said the Sarjeant. "To keep resetting the timer until after the Hall has safely gone."

Some days, the hits just keep on coming.

"I'll stay," the Sarjeant said. "I know my duty. My job is to protect the family."

"No," I said. "It has to be me."

"Why?" said the Armourer. "Why does it always have to be you, Eddie?"

"Because I led us in here," I said. "I know my duty. Anything for the family. Take me to the self-destruct mechanism, Uncle Jack. Sarjeant, get everyone else out of here."

"Fair enough," said the Sarjeant.

"No!" said MacAlpine. "You're not going anywhere!"

He surged forward, his hands reaching for my throat. I whipped out the Merlin Glass, activated it and slapped it over MacAlpine. And the Glass sent him away.

"Where did you send him?" said the Sarjeant.

"Back to the cryogenic chambers," I said. "To play with the other monsters."

"The Glass!" said the Sarjeant. "You could wait till the last minute, then use it to transport you to the Hall just as we're leaving!"

"No," said the Armourer. "I've shut down the shields here, but the castle's main protections still hold. They won't let the Glass transfer anything out of the castle.

I'm sorry, Eddie, if that's what you were counting on. . . ."

"I wasn't," I said. "But we can use it to jump to the mechanism, can't we?"

"Of course," he said. "Take the family home, Sarjeant. Prepare Alpha Red Alpha. As soon as I return, we're leaving."

The Merlin Glass followed the Armourer's instructions and delivered the two of us to a small back room full of strange old-fashioned equipment: great bulky stuff, with lots of vacuum tubes and heavy wiring. One large grey box was ticking down the seconds. The armoured Drood standing next to it hit the reset button, and the timer returned to counting down the minute. The Armourer gave the Drood his marching orders, and sent him back to the Sarjeant through the Glass. Which left him and me and the box.

"Don't ask me what it is, or how it interferes with Alpha Red Alpha," said the Armourer. "The people who worked here originally let their minds run in some pretty strange directions. I could spend months here taking things apart. . . . But we haven't got months."

"It doesn't matter," I said. "I know what to do. Time for you to go, Uncle Jack."

He armoured down to show me his face. He looked like someone grieving at a funeral. "It isn't fair, Eddie. You've done so much for the family. . . . I'm an old man. I should stay."

"No," I said immediately. "They need you to work Alpha Red Alpha. And besides, you're far too valuable to the family. What would the Droods do without their Armourer? Someone has to do this. And I need to do it."

"Why?"

"Penance," I said. "And no, you don't get to ask what for."

"You were always my favourite nephew," said the Armourer. "I don't . . . I don't know what to say to you, Eddie."

"Say good-bye to Molly for me," I said. "Make sure she knows how much I always loved her."

"She knows," said Uncle Jack. "Eddie . . ."

"Yes?" I hit the reset button.

"I have to take the Merlin Glass with me. It's no use to you here, and it's far too valuable to the family to leave behind."

"Of course," I said. "Molly will be able to use it to help Alpha Red Alpha get you home safely."

I handed the Glass over. The Armourer took it reluctantly.

"It was the best toy you ever gave me, Uncle Jack," I said.

He looked like he desperately wanted to say something, but couldn't. So we shook hands, very formally.

"You did good, Eddie," he said. "You're a credit to the family. You will be remembered."

"Then make sure they remember the real me," I said.

The Armourer nodded quickly, activated the Merlin Glass, stepped through it and was gone. I finally got to see what that looked like, as an observer, and it was every bit as freaky and disturbing as people said it was. And I was left alone in Schloss Shreck. Castle Horror.

I pulled up a chair and sat down beside the stubbornly counting self-destruct mechanism. I wondered how I'd know when the Hall was gone. . . . Best give it an hour, and then . . . What we do in Heaven's gaze matters most. And one time pays for all.

I sat in my chair, looking round the room. I didn't armour down; its strength was all that was holding me together. I kept an eye on the descending countdown, making a little game out of how late I could leave it, and looked back over my life. Enjoying my triumphs, cataloguing my sins, regretting all the things I'd meant to do but never got round to doing. I wished I'd made a better fist of running the family, while I had the chance. Wished so many good Droods hadn't died in action, following my plans. And then there were all the many things I'd meant to say to so many people, because you always think you'll have more time. Molly and I never talked enough. Not about the things that really mattered. I'd always meant to marry her, eventually, but it never seemed to be quite the right moment. I hoped she'd understand why I had to do this. Probably not. She never did have much time for guilt or penance.

I wished I'd taken more time to talk with Uncle Jack about all the marvellous things he and Uncle James did. I could have talked with him about my parents . . . but I never did.

I thought about Philip MacAlpine. No doubt running screaming through the stone galleries, trying to find me and stop me before the Hall could leave the Timeless Moment. Fat chance. Would he die when the castle finally blew up, or would Satan's little gift let him survive to drift endlessly in the silver void forever? I smiled, and I'm pretty sure it wasn't a pleasant smile.

I kept hitting the reset, and the seconds kept on counting down.

The door slammed open, and Philip MacAlpine burst into the room. I stood up, keeping my place by the mechanism. He stood swaying before me, grinning broadly, his eyes blazing. He had something very like my Colt repeater in his hand, aimed right at my head.

"Get away from the machine, Eddie. If I'm going down, I'm taking all of you with me."

"Sorry, Phil," I said. "I'm not going anywhere."

"Took me a while to find this," he said, brandishing the gun. "One of the first things I had my people put together for me. A Colt repeater that fires strange-matter bullets. Punch right through that flashy armour of yours. The traitor inside your family really was very helpful. He could provide only a few strange-matter bullets, but I've got enough here to do the job."

"Better not miss," I said.

"I won't," said Philip MacAlpine.

And that was when Molly Metcalf teleported into the room. She appeared right beside MacAlpine, saw what he was doing and, while he was still startled by her sudden arrival out of nowhere, she snatched the gun out of his hand and threw it to me. I caught it easily and turned it on MacAlpine, while Molly moved over to join me. I hit the reset button. MacAlpine glared at me defiantly.

"I'm not sorry. I'm not sorry for any of it. It would have been glorious. . . ."

"No, it wouldn't," I said.

He laughed at me. "You can't hurt me. Nothing in this world can hurt me. I was promised!"

"Yes," I said. "But strange matter isn't from this world."

I shot him twice in the head, and he crashed to the floor and didn't move. I looked at Molly.

"How . . . ?"

"Did you really think I'd leave you here? I told you: I've been to Heaven and Hell and Limbo! Getting into the Timeless Moment was nothing compared to that! Come on; everyone got back home safely, so we can leave this awful place to its own mercy. Time to go home, Eddie."

"Damn right," I said.

CHAPTER TWELVE

All That Remains

When I finally armoured down, back in my bedroom, and Molly saw what had been done to me, she put a hand to her mouth and did her best to keep the shock from her face. She helped me lie down on the bed, biting her lower lip every time I made a pained sound in spite of myself, and then spent the rest of the day sitting with me, working her healing magics. And by the early hours of the next morning, I was well again. So we spent the next few days in bed.

After that, all that was left was the cleaning up. Every field agent in the family went travelling across the world to explain to the various governments and leaders that the satanic conspiracy was gone, never coming back; forget any promises they might have made. And the Great Sacrifice was very definitely off the agenda. A handful of leaders and governments didn't want to give up on such a great idea, and there followed a series of heart attacks and unfortunate accidents, followed by the appointment of new leaders and governments.

In between putting the fear of God into those who needed it, Molly and I travelled all over Europe, seeing the sights and having fun playing tourists. We had to do it the hard way, by plane and car, because the Merlin Glass was broken. The strain of interacting with Alpha Red Alpha had been too much for it, and now the mirror was cracked from side to side. The Armourer sort of thought it might still be possible to use it, but everyone else thought that was a very bad idea. So the Glass remained in the Armoury, under lock and key, because no one wanted to mess with an artefact created by Merlin Satanspawn. Not even my uncle Jack.

Molly and I returned to England some three months later, travelling in a perfectly restored Rolls-Royce Phantom V. Very smooth ride. Very tasty. It was a bright sunny day as Molly and I roared through the back lanes of the southwest countryside. Bright blue sky, not a cloud to be seen, birds singing their little hearts out. Kind of day that made you glad to be alive.

There wasn't any warning.

I drove the Phantom up the long gravel path to the Hall, laughing and joking with Molly. The first indication I had that something was wrong was when I realised how quiet the grounds were. No gryphons, no winged unicorns, no signs of life anywhere. And then I rounded the last corner, and there was the Hall. Or what was left of it.

The Hall was a burnt-out ruin. The walls were broken, shattered, blackened by fire. The windows were blown out. The roof had collapsed and fallen in. Not one wall remained intact. The Hall was a shell, holding death and destruction within. The front doors had been blasted off their hinges and lay broken and charred in the driveway. A single golden figure lay curled in the doorway, the armour half-melted and fused together. I hadn't thought that was possible.

I slammed the Phantom to a halt, and Molly and I got out. For a long moment I couldn't move, held where I was with shock. Molly moved in close beside me. After a while, we went inside to look around.

The Hall had been utterly destroyed. Nothing remained intact. We found a few more golden figures:

dead, melted, some almost shapeless. The Hall was gone, and my family was dead, and I hadn't heard a thing. Too busy playing tourist. I reached out through my torc, trying to reach any other Drood, thinking maybe someone still out in the field might have escaped the slaughter, but no one replied. Not even Ethel.

"Who could have done something like this?" Molly said finally. I didn't have an answer.

Everything I had had been taken from me. All that remained was duty, and revenge. And to be the last Drood.

ABOUT THE AUTHOR

Simon R. Green is a *New York Times* bestselling author. He lives in England.

Connect Online
www.simongreen.co.uk

AVAILABLE NOW FROM

SIMON R. GREEN

LIVE AND LET DROOD

The brand-new book in the series following *For Heaven's Eyes Only*.

Eddie Drood's family has been keeping the forces of evil contained in the shadows for as long as Droods have walked the earth. But now Eddie's entire family has been banished to an alternate dimension. And when he finds out who—or what— attacked his clan, there will be hell to pay...

Praise for the Secret Histories novels:

"Another action-packed melding of spy story and fantasy, featuring suave sleuthing, magical powers, and a generous dash of dry wit."
—*Kirkus Reviews*

Available wherever books are sold or at penguin.com

facebook.com/acerocbooks

R0108

Want to connect with fellow science fiction and fantasy fans?

For news on all your favorite Ace and Roc authors, sneak peeks into the newest releases, book giveaways, and much more—

"Like" Ace and Roc Books on Facebook!

facebook.com/AceRocBooks